I0772383

THE TRUTH IS A LIE

CHERANN WRIGHT

Shutting Sloth Press

To my love. You make all of this possible.

THE TRUTH IS A LIE

a novel

I

---

*"If I had a flower for every time I thought of
you...I could walk through my garden forever."*
—Alfred Lord Tennyson

bby

I KILLED MY SISTER. Allison Clark—Ally for short. The only people who know this are myself, my mother, my aunt, and I suppose my dead sister. I tried to tell them it wasn't me—it was my friend Tina —but their response was, *imaginary friends can't kill people.*

I've lived with the secret of my sister's death since I was a child. So have the other women in my family. For each of us, there's always been a fear that one day someone will find out the truth. That a seven-year-old girl killed her seven-year-old sister. But secrets are like a slow drain in a clogged sink—eventually they leak out.

My mother and Ruby were convinced that I'd just gotten mad at Ally as I often did, and out of anger had pushed her, not knowing the consequences. Then, in order to deal with what I'd done, I'd made up this imaginary friend and decided it was her who'd killed my sister. As I got older, I began to accept the same hard truth. How else could a seven-year-old deal with something so tragic?

But to the outside world, my sister's death was entirely an accident.

I think about it every time I walk past this photo in my upstairs hallway, and today is no different. The picture of my mother—the only one I have in my house—stares back at me as I count to one hundred, giving my daughter ample time to hide from me.

The evening sunlight projects through the arched window and bathes my mother's profile in warm light, making her hair glow. She was thirty-one when she gave birth to me and my twin. Since there were two of us, she wanted our names to be similar. She named me Abbigail—Abby for short. A giggle from down the hallway snaps me back to the game of hide and seek I'm supposed to be playing, and I start counting again from the beginning. "One, two, three, four, five…ten! Ready or not, here I come!"

I tiptoe down the hallway, and the floors protest by popping and cracking like old bones as I sneak into my daughter's room. "Are you under…here?" I squat down and flip up the white bed skirt to peer under the bed. "Nope. Not here."

Next, I crawl on all fours across the plush, pink carpet to look between the dresser and the wall. "Are you hiding…here?"

Nothing.

I move to the closet and swing the door open in one swift motion. "What about here?" Again—nothing. My gaze becomes unfocused for a moment as a hint of panic threatens me.

Ava always hides in here.

I step back out into the hall and listen, hoping I might hear her giggle, but the only sound I hear is the grandfather clock downstairs.

I'm being ridiculous, I know. She's just hiding. And my Ava isn't my sister. I take three deep breaths. I can't afford to let the past snatch away everything I've worked for.

I'd pushed forward from the tragedy and tried to build a normal life for myself—well, as normal as I could. I owe it to Ava. After all, I've taken one of her aunts away, and more or less taken her grandmother too. My mother, Rosemary, now lives in a psychiatric ward. She's been there since my sister died. My aunt, who now lives in my mother's old house next door, had taken me in and raised me after my mother attempted suicide, followed by a complete psychotic break. She'd told me my mother lost her mind and no matter how hard she tried, she couldn't help her find it. The only thing I know is that it was me that took it.

There were times that my aunt wouldn't let me forget.

Some might say that before my sister died, I was like a beautiful flower, but after that horrible day, my petals faded and lost their fragrance. My family shifted from a nourished garden to a plot full of weeds and thorns. There's no way my life could ever be the same.

But I have to make the best of what I have.

Ava.

And I have to keep her safe.

Six years ago, I became a mother to a beautiful little girl, and she is nothing short of being my whole world. In knowing I'm the one who killed my sister, I'm very protective of her. Ava's father thinks I'm overly protective and obsessive. Maybe I am, but I don't care. After she was born, it seems he and I stopped agreeing on everything. I soon found that life's easier when it's just me and her, so I kicked him out.

It's up to me to make sure she has the best life she can. Who else would know what's best when I've seen firsthand how bad things can happen? Life is one of the best teachers.

Instead of walking quietly this time, I stomp into my bedroom, hoping it will force Ava to give away her hiding spot.

Still quiet.

The lack of sound is so pronounced, it feels noisy. The air

becomes suddenly stagnant, and all I can hear is my heart pounding way faster than it should be.

I don't like this game anymore.

She's been quiet for too long. I drop to my knees and look under my bed—just some storage totes. My stomach churns, and heat climbs my body as my throat gets tighter and tighter.

Don't panic.

Just as I'm about to give into the terror and let out a scream, I jerk my closet door open with shaking hands, and giggles burst from inside.

Thank God.

I exhale. Flash a fake smile. Fear got the best of me—again. I push it the rest of the way down, force a bright voice, and reach in and tickle her tiny belly. "I got you."

I'm used to putting on happy voices and cheerful faces. It's a big part of my job as a teacher. Once I'd accepted my horrible past and learned from it, I decided to turn tragedy into something good. Who better to teach unfortunate youth than a person with an unfortunate past? The past can change a person, just as the ocean can change the sand. If you want to overcome the traumas of your past, you have to pick yourself up and give back to the universe.

Ava giggles loudly as I continue to tickle her and wait for my heart rate to return to normal. It isn't the first time this has happened during a simple game of hide-and-seek. As a child, my sister and I loved to play it, and the closet was my favorite place to hide. After she died, I continued to use it for hiding, but not for fun.

For refuge.

My aunt wasn't a nice person. She also used the closet. For punishment.

I spent a lot of time in that dark space, all the way until I was fourteen. Once I outgrew my aunt, she couldn't force me to do it anymore, and I stopped hiding, at least in closets, anyway.

Closets can serve many purposes. Some are merely a place to put personal belongings. Others have much bigger reasons for existing. Monsters live in them. Teenagers use them for kissing games after they spin a bottle. It's a place where people with shopping addictions hide their loot. Alcoholics coined the term closet drinker. Gay people were forced to hide in them, waiting to come out when it was safe. But, for me, the most important use of a closet is to hide my skeletons.

***

Sisters, especially twins, run in my family as far back as the early 1800s; or that is the farthest our family tree has been traced on paper. Some say it goes even farther back to the witch trial days. According to records, each of my ancestors gave birth to exactly two girls, mostly twins, never boys. My grandmother Maria and her sister Sylvia are twins, so are my mother and Ruby, and then there's me and Ally.

In the case of twins, neither of them were ever identical, always fraternal, and any of the girls born in this family, twins or those born a couple of years apart, had a different hair color from each other—one sibling having blond hair, the other dark brown—one with brown eyes, the other with blue. Mom inherited the blond hair, and so did my sister Ally. Those with blond hair were born with a string attached. Beauty, popularity, gifts—and an evil side. I'm not sure that the latter of these is actually true, but the stories passed down speak otherwise.

What I know of my mother is mostly hearsay or what my aunt Ruby has told me. Rumor has it that my mother had trouble getting pregnant. When she gave up on the idea, her husband left her, although there are other whispers about why he left. The other story I'd heard was that my mother not getting pregnant was all his fault, because when she met my father, she was pregnant within the week. When he found out, he left a week later. None of these stories have ever been documented, and most are the words of my aunt. According to her, my mother never took on another man after all that, and I don't remember ever seeing one around.

My sister inherited Rosemary's eyes—bright, blue and beautiful. Mine look nothing like hers—dark with very little white showing in the corners. My aunt claims they shifted to match my soul after what I'd done. She believed in the long line of sisters myth—that there's always a good twin and an evil twin. She and my mother were twins, but she'd never say which one was the good one. Of course, if that myth were true, my mother would be the bad one, because she had the blond hair. Ruby would just say that it must have skipped her generation and wouldn't elaborate further.

Ava continues to giggle, and I glance again at the closet. Even though I hate them, I believe the closet is the most important room in the house. Especially for someone with a skeleton like mine.

I've tried over and over to heal the devastating wound of that day—erase it from my mind for good. But maybe I'm not meant to forget it. The past can cling to the present like a child to its mother.

I sit back on my bottom on the hardwood floor as Ava jumps on me.

"Let's play again, Mommy!"

I look at my watch and take a deep breath. "Well, I don't think dinner is going to fix itself."

"Please, Mommy?"

"I tell you what. Let me fix dinner, and after we eat, we can play it one more time."

"Cross our pinkies?"

"Cross our pinkies, kiss the sky, stick a cupcake in my eye." I hook my pinkie around hers and then I blow a kiss to the sky, followed by the motion of sticking a cupcake in my eye. This satisfies her. "While I cook, you can play with your new dollhouse."

Ava crawls across the hall to the massive dollhouse in the corner of her room. A gift from her father.

Its size matches his ego.

I smile and watch her for a quiet moment before heading downstairs.

As I walk into the kitchen, I pull a hair tie from my wrist and twist my long, dark hair back into a messy ponytail. Focused on what to fix for dinner, I let out an involuntary yelp as my palm slaps my chest. The eyes staring back at me through the thick glass are Aunt Ruby's. The window distorts her face, making her usual scowl even more prominent.

"What the hell, Ruby?" I don't hide the annoyance in my voice.

She doesn't move and waits for me to open the door. I jerk the handle, sling it open, and attempt to get my tone in check. "What do you need? I'm getting ready to start dinner."

Ruby limps up the last step into the doorway and stands with her hands clasped in front of her. She's had the limp as long as I can remember, claiming it was a freak accident in her early twenties. A bitter look creeps into her face before she speaks. "It's a disgrace the way you treat me. I would never have spoken to my mama that way." Her eyebrows pinch to the center of her face, and her lips press into a thin line, barely visible through her frown.

"You're not my mama."

Her glare deepens. "You seem to forget I'm the one that raised you."

Ruby did raise me, and she wasn't always bitter or grumpy. She could be fun when she let her guard down—but even now, she doesn't allow that to happen very often. I don't think she truly knew how to be a mother. The job was thrown into her lap unexpectedly, and her life changed forever the day my mother lost herself. She is at her best when she's with Ava. I guess it's like that with parents and grandparents—grandparents try to make up for their lack of parenting, or lack of knowledge from when they were the parent. Grandchildren can get away with murder. I know Ruby loves me, but I don't think she loves herself.

Regardless, I refuse to engage in yet another useless conversation with her. It's best to get straight to the point, or she digs up the past quicker than a tiller turns a garden. I smooth out my tone. "I said, I need to start dinner. What do you need, Ruby?"

"I have to go pay some bills in the morning. This weather's causing my foot to ache something awful. I don't think I can drive."

"I have to work, Ruby. If you can't drive, then you'll have to call a cab."

"I can't afford no damn cab." Ruby crosses her arms in front of her chest as she sticks out her chin.

"Then I don't know what to tell you."

"I'm not going to live forever, you know. One day you'll regret not spending more time with me."

Ruby is the tour master of guilt trips.

"I'm not doing this with you right now. You can either come in and be nice or go home." I keep my tone firm.

Ruby is often like that annoying itch that just won't go away, no matter how hard you scratch, and regardless of whether you scratch it often. Sometimes she stings, and others, she burns, and when you indulge in her whims, she festers under your skin until you blow up and say something you shouldn't. She can't help it; it's just how she is.

Ruby puffs through her tight lips, making them flap and then looks around the kitchen. Money isn't an issue for her, since she inherited a fortune from our ancestors. Although she's rich, she's a tight wad. She lives on foods like egg sandwiches, potatoes, and soup. Even those things are highway robbery, according to her. Her only indulgences are one glass of wine every day, exactly five cigarettes, and a new pair of shoes every other month. She's the kind of person who won't spend money but will find a way to take it with her when she dies to keep others from getting it.

"Where's Ava Maria?"

"She's in her room. Leave her alone for now, she's doing her homework," I lie.

"Homework, for a six-year-old? What kind of idiot teacher gives homework in kindergarten?" She wobbles a few more steps into the kitchen, and I close the door behind her before taking in a deep inhale to curb frustration.

"Ruby. Keep your voice down or Ava might hear you. She loves her teacher."

"I call it like I see it. Haven't met a teacher yet that wasn't worthless. They're overpaid and only have to work nine months a year. They don't do anything, even then."

I catch myself giving Ruby the same look I'd give a cockroach crawling across the floor. I shift my face back to neutral. Ruby sometimes reminds me of my third-grade teacher, who I hated because she was more like a witch than a teacher. She often scolded her students with her evil stare. I even remember crawling under my desk one day to avoid it. Now that I'm grown, Ruby doesn't intimidate me as much as she used to.

"You seem to forget that I'm a teacher."

Another puff escapes her, this time through her nose. She's every bit what most people would describe as the modern-day Karen—short, dark hair, Tammy Faye eyelashes, and long manicured nails. I'm not sure who Karen is or what she did to deserve having her named associated with a person like my aunt, but it's the only way I know how to describe her. She's too cheap to have someone do her nails or visit a beauty salon, so she does them herself. She's also the sort of person who believes everything should revolve around her and the world owes her something.

"There's no reason for you to be here. Come back when you're in a better mood." *As if that will ever happen.* My lips motion the words, then I bite my tongue. I step behind her, open the door and stand holding the doorknob. "I'll see you tomorrow."

She scoots toward the door, her face consumed with a frown as she nods. "It's just a shame."

I gnaw on my tongue some more but remain silent as she leaves and waste no time in closing the door behind her.

Spaghetti is what I decide on for dinner—quick and easy. Once I put water on the stove to boil, I tiptoe upstairs and down the hall to check on Ava. The steps squeak under my feet. The house is old, but a lot of work has gone into it over the last two years.

As I get closer to her room, I hear her talking. My mouth lifts into a smile as I listen to her imagination at work.

"Here, this one is my favorite—you can play with it. Let's pretend we're getting ready to go for some ice-cream," Ava chatters.

I peek around the door and watch Ava bounce the doll across the floor of the doll house and down the tiny stairs. A faint simmer from the pot on the stove sizzles, and I tiptoe back away from the door. As I step away, Ava giggles.

"Come on, Ally. It's the ice cream truck."

I halt in place as my heart picks up the pace and thuds against my chest. I listen to see if Ava speaks again, hoping that what I thought I heard was just my mind playing tricks. She doesn't speak, but instead hums the 'My Little Pony' theme song. I stay frozen as she starts to whisper, and I strain my ears but can't make out what she's saying. With light steps, I move back to the edge of her door. "Who are you talking to, Ava?"

Ava sits with her legs in a *W* position in the middle of the floor, holding a miniature doll in each hand. "My friend."

"Who's your friend?"

She looks to her left, then back down at her dolls. "Ally."

A tingling sensation radiates from the back of my neck and down my spine as the rest of my body waivers. "Where did you hear that name?" My words come out uneven, and I clear my throat.

Ava hitches a shoulder. "She told me."

"Who?"

"Ally."

The tingling moves to my limbs, and I try to convince myself that this is just a coincidence. *It's a name she's heard on TV.* Rather than push any further, I change the subject. "You want to come and help me finish dinner?"

"Yeah," Ava squeals. She jumps up from the floor and walks to the door, then pauses, turns, and waves at the room behind her. "Bye, Ally."

I stare at the floor as Ava skips past me, and I feel a numbing tingle travel up the backside of my head. With a shudder, I leave the room.

After we've eaten dinner, played five more games of hide-and-seek, and read two stories, Ava snuggles down in the covers while I tuck her in for the night. I walk downstairs and prepare for the two-time ritual of Ava getting out of bed. I've not made it to the bottom of the stairs before she gets up the first time.

"Mommy, I'm thirsty."

We've worked out a routine that allows her only two attempts to get out of bed. She knows she has to choose her excuses wisely, because if she gets up after the second attempt, she loses screen time. The first attempt is often used to ask for water, and the second can vary. Either it's too dark, or we have to check under the bed and in the closet for monsters. She's getting clever, because tonight she asks for something new.

"Mommy." Ava has tiptoed down the stairs, managing not to wake their creaks and pops, and has sneaked into the room.

I look up from my phone. "What do you need, honey?"

"I think I could go to sleep like this—" Ava attempts to snap her thumb and middle finger together. "If you read me one more story." She tries two more times to snap her fingers, then gives up.

"Oh, really?" I ask with a teasing smile.

"Yes." She nods her head up and down in an exaggerated motion.

"Okay. Then it's off to sleep for you. Understand?"

We go back upstairs, and I make the mistake of letting her pick the story. She chooses the longest book in the stack. I'll have to narrow her choices down to certain books next time. Once I'm halfway through the story, Ava falls asleep. I kiss her on the forehead and pull her door around.

Since I have some down time before bed, I sneak into my closet, take down a small storage box from the top shelf and carry it downstairs.

As I sit in my favorite corner of the couch, I open the box and remove a mini external hard drive with trembling fingers. Stored on it are some old childhood videos that I'd converted years ago. I prop my laptop on a throw pillow in my lap and plug it into the USB port. I can't bring myself to watch all of the videos—just one.

The last video taken of my sister.

The one where she's dressed in pink, hands crisscrossed and resting on her chest, her eyes forever closed. Eyes that would never show the beauty or mischief behind them ever again.

Her coffin is white with gold trim. The fabric that surrounds her body is ivory with pale pink flowers.

I'm not sure why, but I often tear open old scars by watching the home movie anytime I get too comfortable or happy. Maybe I owe it to my sister. Self-punishment is often much worse than anything anyone else can put a person through. At least, that's what my aunt taught me when she started the ritual of watching it. She believed that if she reminded me enough, I would never repeat my mistake.

I've watched the video so many times that I can close my eyes and state verbatim what is happening. My aunt's voice behind the camera says, "This didn't have to happen." My mother sits in a chair facing the coffin, and stares at it blankly. I sit next to her, my body slumped over and broken. I glance from my sister's casket to my mother's face—she won't look at me. Desperate for her to see me, I lean my head over to rest against her arm, and yet she still doesn't acknowledge me. She doesn't acknowledge anything. I'm not sure if my mother ever looked at me after that day.

When I've had enough self-torture, I click the red dot in the corner to close the movie window and sit the laptop next to me on the couch. I stare at the wallpaper on the screen, which is a picture of me and Ava, then check the time. It's still early enough to have a small glass of wine before bed. I go to the kitchen and pour some sweet red and return to the couch. With my feet folded under me, I stare at our picture. Ava has my sister's eyes. In fact, they look more like Ally's than mine.

I stare long enough that the wallpaper turns to a screen saver that comprises photos which scroll across the computer screen. I become engrossed in Ava's baby pictures as they move left to right, and I sip on my wine. A smile spreads across my face as each one comes into view. She's the only thing that brings me genuine joy these days. I'm not sure how I survived before her.

Relaxed now, I untuck my feet and reach to close the laptop. Just as my hand touches it, the photos glitch, and a video begins to play, the volume cranked to maximum level. My empty glass falls on the sofa, spilling a few droplets as I scramble to turn down the volume. Giggles and squeals blare from the computer's speaker. What I'm seeing finally registers, and my blood freezes. It's a video of my sister and me spraying each other with water guns. Frantic, I try to turn it off, but it doesn't work. I pound my finger into the button over and over. Nothing. I slam the screen shut, my breath and heart racing with one another.

The room falls silent and suddenly cold.

2

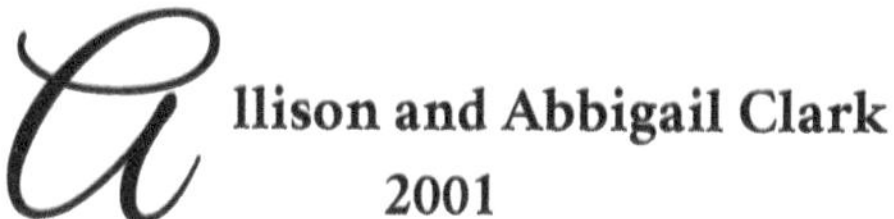**llison and Abbigail Clark**
2001

ABBY GIGGLES as she glances down at her fingers. They look as if a rainbow has exploded all over them. Ally had begged to paint Abby's nails, saying she could make them look like the colors on a unicorn's tail. The skin on Abby's fingers now has as much color on them as her nails do.

"What're you girls doing in here?" their mother, Rosemary, asks as she walks into the girls' pink and purple room. Abby and Ally's room is the largest bedroom in the house. They each have their own beds on opposite walls. The wall behind Ally's bed is painted pink, and the wall behind Abby's is the color of lilacs. Their bedroom takes in most of the top floor of the house, and it's right next to a playroom and their own bathroom, which means they have lots of space, and their mother's room is just down the hall.

"I'm going to fix Abby up like a princess. See, look at her nails," Ally says, moving Abby's hand to where their mother can see.

15

Strung across the floor of the bedroom are princess costumes, make-up compacts, several bottles of fingernail polish, and an assortment of dress-up shoes. "Want me to do yours next, Rosemary?"

Rosemary smiles. She liked Abby and Ally to call her by her real name, though Abby still likes calling her *Mom* sometimes. Rosemary touches a hand lightly over her mouth as her whole face shifts into one big smile. She lets out a small chuckle, then gains her composure. "Can you make them look as good as Abby's?"

Abby grins.

"Yes." Ally nods her head up and down in quick succession.

"Can I pick my colors?"

"Yep. But you still have to pick between these." Ally scoots toward five different colors of fingernail polish a few feet out in front of her. Pink, yellow, blue, green, and purple—all pastels.

"See, Mom, I picked yellow, pink, and blue." Abby wiggles her fingers. "You want to match me?"

"Why yes—I do."

Rosemary pulls her long, flowing skirt outward as she sits crisscross on the floor, wrapping it around her knees. She always wears bright colors that don't match, and scarves and gaudy jewelry. Her handbags are large enough to carry a good-sized animal. The words most people use when they talk about Rosemary are *eccentric, flighty and airhead.* She doesn't care what others think of her. The only things she cares about are the twins and her art—maybe those funny smelling cigarettes she smokes that make her giggle sometimes whenever she's creating her art.

Rosemary picks up the bottle of blue polish and holds it up close to her face. "This blue will match perfectly. Don't you think?" Tied around her head is a multi-colored scarf, mostly blue, that hangs down across her shoulder and right breast. "Okay, Ally, work your magic." She spreads her fingers wide and holds them out in front of her.

Ally nods and opens the three bottles of fingernail polish one-by-one and begins to paint, taking in turns with the different colors.

"What do you think?" Ally asks as she starts to blow on Rosemary's hands.

"Beautiful," Rosemary says. "What do you think, Abby?"

"I think you look just like me." Abby holds up both hands, palms facing her chest and wiggles her tiny fingers. "You want to dress up with us, too?"

She grins. "Well now, look at me. I always dress like a princess —don't you think?" Rosemary stands and twirls holding her skirt out to each side with the tips of her fingers and then bows.

Ally and Abby giggle.

"Aunt Ruby is going to be moving into the house down the street today. She can't wait to meet you two. I'm going to go downstairs and make some sandwiches to take over there later for her and the movers. Would my two princesses like a sandwich?"

"Yeah," Ally says first. "Turkey and cheese."

"No cheese for me," Abby says.

"Okay. When your nails are dry, why don't you come down and I'll bring your sandwiches to the back garden. It's a nice day outside."

Abby blows on her fingertips some more as their mother leaves the room flapping her hands back and forth letting the air dry hers. Ally jumps up to leave, and Abby snaps at her. "Ally, you have to help me clean this up. I'm not doing it by myself."

"We'll get it later."

"No, Ally. If we leave this mess, Mom will get mad and ground us."

Ally hitches her shoulder. "Then you pick it up. I don't want to."

"Allison! Get back here."

Ally skips down the hall and then the stairs leaving Abby to clean up the mess.

Abby grinds her teeth and then sighs before getting to work. Once she's cleaned up what was mostly Ally's clutter, she goes downstairs. She stomps through the kitchen and across the narrow stone walkway of the plant-inhabited sunroom, and out into the back garden. Just as she steps outside, the gagging scent of her mother's new potted plant fill her nostrils. She pinches her nose as she sits down.

"There you are. What have you been doing? Your bread is getting stale," Rosemary says.

Abby shrugs her shoulders and gives Ally a mean glare before sitting down across from her.

"Did you girls notice my Titum Arum? It's starting to open up."

Both girls turn to look at the massive, funny looking plant that has a height almost as tall as the roofline on the sunroom.

Rosemary continues. "Keep an eye on it, because it only blooms once a year. In two to three days, it will be gone."

"Why does it stink so bad?" Ally asks.

"Well, the smell is probably why it's known as the Corpse flower. It only grows in the rainforest."

Ally crinkles her nose at the flower that smells more like a rotting, dead animal than a beautiful flower. "It's killing the smell of the good flowers."

"Ah, yes," Rosemary says matter of factly. "Living creatures are like that sometimes. Some are beautiful on the outside, but underneath can be nasty and fool everyone around them. It just goes to show that you can't always believe what's on the surface."

Abby, still sulking, picks up her sandwich while holding her nose, all the while giving Ally a stare-down. How can she sit there looking all smug after leaving her to clear everything up like always?

Rosemary stands and moves a glass of lemonade in front of Abby. "I'm going to go finish in the kitchen. You girls eat your sandwiches and then play outside for a while. I'll come get you when it's time to go meet Aunt Ruby."

"Okay," they both say. Abby deepens her squint at Ally.

Rosemary sashays down the stone path, zigzagging through the flowers and shrubs, then disappears into the congested sunroom.

"Stop it, Abby!" Ally says.

"Why? Does it bother you?" Abby glares at Ally even harder, this time with wide eyes.

"No. It's just stupid."

"I'm not doing anything." Her eyes remain fixed on Ally without blinking while her legs swing rapidly under the table.

"Then stop staring at me."

"It's a free country. I can do what I want."

Ally pounds her fist into the iron table. "I said stop it."

Her fist doesn't make much of a sound, but Abby looks down to check there's no damage. The table is a vintage garden table, painted ornate white with a floral pattern. It belonged to their grandmother when she lived in the house.

Abby laughs. "What are you going to do about it?"

A rustling noise comes from the direction of the back fence, and they jerk their heads to look. The back yard is a giant maze of flowering bushes, small trees and Rosemary's yard sculptures. Wind chimes hang from every tree made from silverware, glass bottles, and seashells. There's even one made from the small bones of animals. The girls' favorite sculpture is one that stands as tall as their mom, made from slender pieces of metal, twisted and shaped like a fairy. It's painted shiny blue, and when the sun hits it, it reflects other colors. She looks like she's dancing.

Ally and Abby look at each other, then back to the fence. Something moves through the cracks in between the wooden boards, and Abby looks at Ally, as fear stirs in her tummy.

"Go see what it is," Abby hisses.

"I'm not going by myself. Go with me." Ally's eyes are wide and pleading.

They both ease to standing, and Ally reaches out her hand. Something white begins to shift down the fence towards the back gate. Abby's heart feels like it's going to jump out of her chest as she takes hold of Ally's clammy hand, and they tiptoe to the gate.

"Who's there?" Ally asks as she twirls a thick strand of blond hair around her index finger.

No sound comes from the other side of the fence, but the object continues to shuffle towards the gate. They freeze, and Abby whispers, "Maybe we should get Rosemary?"

"Don't be a baby, Abby. Let's see who it is."

Whoever is on the other side of the fence stops moving just at the gate. The girls pause in front of the arched door, and Ally reaches out to unlock it as Abby swallows hard. She eases the gate open, and they both keep their bodies behind it. A sudden whiff of the stinky corpse flower wafts in the air behind them, and Abby grabs a handful of her dark hair before draping it across her nose.

Ally peeks around the gate and her shoulders relax as she drops Abby's hand. "Oh. Hi."

Abby steps out into view to see a girl with short brown hair who stands a few inches taller than them. The girl doesn't smile but waves her hand just a couple of inches from side to side, then lets her hand fall back down.

"I'm Ally. This is my sister Abby. You want to come in and play?"

She nods her head only slightly, then says, "I'm only allowed to play out here. Can you come over there?" She points to the small piece of land just beyond their fence. It's secluded by a cluster of bushes and trees.

Ally looks to Abby before she speaks. "We can't go far. Mom won't let us go past the side fence over there." She points across the yard to their right. There's a small narrow field behind their house that belongs to their neighbors and at the edge of it is a small stream. They don't mind if the girls play back there if they don't leave their toys lying around. Rosemary's only rules are, they can't play in the stream unless she's with them and they must stay within hearing distance.

"Sure," Ally says.

They step through the gate and follow their newly made friend over to a tree a few yards from the fence. Their neighbors don't have kids, but they hung a swing in the tree just for Abby and Ally.

The girl sits down on the swing. "Can you swing me? Then I'll swing you guys."

"Sure," Abby says, and begins to push her. "What's your name?"

"I'm Tina."

3

 bby

DAWN BREAKS open like a fresh bleeding wound as the sun peeks through the window, giving the room a reddish glow. Lying in bed with the covers twisted around me, I'm not sure where my fitful mind went during the night, but it wasn't to sleep—at least not much, anyway. My night of so-called rest was a mixture of unwanted dreams and relentless tossing and turning. I can't stop replaying the short video clip over and over in my mind. It's the very reason I don't watch them.

They're too haunting.

Seeing my sister laughing and alive only makes old wounds burst open. It peels away the scabs I've created to keep from missing her so much. Hearing her laughter for the first time in years is like hearing a familiar song. Sweet, innocent, and torturous. Maybe it's a twin thing, but the grief it causes lingers like a painful disease.

After pressing my palms against my eye sockets, I blow out a puff of air, attempting to get my thoughts together for the day. I stare at the tall ceiling of my old bedroom, finding faces and shapes in the light texture of the paint. I always locate the same three faces each time and most of them look mean, as though they're frowning at me for lying in bed. My alarm hasn't sounded, but I know it must be minutes from blaring its annoying sounds. As soon as I reach to pick up my phone, the pings and whistles begin to sound in short, quick increments. I turn it off, throw back the covers, and roll out of bed.

With slippered feet, I pad across the old floor, complete with scuffs and wear. They sound as old as they appear as I walk across the hall into Ava's room. Her room is the only one in the house with carpet. She hated the cold, hard floors. Since she's making up for the both of us on sleep, I let her snooze a while longer and go downstairs to make some coffee.

With a very full cup, I make my way to the adjacent living room, stop, then glare at the laptop resting on the table by the couch. I need to prepare my lessons for the day, and I don't even feel like logging in. I sit my coffee on the end table and plop down beside it as a quick breath escapes me. I push down apprehension and ease it open—it's just the wallpaper of me and Ava. Another quick exhale and I relax.

Once I've completed my lesson plans, I wake Ava, get us both dressed, and head off to school. The morning drive takes me through the old, quiet streets of Meadowbrook, which are filled with antique shops, antique houses, and antique people. They're the best kind of neighbors to have, because they're usually quiet and keep to themselves, except for Ruby. Sitting high above every-thing is an old, domed courthouse that has been converted to a library that Ava and I visit once a week. It's her favorite place to go —mine too. A good book is always the perfect place to escape to, whenever my mind slows down long enough to allow me to hide there.

After arriving at school, I give a quick kiss on the top of Ava's head then direct her towards her classroom before heading to the small meeting room. Megan is already there, having what she calls the *breakfast of champions.*

"This school district treats its employees like a bunch of mushrooms." Megan pops a cheez-it cracker in her mouth.

"Mushrooms?" I ask and make an attempt at a convincing smile.

"They keep us in the dark and feed us a bunch of shit." Megan cackles and gulps down a drink of soda.

I plop down in the chair next to her and pour myself a pile of crackers onto a paper towel.

"What's wrong?" Megan asks. "You're eating junk food."

"I didn't sleep very well."

"The ex-husband invading your dreams again?"

I smile. "When is he not? No, I think I just need a vacation. I'm super stressed and not sure why."

"I think you just need to get laid. I'm sure your ex would oblige."

I laugh and then shudder. "I'm not going down that road—then he would just want more."

"Then find another plaything," Megan teases. "I'm sure he isn't remaining celibate. Men never do."

"That's not something I want to think about."

"Then let me set you up with one of my friends. They're a little younger than you, and they definitely won't want any strings. Just use and abuse them and send them on their way. Or you could go my direction and I could set you up with one of my girlfriends. You would definitely have a good time."

"Ha. Tempting, but—"

The door to the meeting room opens, and Kris, the school counselor, walks in. Megan and I both giggle and end the conversation as my mood feels a little lighter. Megan's humor always lifts my spirits.

"Do you ever feel like a mushroom, Kris?" Megan asks as she shoots me a mischievous grin.

Kris closes the door behind her, then huffs. "Megan, be serious." She sits down across from the two of us with her usual put-together posture and serious glare.

Kris is a tall, thin brunette with a pixie haircut. She wears only dress slacks, button-ups and turtlenecks. Sometimes two tops together. Kris is pretty, but sometimes her attitude makes her ugly. She's never gets overly excited, and her tone remains calm in any situation, even if her words are harsh. A storm could rip the roof off over our heads, and her voice wouldn't falter from her arrogant monotone.

"These weekly group meetings are already a waste of our time. Why are we being forced to have this extra meeting?" Megan taps her can of soda down on the table and looks at me, then back to Kris as she licks the cheese dust from her fingers.

"Now, how would I know?" Kris's tone is condescending. She's the sort of person that you either like or hate. I haven't decided what I think of her yet. She's been here almost a year, but my view of her seesaws between, *I sort of like her,* to *she doesn't like me.* Other times, she lays the charm on too thick. At our first introduction, she seemed like a goody-two-shoes and unapproachable. She gave me the impression she believed she was smarter and better than everyone else. I can't quite put my finger on it, but something about her rubs me the wrong way.

Regardless, I have to work with her, so I keep it professional. I don't share any personal information with her, and neither does Megan.

Megan continues to ramble. "And, Abby, that husband of yours is as useless as tits on a bull when it comes to us. He keeps us in the dark more than anyone."

"I agree. And that's *ex*-husband." I give Megan a wide-eyed look then a wink. The principal being my ex-husband is no secret, but Megan and I are close, so she knows the truth behind our breakup. Well, the parts I tell her, anyway.

Megan is cute, petite, and loud. If it pops in her head, it comes out of her mouth. She's also comical and rarely ever takes anything seriously. Her style shows it. Some days she dresses the part and others, she comes to work dressed like it's the weekend. Jeans, t-shirt, and sometimes sweats. To be fair, she's the one that does most of the wrestling on the floor with the kids when they need a time out.

"Ladies." Kris props both elbows on the table, sits her chin on top of her curled hands, and looks at us as if we are two disobedient children. "Let's be serious. It must be important, or he wouldn't have called this meeting."

"Okay," Megan and I both say in unison and in the same appeasing manner.

The door to the meeting room swings open with a jolt. The school building is old, and there isn't a door in the place that doesn't stick. Most require a heavy shove.

"Sorry, ladies," says Jared. "I meant to get here sooner, but the superintendent called. Of course, he's his usual wind-bag self." He pulls out the rolling desk chair, plops down and lays back. An aggressive exhale escapes him.

I give my ex-husband an eye roll and look at Megan, who snickers and covers her mouth with her clasped hands.

Jared became principal after we divorced. Married couples can't work as teacher and principal, but apparently divorced one's can. Doesn't make sense. Ava was attending our preschool when he got hired, so I couldn't protest because she was so excited when she found out. I don't hate him; I just know what is best for our daughter.

Jared insists we have weekly meetings to appease the administrators at the board office and their constant school improvement ideas. He says it shows that we are working as a team. I think it's his way of telling me what to do. He only forces us to do it twice when our job is about to get harder. Despite being my ex-husband, he really isn't a bad boss to work for. Most of the teachers love him. As much as I hate the meetings, I'm anxious to find out what he has to say.

"We're getting two new students, and we need to prepare." His tone speaks volumes.

I look at Megan and our eyes reflect the same expression. Wide, intense, and full of dread. No one speaks. A special meeting to prepare means, get ready to go home at the end of the day exhausted, disgruntled and covered in bruises. It usually means there are major behavioral issues involved.

"This puts us over cap, Mr. Brooks," Megan says. "Please tell us you let your balls drop with the superintendent and got him to agree to hiring another teacher."

"Now, Megan. I don't think that's how we're going to get what we want," Kris says.

Jared presses his lips together and shifts his mouth toward one side of his face. "Fraid not."

He stands and removes his suit jacket, and without loosening his tie, unbuttons the top button of his shirt with his well-manicured hands. His dark, silk tie matches his equally dark eyes—a feature he often receives compliments on and one that drew me in right away. My own eyes scan the way the white shirt hugs his broad shoulders and tapers inward to his small waist, then my gaze briefly pauses just below his belt—it hangs slightly to the right. Looking at his penis is a habit I could never seem to break. I look away before he catches me. Jared's looks and our sex life were never a problem.

"Jared?" I say in an even tone as I reach for a cracker to distract my eyes. "Did you tell him we can't handle any more students on the number of staff that we have?"

"Yeah," Megan agrees.

Jared holds up both hands as if he's patting the air and sits back down. "I did, and before you all get your undies in a bunch, let me finish. He did agree to hiring another teacher's aide."

"That's not good enough," Megan interrupts.

"Ladies. We can't change it, so let me give you the background on these students, then we will discuss a plan."

I attempt to erase the disgusted look from my face and slump back in my seat. Megan crisscrosses her arms in front of her body, while Kris pulls at her turtleneck.

"These students are twins—a boy and a girl. They're seven years old and both have multiple disabilities." Jared passes each of us two thick packets. "Here are their educational plans from their previous school."

"Jesus." Megan picks up the corner of the packet and lets the pages fall one by one. "Whomever wrote these is an overachiever. Who has this kind of time?"

"Go ahead and skim through these as quickly as you can, then I'll fill you in on my conversation with their former principal. Their father is bringing them by to tour the school and meet their teachers."

"And when are they coming?" I ask.

Jared flips his watch around in front of his face. "About an hour."

Megan's eyes grow wide as she starts to say something, but she stops when Kris gives her a stern look.

"Let's just look at their plans." Kris calmly picks up one of the packets and begins to read.

The rest of us follow. I pick up the first plan and read the student's name. Mason Robert Harper, seven years old. I make a note of the birthdate. He's almost eight. Disabilities—Emotional Behavior Disorder, Oppositional Defiant Disorder, and Attention Deficit Hyperactivity Disorder. Megan must be reading the little boy's plan as well, because we both look at each other with raised eyebrows and exhale at the same time. I read through the rest of the packet, including his behavior plan. He's going to be a handful.

Next, I pick up the sister's plan, Mia Rose Harper. Disabilities—visually impaired, Growth Hormone Deficiency, and Emotional Behavior Disorder. I look up at my ex-husband. "Jared, did you ask for two instructional assistants? Because we are going to need it. Mia needs all day assistance because she's legally blind."

"She can still see—she's just going to require a lot of accommodations. I'll have to pull someone from one of the other classrooms. At least part of the day."

"Mr. B?" Megan says.

"Let's just wait and meet them, then we'll see what we need to do." Jared looks at his watch, then gathers his things and stands. "I need to make a phone call before they get here." He stands, turns and my eyes land on the other part of his body that I can't seem to avoid looking at. His ass. As he's opening the door, the office secretary steps into view, her eyes wide.

"What is it, Kelly?" Jared asks.

"I'm afraid they're already here. The father just dropped them off and said he had an appointment, but he'll be right back."

"What the f—!"

"Megan." Kris cuts her off as she draws out Megan's name, long and smooth. Her eyebrows pull close and down, creating a crease in her forehead like a scolding mother.

"No one can hear me. Don't get your panties in a wad, Kris."

"Ladies." Jared's tone comes across smooth as molasses. "Let's go meet our new students so we can get back to our *other* students."

Megan huffs, then stands, and we walk down the hall behind Jared.

We step into Kris's office where Kelly left two children along with one of the first-grade aides. The space is much smaller than a classroom but sits towards the entrance of the building. Kelly introduces everyone in her soft, inviting tone. "Everyone, this is Mason and Mia."

I smile at each of them as I place my hand to my chest. "I'm Ms. Clark. I'll be one of your teachers."

Mia is significantly smaller than Mason. According to her file, she is taking growth hormone treatments which are helping, but it is obvious by her features that her size has been affected due to her hormone deficiency.

The little boy rolls his eyes and looks away. "Can I go home now?"

"You just got here. Wouldn't you like to look around the school and see your classroom?" I squat down so that I'm closer to eye level with both Mason and Mia.

Kris crouches down next to me while Megan and Jared remain by the door.

Mason turns toward me, his forehead scrunched, eyes narrowed. "No. I hate teachers. They suck."

"Okay, then," I hear Megan whisper behind me.

I turn to look at her with a crooked grin and raise one eyebrow.

"Aw, Mason. You should give us a chance before you say you hate us." Kris keeps her voice low and consoling.

Mason turns to look at me once more, this time making eye contact. "I hate you. You're a shithead." Then he turns to Kris and says even louder. "You look just like *her* and I hate you, too."

"Come now, Mason. I know you're probably scared and it's possible you don't mean that," Kris continues, her tone indulgent.

"Fuck you! You look like a penis wearing a turtleneck." Mason turns his head to the side and grins as though he's pleased with himself.

Megan snorts and presses her hand over her mouth behind me, and I turn my head away to keep from laughing. Jared turns his back to the room, but I see his shoulders bouncing from his muffled laugh.

I tuck my lips between my teeth and press down, trying to keep a straight face. Kris's eyes shoot sideways, and I detect irritation.

"You don't have to like me, but I believe you will like it here if you give it time." Kris stands. "How about we walk you through the school, and I'll show you the cafeteria and our huge playground? It's new."

I stand as well, and Mia shuffles to me, then reaches up and slides her hand into mine. I pause in surprise and instinctively look at Jared, then catch myself and look down to the top of the girl's head. She looks up at me and gives me a sheepish smile. Mia rotates my hand around to hold my palm close to her face. With an index finger, she traces the lines on my hand and says, "you have an *M* on your hand."

My eyes furrow in confusion and I lean down to look at my palm so that I'm closer to her level. "What do you mean?"

She traces it again. "See."

"Oh yeah, I do." I hold my face close to Mia's and smile. "I've had it as long as I can remember. My daughter pointed it out too because she has one just like it."

"My friend showed me, but my hand looks different." Mia holds her hand up and puts her palm close to my face. "See. Mine kind of looks like an *M*."

I raise up slightly because Mia had shoved her palm so close to my face that I could smell her hand rather than see it. It smelled like a fruit rollup. "Yeah—it sort of does." I stand back up. "Does your friend go to school here?"

"No. She said she can come and see me, though."

"What's your friend's name?" Megan asks.

"Ally."

A chilling sensation travels through my body, just as it had yesterday when I'd heard Ava say the same name. I catch the frown that has taken over my face and shift it back to neutral.

"Who's Ally, Mia?" Jared asks.

"She came to see me last night after Daddy showed me pictures of our new school."

I stand and look at Jared, then toward Megan. They're already distracted by Mason kicking the wall a few feet down the hallway.

I stare, stunned for a moment. Mason's metronome, foot tapping against the wall begins to register, getting louder. I bite my tongue to keep from snapping at him. Jared must have seen my expression because he walks down the hall and attempts to direct him towards the classroom.

Mia reaches up and takes my hand again. "Ally said to tell you hi."

4

J ared

I YANK at the knot of my tie before I even make it through the front door of my house after a long, tough day at work. As the principal of Smokey Valley Elementary, I wear numerous hats and some days, like today, I'm just not sure which one I should don.

My tired brain asks me at around this same time every day whether I'm doing the right thing in staying. My job requires the ability to act as ground control, deflecting the demands of helicopter parents whose children are perfect angels. Most days, my job can be very rewarding, especially when a child looks up at me with wide, loving eyes. Then there are other days I hate my job, but I'll never tell anyone this. I get tired of plastering on a fake smile while getting my ass chewed and completing the demands of others. Then there's the endless drama that can consume my day needlessly.

Don't get me wrong, being around so many women does have its perks. I never have to worry about what to eat for lunch or finding medication if I feel a migraine coming on. I have a nice pick of work wives that take good care of me—except for the one I wish for. Seeing my ex-wife every day is probably the biggest reason I often hate my job. She despises me—but I still love her.

To this day, I'm still not sure why Abby pushed me out of her life. I suppose I just couldn't add up to be enough for her, or at least, that's how I feel. We've known each other since we were kids, although briefly back then. I thought I knew her better than I knew myself, but it turns out I was wrong. It seems I don't know her at all.

I take off my shoes and make my way to the kitchen, trying not to let my post-work thoughts drift to Abby. Most days I can look at her and get through my day without her getting under my skin. Then there are days like today when all I have to do is look at her, and it knocks the wind out of me. Maybe it's because for a moment today, I thought I saw her look at me like she used to. A familiar look in her eye when that little girl took her hand. It was as if she forgot to hate me for a second. The sort of moment when something exciting happens and the first thing you want to do is look into the eyes of someone you love and share it with them. And before that, I saw her gaze land on areas of my body that weren't my face. If attraction and amazing sex were the only thing a good marriage required, we'd still be together. That was never the issue. In fact, I think if Abby would let her guard down for two seconds, we'd be naked together just as fast.

That's not going to happen.

I lay my computer bag and keys on the table and slip off my Wingtip Oxfords. Tie and shoes in hand, I sprint up the stairs of my small duplex apartment to shower away countless grimy handprints. Children from the ages of three to seven haven't learned personal space and there's never a shortage on snotty hugs. After stripping down the rest of the way, I turn on the shower to let it warm.

I allow the water to pour over the top of my head for an obscene amount of time. It's barely cool enough not to scold. With a thick lather of shampoo, I scrub my scalp with vigor, as if it will scrape away the days worries and stresses. The squeak of the shower door sliding open forces me to peek through a partially opened eyelid. This might alarm a person that lives alone, but this guest has been showing up like this for over a month now.

A long, slender leg steps into the shower, and then another to match. My eyes travel up the curves of her hips, waist and breast before stopping at her long slender neck. It looks different without the turtleneck. I bend down to kiss it.

"I thought you could use a back rub," Kris says.

"I hope you're here to rub more than that."

Kris grabs the bar of soap and rolls it around in her hands, creating a thick, fluffy lather. I wait for her to rub it on my body, but she doesn't. Instead, she rubs it over her breasts, stomach, between her legs and down her inner thighs. She presses her body to mine, arms wrapping around my neck as she raises one leg and rubs it up the side of my hips and around my buttock. She presses against me, her body slick and soft, and I push her back against the wall of the shower, gripping her thigh and lifting her from the shower floor. She reaches down and guides me inside her, then wraps both legs around me. The rest of my day begins to melt away.

What Kris and I share is a mutual understanding of a purely physical relationship. She came into a restaurant one evening where I was eating alone to pick up take-out, sat down and boldly suggested that I follow her back to her place. I believe her exact words were, *it's a shame for two beautiful people to spend all their nights alone.* Talk about boosting one's confidence. As tempting as it was, I first turned her down because of our working relationship. She was very persuasive in that we are two consenting adults and that we would never allow it to interfere with our jobs. I don't think either of us intend on it becoming anything more.

Kris and I never talk about work, and our hook-ups are only to fulfill one purpose. Sex. We both fuck away our stresses from the day, then we part ways. Her demeanor at school is calm and always buttoned up and professional. In bed, she's a different person. I sometimes feel that she releases her aggression on me—not that I mind.

I know nothing about her personal life. We don't make it a habit of having meaningful conversations. The most I know about her is that she moved from North Carolina's coast to our deep Appalachian town almost a year ago because she needed to see something other than sand and ocean—a bit of information that came out during her interview. Other than that, all I care about is that we keep this between us, it remains casual, and it never invades our jobs. She doesn't seem to mind.

Kris remains in the shower while I throw on a pair of jeans and t-shirt. I rub the towel over my short hair a few times, then comb it into its usual side part. Its color is becoming more peppered with gray since I started my principal's job. I always thought people were being over dramatic when they said that happened. I'm eating my words.

"I have to go pick up Ava. Lock up when you leave?" I call out.

"You got it."

Our parting of ways is usually as simple as that. Tomorrow, we will go to work, do our jobs, and this evening never happened. I wouldn't even call her one of my work wives. She does nothing extra for me on the job, and we rarely speak at work. In fact, we rarely speak at all.

I pull my car in front of what used to be my home. Well, mine and Abby's. We bought this Gothic style house because it was dirt cheap—not because it was just a few blocks from her crazy aunt.

Abby had said that her Aunt Ruby had rented this same house when she first moved to town more than twenty years ago. She lived in it until Abby's mother became ill.

The house has more space than the two of us would ever need. At first, Abby was reluctant to buy it because of all the stigma behind its stories. Around town, the house is a legend. Rumors said it was haunted—it looks it, too.

It stands taller than all the surrounding houses, except for the mansion in the far corner of the street. In the center of the house is a steep A-frame roof that stands a story taller than the rest of the house. Spread across the front are massive, arched windows that look like what one might see in a cathedral. When you enter the front door, you're met with soaring ceilings and an impressive black walnut staircase. I think it was the stairs that sold Abby on buying it. She remembered seeing them when she was very young, and they were similar to the ones in her early childhood home.

I walk up the wide steps to the antique wooden door and knock on the stained glass. As we worked on renovating the house, Abby and I wanted to keep as much of the original house intact as possible. It took a lot more work, but it turned out beautifully. It still looks haunted, but it's a nice haunted.

The door opens and my breathing stops. Abby appears in the doorway, her hair thrown up into a loose knot, wearing flattering pajama bottoms and a thin white t-shirt. Seeing her this way takes me back to lazy mornings spent tangled up together. Sunday morning sex, then lying in bed until we couldn't stand to any longer, followed by flirting in the kitchen while we fixed breakfast. I have to peel my eyes away.

Abby slaps her forehead. "Sorry, I forgot to tell you to pick Ava up at Ruby's. Ruby has been begging to spend a little time with Ava for weeks now, so I thought she could go this evening for a few minutes."

Ruby is good with Ava, but one thing Abby and I agree on is, we don't want Ruby's grumpy nature rubbing off on our daughter.

"Oh, okay." I seem to always fumble for words when I'm alone with Abby. Something about the way she looks right now makes me stutter like a teenage, nerdy boy with braces trying to talk to a pretty girl. I just nod, smile, and turn to walk back down the steps.

"Jared?"

"Yes?" I turn around a little too eagerly, like a dog eager for a bone.

"Don't let her stay up too late. Last time she said you let her stay up until 10:30. And…you let her have a candy bar at breakfast." Abby gives me a scolding look.

I wince and turn. If I were a dog, my ears would be falling slack, and my tail would be tucked between my legs. I walk to my car, feeling like a chastised child. I don't know why, but I just bite my tongue.

It's like that when I'm with Abby. I lose my confidence, but I don't think it's because she intentionally tries to make me feel that way. It goes back much further than that. All I wanted when I was a child was to be loved, nurtured—taken care of. But all I received was rejection. Then, when Abby decided that she no longer wanted to be married to me, I felt that same rejection all over again. Now, I question whether I'm worthy of love, period.

As I walk onto Ruby's front porch, which is over-stuffed with outdoor furniture, I hear the TV blaring a familiar cartoon theme song inside. There's no mistaking one of Ava's favorite cartoons about a yellow, square sponge that lives under the sea. I knock loudly, twice, then I hear little feet stomping up to the door.

Ava opens and squeals, "Daddy!"

I squat down and give her a huge hug and kiss. When I was a child, hugs were in short supply. In fact, any sort of affection seemed to be off limits, unless you would call a backhand across the face affection. It seemed to be the only kind my drunken father knew how to give. I swore I would never be like him. Because of his treatment, I make sure that I hug and kiss Ava daily, and on the days I don't see her, I make up for it by kissing each cheek for each day we aren't together. We rarely ever go more than two days without seeing one another.

"Where's your Aunt Ruby?"

"We're playing hide-and-go-seek. But she's still hiding."

"So, how long has she been hiding?"

"A while—until I'm told I should let her out."

I frown and look back through the house. "Ava. Where's your aunt?"

Ava puts her finger over her mouth to shush me, then takes my hand and leads me around to the side of the massive, walnut staircase, very similar to the one in the house I just left. She stops in front of a door, which I assume leads to a closet under the stairs. About chest height is an old-fashioned latch and hook that is secured in place. It's high enough that Ava would have had to use a chair to reach it.

"She's in there," Ava whispers and points.

"Ava! Did you lock Aunt Ruby in there?" I immediately flip the latch up from its hook and open the door. Sitting crouched inside is Ruby.

Ruby attempts to stand but remains in a semi-stooped position as she walks out of the closet, struggling to straighten her back.

"I told you, Daddy, we were playing hide and seek."

Ruby purses her lips. "Yeah, we were playing. But I think Little Miss Ava got sidetracked watching TV and forgot that she locked me in here."

"Ava, did you?" I ask, feeling as though I should be scolding her, but instead, I fight to hold back a laugh. I pretend as though I'm a little concerned.

"She's alright," Ruby says. "All kids get distracted." She waves her hand as if to brush it off as no big deal.

I try to be a good parent. "Ava, you shouldn't lock anyone in a closet. It's okay to play, but you probably wouldn't like it if someone did that to you."

Ava frowns. "It wasn't my idea, Daddy, it was Ally's. She told me I should leave her in there a while longer because she used to lock Mommy in there."

"What are you talking about, Ava?" Ruby's eyes narrow in confusion and something else. Fear?

"I'm sure she's just talking about one of her friends at school." I grab Ava and pick her up just as I used to do when she was two years old. I have no desire to get into a long conversation with Ruby about how we should be raising our daughter. She doesn't do it much with me, but often scolds Abby on her parenting skills.

"No, Daddy—"

"We really need to go, Ava. Tell Aunt Ruby you're sorry about forgetting her in the closet."

"But, Dad."

"Ava," I say in a Daddy voice, and she listens.

"Soorrrry."

"It's okay, my dear. We'll play again sometime," Ruby says, but before she even finishes the sentence, we are already heading for the door.

Ava and I head across town, and I realize my apartment doesn't have a lot of food, so I let her pick where we eat for dinner. That was a mistake, because she always chooses McDonalds. Happy meals are the bane of my existence.

I pour out five packets of ketchup onto a napkin, and Ava proceeds to dip one french fry ten times as she counts, nibbling in between each dip.

"So, what's going on in the world of kindergarten lately?"

She lifts her shoulders toward her ears, not looking up from playing in her ketchup.

"Any new boyfriends to tell me about?"

She giggles. "Daaaad."

"What? I'm just asking." I give Ava a wink and a smile.

"No. All the boys in my class are mean." Ava crinkles her nose.

"So, who do you like to hang out with?" I slide the box of chicken nuggets and sliced apples in Ava's direction, trying to encourage her to eat something besides French fries.

"Sarah. Duh." Ava rolls her eyes and ignores the other food in front of her.

I pretty much knew this would be the answer, since she and Sarah are thick as thieves on the playground and cafeteria.

"I have a new friend, but she doesn't go to school." Ava's legs swing back and forth like a pendulum.

"Really. Then how did you meet?"

"She comes to see me at the house."

I cock my head to one side as my eyebrows furrow. "Have I met her?"

"No. She knows Mommy, but she doesn't want to let Mommy see her."

"Aww…one of those sorts of friends. The kind that only you can see?"

"No. I think she lets other kids see her."

"And what do you two do together?"

"We just play." The table between us continues to shake as Ava swings her feet. She picks up a chicken nugget and rakes it through her ketchup, smearing it across the napkin and onto the table.

"Careful, honey." I reach for a stack of napkins and clean it up. "Is this friend a boy or girl?"

"Girl."

"Do you think she'll let me see her?"

Ava lifts both shoulders toward her ears again as she takes a bite of her ketchup-drenched nugget. "Maybe."

"What's your friend's name?"

"Daddy, I need to pee, bad." Ava bounces up and down in her chair as if she can't hold it any longer.

"Okay, come on."

She hops up from her seat and bounces toward the bathroom.

"Hang on—let me check to see if anyone is in there." I knock on the door and hear no answer, then I open it and call out a quick, "hello?" carrying out Abby's instructions for when Ava needs to use a public restroom. Next, I take a few steps in and check under the stalls for feet. Once I'm sure it's empty, I then stand outside the door to keep anyone out until she's finished. Abby insists that anything can happen in a restroom within a matter of seconds. She was beyond insistent about it—almost obsessive.

We finish eating and dump our trays before heading back to my duplex. I swear Ava to secrecy when we stop for a small cone of ice-cream at a local custard joint. "Don't tell your mother."

After building numerous misshaped structures with magnetic blocks and reading some of Ava's favorite stories, I tuck her into bed. Her room at my place doesn't have a lot of her personal belongings, but I bought similar bedroom accessories to what she has at Abby's, so she'd feel at home here, too. I try my best to stick to the same routine she's had since she was born. It's the one thing I still cling to of my old life. As I'm tiptoeing out of her room and pulling the door around, I pause to ask her one more question, but change my mind when I see that she is already asleep.

I'd meant to ask her again what her imaginary friend's name was.

5

I CLOSE the door behind Jared and Ava and plop my back against it, then my head taps against the glass. Normally I hate it when Ava goes to her father's, but today, I welcome the solitude. With everything that's happened the last couple of days, I don't think I can be a very attentive mom.

I wasn't always the person I am now, but my past forced me to be a liar. In public, I'm buttoned up, beautiful, and completely put together. In private, I'm quite the opposite. I'm broken, ashamed, and falling apart at the seams.

Years of the things I've told myself twists like a bowtie. On the outside, things look appealing, but underneath, everything is layered, knotted and permanently scared. I don't even like the real me. I sometimes wish I could forget that I'm broken and actually be who I pretend to be. That could only happen if the past were to rewrite itself with a better beginning.

My nerves are buzzing like a pent-up bee, so I decide to make some coffee and add a double shot of honey whiskey to it, then sit down at the kitchen table. The first sip hits my mouth and burns my taste buds, then the second wave of heat from the whiskey stings my tonsils and warms my chest. I savor the combination of pain and flavor. With an attempt to come down from my day, I sift through my thoughts for a moment. Of course, my thoughts fly straight to places better left uncharted.

Jared.

I unconsciously feel for the faint ridge around my left finger where a ring used to be. When we were married, it was a nervous habit to rotate it around and around.

He looked amazing today—of course, he always does. I miss him—sometimes too much. I've never really moved on, but I'm sure he has. I'm not so naive that I try to convince myself he leads a celibate life—I know he probably has a woman in his bed whenever he feels the urge—even though I haven't been with anyone since him. The solo life I lead now is a choice I made out of regret, guilt, and circumstance. Living alone is how I make myself pay for the sins of my past. And, it's a way of keeping the past buried as it should be.

Jared knows very little of all that, and I want it to stay that way. He doesn't even know I had a sister, much less the fact that I was the one responsible for her death. We rarely deserve the lives we lead and end up paying for them with the debts accumulated by our sins. My price for appeasing the guilt is distancing myself from Jared and complete happiness.

I built an imaginary wall around myself years ago—it's the one sure thing that keeps me safe and sane—at least that's what I tell myself. At one point I allowed Jared to enter inside my walls, but I realized he was breaking them down, so I forced him to exit, and reinforced them with new, thickened layers of shame and guilt—the kind that's impenetrable.

I realize I'm retreating too far into my thoughts, so I shake them off and try to distract myself. I stand and look around the large kitchen, which has been by far the hardest in the house to remodel. Through its renovation, my goal was to keep the vintage look yet add all the modern amenities. The one thing it's lacking is a pantry and storage space. My plans are to eventually make use of the basement by converting it to a wine and food cellar. Every room in the house has been completely redone except for one spare bedroom, the basement, and a small room in the attic.

The quietness of the house suddenly seems too loud, just as my thoughts are. As I aimlessly roam around my kitchen, my eyes land on the basement door. I stare at it, and this act alone gives me a dreaded feeling. I hate the basement. Something about it scares the hell out of me. But why?

I look at the door as if something might appear with the answer. I'm always telling Ava as we're searching for monsters under her bed that facing your fear will make you big and strong. I'm such a hypocrite—because I sure don't. One day, she's going to see right through it.

I continue to eye the door and scold myself for being such a wimp. Maybe busying myself down there could be a perfect distraction—at least my mind won't be able to concentrate on anything other than the fact that it creeps me out. I chew on my bottom lip, continue to stare, and debate it some more. There are some boxes down there I have yet to unpack since moving in, and now could be as good of time as any to start clearing out the space. Who knows what I have packed away down there that I haven't seen in years?

When I was little, I remember this old house being down the street from ours. It stood empty for years and the tales of it being haunted were common. Rumors had it that it was too haunted for anyone to want to live in. Since I've lived here, I haven't encountered anything that really spooked me enough to run.

Except for last night.

When Ava mentioned an imaginary friend with the same name as my dead sister.

When Aunt Ruby moved back into town, she rented this house for a short while and her payment was dirt cheap. She said she didn't believe in all that stuff. When I came to meet Ruby for the first time, I remember thinking the house was scary, and so was she. The house and she were the perfect match for each other. After my mother went into the hospital, my aunt moved into our house, and minus a brief renter or two, it remained empty all those years until Jared and I bought it.

To the left of the basement is a set of back stairs that leads to the second floor. Ava loves the stairs in the house. Her favorite thing to do is sneak up the back stairs and down the front stairs, then she pops into the kitchen as she yells *Boo*.

The basement staircase, however, is something she isn't allowed to play on or around. In fact, she isn't supposed to open the basement door, ever. I flip the switch to light the stairs and open the door. The hairs on my arms immediately rise, followed by a shudder. A flood of mixed emotions threatens to surface—the same I always get when locked in a small, claustrophobic space. The kind I used to get being locked in a closet. In fact, it feels as if an unwanted memory is lurking down there, and I don't want to know what it is.

I hesitate, take a deep breath, and swallow it down, then force myself to take the first step. I freeze, and my heart kicks in even faster before I turn and dart back into the kitchen.

I stand frozen, staring at the open door. I feel the urge to go, yet it scares the hell out of me. Something is pulling me to do it, yet my fear is warning me to stay away. I squeeze my fingertips hard. *How am I ever going to teach my daughter to face her fears if I can't even do it myself? Why does this space freak me out so much?* The same threatening memory attempts to rise again, and I squeeze my eyes shut and blink it away. I stare down the dimly lit stairs and violently shake my hands, as though it will shake away my anxiety.

"Face your fears, Abby. You have to—for Ava." I say the three words, *face your fears* two more times and take the first step, again. Then another and another, all while gripping the handrail with white-knuckled fingers.

The basement looks and smells just as expected when it comes to a hundred-year-old house. The walls are just like the ones on the outside of the house. Aged, red brick, complete with white efflorescence spotting its surfaces. You can still smell a hint of moth balls from days gone by.

Mixed in with the aging smells, I get a whiff of another strange odor and I have to sniff several times to determine what it smells like. The foul stench makes me wince. It smells similar to rotting flesh—a smell that I haven't encountered since I was a kid.

The same that came with the rare flower that Rosemary had in our back garden. I cautiously sniff again, and as quickly as the odor came, it disappears.

I frown as I descend the last few steps, which creak and protest under my feet. Six small windows, two on each wall, do very little to shed any light. When I reach the bottom, I pull a string hanging down from the ceiling, and the bulb at the top of the stairs flickers and goes dark.

My eyebrows greet one another as I stare back at it. The now single light above my head does very little to illuminate the space. I move through the room toward another string hanging from the ceiling, and the cold stone floor feels uneven under my feet. With a yank of the string, the light flashes, pops, and then goes dark. The large room seems to shrink around me as the shadows and corners appear to come alive. A sudden lack of air creeps in around me. I hate this space. I've only been down here a handful of times, and even then, I chickened out and ran back upstairs.

My chest tightens and my mouth goes dry as the sensation of

being inside a dark closet catapult to the front of my mind and memory. The closet that I'd spent a few lonely times in as a child wasn't a tiny space, in fact it, was quite large for a closet. It had a faint light bulb in the center with a long chain. It produced very little light, making the corners dark and suffocating. I remember being terrified of the things that could be hiding in them.

The dark has been my enemy ever since.

Standing here now reminds me of why I never come down here, and why I haven't attempted to do anything with the space before now. I don't even think Jared did much exploring. He seems even more creeped out by the basement than I am.

I'm not sure why.

Out of instinct and habit, I again grip my finger to twirl the absent ring. With no ring there, I find myself resorting back to old rituals. With the index finger and thumb of my left hand, I squeeze the tips of my fingers on my right-hand one by one. First, I squeeze the tip of my thumb, pressing on the nail to the point I feel a sharp quick pain. Then I move on to the index finger and then the next until I have pinched each one. When I finish one hand I switch to the other and repeat the same thing. I started this habit years ago whenever I felt overwhelmed or anxious. It was a habit I could hide easily, but also one where I could feel a hint of pain to take my focus elsewhere. Inflicting pain on myself has often been a soothing source of comfort.

As I shift my habit into self-talk, I tell myself that I'm eventually going to have to do something with this area of the house. I can't be afraid of it forever. It isn't a closet, and I can leave anytime I want to. The space is too big to just let it go to waste.

Rather than deal with the dark, I run back upstairs and dig out a portable work light I used during renovations. If I can see the room better, ideas will come to me about what to do with it. I dig the light out of the utility room and head back down the dark stairs. The basement only has two outlets, so I find one of them and plug it in. That's something I'll need to add.

When I flick the switch on the light box, the room takes on a warmer, appealing atmosphere, yet light doesn't seem to penetrate the corners of the room. The floors remind me of the cobblestone streets in Italy where Jared and I spent our honeymoon. The white salty substance growing on the walls now gives the brick character rather than scarring it. I walk along the walls and run my hand over the cool rough brick, making my way to the farthest corner of the room. Lower to the floor, I find numerous childlike drawings that appear to have been done in chalk. The figures resemble stick people and oddly shaped animals. The drawings run along the wall to the corner and continue on the adjacent wall. Most of them seem random with no pattern. There's something about them that seems ghostlike, and a chill prickles the hair on my arms.

In the center of the back wall is a dark, wooden, plank door that resembles something you would find on a barn loft with a dark bronze doorknob and hinges. Up high, almost out of my reach, is a slide lock. I remember the door being thick and very heavy. I've only opened it on a few occasions and glanced inside. I had enough to keep myself busy without worrying about what to do with it. The room behind the door is pitch black and has the atmosphere of a crypt. My heart begins to thud again.

Before I open the door, I grab the handle on the work light and carry it with me. Maybe it won't be so creepy when lit up. As I open the hefty door, it makes an eerie, popping sound. I shudder, and a tingling sensation lifts the hairs on my arms. This room feels even cooler than the rest of the basement, and the smell of moth balls is much stronger in here. It's at least ten feet by ten feet, maybe more, and the cobblestone in this space have less wear.

In the center of the back wall is another door directly across from this door. It opens to a set of concrete steps that lead up and outside. At the top is yet another set of doors that opens out and upward toward the sky. I'm assuming its purpose was to give quick access to shelter from a storm. Both doors stay locked, with the one outside secured by padlock.

As I move to the center of the room, I reach the end of the cord on my light—it's stretched as far as it will go. I sit it down in the middle of the floor, aiming it toward the left corner, and walk that direction. My knees crackle as I squat down and run my hand over the smooth stones. They're cold and slick. Directly on the floor stones, I find more drawings, and these have been drawn with more detail. On the first stone is a stick figure woman. I can tell because her head is drawn bigger than her body, and her hair made out of squiggly lines. Her face is drawn with slanted eyebrows and a mean frown. Under the drawing is one word drawn sloppily but readable.

Witch.

Next to it is a smaller stick figure with similar hair. The eyes are drawn in a large, drooping fashion, and shapes resembling teardrops are drawn underneath the eyes. Then there's another girl drawn the same, only she has a smile on her face. There are no words drawn underneath these.

Continuing to squat while moving my feet, I find more drawings. This part of the floor is dark, so I move to the light and aim it toward them. Four stones sit side by side, each containing their own sketches. They remind me of those car decal stickers on the back of Mom vans depicting each member of the family.

The first two stick figures are similar in size and larger than the other two. They're all very similar to the drawing in the opposite corner, only underneath these, are names. A wave of nausea rises from my stomach and lodges in my throat. The smaller drawings display the names "Abby" and "Ally" at the bottom.

"What the hell?" I mutter.

My eyes move to the next two stick figures. Underneath the

larger one is the name "Angel", and the last, I almost shout out loud.

Tina!

I gasp as I recoil from the picture.

I stare at it, and as I do, a haunting thought, or better yet, a memory, enters the back of my mind and lingers there.

6

 bby and Ally
2001

"I think she looks like a witch," Ally whispers as she slings her side ponytail back over her shoulder.

"Shhh." Abby presses her index finger against her lips. "She might hear you."

Ally shrugs her shoulders and frowns. "So?"

"What are you girls whispering about?" Ruby says as she rounds the corner from the kitchen to the living room. Her face is set into a smile but lacks sincerity. It seems as if it isn't used to performing it very often. "Your mom and I used to whisper and keep secrets all the time. It must be a twin thing."

Ally's face turns a light shade of pink. "Nothing," she spits out.

"Then why is your face turning five shades of red? You clearly said something you didn't want me to hear." Ruby holds her coffee mug between two hands and wiggles her way in between the two girls on the couch. "So, why don't you two scoot back and tell me something about yourselves?"

The girls look at one another, then flop back on the couch; half sitting, half lying, as Ally bounces her legs from the knees down. She smooths out the outer layer of her pink skorts, then picks at the sequence of her blingy top.

"You girls don't have to be shy with your Aunt Ruby. You can tell me anything. How about we start with, which one of you is the angel, and which is the devil?" Ruby raises her eyebrows and gives a crooked smile. "Hmm? Twins always have a rule follower and a rule breaker."

"Abby always breaks more rules than me." Ally speaks up quickly.

"Uh-uh." Abby leaps forward from the back of the couch and gives Ally a scowling look. "You do!"

Ruby cackles. "The fox, the finder, the stink lays behind her."

"Huh?" Ally twists her face and scrunches her eyebrows.

"What this means, little girl, is if one person accuses another of something, then they are usually the guilty one."

Ally frowns and crosses her arms in front of her chest as Abby gives Ally a smug smile and bobbles her head.

Ruby laughs again. "Relax. You're both children, so that means you both break the rules from time to time, but I'm going to say that, Ally, you are the outspoken one. Am I right?"

Both girls nod.

"Well, here's how I know. Take, for example, your clothes. Ally's has a lot more bling, and Abby, your clothing is much more conservative. You don't like all that flashy stuff, do you?

Abby nods again.

Ruby takes hold of Ally's hand and fumbles with the ring on her middle finger. "I'm assuming this is a mood ring?"

This time Ally nods.

"Right now, it's more of a yellow, which means you're a bit restless and unsure about your situation. The fact that you wear such a ring means that you're also more vocal than Abby. You usually don't have a problem telling people what you think."

Ally shrugs, but Abby says, "She's definitely mouthier." Her comment draws a mean look from Ally.

"Who was the rule breaker between you and Mom?" Abby asks, curiosity stirring inside her.

"Well, your mother, of course."

"Aunt Ruby is probably right on this one. I was the one who always got into trouble." Rosemary says as she walks into the room, sipping a cup of coffee. She takes a seat on the loveseat adjacent to the couch.

"I'm glad to hear you admit that after all these years," Ruby says.

"Mom, can we go outside and play now?" Ally asks.

Rosemary looks at Ruby. "Have you checked the back yard closely? Is it safe for them to play in?"

"Oh, yeah. There's a set of doors that lead to the basement, but they should be locked. The yard is just a little overgrown, that's all."

"I guess so. Just stay in the yard," Rosemary says.

The girls spring from the couch and run from the room before Rosemary even finishes the sentence, their tiny voices echoing off the bare walls.

Abby pauses to pull her socks up after closing the living room door behind them, and she listens to the grown-up voices as they continue to talk without them.

"You're going to have your hands full with those two in a few years," Ruby says.

Rosemary exhales a long sigh. "I know. They're you and I made over. I keep waiting for something bad to happen."

Abby frowns and busies herself with getting her sock just so.

"Well, I'm sure if anything were going to happen to one of them, you'd know it beforehand. You worry too much."

"I've stopped having visions. I don't want them—in fact, I've learned how to shut them out altogether."

"Do you think that's wise?"

"Yes. My life is so much more peaceful not knowing anything." Rosemary quickly changes the subject. "So, which room would you like to start unpacking first?"

"I say you start in here and I'll move to the kitchen."

"Deal. Peek out back and check on the girls now and then. Will ya?"

"Oh, they'll be fine, but I will if it makes you feel better," Ruby says.

Abby swallows and gives her head a little shake before running to catch up with her sister. *Grown-ups are weird.*

Outside, the girls explore the massive backyard where the lawn is patchy and full of more weeds than grass. They follow the stone path that runs close to the house, which also winds and curves in all directions throughout the backyard. Ally squats down next to the back of the house to peek in a window close to the ground.

"What do you see?" Abby asks.

"Nothing. It's too dark."

"Let me see," Abby says.

After Ally stands and backs away from the window, Abby squats low to the ground, cups her hands around the sides of her face, and presses close to the glass. Just as she gets into position, Ally gooses her and screams, "Rrrrr."

Abby jumps to standing. "Stop it, Ally," she whines.

Ally laughs and skips away, leaving Abby standing beside the house huffing and puffing. She kicks pebbles around on the path for several minutes, then attempts to look in the window again. It's pitch-black on the other side. She stands and shivers, feeling the air around her growing suddenly cold, and she moves out of the shade into the sun.

As Abby walks in zigzags along the stone path farther into the yard, the smell of something that reminds her of her mother's stinky corpse flower starts to get up her nose. She looks around to see if there is one around somewhere, but there's nothing that looks like the unique plant at her house. While searching, she hears her sister giggling, then another voice besides her sister's. She cups a hand over her eyes to block out the sun and scans the huge back yard. As she walks around a fat bush, she spots Ally and another girl in the far corner of the patchy lawn under a tree. The tall grass tickles her shins as she walks toward them.

"Hi, Abby," Tina calls out.

Abby picks up the pace and joins them under the tree. "What are you doing here?"

"I live here, silly."

"In this house?" Abby asks.

Tina pauses and looks at the house as if she's thinking. "Sort of."

"Huh?" Ally asks.

Tina's eyes dart between the two of them. "Sometimes I live here, and sometimes I don't."

"That doesn't make sense," Abby says.

"It doesn't make sense to me either. No one is supposed to see me, but I'm glad you two can."

"Me too," Ally says.

"What's under your shirt?" Abby asks.

Tina looks down and then back to the two girls. "Can you keep a secret?"

"Yeah," they both say.

Tina lifts her shirt to reveal an odd-shaped object hanging from a strap around her neck. "It's an old camera. Look!" Maneuvering the strap free, she presses the top of the black box, and a compartment pops up, revealing a flash. "Here, let's all sit under this tree, and I'll show you."

The three girls sit on the ground shoulder-to-shoulder, Tina in the center. She turns the front of the camera towards them. "You ready? On the count of three, smile. One, two, three."

The camera clicks, then makes a whirring sound and spits a piece of paper out of the front.

"Cool," Abby squeals, awestruck. "Where did you find this?"

"It was a gift."

"Can I see it?" Ally asks.

"Maybe later." Tina tucks the camera back under her shirt.

"Can you play with us?" Abby asks.

"Sure. Want me to show you around?"

"Yeah," Abby answers first.

The three girls roam around the yard, picking up rocks and climbing on and around toppled concrete benches and fountains. They make their way closer to the back of the house and spot two doors laid over at an angle. Abby gasps. They look as if they could open up and allow someone to walk into the ground.

"What's this?" Ally asks as she runs toward them, and the other two follow. The set of wooden doors lay side by side with an iron ring handle mounted toward the bottom of the right door.

Ally's eyes are wide as she turns to Tina. "Do these lead underground?"

Tina nods.

"Cool! Can we look?" Ally asks.

"Ally, I don't think Mom would want us doing that," Abby warns.

"It's okay," Tina says. "Let me show you. Here, help me." She pulls on the handle, and Ally joins in by grabbing the edge of the door as they pull it up and back together, revealing a set of concrete steps. The steps get darker as they descend, and another wooden door stands at the bottom. "Come on."

Tina and Ally descend first, then after a short hesitation, Abby follows. As they move down the steps, the damp air drastically cools, making them shiver. They make it to the bottom, and Tina pushes on the other door using her shoulder. It creaks as it opens.

The room in front of them is pitch-black and has the distinct smell of moth balls. Abby grabs her nose. "Ew."

Tina and Ally step into the room first, then Tina calls, "Come on, Abby. What's the matter?"

"She's chicken." Ally laughs.

"I am not." Abby frowns before moving down to join them.

They tiptoe on into the dark room, then Tina whispers, "Want to see something funny?"

Ally squeaks, "Yeah."

"Shh. Follow me and take my hand, Ally," Tina whispers. "Abby, you stay here." Tina drags Ally back through the door, then quickly pulls the door closed behind her, closing Abby inside the dark room.

Abby freezes at the sound of their retreating footsteps up the stairs, and the slam of the outside door above her. She strains her ears to hear the two of them giggling.

"Can she get out?" Ally asks.

"Sure," Tina says, then Abby hears a scrambling sound above her and a grinding from the metal rod that secures the doors in place. "Now she can't."

Barely able to feel her shaking legs, Abby flees to the top of the stairs and pounds on the doors with her fists.

"Let me out, Ally." Abby's voice is frantic, and she hates that she can hear the crying in her tone. They'll both think she's a baby now. It hurts her chest to breathe. It feels like someone heavy is sitting on it.

"We better let her out or I'll get in trouble," Ally says above her.

"Oh, come on. This is fun." Tina sounds disappointed.

"Tina, I will get into so much trouble! We have to let her out."

"Okay. We're only having fun. I'll open it now."

Another metallic scarping sound from the door echoes from

above, and daylight finally filters through the steps as Abby lets out all the air left in her lungs.

"I'm telling Mom, Ally." Abby heaves herself through the entrance and back outside, her face moist with tears, and her breathing hard and fast. She looks from Tina, then back to Ally.

"Please don't tell on Ally. It was me that did it. I didn't think you would get that scared," Tina pleads with a look of wide-eyed innocence on her face.

"Come on, Abby. We were only playing," Ally says.

"Yeah, Abby. You don't want to get your sister into trouble, do you? Remember, only you two can see me. Ally will get all the blame. Or, they might think you're crazy if you tell them about me."

Abby looks at both girls again, her breath calming to normal as she debates what to do. After a long silence, other than her gasps of air, she glares at Ally. "Don't ever do that again, or I'm telling."

"I won't." Ally walks over and places one arm around Abby's shoulders, then pats her on the top of her head. "I promise."

7

 osemary

THE THERAPY ROOM is very similar to the rest of the hospital—stale and mundane like a prison—and my chest fills with dread as I shuffle along the corridor toward it behind Angie, the nursing assistant for my floor. My mind is already picturing the gloom of the room before I even arrive in it. It's small and rectangular, made of concrete block and mortar, painted a dirty white. Its bare walls hold only a single poster, one with a picturesque background sporting a quote by Henry David Thoreau that says, *I took a walk in the woods and came out taller than the trees*. Posters like this are placed sporadically throughout the hospital, each with a quote that's supposed to invoke positive emotions. When you've been here as long as I have, they lose their meaning and become part of the madness that lives inside these walls.

Serenity Oaks Mental Hospital, formerly known as Serenity Oaks Asylum, has been my home for twenty-two years. Its name

60

has changed several times throughout its history in order to make it sound more appealing to an outsider. One of the first changes that occurred was to delete the word *asylum* from its title. The original meaning of the word *asylum* means *retreat* or *sanctuary*. Tales of its history says that it was anything but. The history of the hospital dates back to the late 1800s when most of its residents were placed here against their will. Its legend is rich and haunting.

Stories passed down for decades make for interesting campfire tales to the locals. Anyone who grew up around this town can retell stories told to them by their parents, which had in turn been told to them by their parents, and so on. Stories about wives being committed because they practiced a different religion than her husband and needed to be tortured into changing her belief. Another tells of a parent who committed their son because they claimed he would masturbate himself into complete exhaustion. Most of the hospital's patients were women because they wouldn't obey their husbands. They were packed in groups of up to ten women inside tiny rooms like cans of sardines, and in those times, as many as three-hundred women lived at Serenity Oaks. Male doctors would be the ones to "fix" them.

For the longest time, the hospital was named after one of the doctors who practiced here, contributing his knowledge in mostly immoral ways. Everyone knew him as Doctor Specter. Later, after the truth came out about his treatments, he'd acquired the nickname Doctor Jecter Specter. I suppose it was to mimic Jekyll and Hyde.

During his long reign at the hospital, the straight jacket was the common attire. There was the usual administering of electroshock therapy, but other tales abounded of treatments such as spinning patients at high speeds on a wheel or harnessing them in place, then swinging them until they threw up. Some were branded with hot irons in order to bring patients to their senses. The worst was *malarial treatments*. This cutting-edge doctor believed that injecting a patient with the disease would bring on malarial fever. This was Dr. Jecter Specter's solution and what he believed was the only cure for syphilis.

The current nurses in the hospital often joke about their own solutions to the problem—commit the whoring husbands that gave syphilis to their wives in the first place.

Sometimes I laugh with the staff members, but only on days where laughing feels bearable, and only with the ones I like. I don't mind Angie.

"What do you think of the new doctor, Rosemary? Do you think you might like her?" Angie asks.

I give her a dissatisfied look.

Angie has the patience of a nursing mother. She opens the door to the claustrophobic therapy room as I scoot my feet across the slick tile floor. There's only one window, and in the center of the room are two worn-out wingback chairs, facing each other, with a small table in between. I don't acknowledge Dr. Black sitting in one of them. Instead, I shuffle my feet to the window, my slippers making a swishing sound that echoes in the bare space. I fix my eyes on the sun moving downward on the horizon. My appointments for therapy used to be in the mornings, but they now happen late in the evening, just in time to interrupt my evening painting.

I hate it.

"Good evening, Rose."

This is only my third visit with Dr. Black, but she greets me in the same annoying way she always does. I hate to be called Rose. *My name is Rosemary. I'm not your stupid flower.*

Only one other person has called me Rose, and I forbid it after she betrayed me in the worst possible way.

Dr. Black wouldn't know that I hate to be called Rose, since I've never spoken to her. I've never spoken to anyone here. The only person I even try to communicate with is my weekly visitor—and even then, it's through the game of Scrabble. He's the only person I trust—and Angie.

"We'll be finished in an hour, Angie. Come back and get her then." Dr. Black flicks her hand at Angie as if to say *be gone with you,* along with her usual snooty expression.

I don't like this stuck-up doctor at all.

"I'll be back, Rosemary. You have a good session with Dr. Black, okay?" Angie says kindly as she closes the door behind her.

I stare out the window at a thin cluster of tree branches, giving a spotty view of the courtyard below. A tiny, spotted Wren lands on one of the branches, bouncing and chirping, as if fussing at me for being too close.

My previous doctor of twelve years took an early retirement and left without an explanation. According to Angie, she submitted the paperwork, used her remaining sick days and never returned. No one heard from her after that. Now, I'm stuck with this woman who reminds me of a young, jacked-up version of Mother Kardashian. She must have taken voice lessons for psychotherapists. It's in a low monotone and could put a Tasmanian devil to sleep. I bet she's even boring in bed.

"Do you think you might talk to me today, Rose?"

I can feel her eyes boring into me as I ignore her. I continue to stand with my back to her with no intention of engaging in her psychobabble nonsense.

"Rose? Why don't you come sit down?"

I shift my body more so that my back is all that she can see, no longer giving her a view of my profile. I hate Dr. Black. Why can't she just let me live here without expecting me to engage? I'm perfectly happy with living inside my head.

I stop staring out the window and stare at the palm of my right hand as I hold it close to my face. With my left index finger, I trace the letter that covers the majority of my right palm—each hand etched with the letter *M*. It's a nervous habit I adopted when I was a teenager.

It probably brought me comfort because of what my mom used to tell me. My mother claimed to be a person who could see or hear voices or beings that others couldn't, and that these beings would reveal truths to her—often even when she didn't want them to. She told me and my sister that if you are a person born with a letter or number on your hand, you are endowed with extraordinary intuition and gifts. Those gifts are much more prominent in people blessed with the letter *M*, and not just on one hand, but both. If the *M* covers the entire palm of both hands, the stronger your ability to see and hear the truths around you.

Long before I came here, my mother, Maria, was a patient in this same hospital—long after the treatment of its patients was considered inhumane, but still during a time when women had no rights.

"Rose." Dr. Black speaks a little louder, but the boring tone is the same. "I would really appreciate it if you would come sit down."

I sway my body right to left and back and forth like a rotating chair as I continue to trace the letter on my palm. Dr. Black makes the request again, only this time, a little more demandingly. I take a deep breath and walk toward the empty chair with my shoulder raised to my ear and my face turned away.

"Thank you, Rose. I appreciate that." Dr. Black retrieves her notepad and pen from the table between us, then leans back in her chair as she crosses one leg over the other. My former doctor used to sit in the same chair. She was a lot closer to my age. This doctor is at least twenty years younger and doesn't even look like a doctor in my book. In fact, she looks like someone who spends way too much time on her appearance.

Each time Dr. Sarah Foster and I had met, she would bring a deck of cards to play with. They weren't your typical playing cards, as they always had a theme. It was her way of discovering more about me. We didn't have to talk, but our communication came from the pictures on the cards. They bore different themes such as Alice in Wonderland, Mandalas, various animals, or famous art. She and I both found the cards with mythical creatures as a favorite. Through this form of communication, she discovered that I loved art and books. That led to her bringing me art supplies where we would both paint and sketch. We learned a lot about each other that way. She'd also read me short stories by Ernest Hemingway and Edgar Allan Poe. *The Black Cat* was my favorite. It was as if she could see into my mind and knew what I liked.

Dr. Black has tried none of these things to communicate with me. She spends the entire hour staring at me while asking stupid questions and doodling on her notepad. I spend most of my time with her tuned out. I close my eyes and become engaged in the sound of a bird outside the window.

The sound takes me back, and I've soon disappeared into my back garden with a set of pliers in one hand and a long slender piece of metal in the other. I twist and curve the strip of metal into the shape of a wing and attach it to several more. The beautiful piece of art is slowly growing into a life-sized fairy. Ally and Abby are running and giggling down the paths behind me, through the bushes and trees. A breeze brushes a strand of hair across my lips, and it tickles. I brush it aside and watch the girls zig and zag to and from one another, as the smell of my garden fills my senses. Their laugh is like a beautiful song, light and carefree. I swim in the sounds and smells of home—a time when life was perfect.

"Rose? Rose? Are you in there?" Dr. Black leans forward in her chair, and I can tell she's closer to me now, even though I keep my eyes closed. She lowers her voice. "I think you are in there, Rose. What is it you think you're going to gain by not talking?" She smacks the notepad onto the table more loudly than she should, making me jump, along with her pen. "If you won't talk, then maybe you would like to write something."

I respond by keeping my eyes closed and move my eyeballs from side to side.

"Dr. Foster said that you liked to draw."

I still don't give her the courtesy of opening my eyes.

She huffs out a quick breath. "So here's what I think needs to happen, because obviously, your former therapist didn't get you to talk. My priority is going to be just that. If you would like to continue to have rewards given to you, then you're going to have to earn them. You scratch my back, I'll scratch yours. No more freebies."

I open my eyes but send them straight to the window. She moves from her chair in a low crouch to the table and sits directly in front of me as she leans in and puts her face closer to mine. "I know you're in there, Rose, and I know you understand me. It's time to find out why you're hiding in there. *What* are you hiding in there?"

I stand, walk back to the window, and cross my arms over my chest.

"These sessions are going to get pretty boring for the both of us, Rose, if you don't start talking. Why don't we start with something simple? Just try saying your name. That's not asking too much."

I resort back to my swaying back and forth.

"That's all you have to do—just say your name."

Rose is not my fucking name! The words shout inside my head, and I press the tips of my index fingers against the openings of my ears, determined to block her out for the rest of the session.

I look at the tree in search of the small bird, trying to focus on anything other than the horrid doctor's voice when something happens that hadn't happened in years.

My vision blurs. *It's coming.*

The warning only lasts for a few seconds before I go completely blind. I blink several times, then squeeze my eyes shut and open them again. I still can't see anything. I know it won't last long, but I don't like what it means. Something wants to reveal itself to me. Something that only I can see.

I squeeze my eyes shut again and this time hold them shut to ward it off. But it happens anyway.

"Mmm-mmm-mmm, mmm-mmm-mmm, mmm-mmm-mmm-mmm mmm-mmm-mmm."

A child-like humming makes me stop breathing, but my heart barrels on, and I recognize a familiar children's nursery rhyme. The humming starts over again and as I hear it, the words sing in my head.

"This old man, he played one, he played knick-knack on my thumb."

I look down to my left and my vision returns.

The blond-haired girl standing next to me mimics my earlier swaying back-and-forth movements, as she hums and traces the letter *M* on her hand. When I see her, I'm no longer scared, but I am scared of what it means. I move my right hand away from my ear and drop it down by my side. Her tiny, cool hand slides into mine and I give her a slight smile, then we begin to hum together.

"Mmm-mmm-mmm, mmm-mmm-mmm, mmm-mmm-mmm-mmm-mmm-mmm-mmm. With a knick-knack patty wack give a dog a bone. This old man came rolling home."

She releases my hand and continues to trace the letter on hers and I join in. I feel both joy and terror at seeing my dead daughter for the first time since her death.

And I'm certain it's not a good thing.

bby

As my mind awakens, even before my eyes do, my thoughts begin with Rosemary. I think I dreamed about her. Parts of the dream are choppy and clipped like a poorly edited video, but I was a child again and my mother was dancing around our back garden with the sunlight bouncing off her hair. She was beautiful—like the silhouette of an angel.

When my sister and I were very little, we first called our mother Rosemary just for fun. But she liked hearing us say it, so that's what we called her. From then on, we never called her *Mom*. I barely remember what she looks like. She's like a deep-seated memory that sometimes whispers to me, but it's as if my mind is keeping the details of her a secret. It's not as if I've tried to listen to the voices in my head, in fact, I shut them out when they get too loud. It's easier that way. It keeps me from missing her so much.

The few details that my mind does give me access to, are little things like the way she dressed. All colorful with her long flowing skirts and mismatched, colorful tops. She always wore something in her hair, long and flowing, just as her hair was. Then there was the way she fixed pancakes. It was a Sunday morning ritual. She'd place blueberries into the batter after she poured it onto the griddle to make the shape of a heart. Then in the center of the heart, she'd drop diced strawberries to form two eyes and a smiling mouth. It matched the same hearts my sister and I would draw for her all the time as children. When she'd put them on my plate, she'd say *you make my heart smile.* Now I do the same for Ava.

I've found myself thinking about Rosemary more and more lately. There are times I feel as abandoned as a used Kleenex. Left behind to deal with the whole slimy mess of my life without her. She left me at the worst possible time. I understand that she lost her daughter, but I lost my twin sister—my right arm. That's what it feels like.

My brain is already in full chatter mode, and I haven't even gotten out of bed. I give my body a full stretch and try to wake it to the liveliness my brain has already reached, then throw back the covers. I step into Ava's empty room—I hate it when she's gone.

The room is a mess with toys scattered about the floor, but I ignore it and decide to get some much-needed coffee. When I turn to leave, I catch a sudden distinct smell that makes me pause. It smells very strongly like rosemary. I sniff the air several times and each time the smell intensifies. It makes me turn and look back into Ava's room for the source, but upon scanning it, I don't see anything that would give off this kind of smell. I frown, stare a bit longer, then shake it off and turn again to go downstairs.

My foot hits the top step, and I stumble and catch myself on the banister as a sudden crash followed by glass shattering sounds from behind me.

I step in the direction of the crash, shaking like a frightened child in the dark. I already know which picture has fallen before I even look at the wall.

The only picture I have of my mother.

I pick up my old habit and bring my hands together, pinching the tips of each finger on my right hand and feeling the sting, and then I switch to my left hand. Apprehension forces my feet to slowly tiptoe toward the frame. Why did *this* frame fall now? It's been hanging in the same spot since I moved in.

I catch myself holding my breath, then release it in one long exhale. As I pick up the frame to examine it, shards of glass trickle to the floor. The wire on the back is still secured to the frame, and so is the hook that was holding it. A slight shudder moves through my body at the timing of this exact picture falling. This house has remained quiet up until now, but the last couple of days are making me wonder about all the tales of this place. I shake off the thought, clean up the glass, then carry the picture downstairs with me to make the coffee.

I'd tried visiting my mother in the hospital during my first year of college. It was a mistake. I only saw her from a distance as she was standing with her back to me, painting. As soon as I saw *what*, or rather *who*, she was painting, I left. My sister at seven years old, wearing the same clothing she died in.

I often wonder what my mother is like—now—after all these years. Would she even recognize me? If I showed up one day to see her, would she be happy to see me, or would she turn me away? She believes I killed her daughter.

Seeing evidence of Tina has brought me some kernels of hope. What really happened back then?

My discovery from last night comes flooding back to me. The childish drawings and names. Tina's name. Right after my sister died, I swore over and over I hadn't been the one to kill her. I pleaded with my mother and my aunt, trying to convince them it wasn't me. *It was Tina.* They told me Tina wasn't real and that she was someone I made up in order to deal with what actually happened. *Then who put those drawings there and wrote Tina's name?* The question screams inside my head.

I never saw Tina again after the day my sister died. She disappeared. I searched all the places we would play together, but it was as if she'd never existed. As time went by, and after my mother was committed to a mental hospital, I had to succumb to the idea that maybe it was me—that maybe I *did* make her up in order to deal with what I'd done.

But now, there is proof that Tina existed—or at least existed to me. Question is, how did those drawings and scribbles come to be in the basement of this house? I only remember being down there that one time when my sister and Tina locked me in it. The memory of it is so vivid now.

Tina had convinced me and my sister that no-one else could see her. I don't remember ever introducing her to Rosemary. She always disappeared when someone else was around. I ponder on the memory a bit longer, trying to remember more about the day they'd locked me in the basement, but can't pull any other details to the surface.

After checking the time, I get ready for school and go in long before students arrive. With Jared being the principal, he'll show up early with Ava, and I can spend some time with her before my teaching day begins. Getting prepared for school is much quicker on my own, so I arrive at the school around the same time as Jared. Ava runs to me before I even step from my car.

"Good morning, my girl," I say as I wrap Ava up in a long hug, feeling as if a piece of me has returned. "Did you sleep okay?"

"Uh-huh, and Daddy made me pancakes for breakfast. Just like the kind you make, except he didn't have blueberries, so he used chocolate chips."

I throw Jared a raised eyebrow. I can't help but grin slightly, because Ava seems so happy. He shrugs his shoulders, winks, then shoots his eyes to the ground as if unsure about his reaction. My heart quickens a few beats, and I look away.

I'm amazed at how this man can still turn me into a blubbering, adolescent schoolgirl. You would think being separated as long as we have, those sorts of jitters would have faded by now. I think they're worse.

Our history together goes all the way back to our childhood. We even played together a couple of times as kids. Then he moved away but moved back just after junior high. He came back tall, skinny and awkward, barely recognizable. All the girls went crazy over him. We went from being playmates, to being shy and backward around each other.

We both come from our own kind of broken home. My mother's crazy, my aunt is in far-left field sometimes, and according to Jared, his father's an abusive asshole—emotional as well as physical. Neither one of us is what you would call completely stable. I often wondered when we were married if two broken people could make a whole person. Neither of us had a great childhood. I know all about his, or at least part of it, but he knows very little of mine.

"Is it time for school to start yet, Mommy?" Ava asks as we make our way inside the building.

I check my watch. "Not quite. We'll go to the staff room, and then would you like me to walk you to class?"

Ava nods her head up and down as we enter, closely followed by Megan.

"Good morning, Abby, and mini-Abby," Megan says as she pats Ava on top of the head, then looks back at me. "You ready for our new students?"

"I guess." I look at Megan's choice of clothing for the day. Leggings, long-sleeved t-shirt and tennis shoes. "I see you chose wrestling clothes."

"You never know. I have a feeling this Mason might be a runner. Better be prepared."

I nod. "I have a feeling you might be right. I'm going to walk Ava down to her class real quick. I'll be right back."

"I'll be right here preparing for battle." She salutes.

Megan has been my instructional assistant for over two years. She could easily do my job and more. I asked her in the past why she wouldn't just go on to college to get her teaching certification. Her response was, "No way. I get to do exactly what you do, but without all the stupid paperwork and meetings."

I return back to class and help Megan tidy up before heading to the cafeteria to gather my students. As Megan and I enter the large room packed with long tables, clustered and crowded with children, I spot Jared and one of our new students at the far end of the room. Mason has his back turned to Jared and is kicking the wall as Jared squats down close to him. I give Megan an eyeroll, and she walks over to join them while I give the signal for my students to line up. Mia walks past the entire line of kids straight toward me and takes my hand.

"Good morning, Mia." I smile before walking at a backward pace out of the cafeteria, leading the students in their single file line to class. "Are you excited about your first day of school?"

"Yep." She gives an exaggerated nod.

We continue to walk until Mia tugs on my hand. "Ms. Clark?"

I pause and look down at her. "Yes, Mia?"

Mia looks up at me as she tugs on my hand harder, prompting me to stop and lower my face down closer to her level. "You don't *seem* scared, Ms. Clark?"

"Scared? What do you mean, Mia?"

"Ally said you were scared earlier, but you don't seem to be scared now."

My eyebrows involuntarily furrow, and I remove my hand from Mia's as I turn to walk forward. I realize I'm still frowning when I ask, "You think I was scared earlier? What makes you think that?"

"I told you. Ally told me. She said that she comes to see you—and your daughter."

Nausea hits me as a rush of adrenaline makes my heart pound faster. I continue to walk but can't make myself speak.

Mia has her other hand raised with her index finger pointed, moving it around as if she is drawing something in the air—something I've noticed her doing before. "She said you got scared when that picture fell."

My heart stops as my mind speeds ahead. After a full minute, I'm finally able to speak. "What are you talking about?"

"Ally said she played a joke on you and made a picture fall. She said she was sorry that it scared you, though."

I open my mouth to speak, but no words escape. As I attempt to use words again, I hear little feet stomp past me in a sprint, and when I look to see who it is, Mason speeds by and flips Mia's hair with his hand.

"I hate school. I want to go home." Mason screams the words as Megan sprints down the hall behind him.

"You may have your hands full with this student." Jared steps beside me. His eyes reflect a sympathetic look. "I have to leave for a meeting and Kris is out with a family illness, but our new teacher's assistant, Miss Emily, is going to come in and assist you." Jared tilts his head to the side then adds, "Just in case."

My face must tattle my current state of shock after Mia's revelation, because Jared turns his whole body to look at me.

"Are you all right? You look very pale."

I try to speak, then have to clear my throat. "Yes. I'm fine. You go do what you need to do. We can handle this." My voice fights against nausea as I try to make it sound normal. At this point in my day, all I want to do is go home and bury my head under the covers. It's going to be a long one.

"Alright, then, if you're sure. I'll have my cell on me if you need anything." Jared walks toward the gray double doors at the front of the school building, which squeak as he walks through. I continue to stare at the door, then the chatter of tiny voices brings me back. I hadn't even realized I'd stopped walking, and my line of students are getting antsy behind me. Still unable to bring myself to ask Mia more questions, I walk the students to class as Miss Emily hurries around the line of students to join Megan.

As I get the students settled into their seats, Emily and Megan enter with a much calmer Mason, and show him where his seat is. His demeanor seems more cooperative, and he willingly sits down. I give Megan a hopeful look that he's moved beyond his urge to leave the school building.

Surprisingly, the day moves along smoother than I'd anticipated. With a few minutes left before home time, I sit down at my desk to jot down a few notes to send home to parents, and Mia approaches my desk. I've avoided her all day and let Megan take care of her needs. She comes around behind my desk and stands next to me.

"What do you need, Mia?"

"Are you mad at me, Ms. Clark?"

"Why no, Mia. I could never be upset with you. Why do you ask?"

Mia shrugs her shoulders. "Your face looked mad this morning."

"No, dear, I'm definitely not mad at you."

Mia moves in closer to me, then reaches out and shuffles some pens in a cup on my desk. The noisy rattle penetrates my nerves. "I thought it made you mad when I told you about what Ally did."

"No, not at all," I lie and take a deep breath, trying to hide it. Curiosity battles with apprehension inside my head. Curiosity wins. I rotate my chair so that my body is facing Mia. "So—what does this Ally look like? Are you able to see her?"

"Oh, yes. I can see her better than I can see real people."

"She's not real?"

"No. I see people that aren't real—anymore. They used to be, but not anymore."

The tingling sensation returns on the surface of my skin. Once again, curiosity continues to win the war going on inside my head, and despite my fear, I ask, "What does she look like?"

"Which one, silly?" Mia giggles. "There's two Ally's. This Ally has dark hair and dark eyes—like you."

I pause, press my lips together, and stifle a sound as I hold my breath. Thoughts crash around inside my head all at once, but only one in particular stands out. *Not my sister. Ally had blond hair and blue eyes.*

9

bby and Ally
2001

"READY OR NOT, HERE I COME," Abby calls as she emerges from her bedroom. She steps into the hall and looks one direction, then the other, listening for Ally. The only thing she can hear is the pendulum swinging back and forth on the grandfather clock downstairs. She tiptoes from the stairs to the playroom.

"Girls? Are you up here?" Rosemary calls as she climbs the stairs.

"Yeah," Abby calls back.

Rosemary steps into view. "I'm running over to Ruby's for a bit. Keep the door locked and stay in the house. I'll be back in less than an hour."

"Okay, Rosemary," Abby says.

"Where's your sister?"

"She's hiding."

Rosemary snickers and shifts her voice to a whisper as she

tiptoes closer to Abby. "I'll help you find her." She places her index finger over her lips and gives Abby a mischievous grin, then says loudly, "Ally, did you hear me?"

Abby giggles.

"Yeah." Ally's muffled answer comes from somewhere in the girls' bathroom.

Rosemary bows and gives Abby a wink, then descends the stairs, calling behind her. "Don't open the door for anyone. You girls understand?"

"Yeah," both girl's answer.

Abby sprints to the bathroom and swings open the linen closet. "Found ya."

"No fair." Ally climbs out, propping both fists on her hips, standing just as their mother does when she's upset with them. "It's my turn to go again."

"Uh-uh." Abby says. "You had your turn. It's my turn to hide."

"Rosemary gave away my hiding spot, soooo…it's…my…turn." Ally stomps her foot in a rhythm as she says the last three words.

"Can I play?"

Both girls jump and turn to look toward the stairs. Tina steps up the last step and moves toward them.

"How did you get in our house?" Abby asks.

"Silly girl. I can go wherever I want to."

"Does that mean you're a ghost?" Ally asks.

"You could say that, but it's mostly that I just know how to get around. Can I play hide-and-seek with you?"

"Sure," Ally says.

"Ally, don't you think Rosemary will get mad that we have someone else in the house?"

"She can't see me—remember?"

"Oh, yeah."

"You two hide, and I'll count," Tina says.

Abby and Ally look at each other. "Okay."

Tina places her forearm over her eyes, then turns and rests it against the wall as she begins to count. "One, two, three, four, five—"

Ally runs into their bedroom, and Abby sprints on down the hall to their playroom.

Tina turns her head and peaks under her forearm. She counts on to twenty then yells, "Ready or not, here I come," then walks straight to the first door in the hall and steps into the girls' bedroom. She spots the lump under the blanket, then grips a fistful and jerks it away. "Found you."

***

"Aw. I didn't think you would find me here," Ally whines.

"It was a good spot," Tina says.

"You want to go find Abby now?" Ally asks.

"Nah, I'm bored. I don't want to play anymore. Let's go downstairs and find something else to do."

"What about finding Abby?"

"She'll figure it out in a minute." Tina waves her hand as if to brush her off. "Come on—show me around." She grabs Ally by the hand and begins to drag her toward the stairs. Ally looks behind her with a frown as they walk away.

They reach the bottom of the stairs, and Tina moves through the foyer and begins to roam freely. She comes to a wooden door underneath the stairs and grabs the handle. "What's in here?"

"It's just a closet."

Tina opens it and steps inside. "This is creepy. Wouldn't want to be locked in here." She closes the door and roams some more. She opens two more doors. Each are a spare bedroom with walls painted in lush color, one in a deep burgundy, and the other dark green.

Next, they move to the large living room that's painted and decked out in lush, deep purples, both ceiling and walls. Every room on the first floor is painted in a different color and filled with colorful tapestries. Tina spins and stares up at the soaring ceiling. "Wow. This feels like being in a castle."

Ally continues to follow behind Tina as she opens doors and drawers, trying to keep the questioning look off her face. Rosemary would throw a fit if she or Abby did anything like this while visiting another person's home. She has a rule that people should never rummage through another person's private belongings.

"Your house is so cool," Tina says.

Ally shrugs. "I guess so." She glances back toward the stairs. "Maybe we should tell Abby that we aren't playing anymore. She'll be upset if she finds out we didn't tell her."

"Oh, she'll be okay. She's not a baby." Tina's face looks annoyed. She heads toward the kitchen, leaving Ally to debate with herself. Ally huffs, then follows Tina.

"Do you have any snacks? I'm hungry."

"Sure, there's all kinds of stuff in the pantry. Here, I'll show you."

They enter the massive closet lined with shelves. Ally asks, "What would you like? We have cereal, chips, peanut butter crackers—"

Tina steps beside Ally, her eyes stretched wide open as she looks around at all the stuff. "Wow, this is like a grocery store. You have so much food." She spins one direction then the other, looking at shelves above and at her feet. "Do you have Cocoa Puffs?"

"Yep."

"I'll take that."

Ally brings the box of cereal to the kitchen, followed by a bowl and spoon. She indicates for Tina to take a seat in a tall chair at the cluttered island before opening the refrigerator door to retrieve a jug of milk and pours it into Tina's bowl.

"Aren't you going to have some?" Tina asks.

"I'm not hungry."

"You can't make me eat by myself. That would be rude." Tina frowns at Ally. "I'm your guest, so you have to do what I say, and I say you have to eat a bowl of cereal."

Ally stares back at Tina, flattening her lips together into a frown.

"Hasn't your mom ever taught you that? You have to give your guests whatever they want."

Ally shakes her head. "Rosemary only says we have to be kind and welcoming."

"And that means you have to do what your guest wishes, and I wish for you to eat a bowl of cereal with me." Tina crosses her arms over her chest and bounces her shoulders one time.

Ally huffs then goes to the cabinet to get another bowl, pours some cereal and milk and takes a big mouth full. "Better?" She mumbles the word, her cheeks puffed out, and droplets of milk trickle down her chin.

"Why did you leave me?" Abby barks from the doorway of the kitchen, her fists propped on both sides of her waist, her face consumed with a frown.

Tina drops her spoon into the bowl of cereal and leans back in her chair. "I wanted to tell you that we were going downstairs, but Ally wanted to leave you up there, hiding."

Ally chokes on her mouthful of food, spilling milk from the corner of her mouth. "I did not! You're lying!"

"I'm telling Rosemary," Abby threatens.

"I didn't, Abby, I promise." Ally turns to Tina. "Why are you lying?"

"I'm not lying, Ally. You said she'd be alright and that she'd figure it out," Tina insists.

"That wasn't me, that was you!"

Abby narrows her eyes as if weighing the evidence carefully before rendering judgment. "I believe Tina, because you've done it to me before, Ally."

Ally pales. "I promise, Abby. She's lying."

"If she did it to you before, then you know she would do it again." Tina's words flow across her lips, smooth and soft.

Abby looks at Ally. "I believe Tina, and I'm never playing hide-and-seek with you again." She marches around the island, her feet smacking the tile, and stands next to Tina, glaring at Ally.

Ally huffs through her nose, giving Tina a squinted stare, then stomps toward the stairs. She exaggerates each step as she climbs and mumbles under her breath. "I'm not your friend anymore, Tina."

"Thank you for believing me, Abby," Tina says as she places one arm around Abby's shoulders. "I think you and me are going to be best friends."

10

osemary

Over the years, the hospital has added multiple wings, and now it's like living in a maze—it's easy to lose your bearings, which doesn't seem to be much of a stretch for me these days. One thing that never changes—the smell. Most areas smell like antiseptic and urine.

This morning, I spent some time with my usual Thursday guest, and now I'm getting to do the one activity I enjoy the most —painting. Even though the recreation room has several patients participating in various activities, I can tune them all out and focus on painting memories. For me, painting is the only therapy I need. I get to hide inside each piece.

"Why are you harassing me?" Ewelina's deep Polish accent echoes across the room. "Angie! Angie! This fucking twat is harassing me again!"

I look away from my painting, then roll my eyes as Ewelina

shuffles into the community room in front of Grace, who's holding a magazine and shaking it in the air. Grace, a petite woman with a scrunched-up face and stringy, brown hair, is scooting along right on Ewelina's heels and rambling on about some celebrity—she's obsessed with them.

"Evelyn. Evelyn. Slow down," Grace calls from behind Ewelina as she picks up the pace.

Ewelina stops, swings her body swiftly around in front of Grace, and sticks her chin forward. "My fucking name is Ewelina. That's *Eh-vah-LIY-Naa.*" She says her name loud and slow the second time, stressing each syllable. "If you can't say my fucking name right, don't say it at all." She ignores the shocked expression on the timid woman's face and slings her body back around, reminding me of some drunken, cartoon character pivoting to walk a straight line. She walks away from Grace while pointing behind her. "Angie! I told you to keep this annoying bug away from me."

What I know about Ewelina is that she's from Poland but speaks very good English despite her thick accent. In fact, she can speak several languages. She's a woman with sharp edges that can cut anyone down when she doesn't want to interact with them. She became a patient here a few months ago, and now follows me around every chance she gets. I assume she's a couple of years older than I am but gets around far better and does enough talking for the both of us. According to Angie, she was in a different hospital somewhere in Virginia and her family had her transferred here.

No one needs good hearing around Ewelina. She's loud. She also thinks that anyone who speaks to her is harassing her—except for me, because I've never spoken to her. For some reason, she's attached herself to me. Maybe that's why.

"Matthew McConaughey told me I was sexy. Look, he says it right here. *When I see grace in a woman, that's very sexy.*" Grace reads the words with a southern drawl as if trying to sound like the actor, and shakes the magazine at Ewelina, continuing to scoot behind her.

Ewelina sticks her index fingers in her ears and shuffles her feet even faster toward the window where I'm standing. She's lanky and probably a head taller than me. Her face droops in a permanent scowl, and her voice is halfway to the depths of a man's.

"It's all right, Ewelina, calm down—and watch your language." Angie pats the air instead of Ewelina's arm—she hates to be touched. Angie steps in and hooks her arm into the crook of Grace's skinny elbow and guides her in a different direction. "Why don't you show me, Grace?"

Ewelina makes me think of my mother. She's one of those people who hears voices that aren't there, and I think she talks all the time to drown them out. My mother was the same. She claimed the voices were her ancestors guiding her through life. To an outsider, she just seemed crazy. Strange thing was the voices she heard were almost always right. If they told her something was going to happen, it did.

Ewelina isn't crazy—or at least I don't think so. She's just loud and obnoxious. I'm guessing the only reason she's here is because of her interaction with people who aren't there. But I often wonder what actually defines one as crazy? It has different meanings for different people.

There was a time in my life when I saw things that were unexplainable—revelations—but I learned to tune them out. I never wanted the gift to begin with. The only gifts it ever seemed to give me were heartbreak and tragedy. I learned life was easier to deny that I had the ability, and by ignoring it long enough, it stopped, until recently.

Now I'm seeing my dead daughter.

"Can you believe her? She actually thinks that Matthew

McConaughey would want anything to do with her dried-up puss." Ewelina puffs through her lips and they flap. "She's got the face of a boar's ass and I bet her tits look like five-day-old, deflated balloons." She stops just behind my canvas and stares at me. "Why do you keep painting that same girl over and over, Rosemary?" She asks the question without looking at the painting. "Don't you get tired of doing the same thing day after day?"

I look at her and shake my head, then point to the painting.

Ewelina props both her fists on her hipbones and turns her body to look at it. "Oh. This girl is different. I like the brown hair. Is that your child, too?" Ewelina's last words come out through a deep cough she doesn't bother covering her mouth for, and droplets of spit burst from her.

I wince, then shrug my shoulders.

"Well, she looks a lot like that other girl you paint all the time. You didn't tell me you had another child." She says the last part so loud that I frown at her and look around the room.

At least a dozen other patients are scattered about the brightly lit space. Some are seated at tables engaged in silent card games, while others seem oblivious they're in the world. Two more patients stand and stare out through barred windows, while another gentleman stands at the opposite end of the room and paints as well. He stops to look around his canvas, gives a grimace in Ewelina's direction, then goes back to work.

I frown at Ewelina, exhale disgustedly, and turn away from her.

"Why you got to be like that for, Rosemary?" Ewelina darts around me and crouches in front of my face. "I'm just trying to shoot the shit with you. When you gonna learn to have fun? You and I both know we're the only ones in here that's not crazy."

Ewelina reminds me that I'm not really crazy, even though I'm now seeing my dead daughter. I suppose to some, that would seem crazy, but it really isn't. One has to cling to something to actually keep from going looney in here. Ewelina, on the other hand, claims to hear former patients talking to her. Mostly women. She says they try to tell her about the different ways they were tortured in this place. I'm not sure she listens to the voices, because I often see her with her fingers stuck in her ears while she chants, *Hail Mary full of grace, the lord is with you. Blessed are you among women and blessed...Amen.* When the voices are really loud, she says the words in Latin.

"How come you never painted this girl before?" Ewelina asks.

I look at her, and my eyes must have given her an answer that I didn't intend to give.

"Awww, this girl broke your heart. Didn't she?" Ewelina pauses, then starts to wave her hand around her head. "This voice in my head told me about her."

I look at Ewelina and give her a puzzled look.

"Maria told me."

My confused stare shifts to an incredulous glare.

Ewelina stutters and starts to tap her fingers on her head. "I told you, Rosemary, people talk to me inside my head. Is this the girl Maria told me about? The one that is responsible for your other daughter's death?"

I shake my head in short, choppy movements, then duck my chin low and begin to walk away, abandoning my painting while my insides begin to quiver. My pace quickens the closer I get to the door of the recreation room.

"Rosemary!" Ewelina hurries behind me, screaming my name as I dart around the doorway and down the hall.

Angie darts in front of Ewelina. "Maybe you should let her be for now, Ewelina—Rosemary seems upset."

"But—"

"Just give her a little time, okay?" Angie urges.

"But—"

"Just a few minutes. Okay?" Angie's tone remains as though she is soothing a small child.

Ewelina huffs, then I hear nothing else as I turn the corner down another hallway and dart into my room. My thoughts scurry as fast as my feet shuffle. *I don't want to talk about this—with anyone.*

I pace the floor of my small, square room, which isn't like the other patients' rooms. I've been here long enough that the staff over the years have supplied me with numerous wall tapestries. They cover every inch of the walls and ceilings, each rich in multi-colors. Even the light fixtures are covered in blue sheers, which give the room a softer glow.

I scurry back and forth like a fish in an aquarium tank as I wring my hands like that of a person with a compulsive hand-washing disorder. I must look like the stereotypical mental patient right now. Before I can stop it, my lips mouth words, but no sound escapes them.

I haven't told anyone about the death of my daughter. The only recordings of this would be a coroner's report—and the photo album I have tucked away, of course. It's been tucked away for years, and I won't even allow myself to look at it. But today, the urge hits me hard and fast. I move to the door and look out into the hallway in both directions to see if anyone is nearby. It's empty, so I ease the door closed, then slide open the large drawer at the bottom of my wardrobe cabinet. I dig to the very bottom and pull it free.

I grip the front cover along with several pages and the random page I land on isn't the one I wanted to see. It's a clipped newspaper article with a bold headline that reads *Little Girl Dies.*

Traveling down memory lane isn't the path I want to visit after all, and I slam the album closed. It's an avenue I've avoided for a long time—it's broken and unsafe for my sanity. I put it back in the drawer and cover it up. Just as I close the drawer, the door to my room swings open.

"Rosemary. You have a visitor."

11

ared

I DON'T THINK it's possible to help someone find their way if they don't even know they're lost.

Maybe that's why Abby functions in society as well as she does. She has no clue just how lost she is. Abby has been this way ever since I've known her. I was aware of it years ago when we were kids, and we would hang out together. As teenagers, we'd imagine that we were going on some sort of adventure that would take us far away from home. In fact, she never wanted to go home—neither did I. Curfew with my father was at dark, and even if it was getting dark outside, she would always beg me to stay out a little bit longer. I ended up in deep shit with my father many times even though I knew I would be, I stayed out with her anyway.

My father wasn't a nice man—ever. I'm not sure I ever saw him smile, and later in life, I never understood why my mother ever hooked up with him to begin with. He was never good to her, nor me. As I got older and observed the way he treated her, I swore I would never speak to a woman the way my father spoke to my mother. In fact, I vowed that I would never turn out like him and that I would be the best husband and father possible. In the end, I suppose it wasn't enough to make Abby hold on. There are days when I want to tell her how I really feel—that I want her back, but I don't think I can bear her rejecting me a second time.

Abby seemed extremely on edge earlier today at school. She often does, but she's usually good at hiding it. This past couple of days she hasn't been, and something is off. I'm not sure why, but I still feel the need to come to her rescue when I see she's stressed or worried. Old habits just won't die. Or maybe it's because I'm still in love with her.

She grabbed my attention a long time ago and never gave it back.

I'm pretty sure she hates me most of the time. If she knew where I was going right now, she would hate me even more. I've been making this trip across town every week for a couple of years now. I do it purely for selfish reasons. It allows me to feel close to Abby somehow. This woman I'm seeing is the only person I can talk to about her. She knows all about me and Abby, including all the things she and I have lost. She's the only person I'll talk to about the horrible tragedy that tore Abby and me apart—for good.

That awful day that Abby won't ever talk about—not even with herself.

I step up to the glass doors and ring the button to request entry. Before the doors open, I can smell antiseptic and the other inde-scribable smell that always comes with a place like this. A loud buzz indicates that I can enter, so I pull on the heavy glass door, then a second door before I enter a small room. A tall U-shaped counter with one door to the left stands several feet into the room. Behind the counter sits a security guard next to a pale woman who looks as if she's never stepped into the sun. Her short, bobbed hair is bleached, teased and sprayed into place as if she's terrified one hair will go astray. She looks up and gives me a quizzical frown, then recognizes me.

"Good morning, Jared. I'll bet she's already waiting for you. Would you like to meet with her in the courtyard?"

I nod and smile. "Good morning."

Martha leans over and pushes yet another button. I move through the next door to another security guard's post, who sits behind a cluttered desk at the entrance of a long, wide hallway. Mounted on the surface of his desk are two monitors which give multiple views of the hospital grounds. Each screen displays four different pictures. It's hard to make heads or tails of what he's looking at.

"What's up, Jared?"

"Good morning, Jonathan."

Jonathan springs forward in his comfy looking chair, then waves at an elderly man standing a few feet down the hallway. "Jared, this is Melvin, our volunteer guide for the day."

"Good morning, Melvin." I reach out to shake his hand.

"Melvin, can you escort Mr. Brooks here to the courtyard?"

"Sure." The elderly male shuffles his feet toward me, and the smell of old spice aftershave carries with him. "Right this way, Mr. Brooks."

Melvin is a tall, frail looking man with a slight hump in between his shoulder blades. His hands are long, thin, and callused, making it evident he's spent life working with them. If I had to guess, I'd say retirement isn't for him, so he comes here to fill his time.

"Thank you, sir." I fall into stride beside him, forcing me to shift my pace to short, slow steps.

Melvin looks at my name tag, which I'd forgotten to remove before exiting my car. "Meadowbrook Elementary? You a teacher?"

"Um, principal," I say with reluctance. I prefer to have more leisurely conversations with people when they don't know who I am. Most often they either have a child in the school or know such and such who does, which leads to questions that I don't want to deal with when I'm away from school.

"Ah, the big dog. It'd take a mighty tough person to do your job." Melvin's southern drawl is more prominent than most.

"It isn't for the faint of heart." I chuckle. "How about you? I can tell by looking at those hands you've not been a lazy man."

Melvin grins in return as he holds up both hands, looks at them, then opens and squeezes them shut. "They sure feel that way. For a living, I was a mechanic. On the side, I still like to do some woodworking. That's when these old hands will let me. Arthritis makes everything a challenge these days."

We reach the door leading to the part of the courtyard that allows visitors. Melvin steps through the door and holds it open for me to exit, then I step through and spot her immediately. "I see who I'm looking for. Thank you, Melvin. It was nice to meet you."

"Pleased to meet you, sir." Melvin tips his head in a downward gesture, then scoots his way back through the door.

The woman stands from the picnic bench and clasps her hands in front of her. A slight smile passes across her face, and her eyes take on a warm appearance. I don't believe I've ever seen her give a full smile. I catch an occasional lift upward on one side of her mouth, but that's as far as it gets. When I first came to see her, she wouldn't even look at me. In fact, the first time I was introduced, she immediately turned and scrambled back toward the door. She wanted nothing to do with me. I was told that I shouldn't give up because I was the first person to come and see her in years, besides the occasional visit from her sister, and I've heard that Rosemary always turned her away, so she finally stopped coming.

"Hello, Rosemary," I say with outstretched arms, and she shyly steps into them, one arm embracing me for a very brief moment before they fall back to her side.

She's never been one for hugging, or maybe it's just me. Rosemary turns back to the picnic table and sits down, then hikes her feet and legs over the bench as she turns her body toward me. Laid out on the table is our usual game of Scrabble. We spend most of our time playing the game, and then the rest she will use to communicate with me. I don't get a whole lot out of her, but it's enough.

"How've you been, Rosemary?"

She gives a single nod as if to say, "I'm alright," then gives me a questioning look to ask the same.

"I've been busy, but good. Ava came to spend the night with me last night and we went out for our usual happy meal dinner." I roll my eyes like an annoyed teenager. "I snapped a picture of her for you," I say as I take out my phone and open the picture of Ava sitting across from me in the restaurant. Rosemary takes the phone from my hand as if she's cradling a small child and holds it up closer to her face. Her mouth tilts upward with only a hint of a smile, then she hands the phone back to me.

She immediately sifts through the scrabble tiles and picks our four letters. She lays them one at a time in the center of the table. When she's finished, I read the word—*A-B-B-Y*.

"Abby? She's about the same—good, but uptight as always. She seems to be more so lately, and I'm not sure why."

Rosemary seems to frown, but it's as if her mouth struggles to make the right shape for it, just as when she attempts a smile. She points to my phone.

At first, it doesn't register what she's motioning about, and then I realize she's asking to see a picture of Abby. "Oh, a picture?" I stutter. "I think I have a recent one that Ava snapped without her looking and sent me the other day."

This is a first. Rosemary wanting to see a picture of her daughter. The one time I tried to show her one, she turned her head away. I saw how much it seemed to upset her, so I never tried again. I scroll through my photos, knowing good and well I'd saved it. It's a picture that Abby would say was terrible, but I found it to be one of the best pictures I've ever seen of her. Natural with no make-up, hair thrown high on top of her head, her chin propped on her fist, staring off into space as if she were lost in time. I turn the phone to Rosemary.

Rosemary slumps over, her eyes wide and unblinking. For a moment I think I see tears swell in the corners, then she blinks rapidly and shoves the phone back over to me. I look at Rosemary as she looks down at the table, playing with scrabble tiles. Her features are so similar to Abby's. Not the eye color or hair, but the oval shape of her face and the way her eyes slant downward as if she's pouting. Rosemary's droop more from age. I feel a twinge of pain as I look at her. She makes me long for Abby all the more.

"Shall we play?" I ask, trying to break the silence and the solemn mood that has crept in around us.

She nods, then sets up the game as we sit in silence, each of us trying to top the other with a bigger word. My mind is as jumbled as the tiles in front of me as I place four letters to spell the word *M-I-S-S.* Rosemary stares at the board for a moment, then tilts her head back as if in deep thought. I see a sudden shift in her expression as her eyes droop more.

She reaches into the bag of tiles and finds the letters she wants. I'm certain this is against the rules, but I don't say anything. She places the tiles on the game board next to my letters. When she's finished, I read her short sentence. *I-M-I-S-S-A-B-B-Y.*

I look up at Rosemary, and a single tear falls down her cheek.

12

bby

I FOCUS on the pain as I smash and release the tips of each of my fingers, switching hands, then repeating. I didn't even realize I'd walked out of my classroom until Megan taps me on the shoulder, and I jump as if I could leap from my own skin.

"Abby? You okay?"

I've clearly been standing in the middle of the hallway, staring at the opposite wall for God knows how long.

"Huh? Um…yes. I just had to take a short break. Go ahead and get the students started on packing up for home, and I'll step back in the room in a moment."

"You look super pale. You sure you're okay? You're not getting sick, are you?"

"No, no—just catching my breath."

"Alright, if you're sure you're okay." Megan says the words with hesitancy and then eases back through the door. As the door swings open, the noisy chatter of the students reverberates from the room. For the first time as a teacher, I cringe. I feel a sudden need to flee and be alone with my thoughts, but I can't. On the other hand, I want to run as far away from my thoughts as possible —away from what Mia said. Two Ally's? What the hell is she talking about? Dark hair and eyes like me. *No!* I can't think about that right now.

I squeeze on my fingertips so hard that the pain shoots up the length of each finger into the palm of my hand. It still isn't hard enough. I inhale several deep breaths and prepare myself to step back into the chaotic classroom—maybe chaos is what I need.

I manage to get through the last dregs of the school day without a breakdown, even though I felt like I was going to snap. Once all of my students have been put on their correct buses and the parent pickup line is empty, I make it back to my classroom. Megan is packing up to go home, and Ava is sitting in the reading corner on a beanbag, reading a book.

"Well, we survived the first one." Megan laughs. "Not as bad as I thought it would be. I just hope Mason isn't like most students and shows his true colors once he's settled in."

"You and I both know we haven't seen the worst yet. He's just getting warmed up. I would advise wearing your running shoes again tomorrow." I'm joking, but after seven years of teaching and interacting with children diagnosed with an emotional behavior disorder, I've learned to see things through the students' eyes. Mason hates it here, and based on his previous school records, it's just a matter of time before he *shows* us that he hates it here. It's not as though he can help it—it's part of the disorder. He can't regulate his feelings, which is where my job comes in. At the moment, I can't regulate my own, so how am I supposed to help him do it?

"I guess I'd better—I don't see you wearing your wrestling clothes or getting yourself dirty." Megan says the words in a seemingly joking tone, yet there's a seriousness behind them. I see something in her facial expression that makes me question whether or not she really feels that way. I feel my eyebrows furrow slightly and shift my face back to neutral before she catches it. Maybe I'm just being overly sensitive at the moment. I brush it off, but there is something about her statement that makes me wonder if she actually feels this way.

Megan clears her throat and asks. "You sure you're, okay?"

"Yeah, but I do feel like I may be coming down with something," I lie.

"You better not skip out on me tomorrow," Megan jokes, and this time it seems genuine.

"I won't. I'll be here." Even as I give her the answer, I'm not so sure. I'm not sick, but at this point, a mental health day might do me good. I feel as though I'm falling apart. All the weird coincidences are chipping away at me like an ice-pic, one tiny sliver at a time, and it feels as if I could break at any moment.

"Good. See you tomorrow." Megan waves and disappears down the hall.

I turn to look at Ava, who's still sprawled on the bean bag chair reading Hop on Pop, mostly from memory. She hasn't quite learned enough phonics to read it all, but she's far more advanced in reading than most in her class. I smile and listen to her for a moment then walk toward my desk to do a few things before we head home.

Ava slams the book closed behind me. "What else would you like for me to read, Ally?"

I freeze in place, not turning my body around, but just standing and listening. I hear the bean bag shift as Ava stands, then the sound of her putting a book back on the shelf before she slides out another. "Here it is. I like this one, too."

I turn my head slowly to look over my shoulder as Ava plops back down on the bean bag, then she pats the spot next to her.

"Here, Ally, sit down." Ava pauses as she waits for her imaginary friend to sit, then she proceeds to read *If you Give a Mouse a Cookie.*

I feel the color leave my face once again. No wonder everyone keeps telling me I'm pale. The book Ava chooses was one of my sister's favorite books as a child. It might be a coincidence, but it still unnerves me. Ava begins to read the book from memory.

I walk over and sit in my chair, prop my elbows on top of my desk, and rest my forehead into the palms of my hands.

"That bad of a day, huh?" Jared says as he enters the room and startles me. I raise my head to look at him, and my face must look just as it had earlier when he saw me.

"You still don't look so hot. You getting sick?"

I pause for a moment. "Thanks for the compliment," I try to joke. "I must be—Megan asked me the same thing."

"Ava can come home with me if you need to go home and rest."

Ava springs up straighter in her chair. "Can I, Mom? Please?"

I'm not sure what kind of face I pull with Jared, but he mouths the words, "I'm sorry."

I shake my head and give him a slight smile. "It's fine. Maybe some rest would do me good." *Mommy* guilt hits me as soon as I say it, as though I'm neglecting my only child. Jared must read it on my face.

"It'll be okay. Nothing wrong with you taking some time to care for yourself for a change."

I look at Ava's begging, puppy-dog eyes, then say, "Okay. I guess so. Just for tonight."

Ava squeals, then runs around the desk and wraps both arms around my neck. She releases me then goes to Jared, takes his hand and begins to pull on him.

"Come on, Daddy."

Jared laughs. "Okay, munchkin." They reach the door of the classroom, then Jared pauses. "You better get your backpack, Ava."

Ava runs over to the bean bag she was sitting on, throws her backpack onto her back, then says as she waves, "I'll see you later, Ally."

Jared frowns, then throws me a puzzled look.

"Imaginary friends," I whisper, hoping that my lie is convincing.

He stares at me a bit longer with an expression I can't discern, then waves goodbye, and the two of them disappear down the hall. I look down at my hands, realizing I'm abusing my fingertips again. I make myself stop. Unable to summon the energy to complete my paperwork, I pack it into my teacher's bag and decide to go home.

After I enter through the side door of my kitchen, I drop my bag on the kitchen floor and lean over the counter, plopping my head down on my forearms. I melt into it. The house is eerily quiet. I don't like it.

After I've let out a few releasing breaths, a text tone pings on my phone, breaking the silence, and I reluctantly check it to see a text from Ruby. My breath shifts to a frustrated exhale.

I need a ride to town. I can't drive because my foot hurts.

I reply, *I have work to catch up on. You'll have to call a cab.*

I can't deal with Ruby right now. I'd tell her to call an Uber, but she believes that Uber drivers are all sexual predators, and you can't trust them. She replies back with a sad-faced emoji. I'm not surprised. Three bubbles bounce on the screen and I assume she's sitting there waiting for me to respond further. I press the button on the side of the phone and lay it down. A couple of minutes pass, and my phone pings again. I roll my eyes.

What would your mother think?

I put my phone back down again and ignore her. She keeps saying that to me, but I'm not sure my mother ever thinks about me—or that she's even capable of it. I shake the thought, as I often do when it comes to pondering on my mother.

My eyes land on the basement door and I squint as I think

about what I found down there. A sudden urge hits me, the kind that's similar to a severe itch, impossible to ignore. I open the door wide and ease down the steps. When I get to the middle of the room, I flick the switch on the work light I'd left behind yesterday. The room illuminates, but the dark corners keep their presence. A sudden wave of cold air seems to fill the room as if I've opened a refrigerator door and am standing in front of it. I shudder.

I move to the heavy door and open it. The same dank smell wafts from the room. I grab the light and carry it with me inside. The coldness attaches itself to me and follows along.

As I use my phone's flashlight, I find the names and drawings again—they're still there. The same chill washes over me. I suppose I was hoping that what I'd found yesterday was all a dream, but all of the names are there.

Witch. Ally. Abby. Angel. And Tina.

"Who the hell is Angel?" I catch myself speaking aloud and instinctively look around the room for anyone who might catch me talking to myself—or who might answer me. I don't remember anyone from my childhood named Angel. *Maybe it's someone else that lived here and decided to add themself to the drawings. Maybe this Angel knew Tina?*

I'm startled out of my thoughts by the ping of a text tone, so much so that I almost drop my phone. I look at the screen—Ruby. I close my eyes and take a sharp inhale and release, then slide it open.

If you're not going to take me then I guess I'll have to go myself.

I debate on what to reply, then settle on, *Be careful.*

Three dots float on the screen, then disappear. I'm sure I'll pay for this one. She'll sulk for days. The guilt I feel when it comes to the woman who raised me is different from *Mom guilt.* I feel that I owe her my respect, even though she frustrates me most of the time. I love Aunt Ruby, but I often wonder what it would have been like if Rosemary would have been the one around to raise me instead. I know Ruby can't help it—she did the best she could, considering she was thrown into motherhood against her choosing. She had to give up everything—especially the freedom to come and go as she pleased.

I stare at the drawings as questions churn in my mind. Shaking a magic eight ball would give me better answers. At least then I'd have some kind of answer—right or wrong.

As I turn my body in slow circles, searching for anything with answers, a foul odor fills the room. It smells as though something has died and I have a Deja vu moment. The smell becomes so strong that I almost gag. I frantically search the room as the stench swells. Rotting flesh. The Corpse flower that I only knew as a kid keeps coming back to my mind. *There has to be something in this basement emitting that smell.*

Like a dog following a scent, I move away from the drawings to search. It fades. I move back closer, scanning the walls one more time. Something white catches my attention. It appears to be piece of paper wedged between two bricks. I release my nostrils and slide it free.

It's an old polaroid picture. As I turn it over to look, I almost drop it. A picture of a little girl, roughly nine or ten years old, and there's no mistaking the dark eyes staring back at me.

It's Tina.

It takes me a few moments to find my breath again and when I do, it's erratic and choppy at best. If the drawings weren't enough proof, this is. I now have no doubt that Tina wasn't imaginary. She *was* real.

The foul odor disappears.

bby and Ally
2001

"What're you doing?" Abby asks as she opens the closet door under the stairs.

Ally sits in the corner of the dimly lit closet, hugging her knees. "I'm not talking to you."

"Why? I'm the one who should be mad at you for leaving me upstairs all by myself."

"It wasn't my idea—it was Tina's."

Abby pouts. "That's not what she said."

Ally leaps from the closet and sprints up the stairs. "She's lying!"

Abby runs up right behind her. "Why would Tina lie to me? She's my friend."

"I thought she was my friend too, till now. Now I think she's just mean. She's the one who talked me into locking you in that basement. That wasn't my idea, either. Now she's making you think it was me that wanted to leave you up here."

Abby flops down on her bed, placing her legs in a crisscross, then props her elbows on her knees. "Well, I believe Tina."

Ally shrugs a shoulder, plops down on her own bed, then says, "I don't care what you believe, cause you're wrong."

"Fine."

"Are you two girls fighting?" Rosemary breezes into the room.

Abby whips her head around and blurts out, "No."

Ally doesn't move.

"Something tells me you're not being completely honest with me. Why don't you each tell me your side of the story, then maybe we can figure out a solution." Rosemary walks over and stands between the beds.

Abby turns to look at Ally, her face tinted a pale pink. Ally looks back at Abby, who stretches her eyes wide open and does a slight shake of her head, then lips the words, "You can't."

Ally stares back, then exhales. "It's nothing. I'm just mad because Abby took the last pop-tart."

"Well now, pop-tarts aren't worth being mean to each other over. You're sisters, and that's more important than some dried up piece of pastry."

"Okay," both girls say in unison.

Rosemary smiles and claps her hands. "It's time to get ready for bed. Ally, before you go brush your teeth, I think it's your turn tonight to pick out the bedtime story."

"Yay." Ally runs to the bookshelf that sits in the center of the wall where the pink and lilac paint meet. The shelf is also painted half pink and the other half light purple. Ally's is on the purple side. She touches several books then grins and grabs *If You Give a Mouse a Cookie*, then takes it and puts it on her bed. Abby frowns. The book is not Abby's favorite. In fact, she hates it.

"Ally, since you seem to be upset with Abby, why don't you go brush your teeth first, then Abby can go. I'll be back up in just a bit to read to you."

The girls complete their nightly routine in silence, only exchanging mean looks when forced to cross each other's paths. They're climbing under the covers when Rosemary returns and pulls her rocking chair from the corner of the room to her usual spot in between their beds before beginning to read.

Abby lies on her side, clutching her worn out, long-eared bunny. She's had it as long as she can remember, and its outer surface is threadbare. It used to be bright pink, but it's been washed so many times it's almost white. Ally lays flat on her back, the cover tucked up under her armpits and her hands resting at her sides.

By the time Rosemary finishes the story, both girls are sound asleep.

* * *

Abby's startled awake by a loud noise at the foot of her bed. She grips the covers and pulls them up to her chin as she listens. Rosemary must have forgotten to turn on the lamp between her bed and Ally's, so the room has the lighting of a dungeon. She hears another sound, and something moves on the foot of her bed. For a moment she's rooted to her spot, afraid to even breathe. Then she hears footsteps walking across the bedroom floor toward the door. She leaps from bed, flips on the lamp, and then catapults herself into Ally's bed, sure she'd just seen someone disappear through the bedroom door.

"What're you doing?" Ally says sleepily, scooting her body toward the headboard.

Abby's eyes land on her own bed, and her emotions shift from fear to immediate anger. She bounces to her feet and picks up the shredded pieces of her favorite bunny and the kitchen knife lying next to it.

"Why did you do this?" Abby shrieks, holding out both of her hands for her sister to see, her breathing hoarse and erratic.

"I didn't do that!" Ally squeals and scoots to the edge of her bed. "I promise I didn't."

"I hate you!" Hot tears sting Abby's eyes.

The overhead light in the room comes to life. "What is going on in here? Why are you two girls up? And why are you screaming?" Rosemary sounds breathless.

"Look what Ally did to my Whiskers!" Abby turns and shoves the fistful of stuffing and shredded material toward her mother, still gripping the kitchen knife in her other hand.

"Ally!" The color drains from her face. "Why on earth did you do that? I know you were mad at Abby when you went to bed, but this is downright cruel. What got into you?"

"I didn't do it, Rosemary. I promise!"

"If you didn't do it, then how could it have happened? I don't think Abby would have shredded her own favorite toy."

Ally stutters. "I-I don't know. Maybe someone broke in and did it?" She turns to look at Abby. "Maybe it was Tina."

Silence fills the room for a long second.

Rosemary's eyes narrow. "Who's Tina?"

"Tina wouldn't do that—she's my friend."

Rosemary asks again, her voice becoming more insistent. "Who's Tina?"

"She's someone that only we can see," Ally says.

"Well, I don't think imaginary friends can do something like this. That's not how imaginary friends work. They're called imaginary *friends* for a reason." Rosemary purses her lips.

"Not this one. I think she's mean. I think she did it and wants Abby to think it was me." Ally's voice gets higher.

"Ally, it's okay to be upset with your sister, because that's what sisters do, but it's not okay to seek revenge just because you are mad at them. So, first thing tomorrow morning, you're going to fix Whiskers. Do you understand?"

Ally starts to speak, "But—"

"Not another word. You will fix Whisker's first thing in the morning."

Ally plops down on her bed and drops her chin to her chest. "Okay."

"Let me have the knife and all the pieces. I'll take them downstairs, and as soon as breakfast is over Ally, you'll begin your first lesson in sewing. But for now, both of you get back into bed and I'd better not hear another peep tonight."

Both girls sigh, Ally the loudest, and they each crawl back under the covers.

Abby rolls over, picturing the sight of her butchered Whiskers, and sobs wrack her body as she turns her back to the room. She's pretty sure she can hear Ally sniffing, too.

14

osemary

ANGIE SLOWLY OPENS MY DOOR. "Are you ready for your therapy session, Rosemary?"

A distraught look must consume my face because Angie gives me that motherly look of concern.

"Are you okay?"

I smear on a half-hearted smile and nod.

"I know, Rosemary. You don't like this Dr. Black very much, do you? I miss Dr. Sarah, too." Angie tilts her head to the side in sympathy and waves for me to follow. "Come now, let's just get it over with. It's Thursday—ice-cream night. Just think about that while you're in there with her, and it will all just speed by. Okay? I'll walk with you. Keep you company."

We walk down one hallway, then another, as Angie chatters away about her difficult son and how he often has behavior issues. Not many of her words register, as my mind hops from one thought to another—my visit with Jared, then Ewelina's comments about my mother.

My thoughts halt there.

The fact that she's communicating with her continues to gnaw away at me even now. There's a reason my mother is talking to her, but I'm not sure I want to know what it is.

Angie opens the therapy room door, and a strong scent of disgustingly sweet air freshener wafts from the room. I sniff, wince, and don't even try to hide my annoyance.

"Good evening, Rose," Dr. Black says, and there's something about the way she says it that immediately gets under my skin.

I clench my teeth and glance over at Angie once more. She must have picked up on my annoyed expression, because she quickly speaks her concern.

"I'm not sure, but I believe Rosemary prefers to be called by her full name. She isn't a big fan of being called Rose." Angie looks at me questioningly, and I give my head a brief nod.

"Thank you, Angie," Dr. Black says, dismissing her. "We'll be done in an hour."

Angie raises her eyebrows at me, giving me an apologetic look, then leaves, closing the door behind her.

"Have a seat, Rose." Dr. Black motions to the chair.

I ignore her and walk to the window. "So, this is how we're going to play it again? Very well, have it your way."

I stare out the window, and the same Wren from the other day is still building its nest. I assume it's the same bird because once it drops its twig in place, it bounces two times, rotating one way, then another, as it chirps at me. It fixes one beady eye on mine, and I stare back into it. The bird becomes still but shifts its head in small movements, and its eye color changes from green to bronze and then to black. The color shifts remind me that my heart has made the same shift over the years since I've been here.

"Rose?"

I continue to ignore her. I'm good at that. When you've been stuck in one place too long, you practice ignoring people, then when you've done it long enough, it becomes like second nature. It's getting under her skin, so it makes it fun as well.

"Fine." Dr. Black clears her throat, then continues. "So—I was reading over Dr. Foster's notes. It seems you have a long history here, Rose. You weren't always the most hospitable patient, were you?"

The bird outside flies away, and I shift my attention to the palm of my right hand as I try to tune her words out. I trace the *M* and rotate my body back and forth.

"Looking at one of the incidents, it seems not long after you came here you busted a mirror and attempted to cut yourself. Is that correct, Rose?"

I stop rotating and pause the tracing of my hand. I find myself squinting and holding my breath, so I correct it and return to my rocking.

"This tells me that you don't enjoy looking in the mirror. When I visited your room, I noticed there wasn't even a plastic mirror hanging in there. Why don't you like looking at yourself?"

I have no intention of interacting with this woman, but she's right, I despise looking at myself. When I look in the mirror, I no longer see a face full of life. My eyes reflect a hollowness, as if my soul has left my body for good—deep, dark, and empty. They used to be light in color, even blue, but now they resemble a troubled, stormy sky.

There's one thing I know for sure about mirrors: they tell the truth—it's the people looking into them that are the liars. People stare into their mirrors, looking at themselves only at a certain angle—usually straight ahead, seeing only the parts they think are the best versions of themselves, and are foolish enough to believe that that's what other people see. If they'd take the time to look at themselves at all angles, then flaws, horns, and even demons might emerge. That's why I can't look in a mirror anymore.

Demons, regret, and guilt are all I see.

A loud, grinding sound brings me back into the room where I don't wish to be. "Well, Rose, since you won't come and sit with me, then I'm going to come to you." Dr. Black drags her chair across the room toward me, then sits down and glares in my direction. I turn my body so that she gets a full view of my backside, and return to swaying.

"So, as I said earlier, I've been looking over Dr. Foster's notes. You have a daughter, right? What's her name?"

I stop moving and find myself shaking my head. Just how deep has this woman dug into my records? I take a few steps away from the horrid doctor, and my breath becomes erratic. I've never talked about my daughter, not even with Dr. Sarah, which means she took the time to dig through old files—very old. Let the nosey twit dig; that's as far as she's going to get with it.

Dr. Black pauses, but I can feel her eyes boring into my back, again. Her chair makes a low, continuous squeaking sound, and I assume it's caused by the bounce of her foot.

"Rose? I haven't found your daughter's name on any sign-in registries. Why doesn't she come to see you?"

My body sways back and forth even more rapidly as my movements become more aggressive. The bird returns with another twig, and I focus my stare on it as I try to calm myself.

"I think I may have hit a nerve. Why don't you have a seat, and we can sort this out? Maybe we can talk about how it makes you feel that your only daughter won't come to see you."

I continue to move my body as I try to slow down my thoughts. It's like herding mice. Just what is this woman up to? Is she trying to help me or force me to hit her? She should get the hint by now that I have no desire to interact with her. It couldn't be any more obvious than if I'd written it on the walls of this boring room.

"Your daughter may not come to see you, but someone else does. A man. I believe his name is—" Dr. Black pauses, and I hear her flipping pages. "Um, well, it isn't in my notes, but according to logs, he comes to see you quite often. So, since you don't want to talk about family, then how about we start with him? He must be important, since the log says he visits every week."

"I know he's not your son, so is he a nephew? Son-in-law? Why don't you tell me about him?" Dr. Black pauses and remains silent for what seems like forever. "I'll tell you what, how about we play a game of scrabble? I think I saw you playing it with your visitor yesterday."

Is she watching me?

The loud noise invades my ears again as the doctor drags her chair back to the table in the center of the room. I still don't offer to move over and join her.

"Rose, you can either come sit down and join me, or I can have an orderly come in and make you sit down. Which shall it be?"

I release a disgusted exhale and debate on ignoring her some more. She clears her throat loudly, and I give in and walk to the chair opposite her. She proceeds to set up the scrabble board and tiles, laying out seven tiles in front of herself, and then the same number in front of me. I make a mental note that she gives herself some tiles first, which speaks volumes of her character. *Why doesn't this surprise me?*

"Since you don't seem to want to communicate with me, then I'll start us out," Dr. Black says, her droning tone filling the room. She picks up four tiles from her pile and proceeds to place them on the board.

I stare out the window with no intention of playing her little game.

"Well look, Rose, I made your name."

I dart my squinted eyes to the board. *R-O-S-E.* My heart quickens and a shot of adrenaline rushes to my head. It's as though her mouth gets tired before she can get the rest of my name out. Anger boils under the surface as I look at my own tiles sitting in front of me. I find what I need and pick up four of them before snapping them onto the board, not being the least bit gentle, and connecting them to the end of her tiles. Then I dart my defiant eyes up to hers and back to the window. *M-A-R-Y.*

Dr. Black reaches into the tile bag and retrieves four more to replace the tiles she just used, only this time she picks through and chooses the tiles she wants instead of at random. "Is this you trying to tell me that you don't want to be called Rose? I would know this if you would just communicate with me." She sorts through her seven tiles, then picks up four more and lays them in a perpendicular line below the letter *S* in my name. *S-P-E-A-K.*

I shoot my eyes down for a split second, then back to the window as I debate on whether I want to respond, then I reach into the bag to pull out four more tiles. I pick up only one and place it on the board directly on top of the *O* in my name. *N-O.*

"You're a very stubborn woman, Rose—excuse me, Rosemary, as you prefer. See, I can compromise." She gives me a smug look, then picks up the bag of tiles and continues to go against the rules of the game as she sorts through them and plucks the three she's looking for. "Let's see what you think about my next word." She places the three squares on the board, stacking them above the letter *Y.*

I'm done interacting with her and stare across the room. I hear them snap into place, but I don't offer to look.

"Come on, now. You will *want* to see my word—I promise."

I give her a loud exhale, then glance down. My vision blurs and I feel my eyes blaze with fury and shock as I stare back at her.

A-L-L-Y.

Dr. Black takes on a smug expression as she crosses her arms over her chest and leans back into her chair.

"I think we're finished for today, Rosemary."

15

ared

AVA and I step through the front door of the school and pause as rain peppers the metal roof above our heads. I hug Ava in close. "You ready to make a dash for the car?"

"I don't care if I get wet, Daddy."

"I do. I'm sweet and I might melt." I wink as I look down at Ava.

Ava giggles. "Sometimes you're sweet and sometimes you're sour."

"Sour candy melts too." I smile then usher Ava toward the car, and once we're inside, I ask, "What would you like to do now? And don't say McDonalds."

"Aww." Ava plops her head back against her seat. "You pick, Daddy."

"Hmm." I debate for a moment. I've been pondering for quite some time about taking Ava to meet Rosemary, but I worry that

113

Abby would be upset with me. In fact, she'd probably be furious. It's possible it might make her furious enough that she'll want to ban Ava from staying overnight with me.

However, Rosemary seems to thrive when I visit. The staff at the hospital say that her willingness to interact with others has improved since I've been coming. One of the newer staff members, who seems to have taken Rosemary under her wing, all but begged for me to come and see Rosemary more—that her mood on those days is a massive improvement. Imagine what it might do for her to see her granddaughter. Who knows, maybe it would entice her to speak. Wouldn't that be something? I smile at the idea.

If only Abby could see and understand what I see. This could possibly be a turning point for Abby and her mother. If I could bring Ava and grandmother together, then maybe it could bring Abby and her mother together. Rosemary did say that she misses her.

I stay quiet for a moment, deep in thought, going back and forth with the idea. I weigh the pros and cons, and in my head, the pros win. "How good are you at keeping very important secrets? By very important, I mean top secret."

Ava's eyes light up almost as bright as they do on Christmas morning. "I'm very good at keeping secrets. My friend asks me to all the time, and I never tell."

"Is this the same friend you told me about?"

Ava nods.

"But she's a secret?"

"Sort of like that."

"Okay. Then, I want to take you to meet one of my friends, but you can't tell your mother, at least not until *after* I tell her. This friend is sort of a secret for me too. Do you think you can keep it a secret, just for a little while?"

Ava rolls her eyes back into her head as though she's thinking. "Yep. I won't tell Mommy until after you do."

"Good. Then I'm going to take you to meet my special friend. Buckle up."

"Yay!" Ava hops in her seat, then fastens her seatbelt. I pull from the school parking lot and drive toward Serenity Oaks Hospital. Forty minutes later, Ava and I are buzzed through the entrance door, and behind the reception desk, Martha stands when she sees my daughter at my side.

"Well, you brought company. Who's this?"

"This is Ava, my daughter."

"Nice to me you, Ava. Rosemary sure is going to be surprised to see you again so soon and even more surprised to meet this cutie."

I chew my lip, suddenly worried I may have made a big mistake. What if this sends Rosemary over the edge? What if her reaction is distressing to Ava? "She isn't busy, is she?"

"I'll see, but I'm sure it'll be okay."

We wait for Martha to make her call upstairs, then we're buzzed through the second door. Jonathan comes to life when he sees us. "Good afternoon, Jared—and who is this big girl you have with you?"

"Jonathan, this is Ava, Ava, this is Jonathan."

Ava whispers, "Is he a cop?"

Jonathan chuckles. "Something like that, but I'm just a big ol' teddy bear to most. See." He pinches his pot belly with both hands. "Just ask my misses." He waves at the volunteer standing a few feet down the hall—someone different from yesterday. "Can you show these two to the third floor?"

The elderly lady whom I've never seen here before, scoots in our direction and nods but doesn't say a word. She turns to walk toward an elevator at the other end of the hall. We walk behind her at a snail's pace, and Ava looks up at me with wide eyes. She snickers, then pretends to run in an exaggerated, slow motion.

We make it to the third-floor desk, and Angie stands to greet us. "Hey, Jared. Rosemary is so tickled that you've come to see her again so soon."

"How did she react when she learned that I have company with me?"

Angie grins. "Let's just put it this way, I don't think I've ever seen her smile like that." She moves around the desk and leads us down the hall to Rosemary's room. After knocking on her door, she opens it and announces us. On the car ride over, I'd warned Ava that Rosemary doesn't speak much.

Angie was right. Rosemary stands, and I've never seen her smile in this way. It's still not a show-your-teeth smile, but it is genuine. The kind a sweet grandmother would give. Angie quietly slips from the room as Rosemary sits on her bed, then motions for Ava and me to sit in the two chairs along the wall. I'm not sure how she'd acquired them, but they aren't your typical, uncomfortable, hospital seats. They're matching high-back chairs with a thick seating cushion and large armrests. Their multicolored material matches the rest of the tapestry-rich room. Ava looks around in awe at all the colors.

"Rosemary, this is Ava, your granddaughter."

Ava's head snaps to look at me, then back to Rosemary. I smile, then go on to explain. "Ava, this is Rosemary, your grandmother. She is your mother's mother."

Ava tucks her chin toward her chest and looks at Rosemary out of the corner of her eye, suddenly looking very timid. Rosemary smiles a little bigger. She stares at Ava, which only makes Ava freeze and look away. Something about the news has struck a shyness I've never seen before in Ava.

Perhaps I shouldn't have told her.

Rosemary holds up her index finger as if to say *hang on.* She retrieves a three-ring binder from her wardrobe, then sits on the bed as she pats the spot next to her. I move to sit beside her while Ava snuggles in close to my side, away from Rosemary.

The photo album is the kind that stores photos under a plastic, protective layer. On the first page is a five-by-seven photograph of Rosemary when she was young, holding an infant in each arm. Her smile at the camera is pure and beaming. She points to the baby resting in her right arm.

"Is that her?" I ask.

Rosemary nods.

"Is that who?" Ava whispers.

"That's your mother when she was a baby."

Ava's shyness seems to dissipate, and she leans across my lap to look at the picture closer.

"Who is the other baby?" Ava asks, and I look at Rosemary with the same question going through my mind. I wasn't sure about asking, but Ava did it for the both of us.

Rosemary only shakes her head, and her face shifts downward as a forlorn, distant look enters her eyes. She turns the page, and there are several pictures of toddler girls, one with dark hair and dark eyes, and the other with blonde hair and blue eyes. In each of the pictures the girls are smiling and seemingly happy. With each turn of the page, I become more curious about the other little girl. They look nothing alike and yet they do.

Curiosity gets the best of me, so I mouth the words behind Ava's back. *"Were they twins?"*

Rosemary closes her eyes and gives a slight nod as her posture attempts to fold in on itself.

Abby had a twin sister. The thought occurs to me, but I don't say it aloud. I don't say anything more, not wanting Ava to pick up on the information and hoping that she hasn't already. This is something she probably couldn't keep a secret. Why wouldn't Abby tell me this? Maybe she didn't even know she had a twin sister. I can't ask Rosemary—she's obviously still very distraught over it. I begin to wonder if it has something to do with why Rosemary is in here in the first place. It must have been traumatic—why else would Abby keep a twin sister's existence a secret?

A single tear flows down Rosemary's cheek, and she wipes it away, taking a deep breath, then she turns through a few more pages in the album. As she scrolls through, the girls in the pictures begin to grow and age. With the next turn of a page, Ava lays farther over my lap and slaps the photo album with her hand.

"Wait." Ava stands and moves to stand in front of Rosemary and the album. As she points to the blond-haired girl, she says, "That's my friend!"

Rosemary and I exchange puzzled looks, then what happens next shocks all three of us. A squeak escapes Rosemary mouth, then she clears her throat several times. The word comes out as a whisper as she says it. "Ally?"

Ava nods. "Yeah—that's my friend, Ally. She comes to see me, but only me."

"Maybe she just looks like your friend," I say.

"No, Daddy, that's Ally. I'm sure of it. And this picture is, and this one." Ava points to several different pictures.

Rosemary smiles up at Ava and moves her head up and down.

16

bby

A THUMP UPSTAIRS forces me to freeze as I try to convince myself that it was just my imagination. Then comes another indistinguishable sound from overhead. I glance at the basement steps and debate whether I should hide, or sneak up them. The thought makes my pulse kick in even harder. My feet have their own plans and won't budge.

Another sound echoes from upstairs, but this time it seems to have moved to another part of the house. I look around the basement and the only thing I can find to use as a weapon is a large, ancient looking umbrella with a hook for a handle. I grip it tightly and tiptoe up the steps, but the stairs have no intention of being quiet under my feet. My breath stops and starts again with each pop, crack, and step as I ascend. I grip the umbrella harder as though it were a sword. At least that's what I tell myself I can use it for. *Just swing hard like a Samurai.*

119

As I ease the basement door open, I hear one final noise, like the click of the front door, which only makes me grip the makeshift sword tighter. With my left hand, I still manage to squeeze the tips of my finger on the other hand, even as I remain ready to swing. My childhood habit is becoming even more frequent than it was when I was a child—at least it has been lately.

As I round the corner to the living room, then toward the foyer and front stairs, I exhale a long breath, realizing I'd been holding it for a long time.

There's no-one there.

All I can hear is the tick of the antique clock on the wall that once belonged to my mother. Not ready to let my guard down, I climb the front stairs and stop when I reach the top. Progressing with feather-light steps, I wince every time the old floor creaks under my feet.

First, I inspect the guest room and the bathroom opposite it—they look the same as always. I move on down the hall to Ava's room and then my own. Ava's room is still in the same mess as before. When I turn to leave the bathroom, instinct makes me grab my nostrils as the scent of something dead hits me. As I step out outside, my eyes fall onto my bed, and I nearly fall myself.

I struggle to take air into my lungs, despite breathing through my mouth as though I've forgotten how.

I can't be seeing what I think I'm seeing.

I move toward it as if it could jump up and bite me, but I know it can't. I'm not sure it's even real. Propped on my pillow is—Whiskers. My favorite stuffed animal that I took everywhere as a child. Still tattered, worn, and sewn together. I haven't seen this toy in years. In fact, the last time I saw it was around my seventh birthday.

I instinctively look around the room as if I might find Ally standing there looking at me or laughing at me. Then I shake my head, and my upper body shudders at the thought as I attempt to talk myself down from the onset of an anxiety attack.

How did this get here?

The childhood toy isn't the way I remember it. It doesn't give me a soothing sensation as it always did when I was a child. In fact, it gives me the creeps. Its body is covered in stitches like a doll from a horror film. It appears as though it could come to life at any moment with the intent to harm rather than console. My body shifts into that of a feral cat, and I catch myself scoping the room again.

When the paranoia dissipates to a manageable level, I ease toward the toy and hold it in my hands for the first time since I was seven years old. A familiar warmth spreads across my chest, then I feel the need to hug it close to my body, just as I had back then. I remember now. I cried myself to sleep my first night without it. It was as if I'd lost my best friend. Now she's back and I feel both joy and terror at the toy's arrival.

After checking the entire house, as well as the doors and windows twice, my heightened nerves calm to a controllable level. I don't know how anyone could have gotten in. My tour proved that every door and window is locked. I end my journey in the kitchen, still holding and staring at the tattered bunny, and say aloud, "How the fuck did you get here?" Of course it doesn't answer me back, but something about all the weird occurrences lately makes me think that anything's possible.

The only way I can find any answers to all of this is to visit my past, whether I want to or not. The idea sends a dread straight to the pit of my stomach, causing an instant wave of nausea. I catch myself hugging my bunny.

I head up the back stairs and then to my closet, where I keep the external hard drive containing all my childhood home movies. I ignore the dread and give myself a pep talk.

They can't hurt you.

After removing my laptop from my bag, I sit it down on the kitchen table and decide that I need a shot of courage before I embark on this buried journey of the past. I fix myself a fresh cup of coffee and add two shots of whiskey. The large gulp I take before sitting down burns my throat in all the right ways. I bypass the video I watch regularly and click on the first in the list. The file is labeled April 9, 1999.

With a couple of clicks, the face of my dead twin sister fills the screen, then the shot zooms out to the view of my mother's back garden. I conclude right away that Rosemary is the one holding the camera, because she speaks as soon as the video starts. My pulse leaps into overdrive.

"Look at me, girls."

The camera zooms in on both our faces, then zooms out. It's obvious this is one of the first times she's ever used the camera, because she turns it around, aiming it directly at her face, and says, "Is this thing working?" She turns it back around and then it begins to move forward, bouncing with each step. I feel dizzy just trying to watch it.

I stare at the screen of my computer and focus my eyes on Ally's. They seem even bluer than I remember, like a perfect fall sky. We both wave, then run in close to the camera, and Ally screams, "Can I see it?"

"In a minute," Rosemary says. "Go play. I just want to capture you naturally."

I can see her hand wave in front of the camera as she shoos Ally away.

Neither Ally nor I can ignore the camera. We run through the yard, sporadically looking back at our mother. Ally is wearing her usual flashy attire, the kind you could only find in a little girls' store, very popular at the time in every mall in America. The store didn't carry anything that wasn't covered in sequins or glitter. I never wore clothing from there—my attire consisted of plain, blue jean shorts and a light-pink t-shirt.

Ally begins to spin in circles, arms outstretched, and I follow her lead, each of us snapping our heads around as we spin so that we're looking at the camera the whole time. This went for what seemed like forever. I scan the screen for anyone else in the shot.

There's no one.

I click on several more dates, and each one opens with a view of the back garden. We spent a lot of time there as children. In some of the video we're playing, and in others we're drawing at the table or watching old movies from a projector, which displayed on a sheet hung across the back of the house. With each gulp of my laced coffee, I'm able to watch the home movies without feeling overwhelming guilt. I even find myself smiling as I watch a few more. I come across one that makes me pause.

June 1, 2002

The video opens on a close-up of a hand as it moves away from the camera lens to a wide shot of the garden. Again, Rosemary walks away from the camera toward the large fairy sculpture, then begins to work with a piece of metal and a pair of pliers. Ally and I are sitting at the garden table with containers of Playdough and various cookie cutters. It's obvious from the video that Rosemary had set up the camera on a stable surface and just let it record.

She works with small pieces of metal, bending and shaping them into wavy swirls, then attaching them to the head of the sculpture. I watch the video, fascinated at how the fairy's hair took shape. Everyone in the video seems perfectly content.

As I stare at Rosemary, something in the back of the shot catches my attention. A movement through the cracks of the fence. I click the back arrow several times and watch it again. The movement starts in the far right of the screen and moves down the fence toward the gate. Rosemary notices it and stops what she's doing.

She doesn't say a word at first, but moves through the garden toward the gate.

"Is somebody there?" I hear her say in the video.

The movement freezes, and as Rosemary approaches the gate, the object backs away from the fence, leaving it only barely visible, then I can see it move rapidly back the direction it came from.

Rosemary opens the gate and jumps through, then stands very still as she stares in the direction of where the object fled. She gives up, then closes the gate, securing the latch back in place.

I rewind the video and watch it several times, zooming in with the hope that I can see who it is. It's obvious that it's a child. Not the same size as Ally and myself, but not an adult either.

This has to be Tina. But if Tina was supposedly only imaginary, then there's no way she could be caught on camera. I remember the first time we encountered Tina, it happened in the same way. She came nosing around, then Ally and I saw her peeking through the fence. I rewind it a couple more times, then move to another video. The date catches my eye. Mine and Ally's seventh birthday.

June 7, 2002

Giggles and squeals blare from the computer's speaker. The frame is zoomed in on Ally and me spraying each other with water guns, then it zooms out to the whole back garden.

The same video that sporadically played on its own the other night.

Aunt Ruby comes into view carrying a cardboard box full of water balloons, fat and full of water, ready to throw. Three other girls and two boys gather around the table, along with my sister and myself.

My focus shifts to the smallest boy in the group, and it hits me who he is. I smile and bring my face closer to the screen. There's no mistaking the shoulder-length dark hair and long eyelashes.

Jared.

I'd never realized that I'd met him at that age, even if it was only a couple of times. I thought I'd only met him in my early teens, but there he is, at mine and Ally's birthday party. I can't believe I forgot this. It makes me wonder if he remembers being there. He can't, because as far as I know, he doesn't even know I had a sister. Jared moved around a lot all the way up until he turned sixteen, and according to him, he refused to move anymore after that. He stayed wherever he could until he went off to college.

I catch myself smiling at the memory in front of me. This was mine and Ally's last birthday together. The thought punches me in the gut, and my smile makes a turn south as a lump catches in my throat. I try to wash it away with a large gulp of coffee, the whiskey having settled to the bottom of my cup. It burns my throat, and I welcome it.

I look away from the screen, squeezing my eyes shut in an attempt to obliterate the sting of the memories. I don't think I can stand to watch this one, so I reach to click the red dot. As I do, the far background of the frame grabs my focus once more. I lean in and see that the gate of the garden is standing wide open to reveal someone's face peeking around. The hair rises on my arms as I recognize the girl—dark hair and dark eyes. I pause the video and use my thumb and index finger to zoom in on the girl and stare for a long time, then I click play, and the children on the screen run and squeal, chasing each other with water balloons.

No one notices the girl spying on them.

The video goes on for several minutes as the girl stares at the activities, and yet no one sees her. Young Jared smacks a balloon on top of Ally's head, and water splatters all around her. She freezes in place as her mouth forms an *O*, and she scrunches her shoulders toward her ears.

I catch myself giggling out loud as I watch it. I focus again on Jared when he does something that surprises me. He spots the girl peeking around the fence and runs to the opening. She darts out of sight. He stands there for several minutes, moving his hands in different gestures as though he's trying to lure her to come inside. After a short period, he turns and runs back to the party. She doesn't show her face through the opening anymore.

The computer screen goes black as the video ends. I stare at it and disappear inside my mind as one thought emerges.

Jared could see Tina.

17

bby and Ally
2002

ABBY AND ALLY stare across the back garden at the mess they're supposed to help clean up. Neither one of them thinks it's fair they should clean up their own birthday party. Ally turns to walk toward the sunroom door, and Abby snaps.

"Get back here, Ally! I'm not cleaning this up by myself."

"I'm coming back. I have to go pee."

"You're lying," Abby says as she props both fists on her waist. "You always have to go pee every time we're told to clean up."

"I do not!"

"Uh-huh."

"Girls, you better not be fighting out there, or you'll have to kiss and make up." Rosemary's voice comes from somewhere inside the house.

Ally sticks out her tongue at her sister, then runs through the back door.

"Ally!" Abby's bark does nothing to detour Ally from fleeing. "Psssst."

Abby jerks her head around, startled. She squints her eyes and moves them from left to right, scanning the backyard for the source of the sound.

"Psssst."

She hears it again and this time she begins to tiptoe down the stone path, stepping over paper cups and plates and piles of wrapping paper. She tunes her ears and finds the source with a jolt. Tina pops through the opening of the gate, and lets out a *Rrrr!*

"Tina, you scared me." Abby slaps her chest with slight aggravation in her voice. "What are you doing here?"

"I've always been here, silly. I just didn't let you see me until now. You look like you had a cool party."

"Yeah, but now we have to clean up."

"By yourself?"

"No. Ally is supposed to be helping me, but as usual, she said she has to go to the bathroom." Abby rolls her eyes.

"Then I wouldn't start until she comes back."

"If I don't, then I'll be in trouble too."

Tina nods and stays quiet for a moment. "Is Ally still mad at me?" she says, eventually.

Abby shrugs her shoulders. "I don't know—maybe, but I'm not sure."

"Well, it doesn't matter. Come out to the swing with me until she comes back. I promise you won't get in trouble. If your mom gets mad at you, then tell her Ally refused to help, and you weren't going to start until she does."

Abby looks back over her shoulder to see if Ally had come out of the house, but there's no sign of her. She pauses, then follows Tina through the gate to the swing down by the stream.

"I'll swing you first," Tina says.

Abby sits down on the swing, and Tina gathers all of Abby's

long, dark hair into her hands and moves it over Abby's right shoulder, then proceeds to push her. "Who was that boy at your party?"

"Which boy?" Abby asks.

"The one with long hair."

"I think his name's Jared. He just moved here, but he says he's going to move again pretty soon."

"He's cute."

Abby screws up her face. "Ew. I don't like boys—they're mean."

"He didn't seem mean. I thought he was nice."

Abby narrows her eyes. "Could he see you?"

"Yeah, but only him. No one else at your party could."

"Abby!" Ally stands in the opening of the gate in the same posture, hands on hips, just as Abby had earlier. "We're supposed to be cleaning. If you don't help, I'm telling Mom."

"I better go," Abby tells Tina, and jumps off the swing.

"Can I come back later? I want to show you something." Tina looks at Abby, then to Ally as if she were asking her directly.

Ally shrugs her shoulders, her face blank. "I guess so."

Abby and Ally return to the back garden and push themselves through the grueling task of cleaning up. Toward the end, Rosemary comes out to help them after she'd finished cleaning the kitchen. When they're finished, the three sink down on the living room furniture and watch one of their favorite movies until bed. As the ending credits of Monsters, Inc. begin, Rosemary pushes the button on the remote and tells the girls it's time for bed. They don't offer a protest as both of them had sank to lying down, each of them barely coherent enough to respond.

Rosemary allows them to get away with only half brushing their teeth, and neither girl cares about hearing a story before bed. They crawl under the covers, and before their mother is finished telling them goodnight, Abby is already asleep.

Sometime during the night, a noise wakes the girls. Abby leaps from her bed, her heart hammering. With a shaking hand, she switches the lamp on, and Ally's eyes pop open to stare at Abby. She looks too frozen in fear and confusion to do anything else.

Two more cracks sound, and this time there's a definite ping on the window. Someone had thrown something into it.

"Go look," Abby whispers.

"No, you," Ally whispers back.

They both stare at the window, and another tap comes—this time they both see it. "I bet I know who it is." Ally throws back the covers, climbs from bed and creeps toward the window.

"Who?" Abby asks as she falls in behind her, clutching her tattered, sewn bunny close to her chest.

Ally pulls back the curtain and peers down to the back garden below. "I knew it—Tina." The tone she says Tina's name in isn't friendly. She walks away from the window and takes a leap back into bed.

"Come on, Ally, let's go see what she wants."

"You go. I don't want to talk to her."

"Please. I don't want to go by myself. It's dark."

Ally huffs and glares at Abby. "I'm only going because I don't trust her anymore. I think she just wants to cause us trouble."

They tiptoe downstairs, careful not to wake Rosemary, then through the sunroom to the back garden. Tina is sitting at the cast iron table, and resting on it is a funny shaped box, which looks more like a trunk. She smiles and sits up when Abby and Ally appear.

"Hi!"

"What are you doing here?" Abby asks.

Ally frowns.

"I don't sleep much."

"Why?"

Tina shrugs. "Just can't." She turns to Ally then says, "Maybe it's because I'm worried."

"About what?" Abby asks.

Tina doesn't look at Abby but continues to look at her sister instead. "I don't like it when people are mad at me. I'm sorry I lied the other day, Ally. I didn't mean to. I was mad at someone else, and I took it out on you. Can you forgive me?"

"Only if you tell Abby the truth."

Tina frowns, then turns to Abby and says, "I lied. It was supposed to be a joke. I didn't know Ally would get so mad. It was my idea to leave you upstairs during our game of hide-n-seek."

"It's okay. I just want you and Ally to be friends again," Abby says.

"Are we?" Tina stands and pats Ally on the shoulder. "Friends again?"

"I guess so." Ally gives a partial smile that isn't very convincing.

"Good, because I have an idea. Since you two are my best friends in the whole world, I want us to do something to remember each other by." Tina returns to the table and picks up what looks like a small treasure chest. The oblong trunk has a handle on the top and a latch on the front. The outside surface has floral, raised carvings, and Abby runs her fingers over the surface.

"This looks so cool. Where'd you get it?"

Tina shrugs. "Don't remember."

"Are you leaving?" Ally asks.

"I might be."

"Why?" This time it was Abby's turn to ask why.

Tina shrugs her shoulder and dips her head toward the chest in a nonchalant sort of way. "I can't explain it, but I can't stay for much longer. So, have you ever heard of a memory box?"

Both twins look at each other and then shake their head. "What's a memory box?" Abby asks.

"It's where you pick out something you really care about and put it inside a box, then you bury it. You leave it there for a long,

long time, then you dig it up when you're really old. You know, like thirty."

"Why would we do that?" Ally asks.

"It's something I saw on TV. People put things in there that they don't ever want to forget. Or maybe even things that they do want to forget. We don't have to tell each other what we put in there if we don't want to."

"Okay," Abby says. "That sounds cool."

"Let's do it," says Ally.

"Yay," Tina squeals. "Now, let's all pick one special thing to put in the box. They have to be small, or it won't all fit."

Abby scrunches her face as though she's thinking very hard about what to put in the box.

Tina says, "Abby, I'd bet that if you put your bunny in here, it'll be healed when we dig it back up."

Abby clutches it close to her chest as horror crosses her face. She looks to Ally as though asking what she should do.

Ally shrugs her shoulders. "Maybe it will. I don't think it will hurt to try."

Abby fights back the urge to cry.

Ally must see it because she says, "I'll put my mood ring in there if it will make you feel any better." The ring seems to darken even as she says the words. She's never taken it off in over a year. Their mother had given it to her and told her that it belonged to their aunt or great grandmother. It quickly became Ally's favorite thing to wear. She never goes anywhere without it.

Tina sits the box back down on the table and opens it. "I put in the picture I took of the three of us the other day with my camera. See?"

The twins lean over and look inside.

"This is very special to me. I want to always remember you guys just like this."

18

bby

ALLOWING myself to visit memory lane on the same evening as the mysterious reappearance of my childhood toy throws my mind into a frenzy. It prompts memories to resurface that I'd buried deep, but the recollections of that night are far from becoming a complete puzzle. There are lots of missing pieces.

The night Tina showed up at our house with her idea of burying a time capsule, or a memory box as she called it, we'd each chosen one item that we thought would be something we wanted to remember when we were old. I remember putting my bunny in there, and Ally giving up her beloved mood ring, which had apparently belonged to one of our ancestors, but the rest is fuzzy.

One thing I am certain of: I have to dig up the memory box. There has to be more proof of Tina's existence in there.

As each memory of Tina resurfaces, I realize that she was meticulously skilled at being bad while pretending to be good. A master manipulator. At the time, she was roughly two or three years older than me and my sister. A prick of anger stings me as I think about my naivety. Sure, I was just a child, but I'm not sure I'm any stronger now than I was then—I'm susceptible to the same naive trust in people.

I may have a tough exterior, but sometimes internally I feel like a wave of the sea driven by the wind but tossed into the deepest part of the ocean with no direction or stability—at least my mind does. I'm weak when I only ever wanted to be secure, confident—strong. Maybe I can be, if I can prove I'm not the one who killed my sister. If only I can prove without a doubt that Tina was real.

We buried the box in the garden of my childhood home. Ruby's garden now. I don't have a photographic memory, but the recollection of exactly where we buried it is very clear. Underneath a heart-shaped rock in the far back corner of the fence. I have to dig it up—tonight.

Everything that's been happening lately screams for me to find answers. Answers to so many questions. How did Whiskers emerge from the memory box? Who put her on my bed? Why is a new student of mine repeating a name from my past? Why is Rosemary at the forefront of my mind all of a sudden? Who was Tina? And does Jared remember her?

He obviously doesn't remember being at my birthday party as a kid. I didn't even remember him being there. But had he met Tina any other time aside from that day? If *he* could see her, then she had to be real.

My brain continues to hop in random patterns, getting me nowhere. I look at my watch—11:00pm. Ruby will surely be sound asleep. She goes to bed about the same time as a roosting bird. I decide to give it one more hour.

In the meantime, I log onto the teacher portal and request a substitute teacher for the morning. I need a mental health day after all.

I change my clothes and slip into a pair of black pants and a black, long-sleeved shirt. In the mud room, I find some small gardening tools and throw them into a backpack.

I slip out the back door, and the full moon is a welcome sight. I shouldn't need a flashlight as I follow the path outside the back fence toward Ruby's house. I find the loose board in the fence that has been that way since I was a kid, and I slide it aside and slip on through. Tip-toeing along the back fence wall toward the corner, my view of the house is blocked by the large tree, which seems massive compared to its height when I was a child.

I retrieve my tiny flashlight from my backpack and squat down at the corner of the fence, finding the heart-shaped rock right away, but it isn't wedged underneath the fence as I remember. It's been tossed aside, and underneath the fence is a hole where the memory box should be. I search frantically, feeling with my hands.

The memory box is gone.

II

"The more perfect a person is on the outside,
the more demons they have on the inside."
— Sigmund Freud

19

1980

THEY SAY that blood is thicker than water, but sometimes the blood between Rosemary and me is watered down with gasoline and highly flammable. I love Rosemary most of the time, but in others, I hate her because I'm always living in her shadow, and sometimes I'm pretty sure our mother favors her over me. I haven't decided what kind of day it is today, but either way I need to go and speak to her, so I make my way down the hall to our shared bedroom.

The love-hate relationship between the two of us is complicated. Rosemary was born with the blond hair and blue eyes. She was also born with the family's gift, though she doesn't think so. She, and other women before her, often consider it a curse. She describes it as going blind for a moment and then being able to see things too clearly—and seeing them before they happen.

As for me, I'm the other type of female in this family—dark hair, dark eyes, and my gift pales in comparison. I have it, but it's

137

like it's behind a thick piece of glass—I can't seem to access it. My gift appears as a sharp pain in the chest, hard, painful and fast, but I can't see the details of what's trying to reveal itself to me. It's a bit like being given a tornado warning, but knowing the accuracy of it is unpredictable.

I walk into our room and a heavy sigh escapes my lungs as I watch Rosemary. She's laid back on her bed, casually flipping through the pages of Teen Magazine, looking for her next crazed outfit. Her long, blond hair is strewn about the pillow, looking naturally curly and beautiful. My sister seems to have it all—body, brains, and beauty. She'll try out the new style, boys will love it, and then she'll land her next Saturday night date.

The two of us might not look anything alike, but as twin sisters, we were taught to share everything equally, but it's impossible to share something that isn't tangible. It's like trying to split an apple in half, but one side has all the flavor, and the other is just plain. That's how I feel in comparison to her.

Rosemary flips the magazine face down on her chest as if she's gotten caught with her hand in the cookie jar.

"What are you doing?" I ask, narrowing my eyes.

"Nothing. Just looking through this old magazine."

"Let me see." I walk toward the bed, and she presses her hands down onto the magazine and hugs it tight against her chest.

"I said, let me see." I grip the corner of the flimsy pages and yank while Rosemary attempts to hold it tighter.

It breaks free of her grip, leaving another smaller book face down on her chest. The blue cover with gold lettering registers immediately and fury consumes me. "What the hell are you doing reading my diary?"

She doesn't try to prevent me from yanking this one away.

"You like Mike? The tall dweeb with curly hair?" Rosemary taunts.

"You had no right to read my diary, Rosemary."

"Relax, I only read the last page."

I feel the color drain from my face, and my mouth goes dry. "I don't care. You shouldn't have done that."

Rosemary sighs dejectedly and pleads, "Oh, come on, I promise. It was just that one page. I'm really sorry and I won't do it again. I promise."

I take a deep breath and halfway believe that she's sincere, but I tuck my diary under my mattress. "I catch you with it again I'm going to kick your ass."

"Deal. So—now that I know about Mike, I can help you get his attention." Rosemary springs from the bed and stands to face me with a smile. She looks like the cat that swallowed the canary, her blue eyes twinkling. I know that look, which usually lands us in trouble—though it will be me that gets into trouble, because I usually get the blame.

"Let's sneak out tonight," Rosemary says.

"We're both grounded." I shake my head.

"That's why we're sneaking out, dumb-ass."

I sigh, knowing that when Rosemary has an idea, there's no stopping her. I raise a skeptical eyebrow, but deep down, I know I can't say no. Rosemary has always had a way of convincing me to do things I wouldn't otherwise do.

"Come on, Ruby," she pleads, taking my hand and dragging me down onto the bed. "We never do anything fun together anymore. It seems like you're always mad at me."

"The last time you said *let's have some fun*, it got us both grounded—forever."

"And that's why we have to sneak out, because we've been grounded—forever." Rosemary rolls her eyes. "And that was only because we got caught. We won't get caught this time."

She looks at me with the same twinkle in her eye, knowing that she's already won me over. I try one more time to push back against her, reminding her of the consequences of getting caught, but Rosemary has already made up her mind, and I can tell there's no changing it.

"Fine," I say, finally giving in. "But what're we going to do?"

Rosemary's grin widens. "There's a party happening tonight at the old mansion on the corner. It's supposed to be wild. And, Mike is supposed to be there."

My heart quickens and I try to control a giddy smile. "Okay, but we can't get caught."

"Of course—here's what we're going to do," she says. "We'll tell Mom goodnight and stress to her that she can't come into our room because we're working on a surprise for her birthday. Then, we wait for her to knock on the door to tell *us* goodnight, answer her, and really stress to her that she can't come in because of our surprise. She'll go to bed and won't suspect a thing. We wait for her to fall asleep, then we can tiptoe out of the house. We'll leave the back door unlocked so that we can sneak back in after the party."

I'm often good at manipulation, but Rosemary is an excellent schemer. "I guess you thought of everything."

Rosemary's plan goes off without a hitch and our mother is non-the-wiser. Soon we're sneaking across town just after 10:30. We round the corner and the massive old mansion comes into view, looming above all of the other houses around it. Its gable roofs each enclose their own lit windows, making the house look as though it has numerous eyes watching the street in front of it. Music blares from inside its walls as the bass pumps through the air like a heartbeat. The patter of my own heart competes the closer we get to the house and my palms begin to sweat as I dare to hope Mike will notice me.

A dimly lit, wraparound porch encloses the house and is packed with teens who stand in pods, each holding a red solo cup in their hand, some with one in each hand. Girls stand in their prissy postures with two fingers pointed upward, holding cigarettes that they shouldn't dare be smoking. Bodies fill the lawn, doorways and windows.

Rosemary prediction was right, the party is packed.

My eyes begin a frantic search for Mike, and I finally catch sight of him as his gaze lands on Rosemary. He barely glances my way as he rushes towards us. Mike is a head taller than us, slim yet muscular. He wears tight jeans and a red shirt, accentuating his chiseled chest. His curly hair almost reaches his shoulders, and frames what I think is the most beautiful face I've ever seen. I practically have to push my bottom jaw back in place at the sight of him.

"You made it," he says, yet his words are directed solely at Rosemary.

A twinge of anger courses through me, and I push it down and smile anyway.

"Of course we did," she replies with a smile.

His eyes flicker to me for an instant before returning to her.

"Come on, I'll get you a drink," he suggests, extending his hand out to Rosemary.

She grasps it without hesitation, and they leave me feeling like the odd one out. My face flushes and I instantly regret coming— why hadn't I seen that this would happen? As always, Rosemary steals the show and crushes any hope of me hooking up with Mike.

An hour later, I'm sitting in a corner with my third cup of alcohol, buzzing like a bumble bee. I know I should probably pour it out because at this point Rosemary may have to carry me home. I don't care. I finally get up from my corner and stagger around groups of people on the first floor of the old three-story old house.

I maneuver through and around drunken teenagers and manage to make my way up to the second floor, only to find myself standing in front of a large window made up of small panes of glass. The glass is horribly thick and blurred, but that might just be my intoxicated vision. My body sways in place and I realize I'm not just buzzing; I'm drunk. Familiar voices come from one of the bedrooms down the hall, then comes a distinct cackling that I recognize as Rosemary's. It's followed by a low, male rumble in response.

My heart sinks like a boulder in water when I realize they are in that room together, and no doubt doing things I'd rather not know about.

Now I'm certain there's no hope for me and Mike. Resentment festers inside me, and I stomp off, muttering its unfairness under my breath. *What I should do is bust down the door and demand to go home.*

I go back into the kitchen to pour myself another drink when Jack, a tall, skinny guy with glasses, who has hit on me three times since I've been here, says, "Maybe you should slow down just a little."

"Oh yeah, why?" I slur.

"Because I think I've had too much to drink myself, and I don't think I can get you home." He laughs and winks.

I take a big gulp of my drink then step closer to Jack, stopping when my face is only inches from his. "Let's go smoke some weed and make out."

He almost drops his own drink as his eyes expand in disbelief. "Really?"

I grab him by the shirt and begin to drag him outside. "Can you get us some weed or not?"

"S-sure," he stutters.

I lean my back against the porch post so I can remain upright while Jack scurries away. "Wait right here. I'll be right back," he calls behind him. He's back in under two minutes, holding a joint between his thumb and index finger. "Got one." He lights the joint and the end glows bright orange as he takes a long drag, holding it in while trying to talk. "You ever smoked weed before?"

"Pfff," I puff through my lips and teeth. "Sure I have. Let me have it," I lie.

He turns his hand over, shifting the joint around, careful not to touch the smoking end, then holds it up to my mouth. I attempt to pucker my lips, which isn't easy in my drunken state, and suck in hard as the stinging burn travels down my throat. It hits my lungs, making me cough.

"You *haven't* done this before," Jack says.

"First time for everything," I strain to say in between coughs.

He laughs. "Here, try it again, and this time take it slow while trying not to cough. You have to hold it in if you want to get a buzz."

"I think I'm beyond that." I sway in place and do as he says, and before I know it, I'm sliding down the porch post and sitting on the porch floor. Jack sits down next to me, and I reach up and take off his glasses, then look into his brown eyes. "I thought we came out here to make out."

I drape my legs over his, wrap both arms around his neck, and meet his lips with a sloppy kiss. I almost forget about Rosemary and Mike.

Almost.

20

Ruby

1981

I SPRINT into the kitchen to find a snack, not paying attention as I round the corner of the doorway. The coiling cord that stretches across the room from the wall phone clotheslines me across the chest, causing me to stumble backward. I snap, "Rosemary! You've been on the phone for over an hour. Who are you talking to?"

Rosemary waves as if to shush me and shoots me a mean look. I know exactly who she's talking to—the same person she's been talking to every day for three months now.

Mike.

I let a puff escape my lips and clench my teeth. The thought of it sends a new course of jealousy through me. Envy of their relationship has taken up permanent residence inside my head, and I struggle not to wish them ill will. *I'm* supposed to be the one he's with, not her.

Suddenly losing my appetite, I stomp through the kitchen into the back garden, where Maria sits at the wrought-iron table with a newspaper and a cup of coffee. The sun shines across her curly blond hair as several strands whisper around in the light breeze. I pause and debate for a moment about whether I should confide in her about how I feel about Rosemary and Mike.

After a few moments of quiet, she says, "You might as well get it off your chest and come sit down." She lays down her paper and gives me one of her sympathetic smiles, as if she knows why I'm here. She probably does.

"What's wrong, my dear? You seem troubled." Maria sits back in her seat, crossing her white bell-bottomed leg over the other as she grips the cup of coffee in both hands.

"Did you ever like someone, but they didn't like you back?"

"Oh, yes—your father. He didn't even know I existed until I *made* him notice me."

"How did you do that?"

Maria sits down her coffee as the ends of her orange sleeves drape down over the table, and her smile turns into a mischievous grin. "Well, since you're only seventeen, I'll give you the PG version of the story, and maybe when you're older I'll tell you the rest."

I become all ears and scoot forward in my chair. "You mean there's an R version?"

She grins bigger. "Your father was actually dating someone else when we got together, but she definitely wasn't right for him, nor was she very nice. Her name was Lala, and she was spoiled, entitled, and knew she could have anyone she wanted, and she did most of the time. Even while she was dating your father. Everyone could see it but him, so I figured out a way to make him see her for who she really was."

It sounds just as if she's speaking about Rosemary, and I glue myself to her every word and ask again, "How?"

"At that time, I had a friend named Dean who was older than me—college age. He was very handsome."

"Then why didn't *you* date him?"

"Oh no, we'd been friends since we were little, and he was too much like a brother to me. But all the girls certainly swooned over him, including Lala. Anyway, Dean and I set little Miss Lala up. This happened when your father and I were seniors and there was this big, end-of-the-year party. Tons of students from school were there, including your father and Lala. I brought Dean along, and in less than two seconds, every girl at the party was panting over him. So did Lala."

Maria takes a sip of her coffee, keeping me in suspense. "People are often attention seekers, but some more than others, and I knew that Lala was the queen of it. So, it was easy to trap her into a situation that she couldn't resist."

Maria has my full attention. Should I be taking notes? A gust of wind blows through, shifting the newspaper on the table as well as Maria's hair. She gathers the long strands into both hands, twists it around in front of her body, then tucks a few stray strands behind her ear.

"Your father will tell me now that he had a crush on me, too, back then, but he was loyal to whomever he was with. I like to tell myself that he just needed a nudge. That's what I did. But I would say if you asked Lala, she wouldn't agree—it was pretty sneaky and mean."

"What was it?"

"I don't know. Maybe I shouldn't tell you." Maria hesitates, pressing her lips together as her eyes take on an unsure look.

"Oh, come on. You have to now."

Maria giggles, then continues. "We made it to the party with bonfires, music, and of course, some people snuck in booze. Our plan was to get Lala away from your father and then Dean would lay on the charm. He didn't have to work very hard before Lala was flirting back and making excuses to get away from Charles. Then Dean spiked her drink."

I suppress a gasp, trying to look shocked as my mind immediately begins to plot while Maria finishes her story.

"I distracted your father by talking about his car. No man can resist that. I knew enough about them to keep him busy for a while. Dean got Lala drunk and into the back seat of his car. I don't think it took much convincing. Then I pretended to be worried and begged your father to help me find Dean."

"Did he?" I ask, butting in as soon as Maria finished saying the last word.

"Oh yes, but I'm not going to tell you anymore. That's the R rated part." Maria smiles. "But I did feel bad, because your father was heartbroken. That didn't last long. I was there with a shoulder for him to lean on, and the rest is history." Maria picks up her coffee and leans back in her chair.

The wheels in my mind begin to turn like the inner workings of a clock as I begin my plot on how to end my sister's relationship with Mike. I have to figure out a way to make him see her as bad, and me as the one he wants to be with.

21

Ruby

1982

HISTORY CLASS SEEMS to drag on forever as I stare into space. I'm sick of living in my sister's shadow *all* the time. It seems as though her life has always been served to her on a silver platter. She's the sort of person that can fall into a pile of shit and still come out smelling like a spring flower. *Some people* never truly know what it means to struggle in life, because God decided to give them a deck of cards stacked in their favor.

After hearing my mother's story about her revenge on the girl that sounds a lot like my sister, I've decided how I'm going to make Mike see Rosemary differently. I'm going to make him believe that she is fooling around with someone else.

My friend Gretta is known as the biggest gossiper in school. She can't keep a secret and loves stirring up drama just to see people's reactions. She has a new rumor to tell every morning when she comes into school. So, I planted a little one in her ear myself and swore her to secrecy. If you tell her to keep it a secret, then you might as well tell her to shout it through a megaphone.

I told her that Bobby is crushing on Rosemary, and that Rosemary has feelings for Bobby.

I helped the rumors spread even more by sliding little notes into fellow classmates' lockers. Little slips of paper that say things like, *Rosemary hearts Bobby,* and *Bobby's going to come out about his secret crush on Rosemary,* and my favorite is the one that says, *Rosemary's a slut for cheating on Mike with Bobby.* For the last one, I tried to match my sister's handwriting as much as possible, and I slipped it directly into Bobby Anderson's locker—the most popular football jock in school. It was a letter confessing her long-time secret crush on him. It's been obvious for some time that Bobby has had a crush on my sister, but she's been too wrapped up in Mike to notice. This will surely catch everyone's attention.

I've always heard a saying that goes, *wherever there's smoke, there's a fire.* That's what I'm doing, creating a fire, and the notes will surely create the smoke signals I need to make Mike suspicious.

I do feel a little sorry about the idea of this hurting Mike, but not Rosemary. She deserves it for taking him from me to begin with, and I can't wait to watch her crumble.

So far, the plan is working because Bobby's already following my sister around, and she's eating it up.

The bell rings for class change, and as I walk down the crowded hallway filled with body odor and roars of chatter, I spot Mike and Rosemary standing in front of his locker. Mike's body language isn't loving. There's a defensive stance in his posture, and his clenched jaw tells me he isn't happy with my sister. *I wish I could hear what they're saying.*

This weekend is the yearly county fair, and what I have planned should be the final straw. Mike has taken on a temporary job at the fairground, running a gaming booth. He'll be too busy and won't be hanging out with Rosemary, which leaves plenty of opportunity for Bobby to hit on her. The plan is to have one of my friends tell Mike that she saw Rosemary in line at the tilt-a-whirl making out with Bobby. In all honesty, I don't believe Rosemary would actually do anything with Bobby—she may flirt, but I've never known her to cheat. But, with all the rumors I've spread, that's all it'll take to tear them apart,

The sun dips below the horizon, casting a long shadow across the sprawling county fairground. I've been waiting all week for this day to come, not for the cotton candy, the Ferris wheel, or the flashy rides, but for my chance at retribution.

The vibrant lights of the Carnival rides flickers against the darkening sky, and the air fills with the scent of deep-fried dough, popcorn, and the pinging sound of games, laughter and music. It's the perfect setting for my plan. All the noise and chaos will make it hard for Rosemary to prove that she didn't do what she'll be accused of doing.

As I'm waiting on my friend Judy to arrive, I spot a tent with a banner that says *Fortune Teller*. I step closer and squint into the dark interior, and the smell of herbal incense wafts over me so strongly I can taste it. I tiptoe inside and peer at the woman sitting in the middle at a table. The rest of the space is surrounded with candles, giving the tent a warm glow, yet it's still dark enough to make the setting mysterious—even creepy.

The dark-haired woman waves me in. "Come in, please. Let me tell you your fortune."

I hesitate, and she speaks again. "Madame Zhara doesn't bite."

I move closer to the table as she motions for me to sit, and I ease into the squeaky chair. Around the edges of the table, more candles light the center of it with a dancing glow. The woman places her hands in front of me with both palms facing up and tells me to place my hands just as she is on top of hers. I pause, and my eyebrows involuntarily raise when I see the lines across both surfaces of her hands. The letters are etched deeper and larger than my own—even more than my mother's. I glance back up at her, and she nods her head downward as if to say *go ahead*.

I'm second-guessing my decision for coming here, but I lower the backs of my hands into hers anyway, which feels warm to the touch. This time it's *her* eyebrows that raise, and she looks back at me. "You carry the special markings. They may be much smaller than mine, but they're there, and that means the answers you seek are already answered in your mind."

My face shifts into an apprehensive frown, and as soon as she says the words, a sharp pain pounds me in the chest, making me jump. It's the sort of pain that usually comes as a warning. I never know or understand what it's trying to warn me of, but it's usually something bad.

The woman gives me a crooked grin. She traces the line on my left hand, sending a chill across the length of my arms. "Your sister has these as well, and your mother, and your mother's mother. Their gift appears to you to be much more powerful than yours, but that doesn't mean they are—they're just more attuned. So, what is it you want to ask me?"

My face flushes, and I jerk my hands away. I don't want to talk to this woman after all. "I don't have any questions. I was just killing some time until my friend gets here."

"You're not here to ask me what you should do?"

"About what?"

"Your jealousy and anger toward your sister."

My jaw twitches and my mouth goes dry. "I'm not jealous, nor am I angry." I shove my hands under the table.

She peers closely at me. "You have big plans for her tonight."

I stand abruptly and step back, my gaze bouncing from her face back to her hands.

Madame Zhara leans forward, her eyes looking as though they may pierce my soul. "Remember, child, fate favors those who make the right choices. The fair moon above will guide your steps. Choose wisely."

I stumble from the tent and immediately look up at the sky. Despite the glow of the fairground lights, the moon swells larger and brighter.

"What does that old hag know?" I shove her words aside, but not without a slight hint of apprehension as I spot Judy. I wave and sprint over to her. "You ready to go talk to Mike?"

We both look across the way to Mike's booth, and he spots us and waves.

"This is going to be so fun." Judy rubs the palms of her hands together as though she's getting ready to dive into a feast. Her lack of apprehension fades mine away, and I forget all about Madame Zhara's words.

"I'm going to stay back here while you talk to him. If he sees me, he might be suspicious."

Judy nods. "Right. Now what am I saying, again?"

"Just make up some chit-chat bullshit with him then, say something like, *'please don't tell anyone that I'm the one who told you this, but I saw Rosemary and Bobby kissing in line at the tilt-a-whirl.'* But talk to him a little bit first before you say anything. Build up to it. I'm going to find Bobby and tell him that Rosemary is looking for him. I'll make sure they end up at the tilt-a-whirl at the same time, and when Mike hears what you saw, he'll go to find Rosemary, and when he does, he'll find them together."

Judy grins. "I got it. Do you think Mike will punch Bobby?"

I chew my lip. "No. I think he'll hate my sister after this, though."

Judy chuckles, then sprints away and weaves around people toward Mike's booth while I fight the crowd to find Bobby. I knew where he'll be—the same booth that all the stupid teenage jocks flock to. The game with fake rifles to shoot pop-up ducks.

That's where I find him. He isn't playing the game at the

moment, so I walk up, hook my hand in the crook of his arm and drag him a few steps away from the crowd of boys.

"Oh, hey. What's up, Ruby?"

"My sister's looking for you."

"Really?" Bobby's face lights up. "Where is she?" He leans from side to side to look behind me.

"She was as the tilt-a-whirl trying to get someone to ride with her, but none of her friends like to ride it. It gives them all whiplash. You should go ride it with her."

He nods. "Where's Mike?"

"He's too busy being Mike. If you ask me, I think she's just fed up with him. You should go cheer her up. But she's probably not going to tell you she's upset. Don't tell her I told you, but I even saw her crying earlier."

I don't have to convince Bobby any further. He calls out to his buddies and tells them he'll catch them later. The dunking booth next to the tilt-a-whirl is where we find my sister.

"Remember, don't say anything about her being upset. Just ask her to ride."

"Gotcha."

I glance around to look for Mike, but don't see him. With a mix of glee and nerves running through me, I step back out of sight and wait for everything to go down. Bobby walks straight toward Rosemary, and she waves, giving him a stupid, giddy smile. My mouth forms into my own type of smile, but it isn't giddy, it's cunning and victorious.

Rosemary doesn't hesitate and hops in line for the ride with Bobby. I glance to my left and spot Judy and Mike, who both come to a stop when Mike spots Rosemary. The look on his face shifts from worry to immediate rage.

Mike picks up the pace and heads toward my sister while Judy scans the fairground. Is she looking for me? I stay hidden so I can continue to watch the show.

The timing couldn't be more perfect. Rosemary's back is turned to Mike, but she has her hand hooked around Bobby's arm as she throws her head back to laugh. Bobby reaches up to brush a strand of hair out of her face.

She's unaware of what's about to happen.

I watch Bobby's face as it shifts from a full-teeth smile to a look of dreads. The blood drains from his cheeks, making him look even paler than he already is. Like he's just been caught with his hands in Mike's cookie jar.

Rosemary must see the sudden change in Bobby's face, as she turns to see Mike, who looks at her with slumped shoulders, squinty eyes, and a down-turned mouth. She immediately turns her body away from Bobby and moves toward Mike.

Mike shakes his head and slings both hands up as if to wave her away, then he rushes back through the crowd.

"Mike! Wait!"

I taste sweet victory as I dart through the crowd to find Mike and finish out my plan.

Offer my shoulder, and more if he wants it.

bby

I STARE at the wall of my bedroom, and the only difference from an hour ago is that the white image of the window created by the moon's glow has moved from one part of the wall to another. The digital alarm clock that rests on my bedroom dresser reads two-thirty AM. Sleep has forgotten about me, or maybe my mind has forgotten how to find it. Either way, I've flipped my body several times, hoping it will come.

Next to my alarm clock, the tattered bunny seems to be staring at me—Whiskers. When she first reappeared, she creeped me out, to the point I couldn't look at her. But now I've allowed myself to really look at her, it seems as though her eyes are pleading with me to hold her. I think about her being buried and alone all these years and a sudden guilt overwhelms me. I abandoned her. The feeling floods me with a sadness that I'm not expecting, and I throw back the covers, leap from bed and grab her, then hop back in bed as I hug her tightly to my chest. I hug her the way I used to hug her when I was a child. The way I did when scared of the dark or lonely. I snuggle her in as close as one might hold a pet that's been missing, and has suddenly returned home. I squeeze her in an apologetic way as I whisper, *I'm so sorry I abandoned you.*

I begin to cry, and the feeling is so overwhelming that I find myself missing Rosemary. Would she feel like I'm feeling right now if I returned to her? Would she be happy to see me? Maybe she would be put off at first, but after a while. Maybe she would be happy to see me. Maybe she'd hold me just like this.

Tears continue to fall, moistening the cheeks of the bunny as I rub my face on hers. I allow myself to fall into the moment, giving it a chance to completely consume me. When it slowly begins to ease its grip, I feel a small sense of relief. I've been holding back my emotions for days and maybe this is what I needed. I take a few deep breaths and attempt to pull myself back together.

Rosemary used to make us what she called a *special tea* when my sister or I couldn't sleep. I'm not sure how special it was, but now I decide to do the same. I kick back the covers and go downstairs to fix myself some chamomile. Between allowing myself to have a good cry and a cup of tea, maybe I can still get a few hours of sleep.

I carry Whiskers with me and prop her in a seated position on the counter as if she were a small child. I decide to pull the old-fashioned kettle that Rosemary used to make our tea in and prepare it just like she used to. As it heats on the stove, I sit at the table and wait for the soothing whistle the kettle makes when it's ready.

I smile as the whistle first begins as a subtle sputter, then grows louder to a loud squeal. To me, it isn't an annoying sound, rather the sound of my past—the part of my past that I allow myself to remember. Once I've prepared my tea, I sit back down at the table and place Whiskers on the table in front of me. I raise my cup of tea as a toast to her and when I go to take a sip, I get a strong whiff of rosemary—like the herb. I pull the cup away, look at it and the box of tea on the counter, then sniff it again. This time it smells like the tea that it is—chamomile. I frown and sniff again. Still the same.

I stare at Whiskers with eyebrows furrowed. "Is this a sign? Should I go see her?"

Of course, Whiskers doesn't answer, but the question grows louder in my mind, and I seriously begin to debate it. The pros and cons begin to play cat and mouse with one another. She may turn me away or she may be happy to see me. She won't recognize me, or she will and pretend that she doesn't. She hates me or she never stopped loving me.

I lift the cup to sip my tea again, and the smell of rosemary returns. This time it's so strong I can taste it even as I drink. I pull the cup away and look at the box again, only this time I stand and look at the emptied packet I'd left next to the stove. The pouch reads chamomile.

Now, the smell seems to be thick in the air, and as I look around the room, then back to Whiskers, I give into the idea. "I know what I need to do. I need to see Rosemary."

23

osemary
1990

Secrets are like eyeballs, everyone has them, only some choose not to see. They're blind to what's right in front of them, and the same goes for the truth—it's often something we won't even let ourselves see. Fixing or not fixing one's eyesight can be costly, just as refusing to see the truth can often cost a person everything.

As I run the feather duster over the table next to my mother's old chair, I open the drawer to drop in an ink pen and a hair tie, an attempt to declutter. Inside, the scrapbook catches my eye and I decide to take a break from cleaning and plop down in my mother's old chair. It was always her favorite, and it still sits in what was her favorite corner of the living room. My mother's ghost is everywhere here. So's my sister's, and she's not even dead.

My mother, Maria, always said that she and I were more alike, but I think she was wrong—I think Ruby and I are both like our mother in our own ways, but I'm more like her than I care to admit.

I rest the scrapbook on my lap and open to a page that contains a picture of me and Mike at the county fair when we were just teenagers. It only takes a moment for my mind to remember, and my smile lessens when I think about what happened that night. It was years ago, yet I still feel a twinge of anger when I allow myself to think about what my sister did. Her friend Judy had ratted her out the second she thought it would get back to me that she was involved in the plot to sabotage mine and Mike's relationship.

It worked—for a while.

Once Mike calmed down and learned that the rumors were all rooted from my sister's plot to break us up, we became closer than ever. Ruby's plot only backfired. Mike wouldn't even speak to her for a long time after that.

I let out a long sigh and close my eyes, waiting for the tension to ease, but with little success. Two days ago, Ruby found out that I'd had to commit our mother to a mental hospital.

Time had stopped for Maria, and for a while now, she's been living inside her head, never knowing what day of the week it is; her age, or mine. She sees people that aren't there, which isn't out of the ordinary, but it has become a constant thing. She often talks to the dead who, as she says, come to reveal truths to her, but her conversations with them have become more like a vivid account one might read in the diaries of a lunatic.

My mother began having dementia episodes when she was barely forty years old. The illness progressed rapidly, and I've had to be the one to take care of her. Ruby left town and only returns a couple of times per year. When she does visit, she only hangs around for a day or two, and during those couple of days, she spends most of her time catching up with old friends and insists on staying in a hotel.

Mike and I have been together since high school. For years we said that we didn't really want children, but for more than a year now, we've been trying. For me, the fear of having children comes from the fear of the curse. I believe it. At first, I didn't. Not until my mother told me her story. Maria was definitely the bad sister. Blond hair, cruel intentions, and all.

What if I give birth to twins and one of them inherits the curse?

Generations of women in my family have lived right here, in this house—my mother, her mother and her mother's mother. The plush, winged-back chair where I now sit, its material thread-bare, has remained in this corner for just as long. The seat sags in the middle, a sink hole carved out by generations of women. Sitting where all the other women had spent countless hours before me, I find myself reaching far back into my memories.

Several months ago, Maria sat in this very chair and told me one of her final stories. She'd progressed quickly into her battle with dementia and thought she was confessing one of her most horrible sins to a priest. I tried to get her to understand that we weren't sitting in a confession booth, and I wasn't her priest. I told her clearly who I was, but like so many other times, she was too lost inside her head.

"Maria, I'm not your priest. I'm your daughter, Rosemary. Don't you see me?" But she didn't.

"Forgive me father, for I have sinned." Maria tapped her forehead, then moved her hand down across her lips to her chest, tapped it, then tapped from shoulder to shoulder.

I decided to sit back and see where her confession was going, and as she made it, I was more than shocked by what I heard—it confirmed there were two sides to my mother's life story.

"I did something horrible, Father, but my sister deserved all of it. My true confession is that I'm only sorry I didn't succeed in killing her. I know I'm supposed to love her, but I don't—I despise her. I live in her shadow all of the time."

I'd looked at my mother and observed her age outwardly, but

the words she was saying were those of a teenage girl. Her mind had traveled backward as she'd continued, her voice taking on a hateful tone—something I'd never heard before. My mother had always been soft-spoken and kind.

"I wanted her to die, and I tried to make it happen. I did my best to smother her in her sleep, but I suppose when one is fighting for their life, one gains the strength of Hercules." Maria paused and stared straight ahead as if the priest were speaking to her.

"Well, I know it was wrong, but so was what Sylvia did. She stole my place as captain of the cheer squad. It had been mine all through high school, and she decided to take it our senior year. I'm sick of her—she takes everything from me."

Shaking off the memories, I lean my head back against the worn chair as the faint image of my mother slowly fades. Instead of her being taken from me by a sudden death, her mind slipped away before she was actually gone. And as for Aunt Sylvia, I'd never met her. It was said that she and my mother hated each other so badly that she'd left home the day she turned eighteen, married, and never came back. My mother rarely talked about her.

As I continue to sit and mull over my decision to commit our mother to Serenity Oaks, my surroundings begin to blur before shifting to a white haze, then to black. It sends me into a blind panic, literally, and I know what this means.

Something bad is trying to reveal itself to me.

I sit up straighter, attempting to breathe my way through it, and wait for it to pass. These occurrences are happening more often and are stronger than they've ever been. It seems they shifted when Maria started losing her mind. Almost as if she's passed her gift to me.

As I stare into the darkness for what seems like forever, Ruby moves to the forefront of my mind. *She's coming, and she isn't happy with me.*

As soon as the thought arrives, the blindness leaves. I hear the front door swing open and the sound of footsteps echo from the foyer.

Ruby stomps into the room and finds me in our mother's chair. She's decked out in the many colors of the rainbow, her nails and lips painted crimson. A look I've never seen on her before.

"What the hell are you thinking, committing our poor mother to that godawful place? I know she isn't herself, but she doesn't deserve to be there."

My jaw tightens. "Ruby, you haven't been here, so you have no idea what you're talking about. Maria isn't Maria anymore. She's had too many episodes that put her life in danger. She'd wonder out into the streets and into traffic—sometimes naked."

"Then why didn't you hire someone to help with her?"

"I did! Those things happened under their care. You know how she is—when she gets something in her head, there's no stopping her. Besides, I didn't see you coming back here to help take care of her, so it's been Mike and me every step of the way."

Ruby narrows her eyes, which are filled with fury. "You've always been selfish, Rosemary. Everything and everyone revolve around you." She shifts her tone and her body language to that of a mocking, snobby adolescent. "Poor innocent Rosemary. Look at me—I'm so helpless."

"If you only came back here to criticize the way I've done things, then go back to where you've been hiding all these years."

Ruby freezes and speaks through gritted teeth. "I haven't been hiding, I've been busy having a life for once."

"Ruby, this isn't about you or me. It's about our mother. I did the best I could under the circumstance, and if you want to come home and take care of her full time, be my guest. As far as I'm concerned, this is the end of this discussion." I stomp upstairs with the full intention of leaving the discussion behind. Like all the other arguments Ruby and I have had, she won't let it go and stomps up the stairs behind me.

"Here is what I think really happened. Our mother interrupted yours and Mike's fantasy of playing house, and you didn't want that responsibility anymore. Since you all decided to try for kids, she's getting in the way of all your frigging, so you decided to ship her off."

I reach the top of the stairs, my blood boiling at her comment. Before I have a chance to stop myself, I turn and shove Ruby, causing her to teeter backward as she frantically grips for the banister. She kicks her foot out while trying to grab onto anything to stop herself from falling. In the process, her foot lodges between two spindles of the railing, and she lands directly on her back. Her body propels itself downward, twisting her foot at a grotesque angle, and several cracking sounds echo through the air. I know right away what the sound is—bones snapping.

"Fuck! You fucking bitch! You fucking bitch! Get the fuck away from me!" Ruby screams the words over and over through gritted teeth as she writhes in place while I attempt to gently release her mangled foot.

"What the hell is going on here?" Mike calls from the front door before running up the stairs.

"Mike, help! Ruby's foot's stuck and I'm afraid to touch it."

"What happened?"

Ruby spat out the words one at a time as though it causes her great pain to even speak. "Your fucking wife—that's what."

"Ruby, calm down." Mike slides both hands underneath Ruby's shoulders as he lifts her upper body. He scoots her upwards so I can get her free from the railing. Once she is free, Mike cradles her up into his arms like a small child and carries her down the stairs. Ruby rests her head on Mike's shoulder and nuzzles her face in close to his neck before darting her eyes upward. They glare at me as if daggers could catapult from them, then she squeezes her arms tighter around Mike's neck.

I watch from behind, and for a split second, I'm not sorry I pushed her.

24

osemary
1994

A MARRIAGE ISN'T what falls apart between two people—it's the two people who fall apart from the marriage. They stop being friends for one reason or another. Maybe it's because one grows up and the other grows away, or maybe it's because our expectations of marriage are more like that of a fairy tale.

In the beginning, my life with Mike was full of magic and enchantment with all the subplots of lust, sex, and love. Lately, it's as if the wicked witch of the story has cast a spell, turning it into a nightmare—or in our case, into real life.

Mike and I fight over the stupidest things. Things like who should turn off the light when we go to bed, or, if you'd just made the coffee last night, I wouldn't have stubbed my toe as I went to do it this morning. The serious fights lately are about the joys of sex. There is none. Trying for a child has become more like leaving a soda out all night with the lid off. It's gone flat and dry—literally. Before the stress of trying to make a baby and the constant bickering, all Mike had to do was brush up against me and I was ready to go. Now, lubricant is a necessity because sex has become a chore. I still love Mike just as much as ever, but these days I really miss the way things used to be.

I sucked up my pride a month ago and called Ruby on our birthday. Something about turning thirty jolted me into the reality that I need my sister, after all. I gave her a true apology for the first time since her accident on the stairs, which had caused permanent damage to her foot. After several corrective surgeries, doctors said that she would never walk again without a limp. Almost a year has passed since that day, which must have been enough time for her to get over being livid with me. I was surprised when she answered and actually seemed happy to hear from me. Since then, we talk almost every day and in some ways we're closer than we've ever been. Maybe we've both grown up.

It's been nice having my sister back in my life, because I now have her to confide in about the stress Mike and I are going through. I glance at the clock a third time, anxious, because Ruby should be arriving at any time for a visit. She's flying in from New Orleans and plans to stay for a week—the longest she's been home in years. It's the first time I'm truly excited to see her.

"Rose? Are you here?" Ruby calls from the front door.

"In the kitchen," I call back, but I don't wait for her to make her way to me. I step around the doorway and the air gets trapped in my lungs when I see her. The first thing I notice is her limp, but I quickly divert my eyes away from her feet. I don't want to remind her of what I did to her—not that she could forget.

My eyes widen as I take in the rest of her body. She's lost at least twenty pounds and is wearing clothes that show off her petite, yet curvy figure. I involuntarily slouch in on myself, feeling self-conscious. She must have given her twenty pounds to me, because I've definitely let myself go lately, gaining at least that. Everything about her, even with the limp, is spewing confidence, which, for some reason, quashes mine.

I take a deep breath and swallow it down, painting on a lying smile as I step forward to hug her. "It's so good to see you. How was your flight?"

"Oh, you know, there's always a screaming child siting right behind me, but other than that, it beats the hell out of driving." Ruby slings her hair over her shoulder, and I notice the caramel highlights in her hair. It seems she's had a complete makeover since last year, making her look ten years younger.

"I'm so glad you're here," I say, but I'm not feeling as much enthusiasm now. I do my best to push any negative feelings aside and tell myself it's going to be the best visit we've ever had.

The front door opens again, and I look around to see Mike coming in. I plaster on an even faker smile and move around Ruby to greet him. "Hi, honey, I'm glad you're home."

Mike gives me a puzzled look. It's probably the best greeting I've given him in a while. He gives me an apprehensive smile, then I catch his eyes scan Ruby's body before they actually land on her face. "Well, hey, Ruby. Look at you—you look amazing."

My teeth clench tightly, and for a moment, I'm jealous. I quickly get it in check. There's no need for me to be envious of my own sister.

"Thank you, Mike. Well, it was hard to find an exercise routine to get in shape after my accident, but I managed to do it. This gal has officially lost twenty-five pounds." Ruby sashays back and forth as she holds her hands out to the side. She mentions the accident in such a nonchalant tone as though all has been forgiven and there are no hard feelings.

Part of me is relieved, but the other part feels a hint of suspicion that she is so blasé about it. Ruby never lets anything go.

"Good for you, Ruby. I bet you can have the pick of any man you want, not that you couldn't before." Mike smiles.

"Yeah, Ruby, is there a Mister?" I ask, trying to keep my voice even.

"No one in particular. I'm having too much fun playing with them all." Ruby winks at me, and I manage a grin.

"Well, anyone would be lucky to have you," Mike says as he pats Ruby on the back of her shoulder, his hand lingering a little too long.

My enthusiasm about spending the week with my sister dwindles a little more, and I work hard to tell myself that I'm allowing my insecurities to dictate my state of mind. Insecurity can be ugly and can only force others to see you in a negative light. My internal conflict must show in my face, because before I've had a chance to get it in check, Mike frowns at me.

"Everything alright, Rosemary?" Mike asks.

"Oh, yes. I was just debating on what we should do for dinner." I walk over and hook my arm into Mike's and kiss him on the cheek before looking at Ruby. For a second, I think that I see an old familiar look in her eye—the kind she used to get when we were teenagers, and Mike and I would cuddle or kiss. It only lasts for a split second, and I question whether I'd seen it in the first place.

"Let me help, Rose. What would you like for me to do?"

I allow my fears to dissipate as I relax my shoulders and smile at Ruby. "Wouldn't that be a first?" I tease, then tell myself that this is going to be a great visit.

After dinner, the three of us sit around the dining table with a glass of wine and listen to Ruby's stories about New Orleans and how she ended up there. In some ways, I'm envious that she was able to get out of here while I was holding down our mother's house and our mother—sometimes literally. Ruby had zero responsibilities at home after she left for college and then moved away.

"Earth to Rose—you in there?" Ruby snaps her fingers in front of my face.

"Sorry. I guess I'm more tired than I realized."

"Why don't you go to be bed, honey? You cooked, so Ruby and I should do the cleaning up."

"You volunteering me to work?" Ruby laughs and winks at Mike.

I sense my mind shifting in a negative direction as I watch their interactions with one another and realize that once again my insecurities are taking center stage. I find myself wanting to be alone, and rather than risk showing my true feelings, I say, "I think I'll take you up on that. Ruby, I'm sorry to bail out on you, but I say we get up bright and early and go do some shopping in the morning."

Ruby beams. "Yes, Rose. Shopping and visiting the little shops of Meadowbrook would be nice. What time would you like for me to be back here?"

"What do you mean? Why aren't you staying here while you visit?" Mike asks.

"Yeah, I thought so too," I agree.

"No—I don't want to impose on you two lovebirds for a whole week. I'm going to stay in a hotel."

I don't have the energy to argue with her, and in all honesty, I'm relieved. I suppose I should feel guilty that I am, but the uneasy feeling has subsided—not completely, but better.

I say my goodnights and head upstairs to bed, leaving my sister and my husband in the kitchen sounding like a couple of teenagers again as they catch up. As I'm brushing my teeth and looking at my reflection, the mirror turns white, then black. I realize immediately that it isn't the mirror, it's my vision, and now I'm blind. Panic hits me, because I know what this means.

Something bad is going to happen, and this is my warning.

Three numbers flash across the dark space like a flashing marquee sign—*2—7—6*. I stare into nothing and wait as they continue to get brighter, yet everything else around me remains dark, and I start to worry that my vision isn't going to return. The numbers continue to flash over and over, so I press my palms against my eyelids and then open them again. I say the numbers aloud in frustration and as soon as I do, my vision returns.

I haven't had this kind of episode in a long time. I force it out of my mind and convince myself it's because I've been on edge all day.

Something about the whole episode drains me even more than the evening had, and I force myself to push it out of my head. I fall asleep to the sound of Ruby and Mike's innocent banter.

I awake, and my bedroom is dark. I thought I'd left the bathroom light on, but now it isn't. The house is eerily quiet, and Mike isn't in bed. My chest tightens as I get out of bed and throw on a robe before going downstairs.

As I round the corner into the kitchen, I hear Mike and my sister giggling, but I don't see them. I step around the center island and spot them sitting on their knees on the floor, facing each other, their faces dangerously close.

"What're you two doing?"

Mike leaps up from his position and stumbles, almost falling, as he catches himself on the counter. It's obvious he's drunk. "Uh, nothing. Ruby had spilled her drink, so we were cleaning it up."

"So, I guess you decided to stay? There's no way you can drive if you've been drinking."

"I'm going to call a cab."

"Ruby, it's one o'clock in the morning."

Ruby hooks her fingers over the edge of the countertop as she helps herself up. "So?"

"Just go upstairs and go to bed. If you want to insist on staying in a hotel, then do it tomorrow night."

Ruby doesn't argue once she's made it to full standing, then has to steady herself with both hands and lets out a *whoa*. "Maybe I will."

"You need help upstairs?" I ask.

"I got this." Ruby staggers around the island and heads toward the stairs, but not before I catch the look exchanged between her and my husband.

The sort of look that used to be exchanged between him and I.

* * *

Ruby calls me this morning from her hotel and says that she's going to hang out with some of her old friends today. I'm actually relieved because for the last three days, I've spent almost every waking moment with her. The uneasy feeling that I felt the first day of her arrival has grown increasingly worse, and today I've felt physically ill.

I fix myself a cup of herbal tea and settle into the back garden to work on my latest sculpture. I'm putting some of the finishing details to the face of the seated, life-sized mermaid constructed from hundreds of thin wires made of aluminum. When she's finished, she'll rest in the center of a giant fountain in front of the famous courthouse library.

My vision turns white again, then black, and then I'm blind. "No, no, no. Not again." The same three numbers flash again. 2—7—6.

Bile rises in my stomach, and I realize I can't ignore it any longer. I know that whatever is trying to show itself to me isn't going to go away. I finally give in, and it reveals itself to me.

Mike isn't working, and my sister isn't hanging out with her friends—they're together.

I drop my tools and race to room 276 of Ruby's hotel.

I turn into the hotel parking lot and spot my sister's car, but not my husband's.

Maybe I'm wrong.

Part of me wants to turn around and go back home, but I drive around to the back of the hotel, and my gut feeling turns into a deafening alarm.

Mike's Subaru.

I park my car in a spot next to Mike's, shut off the engine, and stare at the building while my heartbeat behaves like a set of drums against my chest. I try to calm the overreaction of my body, but adrenaline has its own agenda. My legs compete with the erratic pace of my heartbeat as I climb the stairs to the second floor, as though I'm racing against the clock. I have to try to save my marriage before anything happens that could undo it forever.

My ears ring as I stand in front of room 276 and attempt to calm myself with a few breaths. I have no idea what I'm going to say when the door opens because my brain can't focus on anything other than wanting to be wrong. With a last hard inhale, I tap on the door, then step to the side to prevent them from seeing me through the peep hole.

I hear my sister's muffled giggle on the other side of the door, and my stomach threatens to wretch. I hear Ruby's voice come closer to the door, then as she swings it open, she says, "It's about ti —" Her words cut off as if she were choking on them as I step into view. She wraps my husband's button-up shirt tighter around her body when I shove around her and storm on into the room.

Mike jumps naked from the bed, looking around as if he's frantic to find something to cover himself. "Rosemary!"

"What are you doing here, Rose?" Ruby asks in a sickly, calm voice, and an icy feeling courses through me as I turn to look at her. Ruby continues to stand next to the hotel door with both arms crisscrossed in front of her body.

"Don't ever call me by that name again!" I say through gritted teeth.

Ruby leans her shoulder against the wall and shifts her face into a devious, satisfied smile.

My eyes squint tighter as I look into hers, and I do a frantic search of her face before the realization sinks in—she'd planned this all along.

25

osemary
1995

RAIN PELTS against the glass as I sit in the seat of the bay window in the center of the dining room. The gloomy sky outside matches my mood as I sit with my arms clutched around myself and rest my head against the cool glass. This place has become my refuge ever since the day I caught my sister with my husband last year. Not just this physical spot, but the mental prison I've been stuck in, where I've wallowed in my own self-pity, hatred, and plots for revenge.

Despite the stress of trying for a child coming between us, I believed that he and I were invincible. Only a week before that horrible day, the doctor had told me during a check-up that pregnancy would surely happen soon. The doctor assured me that the only reason it hadn't already was because I'd been on birth control for so long that my body needed time to adjust.

It's been a little over a year since I caught Mike with Ruby, and more than six months since our divorce was final. The irony now is that I know exactly when my period should arrive and exactly when my body ovulates—not that it does me any good now. My chances of getting pregnant now would surely be inevitable if not for my sister coming in and taking everything from me.

For a short time, Mike begged and pleaded with me to take him back, but I couldn't bring myself to allow him to put his hands on me after I knew they had been all over my sister. But it still doesn't mean I don't miss him.

Ever since that day at the hotel, my days and nights stretch like a worn-out rubber band, never returning to the shape they were before the betrayal. I think back to life before we even thought about having a baby. It was perfect, and we were happy, but apparently happiness was only on loan for a while. Mike allowed my sister to lure him into her bed and defaulted on any happiness we had together.

I dart my eyes back to the letter that I'd received in the mail today. I still can't bring myself to open it—it's from Mike. I thought I was slowly getting over him, but the minute I saw who it was from, my hands began to violently shake while my heart felt as if it would beat out of my chest, and every time I look at it, the sensation starts all over again.

I force myself to stare at it until the shaking subsides, then I pick it up and look at the address on the envelope. A new set of ailments takes over when I look at the return address. New Orleans. Seeing it feels surreal—no—it's more like a nightmare. Physically, it's a bit like food poisoning—I'm feverish and sick. He and my sister are together. It doesn't take long for everything to turn to rage, then I rip the white rectangle open with the kind of aggression I would like to use on the both of them.

Dear Rosemary,

I'm hoping that enough time has passed that you can read this without it causing you grief. For what it's worth, I really am sorry for everything that happened. It was never my intention to hurt you, but things just got so mixed up in my head.

I need to explain to you that what happened between me and Ruby wasn't just a fling. She had called me several months before she came to visit, just needing someone to talk to. She went through a nasty break-up and wanted a man's perspective. I never intended for anything to happen between us. In fact, we mostly talked about you. But somehow, through all of our conversation, feelings started to form, and I didn't even realize it until I saw her.

The reason I am writing to you is not for my sake, but for hers. You are sisters and that should mean something. Please don't hate her for something that was my fault. I beg you. Hate me as much as you want, but please don't go on hating her. She misses you like crazy, but is too proud to call you. All I ask is that you think about it and give her a call sometime.

For what it's worth, I still love you. I know it's wrong to love two people, but I can't help it. I hope this letter finds you well and hope that we will hear from you soon.

Love Mike

At the end of the letter, Mike included a P.S. to tell me that he had gotten one of those high-tech car phones and included his number if I ever decided to give him a call. I wad the letter into a ball and throw it across the room.

Tears burn hot and blur my vision. If each tear had the ability to carry its own emotion or thought, each one would be different —carrying unwanted emotions such as grief, anger, hate, fear, betrayal, jealousy, envy, and even love. But I don't want to love him —I only want to hate him.

He says that he still loves me but has a twisted way of showing it. I curl back into the semi-fetal position and stare out the window as dark begins to creep in. It's dark enough outside now that I catch a glimpse of my reflection in the window, and it's a pathetic sight. The black rings and bags under my eyes make me look like a zombie. I squint as I look into my own eyes, not liking what I see.

The sight of my face in the window lights a fire under me. I'm sick of letting them take away my happiness—my life. I'm not going to allow them to do it anymore. My body tenses from head to toe as I realize what I must do in order to be happy and get my revenge at the same time.

I walk across the dining room in my socked feet, pick up the letter and unfold it. This first thing I will need to do to set my plan in motion is to call Mike.

I don't want Ruby to know when I call, and I'm pretty sure after reading his letter, I can convince him to keep it just between us. If he still loves me like he says he does, then I shouldn't have any problem convincing him that I want to meet up with him one last time. If I time it just right, then a weekend is all I will need, because there's only one final thing I need from Mike to get the closure I deserve—and the sweetest revenge on both of them.

osemary
1996

REVENGE ISN'T the most important thing in my life anymore. For many months, the need for it was so strong I could taste it. In fact, it felt as though it could eat my soul from the inside out.

Now, as I stare down at the two tiny bundles that rest in the crook of each arm, it's as though revenge dissolved into thin air. Now, that feeling has shifted to a love so intense that it almost hurts—but it's a good hurt. I don't ever want to feel anything else. The only thing that matters is that I become the best mother I can be to these two precious girls.

I know now that I was the one born with the family curse—I was the bad twin. The one that generations of ancestors said I would be—blond, blue-eyed, and bad. I was on the path to proving them right by telling Mike and Ruby that the twins belong to him. But I refuse to be that person—the one who intentionally rips two people apart. Mike only attempted to call me one time, and I made it perfectly clear that I wanted nothing to do with him. He never tried again. And now, as far as I know, neither one of them even knows about the twins.

I believe that anyone can break a curse if they really want to. Curses are only real if you believe in them. Before now, I hadn't really given it much thought. I was fine with it either way. I had what I wanted, and I did what I wanted to get it. But now I'm choosing not to be.

I look down at the two babies sleeping peacefully and take in their similarities and differences. They both have heart-shaped mouths, and their lips are a soft, bright pink. I'm often blown away by the differences in their hair color. Ally's is so white it's almost translucent, and Abby's is the complete opposite. Without a doubt, their personalities will be as well.

It's been almost two years since Ruby and I have spoken, and a little over a year since Mike and I said our goodbyes for good. He did just as I figured he would do—came to see me so that I could have my closure. Of course, getting him to sleep with me was even easier. He proved he was just that sort of man when my sister enticed him to bed with her. I didn't have to persuade him to sleep with me. He came with that very intention.

After spending two days in bed together, I broke down and told him it was over—for good. I told him all the reasons he should marry my sister and that our time together was done. He claimed that he still loved me, but it didn't take him very long after our divorce to marry Ruby. At the time, it only drove my plan for revenge harder.

I had every intention of splitting up their marriage, but the day that Ally and Abby were born, my yearning for retribution completely faded. In fact, my desire is now quite the opposite—that my twins will never know who their father really is. If per chance, someday, Ruby and I do make amends, she will be made to believe that I got pregnant and that the father ran off when he found out.

Ally, who is already proving to be the rambunctious one, stirs in my arms. I lean over and place Abby gently down before Ally's restlessness wakes her, then unhook my bra and feed her. Ally is the eater and Abby is the sleeper. As she nurses, her tiny fingers grip a handful of my shirt while her eyes stay locked onto mine. She pauses every so often with a satisfied sigh, her eyes never leaving mine. It's as if she is staring into my soul. Moments like this make me even more adamant about doing the right things and making the right choices.

As I stare into her eyes and smile, something jolts my heart into overdrive, like the sudden onset of a panic attack. Then everything turns white, then dark. My vision blurs for a moment, then leaves entirely. I inhale harshly, trying to push it down while I squeeze my eyes shut, and to my surprise, it forces my vision to return. I throw all my efforts into calming my breathing and open my eyes. It works—my vision is normal. I stopped this unwanted gift once again. I'm getting better and better at pushing it out—stopping it before it shows me anything. It's how I want it.

Ally must sense the sudden shift in my behavior because she unlatches and stares at me with more intent. Babies, even at a few months old, understand rapid shifts in emotions, even if a parent thinks they're hiding it. I smile at her calmly and rub her head while I continue to fight my gift.

I'll continue to fight until it's gone for good.

III

"Out of your vulnerabilities will come your strength."
—Sigmund Freud

27

bby

THE DRUG that is Jared enters my veins like a slow, erotic high I don't want to come down from. I hold back the climax of the orgasm, letting it build as his strong arms hold his weight above me. My eyes scan his chest and flexed muscles, then down to the lowest part of his torso, just to the base of his penis. I lift my legs higher and press my heels into each cheek of his buttocks, guiding him to the rhythm of my own. I wake, my whole-body pulsing as I focus on the aftereffects of the dream. Dreams such as this—dreams about Jared—continue to haunt me, often. He's a want that no matter how hard I try, I can't shake. He and I are like the alcoholic and the shot of whiskey. It's why I avoid being alone with him. It's the only way I can show restraint.

If I could harness the sensations and events of the dream, and it was all I needed to make our marriage work, I'd stay with him forever. Trap time inside one moment and keep the thoughts and perfectness of it for a lifetime. Moments like this last only for a short time. Like sand in an hourglass, or the waves of the ocean, they only leave you with trickles of the memories—ghosts of what once was.

The dreaded thought of peeling myself out of bed comes to me, and I have to force myself to even think about it. Even though I'm not going into work today, I have to leave the house at the regular time because otherwise Ruby will want to know why I'm not. I don't feel like participating in one of her nosy quizzes.

Jared may have known Tina as a child. I can't push the thought out of my mind. How can I find out without him needing to know why?

Jared has always tried to fix me. He means well, but he also knows nothing about my sister. It's not possible for him to fix me if he has no clue why I'm broken to begin with. I press my palms over my eyes. Trying to control my thoughts is like rowing upstream against a downward current, and I'm getting nowhere.

But what if I do ask him and he does remember her?

"Then there will be no doubt that Tina was real." I say the words aloud as if I'm stating them in front of a judge and jury. *It's settled. I'm going to ask him.*

I'm sure I'll get a text from Jared soon when he sees that I've requested a sub to fill in for me today. That's the bad thing about having an ex-husband for a boss—I can't take a day off without him knowing. Since it's my birthday, maybe he won't think too much of it. Turning thirty seems to bother most women, but I should see it as a blessing, a milestone, especially since I'm alive and my sister isn't. At the moment, though, I'm very indifferent about how I feel.

I've laid in bed long enough with my thoughts, so I push myself to get up and go straight to the bathroom to shower and get dressed. As I'm leaving my bedroom, my childhood toy catches my attention in the morning light, and the hair raises on my arms. I'm still creeped out by it and find myself shuddering as I rush from my room to get away from it.

As I leave my room, I'm forced to pause once again as the smell of rosemary fills the air—just as it did in the kitchen last night. I shake my head and ignore it. I head toward the stairs, not quite sure if I've summoned enough courage to follow through with my plan today. As I pass the cluster of pictures on the wall, I'm stopped dead in my tracks.

The same photo of Rosemary falls—again. This time, the glass doesn't shatter. After its last fall, I'd removed the remaining pieces of glass and hung it back in its place.

Once again, I feel like a frightened child that's about to enter a spooky, dark room. My heart beating faster than it should this early in the morning, I bend over and pick up the frame and turn it over. I stare into my mother's blue eyes, seeing Ally's, then look in front of me and behind me, remembering what Mia said. She said that Ally was the one who knocked the picture down before.

Talking to my dead sister is something I've never done before, but now I find myself wanting to shout at her. I look all around me, head low as though I'm trying not to be seen, and the air around me suddenly feels suffocating and cold. Instead of shouting, I whisper, "Ally? Is that you?"

I hear nothing.

It seems that Rosemary is everywhere lately. In my dreams, in my senses, and now as I hold the picture, she's staring straight at me. Maybe all of this is a sign—a sign that it's time to face the fear of her rejecting me and go see her. Her rejecting me isn't the only thing that worries me. It's bringing up the past. The thought forms a lump in my throat, and I shake my head.

No. I can't.

I hang the picture back in its place, and as soon as I walk away, it falls again. This time I pick it up and look at the space in front of me. "Okay. You win—I'm going—alright?"

I carry it downstairs with me and put it in the cabinet to left of the fridge.

Let's see you knock it down now. I grab my bag and keys and leave the house. After rounding the corner toward my car, I halt in place while my heart barrels ahead again, and I nearly drop my keys.

"What the hell, Ruby? You scared me half to death."

Ruby stands in the middle of the path, one hand on her cane, the other on her hip, her overplucked eyebrows squeezed together. "You're running a little late this morning, aren't you? Where's Ava?"

"She spent the night with her father."

She purses her lips. "It's not his day to have her?"

"He's her father. I suppose he can have her whenever he wants." I say this as I step around her and walk to my car.

"Since when?"

"What do you need, Ruby?"

Ruby huffs—something she's good at. "Make sure you lock your door. I'm pretty sure I saw someone wondering around my back yard last night."

I freeze but don't turn around to face her. *Did she see me?* I wouldn't put it past her—she's the queen of busybodies. She probably only pretends to go to bed early and sits near a window, watching the whole neighborhood. *The Woman in the Window*—I think of the book I read just last week.

"I'm sure you were just dreaming, Aunt Ruby. I have to go or I'm going to be late for work," I lie.

She huffs again. I get in my car and close my door before she has a chance to say anything else and back my car out of the drive, leaving her standing there. As I look in my rearview mirror, I see her hobbling down the driveway, her limp quite prominent as she puts on a show that says *poor me.* I'm sure she's attempting to play on my sympathy. *And here I thought she might be here to wish me Happy Birthday.*

I spend the whole morning running errands, but mostly I'm stalling. I have to force myself to shift my focus onto what I actually set out to do today. When I think about doing it, every nerve in my body seems like a strained harp-string ready to snap at a touch. Seeing my mother face-to-face for the first time in twenty-three years, terrifies me. What if she turns me away? Or what if she doesn't even recognize me at all?

Eventually, when I can put it off no longer, I pull in front of Serenity Oak Hospital, something I've actually done several times, but I always chicken out and run, exactly like I want to do right now. I sit in the front seat of my car and clutch my steering wheel as my nerves scatter like bubbles on a rushing river, bursting in a frenzy. With a deep, sharp inhale, I get out of the car and move quickly toward the entrance, only to turn back around and get back into my car. I repeat this act three more times, each time making it a little closer to the door. If there are cameras anywhere in the vicinity, and someone is watching them, they'd probably wonder if I'm actually a patient here.

I think of Ava and the kind of mother I need to be for her, and I begin to repeat the same words as before. *Face your fears. Face your fears. Face your fear.* I chant them in my mind on repeat as I push the button at the entrance of the hospital and before I have a chance to change my mind.

May I help you?

My voice has hidden itself somewhere inside my body, refusing to come out, and I clear my throat and find it. "I'm here to see Rosemary Clark."

"And you are?"

My voice quivers and I'm not sure I can get the words to come out. "Um, um, her daughter—Abbigail."

The door buzzes and I'm quick to jerk on it. It doesn't budge.

"Wait till you hear a click, then open it."

It buzzes again and I do as she says. A wave of cool air and an indecipherable smell waft over me as the second door buzzes, then clicks. For some reason, the noise of it seems incredibly loud—ear piercing, in fact. Maybe it's still my nerves working overtime. My heart insists on competing as it makes itself known loudly in my chest.

The woman stands behind the counter with a clipboard and pen in hand. "Rosemary seems to be very popular this week."

I feel my eyebrows draw together in confusion and correct it quickly when the woman clears her throat as though she wants to take back her words. I suddenly realize this woman may think I'm a horrible daughter for never visiting my mother. I find myself wanting to explain, but there is no explanation. I *am* a horrible daughter.

"Fill out the top portion and sign at the bottom. We have to keep a record of all visitors. I'll need to call up and announce that you're here, then someone will escort you to see her. Have you been here before?"

I have to chase down my voice again and swallow it into place. "It's been a while."

The pale, petite woman behind the counter looks down at the paper I've been writing on and searches for my name. "Well, Abbigail, I'm sure she'll be happy to see you." The woman's voice doesn't match her facial expression. In fact, they seem to defy each other, or maybe it's just me.

She takes the clipboard from me and immediately picks up the phone to announce my arrival to someone inside the hospital.

"Pleased to meet you, Martha." I say the words as I look at her name tag, as though the kind words might sway her judgement of me.

The door to the left clicks, and Martha says, "Jonathan will take care of you on the other side of the door."

Again, I think I read pity in her eyes, or maybe they're saying *shame on you.* I shake it off. Guilt remains my constant companion —there's no escaping it.

I follow the old gentleman down the hallway, feeling the dread churn to nausea in my stomach. The volunteer leading me down the hallway attempts to make small talk, but it does nothing to distract me. If it wasn't too late, I'd bolt back the way I came. He opens the door to a large courtyard surrounded on three sides by the walls of the hospital, and the fourth side is enclosed by a one-story-tall wooden fence, painted white and beautifully decorated with flowering bushes and trees. Spaced out across the grounds are picnic tables strategically placed beneath moderately sized oak trees for shade. It's extremely different from the rest of the hospital—almost like a retreat.

"Pick any table you like, ma'am. I'm sure the person you came to see will be here shortly." The old gentleman tips his head slightly, then disappears.

I look around the courtyard, not sure where to sit. A sharp pain shoots through the palm of my hand, and I realize what I'm doing. I shove my hands into the pockets of my dress.

I decide not to venture too far into the courtyard in case my mother rejects me. Once I've chosen a table, I turn my back to the door. I don't want to see the look on Rosemary's face right away. I'm afraid of what it might tell me.

"Abbigail?" A soft voice moves around in front of me. "You're here to see Rosemary?"

I nod and look up to see a woman with honey-blond hair and a loose ponytail. "Yes."

"Oh, um, hi." She smiles. "I'm Angie. I work with your mother quite a bit."

I stand and offer a hand to shake hers. She takes it, then motions for me to sit back down as she sits down across from me. Her skin is porcelain-pale, as though she spends a lot of time inside this place, rarely in the sun. She and I are similar in height, but her frame is tiny, as if a puff of wind could blow her away. She hesitates before she speaks again.

"I've only been here for a few months, but I've grown very close to Rosemary. I don't want to be nosy or anything, but what made you decide to come see your mother now?"

The question takes me by surprise, and I stutter. "Um, I, I… don't…know. I suppose I felt it was time. In all honesty, I'm not sure she will want to see me."

"She might. You never know with Rosemary." She takes a breath. "She paints portraits all the time of a little girl, well, two different girls, but now that I've met you, I assume that one of them is you. She doesn't speak anymore. Some say she used to mumble a little, but even then, it was only a word or two."

I swallow hard. "Why doesn't she speak?"

"I'm not sure. Some patients resort to being mute because of trauma. I don't have access to her history—I only know what people have told me. But what I can tell you is that I'm very protective of Rosemary. Not sure why, but there's something about her that just drew me in right away. I guess I just wanted to warn you, you know, so that you're not disappointed if she doesn't speak to you. She's been known to turn visitors away, completely refusing to see them. Don't take it personal if she does, but don't give up on coming to see her either if that happens. She usually comes around, well, unless you're her new therapist." Angie lets out a giggle and gives me a wide-eyed smile.

I ponder for a moment, wondering who'd be coming to see her, especially someone that she might turn away. *Ruby?*

"Anyway, I just wanted to give you a heads-up. I'll go up and get her now."

"Thank you, Angie."

She slides from the table, and I immediately place my forearms on it and resort to squeezing my fingertips—hard. I do this as I wait for what seems like forever. Then, I sense someone behind me and my muscles tense as my inhale gets caught in midstream. I don't look up at first as the person moves past me and turns to stand in front of me.

On my exhale, I lift my eyes and look into Rosemary's. The solemn look on her face sends a wave of emotion through me, forcing me to clench my teeth and swallow it down.

"H-hello Rosemary." The words come out just barely more than a whisper as she sits down opposite me and clasps her hands together on the table. My eyes fixate on them as I realize they no longer look young and beautiful like I remember. A memory flashes before my eyes. My sister and I painting her pretty nails. I have to choke down the urge to cry.

We sit in silence as I stare at her hands, and she stares at my face. I close my eyes, summoning the courage to speak without my voice cracking. My eyes flutter open and meet hers. This time, her eyes are soft with just a hint of a smile, making them seem less sad. They're no longer the beautiful blue I remember, but are darker—gray, in fact, as though life has left them. They used to smile even when she wasn't. Another wave hits me, and I have to choke it down again and try to force myself to speak.

I open my mouth, but before any words escape, Rosemary reaches one hand across the table and takes mine. This time, she presses her lips together then smiles. I can't hold back any longer and the tears begin to flow as I press my other hand across my face.

"I'm so sorry, Rosemary. I should have come to see you."

She squeezes my hand harder, and I can't say anything else for several minutes. Once my sobs have ceased, I pull my phone from my purse and open it to my photos. I open a picture of my daughter and turn the phone toward Rosemary and say, "This is—"

"Ava." Rosemary finishes my sentence with a hoarse whisper.

28

osemary

I CAN'T STOP STARING at her. My daughter is more beautiful than I could've ever imagined—more than pictures can show. I watch as she stares at her nervous, twitching hands, her insecurity evident in the way she slouches over the table. Her beauty doesn't seem to penetrate from under the surface the way it should. I stare at this broken person, as though she's still seven years old, and my heart suddenly aches for her. All I can see is scars and boo-boos that she's had to face without me. I should have been there to kiss the boo-boos. I should have been there to prevent, or at least help mend the scars she's had to endure throughout her life.

It's my fault—I shouldn't have left her.

She finally looks at me, and the sadness in her eyes guts me like an autopsied corpse. I instinctively reach out and grab her hand, and her tears flow as if she's crying for the first time since I left.

Like she's still that broken child I walked out on. Guilt forces me to lower my gaze, ashamed of myself.

It takes several minutes before I can look at her again. I squeeze Abby's hand a little harder until her crying subsides. We look at each other, and Abby pulls her hand away, giving me a sheepish smile, then quickly wipes her face. She removes her phone from her pocket, taps the screen several times, and turns the phone toward me. Her voice comes out at the tone and level one might use in a library.

"This is—"

"Ava." I manage to speak the word, despite my throat's protest against using my vocal cords. I feel like an unearthed artifact, buried underneath the weight of my own guilt. I smile at Abby and feel for the first time since losing a daughter, that it's a real, genuine smile. The kind that can be felt at the core of my heart.

Abby looks at me in shock when I say my granddaughter's name. I quickly cut in, my voice still whispery, shaky and foreign from lack of use. It doesn't sound like I remember. "Jared came to see me."

The look on Abby's paling face transitions through three different expressions before she speaks—shock, anger, then confusion. "How? When?"

"Yesterday." I swallow and clear my throat, trying to give my voice some extra assistance. "Well, I mean, I met Ava for the first time yesterday, but before that I'd only seen her in pictures. Jared has kept me up to date on how you are doing." I clear my irritated throat again and attempt to extinguish the flame when I see a spark of rage returning to Abby's eyes. "Don't be angry with him. Best intentions. He w-want's to be close to you." I pause to check the right words are coming out, and I'm so exhausted I'm not sure I can finish what I want to say, but I close my eyes and force out the next words. "He still loves you."

Abby's expression softens a little, though her hand continues to tremble. "She's beautiful, isn't she?"

"Like her mother."

Abby shoots her eyes downward like a shy child avoiding a compliment from a stranger. "Today is your birthday?"

Abby nods and I can tell right away that birthdays aren't something she gets excited about. I don't say any more but look back down at her hands, noticing the mangled cuticles around her fingernails. Abby thumbs through more photos of Ava as she explains where this one and that one was taken. In the mix of photos there are many with Jared and Ava together, and it's obvious when she pauses and a smile spread across her lips, that she still loves him too. Those beautiful, brown eyes. A knot forms in my throat, and I choke it down.

I'll save the tears for later.

We spend the entire afternoon looking at pictures, and I let her do most of the talking as I listen to stories about Ava's milestones and her successes in school. When she's finished showing me pictures, we fall into an awkward silence. As if on cue, Angie enters the courtyard.

"Rosemary, I hate to break this up, but visiting hours are almost over for today. I'm sorry, Miss Abby, but our later hours are on Wednesdays, Fridays, and Saturdays. I do hope you will take advantage of it and come back to see Rosemary."

"Can we have just ten more minutes?" Abby asks with a pleading tone, and I feel my heart leap for joy.

Angie purses her lips. "I do have to check on another patient before I leave today, so I'll come back and walk you out then."

"Thank you."

Once Angie disappears back into the building, Abby asks, "Rosemary, I need to ask you something." She pulls a polaroid picture from her purse.

I look down at her hands as she reaches it to me, and they're shaking again. I take the photograph and glance up at her face, then back down at the small, square photo. She asks, "Do you remember seeing this little girl before?"

I hold it a little closer to my face and squint my eyes in order to see better. I give it a long, hard look. The eyes look familiar, yet I don't recognize her. I hesitate, then shake my head.

A disquieted look creeps into Abby's face, making her complexion paler, and she hesitates as if she's afraid to tell me.

"Do you know who she is?"

Another short hesitation, then she blurts it out. "Her name is Tina."

Horror steals my own expression and causes Abby to slump back away from the table. Despite this, she takes on a determined look and continues, anyway. "This is a picture of the little girl that used to come and see me and Ally when we were kids. The one I tried to tell you and Ruby about."

I hadn't anticipated our visit turning in this direction. I'm not sure where it comes from, but a spark of irritation festers just under the surface. I liked seeing my daughter again as long as we didn't trek down memory lane—nightmare lane. Silence swells between us for a moment, like expanding foam, but she speaks again quickly.

"I found this photo in the house that Jared and I bought a few years ago. I think Aunt Ruby rented it when she first moved back to town. I also found childish drawings in the basement, and among them was her name, along with mine and Ally's. Proof that she existed, and that she knew me and my sister back then. I'm not sure if the drawings were made before Ruby moved into the house, or during, or after."

I stare at Abby, not sure what kind of face I'm pulling but I do my best to keep it neutral despite my pulse and breathing taking on their own reactions.

"This is proof that *she* was real."

My voice leaves me again, and this time not by choice. A tingling moves up my spine and a thought starts to chew away at my attempts to remain neutral and unresponsive. *What if I was wrong all these years?*

"I swore to you back then that she was real, and this picture proves that she was." Abby continues to try to convince me.

I still can't find my voice, so I just stare at her. I have to will myself to speak, and the words escape my throat, sounding scratchier than before. "Ally could see her, too?"

"Yes! Actually, she and Ally didn't get along very well. In fact, Ally didn't like her at all towards the end." Abby's voice quietens as she says the last part.

I'm not sure I want to hear anymore. The very idea that I may have been wrong and left Abby behind is more than I can bear, and all I want to do is run away from it, and from Abby. I was a coward. I couldn't deal with losing one daughter at the hands of the other.

"I'm going to find out who she is," Abby says, her eyes taking on a determined pitch.

Only when Abby looks up do I realize that Angie is standing there.

"I'm sorry to break this up, Rosemary, but Dr. Black is here to see you."

I look up at Angie with a questioning frown.

Angie lets out an audible breath as she sighs and places her warm hand on my arm. "I know this isn't your normal day for therapy, but Dr. Black said that your last session concerned her, and she wanted to make some extra time for you today."

I scoff before I can catch myself. and Abby gives me a worried look.

"It's okay. I didn't realize just how late it'd gotten. I need to meet Jared to pick up Ava." Abby slides her legs from under the picnic table and stands. She's at least three inches taller than me, and although she appears to take care of herself physically, she's stands without confidence, and her posture slouches in on itself as though she's spent too many years trying to hide from the world. She looks down at me as I continue to sit at the table. "It was good to see you, Rosemary. I'll try to come back soon."

"Melvin is standing just inside the door to escort you back to the front of the building," Angie says. "It was nice to meet you, Abby. I hope we'll see you more often."

Abby nods, turns and soon disappears back into the hospital. I fight the urge to chase after her.

"You ready, Rosemary?"

I exhale a puff of frustrated air, not hiding my disgust, then I place my hands on the picnic table and push myself up as my legs protest. We make our way into the hospital and just inside the door, Ewelina is waiting for me.

"Is that your daughter?" Ewelina asks me, not giving me a chance to even nod as she continues. "She looks like a grown-up version of the girl you were painting the other day." She stares at Abby as she walks down the hall and around the corner. "But never mind that. I came to find you because I have to tell you something."

"Can't this wait until later, Ewelina?" Angie asks. "Rosemary has an appointment."

"No, it can't. I need to tell her now." Ewelina's voice is as loud as usual and very insistent. She reminds me of a child begging for a piece of candy.

I stop and give Ewelina a frown, then nod to Angie.

"I'll give you two minutes. I think Rosemary has had a pretty overwhelming day already." Angie says, then walks down the hall, still in view, but out of hearing distance.

Ewelina turns around to face me, and I make the mistake of breathing through my mouth. I get a taste of her stout perfume—a spicy mix of rose petals and lavender. "Maria wants me to tell you something."

I roll my eyes and immediately move to step around her, not wanting to hear what she has to say. I know that her talking to my dead mother isn't a good thing. It can only mean that my mother is wants to warn me about something. She steps back in front of me.

"Your mother is driving me crazy, Rosemary." Ewelina moves in closer to my face as she speaks even lower. "She wants you to know something, but you're not listening to her. You've got to start listening."

I take a step back and huff out of my nose. She only moves with me and leans in even closer. This woman doesn't know the slightest thing about personal space.

I huff again. As she whispers, her Polish accent is even thicker, making it difficult to understand her. "You're just like me, Rose-mary. It's time for you to start listening to those little voices in your head and figure out how to help your daughter. Maria also said it's time for you to suck it up and go see that sister of yours."

29

bby

I'VE FELT like an abandoned child since I was seven years old, but right now, for the first time in years, I feel as though I've been found. It's bittersweet. I only wish now I'd come to see Rosemary sooner. I honestly believed that she didn't want to see me. Why would she if she believed that I'd killed her daughter? The look on her face when I told her about Tina at first was pure disbelief, but I think now she's truly questioning what really happened back then. I think for the first time, she believed me.

I climb into my car and immediately turn on the air conditioning. The weather is unusually hot for early June. My t-shirt is already sticking to the backs of my shoulders as I sit against the black leather seats, waiting for the aircon to do its job. I shoot Jared a text to ask him if he can meet me at the house. I want to ask him about the photo, and what the hell he thinks he's doing sneaking around and visiting *my* mother behind my back. In my opinion, it's borderline stalking. My stomach churns as I think about it, and I grip the steering wheel tightly.

I make it home only a few minutes before Jared and Ava arrive. Ava bursts through the front door and runs to the kitchen where I'm fixing her favorite after-school snack: strawberries, blueberries and peanut butter.

"Happy Birthday, Mommy!" Ava squeals as she gives me a hug. "I can't tell you where me and Daddy went because he wants to tell you first, but here." She hands me a purple gift bag with lavender tissue paper crammed into the top. "Open it."

Jared steps into the kitchen and leans against the doorway as he crosses his arms over his chest. I give him a squinted look and even though I'm frustrated with him, adolescent jitters course through me.

"She's been waiting all day to give that to you."

"Open it!" Ava hops in place, clapping her hands gently together.

"Okay, okay." I sit the bag on the counter, remove the tissue paper, then find a piece of purple construction paper folded into the shape of an envelope. Holding the flap in place is a bright yellow SpongeBob sticker. I peel the sticker free and inside is another piece of purple paper folded oddly several times. Inside, Ava had drawn a giant heart and in the center of each hump are the eyes, and near the bottom of the shape is a smiling mouth. Drawn as though the heart were human, it has two arms and two legs.

"Daddy helped me spell everything, but I wrote it myself."

I read it aloud. *"Happy Birthday, Mom. I love you.* Aww thank you, Ava, this is beautiful." I bend down and pick her up into a tight hug.

"Open the rest, Mommy."

"There's more?" I tease and reach into the bag. I pull out a small jewelry box with *Jared* etched on the top of the box and look straight to my ex-husband. He presses his lips together, then smiles as he shrugs his shoulders.

"Look, Mommy, it has Daddy's name on the top. Did you know there's a whole store named after him?"

I'm pretty sure Ava didn't buy the gift—it came from my ex-husband. The thought makes my pulse quicken. Inside is a thin, white, gold band with twelve round beads, each made of a different color, one bead being larger than the rest.

"It's a fidget ring, Mommy. There's a color for every month and the big bead in the middle is the color of my birthday. Here, put it on and I'll show you how it works."

I glance up at Jared again, as he looks at Ava lovingly, and a lump forms in my throat. My bottom lip begins to quiver, so I tuck it in between my teeth. Despite the effort, my eyes moisten, and I close them tightly, then blink away a tear. I slide the ring onto my index finger, then Ava shows me how the beads spin and move around the ring.

"We thought this might save your fingertips." Jared's words seem nervous.

I give him a questioning frown, but remove it quickly. I thought my nervous habit had been hidden better from others—I guess I was wrong.

"Do you like it, Mommy?"

"I love it, Ava." I give her another hug while still avoiding Jared's eyes. I'm still mad at him for going behind my back. I release Ava and hand her the plate of snacks. "Why don't you take your snacks to your room and play? I need to talk to your father about something."

"Okay." Ava snatches the plate of snacks and runs up the back stairs.

"Coffee? Beer?" I ask as I turn my back, not sure where I want to begin. I hadn't thought our conversation through, and now nerves have suddenly stolen my courage, and it seems, my voice.

"Coffee's fine."

I busy myself as I try to find my words, but Jared beats me to them.

"Abby, I need to talk to you about something as well. In fact, I need to confess something, because Ava will probably tell you anyway, and I think it's better coming from me."

I turn around, my eyebrows lifted to attention because I'm pretty sure I know what he's going to confess.

"I took Ava to meet your mother." Jared's face freezes in a *please don't hate me* expression.

Jared going to see my mother by himself wasn't so bad, but taking Ava without asking is the upsetting part. The fact that he confesses, dampens my irritation a little. "Jared, why? I don't understand."

He drops his eyes to my hands, and I realize that I'm already using the birthday gift. I quickly turn back around to tend to the coffee.

"I don't know. The first time I went I just wanted to meet her, and after visiting her regularly I wanted Ava to meet her, too. I didn't intend for it to become a regular thing, but she seemed so—" He hesitates. "Lonely."

Guilt rears its ugly head again, and I try to breathe it away. Guilt and regret have become permanent guests in my mind that were never invited in the first place and won't leave no matter how hard I try to get rid of them. This, I realize, only feeds them more.

"Honestly, going to see her is..." He hesitates again. "Familiar. Don't ask me how or why, it just is. Even though she doesn't talk, she's still very good company."

I finish pouring our coffee, then carry our cups to the table. There's more of a sting in my voice than I intend, but I can't help it. "It's borderline stalking, and just plain weird."

A beat of silence fills the room. "Maybe, but someone should be visiting her."

"And you think that's you?"

"Why not? You're not going. You've never told me why you and your mother became estranged in the first place, and as far as I know, she's rotting in a mental hospital with no family or friends that care about her."

My throat begins to close. "It's complicated."

"So you've said. If you're not going to go see her, then what's wrong with me going? Ava deserves to know her grandmother."

"Just like she should know her grandfather," I snap, and as soon as I say it, I wish I could take it back. There's no way I would even allow Ava near Jared's father. He's a horrible human being.

His mother passed away years ago, but his father actually lives just on the other side of town. Jared wants nothing to do with him. I can't say that I blame him. I take a deep inhale and shift my tone as I admit, "Well, I actually went to go see her myself today."

Jared shoots me a look of surprise and disbelief.

"Don't look at me like that."

His response surprises me. "How was it?" Jared sits back in his chair and takes a gulp of coffee.

"Good. I think. She was very happy to have met Ava." I take a sip of my own coffee, and the room goes silent—for too long.

"How come you never told me you had a sister?"

Jared's question catapults me out of my thoughts. "What?"

"Your mother showed me and Ava pictures of you *and* your sister. Twin sister. How come you never told me?"

I hop up from the table, turning my back to Jared as I flick the beads on the ring. "It's not something I want to talk about."

"Why not?"

"I just don't!" My words come out harsh, cutting Jared off.

"Well, maybe you should, because Ava claims that your dead sister is her friend."

At Jared's first mention of going to see my mother, I could feel the heat rise in my face, but at the mention of my sister, it turns cold, and my limbs are like ice. I finally find my ability to speak. "What do you mean?"

"When your mother was showing us some pictures, Ava pointed to your sister's picture and said that it was her friend, Ally. She swears that she comes to see her here, and even at school. Have you ever told Ava about your sister?"

"No." The word comes out barely more than a whisper.

"Do you have any pictures around the house that Ava might have found?"

"No. I mean, I have videos, but I've never shown them to her."

"Then how did she recognize her?"

I still don't turn around, and the only form of answer I can give is a shrug of my shoulder and a shake of my head.

"Your mother had her own theory—you know what it was?"

My first instinct is to say no, but I don't say anything.

"She said Ava was the one born with a gift."

30

ared

Sometimes when I'm with Abby, I feel like an actor who's forgotten their lines. I never know what to say, or maybe I'd never learned the lines to begin with. When trying to have a serious conversation with her, no amount of preparation can make communicating with her any easier. Just when I feel like I've learned my part, it's as if she's the one who gets stage fright, then shuts down and that's the end of it.

I've learned that just giving Abby her space often helps her to gather her thoughts. I'd heard stories about her grandmother when I was a kid. She was the woman who knew and saw things. Even though I didn't live here my whole life, I heard that she was a legend around here. Most thought she was strange, while others went to her, desperate to know if they would ever find true love, or if they'd ever be rich. She made a living by it as well as her art, but most often, folks didn't like the outcome of their fortune. Yet, they still flocked to see her.

Abby holds her mug with both hands as she sips from it, and I observe the tired look in her eyes and face. She hasn't been sleeping—I can see it. I know that Abby is struggling with something, but she refuses to let anyone in, especially me. She's always been guarded, but lately she seems on high alert. There has always been a wall between me and her innermost thoughts. She guards the wall like Fort Knox.

After she became a mother, those walls grew thicker. It was as if the woman I'd married disappeared and someone new took her place. She became obsessed with motherhood and lost all desire to be a wife. I could never understand why she couldn't be both. Now that I know she had a twin sister who died, maybe her becoming an extremely protective mother was rooted partly in that. Rosemary couldn't tell me what happened regarding the circumstances around Ally's death, especially since Ava pointed out that this Ally was her friend.

I break our silence. "So, were the rumors about your mother true? Could she see or hear people that weren't there?"

"My mother? No. My grandmother, yes. I never heard of my mother doing it. But Ruby said she could when she was much younger."

"How so?"

"I don't know, but Ruby claimed that Rosemary used to be very good at it, but just one day stopped. But you know, I don't remember very much about my mother."

I sense that Abby is holding back from talking about her mother, but I'm not going to push the point. It's just nice to have her talking to me, period. A troubled look crosses her face, and I catch my mind going to places it shouldn't go. *God, I want to reach out and touch her so badly—hold her, kiss her.* I'm lost in this thought when what Abby says next catches me off-guard.

"Ava began talking about Ally a few days ago. I actually heard her talking to her in her room."

"You mean you could hear both of them?"

"No, no, but I heard Ava call Ally by her name. At first, I just passed it off as some character from a book or TV. Now, I don't know what to make of it since she says her imaginary friend looks like my dead sister."

In my mind, the whole idea of Ava talking to a dead relative is preposterous, but strange things happen every day to all sorts of people. As a kid I didn't see imaginary friends, but I did pretend they were there, and talked to them all the time. It was my way of coping with my asshole father. Maybe Ava needs something similar to cope with having divorced parents and two homes. I can't believe I'm going to say it aloud, but I do it anyway. "Maybe she can."

"Can what?"

"See your dead sister. You said your grandmother could do it—maybe Ava can too."

I stand and walk to the counter next to Abby to refill my coffee, then remain there. The scent of her shampoo washes over me. That familiar smell that always has a hint of apple to it. I breathe it in. I become hyper aware that our elbows are lightly touching, and hope that she won't move away.

"So, how was your visit with you mother after all this time?"

Abby hesitates, but only for a second. "It was much better than I expected it to be. I honestly expected her to turn me away, but she didn't. I talked to someone named Angie before I saw her, and she told me that my mother hadn't spoken in years. But she spoke to me—I mean, she was quiet for the most part, but she did speak to me." Abby pauses and swallows hard. "She's aged so much." She lets out a heavy sigh.

"Your mother went for years without speaking. Maybe seeing you is what she was waiting for. With me, she would occasionally make a remark here and there but never audible." I look down at Abby as she turns her face away, but not before I'm able to see her biting her bottom lip as she presses her eyes closed. She's doing everything she can to keep from crying. I suddenly feel guilty for what I just said. "Abby, I'm sorry. It wasn't my intention to upset you."

Seeing her mother after all these years must have stirred up all kinds of mixed emotions. The fact that she'd never told me she had a sister and avoided seeing her mother must mean there's more than just having a sister who died.

I hear Abby stifle a sob and can't stop myself. I sit down my coffee then turn and wrap both my arms around her and pull her close to me. She doesn't resist and leans into me, letting herself cry quietly.

I squeeze her tighter and soak in the moment. The way she feels in my arms—she feels like home. I rub one hand over her back and shoulders and feel her press in closer, then her arms wrap around my waist. We stand clutched in each other's embrace for a long while and I become hyper aware of the shape of her body, the parts that are touching mine, and a familiar desire consumes me. She must have felt it too, because she raises her face to look at me, and I don't even second guess myself as I lean down and press my lips to hers. Our bodies press hard against one another, and the kiss deepens with a hunger as if we haven't eaten in days—as though we're starving for each other.

"What'cha doing?" Ava asks behind me.

Neither one of us heard Ava come downstairs. I pull my face from Abby's and stare down at her, trying to catch my breath. "Noth—" I have to clear my throat and try again. "Nothing. Your mother had something in her eye, and I was trying to get it out." I try to sound casual and reluctantly release my ex-wife. I quickly untuck my shirt and pull it down over my pants to hide the effect of our kiss.

Abby glances down at the front of my pants, then looks away as she tucks her lips between her teeth, trying to hide her smile.

"Are you staying for dinner, Daddy?" Ava asks.

I look at Abby for an answer.

Abby's face makes a sudden unexpected shift. "No, honey. Your father said that he had to go."

A punch in the gut wouldn't hurt as bad as this just did. I stare down at Abby, but she doesn't look at me. The invisible wall that she has maintained for so long—the one that I just thought I'd crumbled—has suddenly rebuilt itself. She avoids my face, steps around me, and speaks to Ava. "I thought you and I might go grab some McDonald's and ice-cream. How does that sound?"

"Yeah." Ava squeals and then hops in place. "Why can't you go, Daddy?"

I swipe my fingertips across my lips, still feeling the kiss on them, and smear on a fake smile. Disappointment makes it hard to pretend, but I've gotten pretty good at it—it's a way of life. I don't know why I keep getting my hopes up. I feel like a piece of bait on the end of a hook that gets only a nibble, but never catching the fish. Or worse, I feel like the fish with a hook caught in my mouth, bleeding, and unable to break my heart free from this woman.

"I have some things I need to do, honey. You go have fun with your mother." I force the words from my mouth as lovingly as I can, take one last gulp of my coffee, then kiss Ava on the head without looking back at Abby. The last thing I want her to see is just how hard she stung me.

31

I OFTEN WALK DOWN the halls of this hospital like a ghost, rarely being noticed. Not allowing myself to speak for years helped me establish this sort of existence, which has always worked for me, but all of the interaction lately has left me mentally drained. Right now, I feel as though I'm wearing a bright red bullseye on my chest, and guilt has multiple arrows aimed at it—they're all firing at once. I think I'd rather be a ghost. Having a non-existence is easier than facing what I'm now learning I've done.

I was wrong about everything.

Angie interrupts my thoughts. "Did you have a nice visit with your daughter?"

I nod and attempt to paint on a smile, then we turn the corner and the realization of where I'm going in this moment forces my face into a familiar scowl.

"What's that look about?" Angie asks.

I look out in front of us at the therapy room door and pause in the hallway.

"Ah—I see. I'm not quite sure why she insisted on seeing you again today. I've never known any of our doctors to see their patients more than twice in one week. Maybe she isn't as bad as you think she is."

I can't control the look of disgust that crosses my face.

Angie turns on her motherly smile. "You don't seem yourself after your visit with your daughter. Maybe you could actually use this time with Dr. Black to get some things off your chest?"

My head shakes a firm *no,* as if the reflex were separate from my body and acted on its own. I take a sharp inhale, then let it out swiftly to say without words, *let's get this over with.*

Angie opens the door to the same suffocating room, and I lock eyes with Dr. Black right away. After the way our last session ended, I decide, instead of walking to the window to ignore her as I always do, I will sit down in the chair across from her and stare her down. It doesn't seem to intimidate her, but I continue to do it anyway.

Dr. Black doesn't even speak to Angie this time, she just gives her a lifting of the eyebrows, then shifts her eyes back to me. She wastes no time getting straight to the point.

"Hello, Rose."

I continue to stare at her as though we're in a non-blinking contest. She never wavers and neither do I.

"What do say we just jump straight into it and dive a little deeper into what happened to bring you here?"

I continue to stare, never breaking eye contact.

"According to Dr. Foster, you had twin daughters—one was named Ally, and the other, Abby, but one of those daughters died just before you ended up in here. Is that correct?"

I stare ahead, unblinking.

"What I find strange is that Dr. Foster didn't seem to believe your daughter's death was an accident like the police report said. She seemed to think that your daughter's death was more tragic than that. Perhaps her death happened at the hands of your other daughter?"

Her words feel like several punches to the gut, forcing my eyes to dart to the notepad on her lap. I can only make out scribbles.

"Is this why she never comes to see you? Because you believed that yourself? I will say it makes me question it as well. Why else would a mother write off her own child when she is only seven years old?" Dr. Black sits in her chair with a perfect, straight spine, her back never touching the tall cushion, and her face wearing a consistent, smug expression.

The room begins to spin, or maybe it's my head. I start to wonder if her words are those of a professional who is supposed to be here to help me. They seem the complete opposite. Even though there's some truth behind her words, they come from her mouth with malice and intent. Intent of what, I'm not sure, but it certainly seems as though she wishes to cause me emotional harm. Why else is she pressing the topic?

There's no attempt on my behalf to mask the hateful look that crosses my face, and if looks could transform themselves into physical acts, her face would have a red handprint across it. There's no way anyone can know the actual truth about that day. Police reports ruled it as an accident and nothing more. It must be speculation on her part. *Did Dr. Sarah suspect this? If she did, she never said the words aloud.*

I decide that I've had enough and stand from my chair so that I'm towering over her, sending her the message that we're finished. She stares up at me, never wavering. I swallow hard and use my voice in a way I haven't used in years. "I have no desire to talk to you now, or ever."

Dr. Black's lips slowly curl into a twisted smile as her left eyebrow remains cocked. "Well, look who *can* talk. See—therapy is working already, Rose." She shifts her head to the side, still wearing the defiant grin.

"My fucking name isn't Rose." My words surprise even me.

"Well, if you continue to stand over me like that with the intent of intimidating me, then I may have to call in some help. A non-compliant patient can call for restraints. Maybe even force me to prescribe some calming medication to prevent you from being a threat to others or yourself. So, I suggest you sit back down."

Behind Dr. Black's chair, standing under the window, Ally appears just as she had the last time I was in this room. She lifts her blue eyes to look at me, and without saying a word, brushes a finger across her lips.

"Shh."

32

ared

I LEAVE Abby's house feeling wounded, and it's no one's fault but my own. I'd taken advantage of a weak moment, knowing it had nowhere to go other than to backfire on me. I set myself up for failure by allowing myself to believe that she still might want me. I feel beaten down, angry, and once again like a beggared dog with my tail tucked between my legs. It's time for me to walk away for good. I can't keep allowing her to reel me in, only to throw me back out again.

Needing my wounds licked, I pull my phone from my pocket and send a two-word text.

My place?

The return text comes before I even have a chance to put my phone back in my pocket.

On my way.

After I walk through the front door, I head straight upstairs, strip down naked, and lie back on the bed while I wait for my guest. The front door releases a faint sound as it opens, then comes the sound of hard, soled shoes as they travel into the kitchen. Next, glass jars against glass as the refrigerator door opens, then closes. Her footsteps climb the stairs, then Kris appears in the bedroom door, wearing a red raincoat that cuts off just above the mid-thigh of her bare long legs—at the end of those are high-heeled shoes the same color as her jacket. She crosses her arms in front of her chest gripping a beer in one hand as she leans against the door frame, then my eyes follow one, final sexy move as she crosses one leg in front of the other. Her eyes scan my naked body as a pleasing grin shifts across her face. She lifts the bottle of beer to her lips and takes one swallow, then sits it on the bookshelf next to her.

Not saying a word, her fingers perform slow, seductive movements as she unsnaps her raincoat one at a time. As each one opens, beginning from the top down, her naked body comes fully into view, then the jacket slides from her shoulders to the floor. Her red high heels are the only thing left on her body. She moves toward the bed, and neither of us speak. She low crawls across my body, and just as I needed, she begins to lick my wounds.

When we're finished and attempting to catch our breath, we both lie on our backs, staring at the ceiling. After a period of silence, Kris rolls onto her side. "Better now?"

I shake my head, turn to look at her and mumble, "Much."

"Good. I aim to please." Kris runs her fingers over the thin line of hair that runs from my chest to my lower abdomen, then traces the same line back up again. "I was surprised to hear from you. And judging by the way you just laid me, you didn't have a very good day. You seemed fine when you left school today, so I'm guessing you had a fight with Abby."

I feel my eyes narrow in annoyed confusion. I'm not sure it's because she brought up Abby's name now, or that she brought it up, period. We don't discuss our personal lives, and we certainly don't discuss Abby. "Why do you ask?"

"No reason. It's just that you seemed to be in a good mood earlier, and now that you've been to Abby's house, your mood seems to have changed."

Confusion sinks in a little deeper, and I look back toward the ceiling. "I don't remember telling you I went to Abby's house. In fact, I don't believe we've spoken at all."

"I know—I just assumed you might like to talk about it." Kris props her head on her elbow and drapes her other arm so that it rests in the curve between her ribs and hips. "I mean, all we do is fuck. It'd be nice to talk once in a while."

"Since when do we care about talking?" This is not a path I want to walk down with Kris, and I definitely don't want a relationship with her. "We've got a good thing going."

"Don't you think it would be nice to have a conversation once in a while? I mean, it's obvious that you still have feelings for Abby. I can be a good shoulder as well."

I say, more harshly than I intended, "I don't need your shoulder." I catch my tone, pause, inhale and start again. "She's the mother of my child, so there's always going to be a connection between the two of us."

"Pardon me." Kris's words come out smooth but cold as she rolls over and hops from the bed. Without looking back, she goes into my bathroom and closes the door behind her.

I frown and stare at the closed door, wondering what just took place, then shake it off, spring from the mattress, and pull on my boxers. I hear the shower turn on, so I head downstairs. The beer cap makes a hissing sound as I pop it open, then I chug half of it.

As an attempt to distract myself, I grab my phone and take a seat at the kitchen table. Out of habit, the first thing I check for is to see if Abby has texted. I guess there was some small hope that she'd say she was sorry. I'm delusional—of course she didn't. I'm not sure why I even expected it. I check my emails and see way too many work-related requests, and put my phone back down.

Despite my attempts to avoid thinking about Abby, our conversations flood back, anyway. I thought I'd put it to bed for the night when Kris had crawled into mine. I saw the look in her eyes when she looked up at me, just before I kissed her. There was something there—something familiar. I know I didn't read it wrong.

Kris enters the room wearing my shirt from today, and it catches me off-guard—it's as if she plans on staying. She sits down at the table with her beer. "I really didn't mean to upset you earlier. But if I'm going to fuck someone, I do like to know a little bit about them."

I flinch and attempt to keep my expression neutral as I wonder about the sudden shift in Kris's need for more. *I liked this situation better when it was just physical.* Her eyes take on a different look—it seems almost desperate, and I suddenly feel guilty. Maybe she's just needing to talk, and it's me that's being the asshole—all because of Abby.

People tend to do that—deflect their emotions onto others all to save themselves from their own thoughts and feelings. When our lives seem to bring us down or even break us, we need someone to pick us up. In this case, the person I need to pick myself up from is Abby, not Kris. Maybe she just needs some of the same from me.

"I'm the one that should be sorry. I suppose I did have a bad day and took it out on you."

"It's okay." Kris smiles, takes one of my hands in hers, and my guard falls a little.

"You were right. It's Abby. We've been divorced for more than three years, and she still gets under my skin. I don't know why." I start to talk, and then my words seem to pour out of me. "Abby's been estranged from her mother since she was a kid, but I felt like Ava should know her grandmother. So, I started going to see her a couple of years ago and introduced her to Ava for the first time the other day. Abby found out, and she isn't happy with me."

"Not to sound like your counselor, but do you think that was your decision to make?"

The saying, *truth hurts,* seems to slap me, and I know that Kris is right. "No, probably not. I just wanted her to know her mother again—the Rosemary that I've gotten to know. I thought I was doing Abby a favor. Maybe bring her and her mother back together again."

"But isn't this woman in a mental hospital? Maybe Abby knows why, and she doesn't want Ava exposed to any of that. Maybe there's more to the story than you know about."

I open my mouth to respond, but then realize that Kris mentions the words mental hospital. I don't believe I've said anything about Rosemary being in a hospital, ever. My face must give away my apprehension.

"Don't worry—I haven't told anyone. Abby confided in me one day about her mother, and like I told her, the secret is safe with me."

I force my face to lie by conjuring a fake smile, but the sudden spewing of my thoughts and feelings shrink back to where they came, and I simply nod. Something about the fact that Abby would confide in essentially a stranger about her mother and not me, hurts way more than it should.

33

bby

THE SIDEWALKS that line the streets near my home come to life as the lampposts begin to switch off, prompted by the sun swelling over the mountain. My motivation for my morning run isn't to soak up the sweet scents of morning but driven more by my low self-esteem. When it comes to exercise or bettering myself at my job, I feel inadequate, so I try to make up for it by pounding through five miles or spend my morning developing a top-notch lesson plan with all the bells and whistles that will impress an observer or an outsider.

I've always spent way too much time trying to impress and appear more put together than I actually am. I started competing with myself at a young age, my mind constantly telling me that I'll never be good enough, yet I push harder to try to be. My brain works like the angel on one shoulder and the devil on the other— in constant war, going back and forth like talking heads. But who better to challenge a person than the self? This constant war going on inside my head exhausts me to the point I want to give up. Ava is my only reason for not doing just that.

What happened last night with Jared can't happen again. I proved to myself just how weak I am. However amazing it was, I'm way too messed up right now to be in any kind of relationship. Now, my focus is going to be on proving that I am not a killer.

For now, this is a search I must do on my own, because if it leads to a dead end, then only three people will know what happened back then. *What if all of this is just me wishing for it to be true, and the picture of whom I know as Tina is nothing more than a picture left behind in some old house? What if I saw this photo briefly in my past and somehow shifted that image in my mind to an imaginary friend?*

A daily alarm that I depend on to tell me when it's time to head to work, brings me out of my thoughts. It's finally Friday, and this weekend is Jared's weekend to have Ava. I hate the thought of her being away from me again so soon, and for another two days. The *Mom* guilt is already trying to creep in from me being relieved for the break.

"Come on, Ava—we're going to be late for school," I call from the foot of the stairs. Her tiny hand grips the railing as she descends the stairs in her early morning, I'm-not-ready-to-function-yet, fashion. I always set my alarm earlier than it has to be, because she moves at the pace of a snail. She stops about midway and tugs at her backpack, which hangs crooked off of one shoulder, then sits down to attempt to tie her shoe.

I stifle an impatient groan. "Ava, honey, we have to go." I sprint up the stairs and tie her shoe, and in turn she fusses at me, telling me she wants to do it herself.

"We don't have time, Ava. I'll do it this time, and next time you can do it."

Ava whines and mumbles words that are inaudible. They're

usually the opposite of what I need her to do. I ignore her protests and stand with the door open as I watch her drag her feet toward me, all the while taking deep breaths to keep from snapping at her to hurry up.

We finally make it to school, and I smile at her teacher when they greet me at Ava's classroom door. I whisper as I continue to hold a full smile so that Ava can't hear me. "She's a little moody this morning."

Her teacher smiles and whispers back, "Then she and I will get along just fine," and she winks. "I'm pretty sure it's a full moon."

I lift my head in a *now I get it* gesture and laugh. Only teachers understand the true effect of what a full moon means. It turns even the most friendly and docile students into water-soaked gremlins.

Once I've gathered my students, marched them down the hall-way, single-file, and settled them into their school day, I dive into my job and forget my worries. At least for now. The morning runs smoothly—no strange encounters with Mia, and despite the full moon's effects, Mason is more well behaved than usual. Maybe the full moon has the opposite effect on him. It all comes to a halt when Ava's teacher comes to my door and motions me to step into the hall.

Ava is next to her, crying. I squat down and place my hands on both of her shoulders. "What's wrong, Ava?"

She rubs her eye with the back of her hand and takes in short, quick breaths, and says in between each one, "I—want—to—go—home."

I look up at her teacher, and she shrugs. "I'm not sure what's going on. The students were in their learning centers and another student came over to tell me that Ava was crying but doesn't want to tell me what happened."

"Ava—do you want to tell me what's going on?"

Ava shakes her head, continuing to rub her eye. "Can I stay here, Mommy?"

I look up at her teacher, searching for the answer, and she responds with a nod.

"Sure, honey, just until you feel better. Then you have to go back to class. Okay?"

Ava nods and looks down at the floor as I give her teacher a puzzled look. She shrugs and shakes her head, making it obvious that she has no clue what happened.

"Honey, why don't you go sit in the reading corner?" I squeeze her shoulders then stand and watch her as she timidly walks across the room and sits on a bean bag next to Mia. Mia smiles at her, and Ava responds with her own forced grin. I turn back to her teacher, and she explains as best she can what she observed.

"I'm not sure what happened. Ava was working in the writing center in her journal when another student informed me that she was crying."

"Did you look to see what she drew in her writing journal?"

"No, but I'll look. If I see anything out of the ordinary, I'll bring it to you at lunch."

"Okay. She can stay with me for now, then I'll talk to her and walk her down to the cafeteria."

I close the door, and as I walk past Megan, she gives me a questioning look. I shrug my shoulders, then observe Ava and Mia together. Ava has stopped crying, and Mia is talking to her as if she's known her all of her life. I wonder how children do that so easily. Meet as strangers and immediately become friends. What is it about becoming an adult that robs a person of the ability to interact with strangers without prejudice, reservations, or judgement? We somehow lose the ability to trust. If only grown-up life were as simple.

Megan stands and begins to perform our daily routine of lining the students up for lunch. Ava and Mia stand from their bean bags, clasp hands and sprint to get in line. She seems to be back to normal. My worry subsides, but what had upset her so badly?

While Megan takes the students to lunch, I slip down to Ava's classroom to take a look at her writing journal. It usually consists of drawings based around a story the class is reading or a writing prompt the teacher has given them. Her teacher hands me the journal before she slips out to get some lunch.

Written on an easel is the day's prompt that says, *If I had three wishes, I'd wish for ___. Pick the one you wish for most and draw a circle around it.* I flip through Ava's journal and find the drawing from today. I find it easily, because as part of their daily writing, the students must copy the day of the week as well as the date.

Three drawings have misspelled words underneath, yet Ava has sounded each word out well enough that I'm able to decipher what they're supposed to say—then some of the words are clear because she used the classroom word wall to help with spelling. One drawing is of a pink bicycle complete with pink tassels on the handlebars, and underneath are the letters *bik.* The second drawing resembles a pony and underneath are the words *mi little pone.* The third drawing is a stick figure drawn with squiggly hair and a blue dress. The hair is colored in with black crayon and so are the eyes. This one has a circle drawn around it.

Underneath the drawing are five words and as I read them, I almost drop the journal.

I w a n t my s i s y b a c.

34

osemary

I SQUINT at Ally in confusion as the look in her eyes makes me sit back down in my chair, just as a compliant patient should.

"I don't think you should talk to her, Rosemary. I don't like her," Ally whispers.

I blink twice at Ally as if to say, *I agree.*

"Are you going to respond, Rosemary?" Dr. Black asks. Her approach to being nice and using the correct pronunciation of my name does nothing to coerce me into talking. I remain silent and look at my daughter, who smiles at me.

"Dr. Foster discovered why you stopped talking. She said you knew that one of your daughters may have been responsible for your other daughter's death. And then, you walked out on her—abandoned her. Didn't you?"

My pulse quickens and my breathing shifts to an uneasy pace.

"What kind of mother does something like that? Abandons

their child so young. You just couldn't handle learning of the heinous act your child had just committed. Not at only seven years old."

I'm starting to question her intentions as well. A sickening feeling plants itself in my stomach. *Why is this doctor trying to get me to admit what I've already believed all these years? How is this supposed to help me? I didn't tell Dr. Sarah any of this.*

Aside from Ally's warning, a voice inside my head is also cautioning me not to talk to the doctor. I keep my lips pressed firmly closed, not taking a bite of the doctor's bait to engage.

"What are you staring at, Rose?" She turns and looks behind her, then back to me, her eyes squinted.

I give her a blank stare.

"So, let's dig a little deeper into why you're here, Rose. Here's what I've gathered about your past. You had two daughters who liked to fight more than the average siblings, and the day that one of your daughters died, the other one got mad and pushed it too far. Am I right?"

Dr. Black's words fuel my anger. Having her say aloud what I'd allowed myself to believe back then makes me want to defend Abby now. Defend her as I should have then. "You're wrong!" I snap.

"Shhhh." Ally attempts to stop me.

"My daughters loved each other," I croak. "Why are you accusing her with these lies? I'll have your license." I say the words in an alarmingly calm manner—the sort of calm before the threat of a storm.

Dr. Black's cocky grin only feeds the waiting storm more. If it weren't for Ally looking at me with a pleading expression, I would stand again and tower over her—and stop fighting the urge to slap the grin from her face.

I take a calming breath and chew on the inside of my lip. The voice inside my head screams for me let it go for now; warns me to finish the session without engaging. I've got to find out just who Dr. Black is and why she's so interested in the day my daughter died. *Just where did she learn what she thinks she knows?* I resort back to being the old Rosemary.

Silent.

She continues to talk, repeating the same accusation just in different ways, but I don't engage. I remain silent through the rest of the session as she proceeds to tell me that she thinks we're making progress. We have, but not like she thinks. The only progress I see is that she's talked, and I've plotted on how to get out of here. I'm going to find a way to go to Abby, because something tells me that her search for answers and this doctor's sudden interest in my daughters isn't a coincidence. I'm not sure why, but the feeling I got years ago when I was betrayed in the worst possible way, returns. It's deep, and it's warning me to protect Abby like I didn't back then.

Angie knocks on the door and tiptoes into the room like a timid child asking for candy. "Shall I escort Rosemary back to her room now?"

Dr. Black doesn't remove her eyes from me as she says, "I guess we might as well be finished—Rose refuses to help herself."

I return my gaze back to the doctor's eyes again, my stare unwavering as I fight the desire to physically retaliate. I stand and Ally says one final thing.

"You have to get out of this place."

As I'm walking from the room, the doctor speaks with malice in her voice. "Oh, Rose?"

I don't turn around, just continue to move toward the door.

"I'm only here to help you."

As I leave the room and Angie closes the door behind us, we turn the corner to another hallway before she speaks. "You seem just as troubled as you were before you saw the doctor, Rosemary. Is everything alright?"

I nod, then point toward the recreation room.

"Alright, if you're sure. Your canvas and paints are all set up for you, and I'll come back to check on you later."

I give Angie a forced smile and enter the large room, but instead of going to my canvas, I search for Ewelina. She's sitting in the first of six rocking chairs along the far wall, with a set of crocheting needles in her hands. She's the only person in this place I can trust. I could probably trust Angie, but she works here, and I wouldn't want to risk her losing her job. She's been far too good to me.

I sit down in the empty chair next to her as she knits away on what appears to be a blue hat of some sort. She stops, drops the needles into her lap and holds it up as she asks, "You like my chook, Rosemary?"

I give her a confused look.

"It's a chook—you know, a toque—you wear it on your head. I think you call them a boggan or a bean, or whatever the hell Americans call it."

I raise my eyebrows and press my lips together, trying not to laugh. It looks large enough to fit the head of a camel and shaped as though it would as well. I nod my head up and down and pretend to like it and clear my throat. I don't think I'm very convincing, because she puffs and tosses it and the needles into a basket next to her chair, then clenches and unclenches her old hands as she says, "Never mind. You're right—it sucks."

I snicker and scan the room, then turn to Ewelina and whisper to her for the first time—ever. "I need your help."

"O matko, Rosemary! It's about damn time you use that voice box of yours." Ewelina shoots forward in her chair as I give her a quick *shhh.* She lowers her voice to a whisper. "Whatever you need —we kobiety have to stick together."

I frown.

"We women, Rosemary—we girls have to stick together. What do you want me to do?"

I've never communicated with words to any of the patients. In fact, spending years in silence, doing without and basically making myself invisible, has conditioned the other patients to ignore me. Most don't even look my way. However, I spy another patient rocking three chairs from ours staring at me as though she has witnessed a miracle. I assume she's waiting for me to speak again. I lean back in my rocking chair and shake my head as if to say *not here*.

"What's the matter?" Ewelina looks around the room and then she stops to look at the woman, who continues to stare. She barks, "Mind your own business, nosy twat."

I shoot Ewelina a scolding glance.

"I'll take care of you, Rosemary."

I slap my palm over my face and shake my head as I suddenly realize who she reminds me of. A female version of the character Max Goldman from the movie Grumpy Old Men. Ewelina has never had much tact when it comes to saying what she thinks. She doesn't own a filter for her mouth. Rather than fight the battle, I nod my head toward the door, stand, and urge Ewelina to follow.

We turn down the hallway that leads to my room, and Ewelina says, "This must be dire. You never invite me to your room."

I nod but don't say anything else until we step inside my little space and the door is closed. Ewelina stands in the middle of the room, rotating her body to look at the walls and ceiling, which are both covered in massive tapestries and sheers. "You were one of those hippies back in the day, weren't you? I bet you even smoked that wacky shit too, didn't you, Rosemary?"

"I told you, I need your help."

Ewelina flops down in a chair, her eyes still transfixed on the walls.

I snap my fingers. "Ewelina!"

"I'm listening. Don't get your kitchen in a twist."

"I need to get out of here."

"Are you crazy? Of course you are—you're in here." Ewelina laughs at her own words, and I give her a displeased look. "Okay, okay," she says, and clears her throat.

"You were right. I think I need to get out of here and find my sister. What exactly did you mean when you said I needed to go see my sister? What did my mother tell you?"

Ewelina stands and walks behind my bed to rub her hands over the multi-colored tapestry which displays a bohemian mandala. "This thing messes with your head, Rosemary. We've got to get us some smoke and check it out."

"Ewelina." I say her name as though she's a child ignoring the demand of a parent. "I need you to focus."

"Alright, alright. Maria said that you need to talk to your sister about someone named Tina. Maria said that your daughter was right—that little girl was real, and your sister might know who she is.

I give her a questioning frown.

"She said, think about the triangle."

bby

I SLAM the journal shut and hold it to my chest while the rest of my body remains frozen in place. The only thing that seems to be in overdrive is my heartbeat and my thoughts. Both race to the tune of confusion, prompting me to go to the only person who will understand—the only person in the building who will know what this means.

I march down the hallway, avoiding eye contact with anyone, and head straight toward Jared's office. I bypass the school secretary's desk, and Kelly gives me a quizzical look as I step into Jared's tiny office. The four walls that enclose his claustrophobic space are still covered in brown paneling, which has been hanging since the school was built. It feels more like a cardboard box instead of an office—smells like it, too.

"We have to talk." As the demanding words leave my mouth, I

realize that Kris is sitting behind his office door with a stiff posture. I look to Jared, then back at Kris and feel as though I've walked in on something I shouldn't. At this moment, I don't care and make a demand of her as well. "I need to speak with Jared in private."

"Abby, we were in the middle of something important," Kris says.

"I don't care—this is more important. It concerns our daughter." I bark the words with an assertiveness that surprises even me.

Kris gives me a dissatisfied look, then turns to Jared as if expecting him to step in and defend her.

Instead, he asks, "Kris, can you give us a moment?"

She looks at Jared with a look that I can't quite decipher—confusion? It seems more of an expectant look as though she's shocked that he would choose me over her. Something about it gives me a sense of satisfaction—I'm not sure why.

Kris huffs as she stands and leaves the tiny office. I shut the door behind her, and the small space feels even more suffocating. No wonder Jared rarely has his office door closed.

"What's wrong, Abby?" he asks as soon as the door clicks.

"Ava's teacher brought her to my class crying this morning, but Ava wouldn't tell me why. Her teacher said it started when Ava was writing in her journal, so I looked at what she was working on for today." I open the journal and lay it on the desk in front of Jared.

His expression shifts from mild curiosity to wide-eyed questioning.

"Yeah," I say as we both stare at each other for a moment, searching for something to say.

"Where the hell did this come from?"

"You tell me."

"How would I know?" Jared's tone turns defensive.

"Have you been talking to her? Did you tell her?"

"No! Why would I?"

"How else would she know about this?"

"What about your crazy aunt? Would she tell her?"

"She hasn't been around her—at least not much without me around. Besides, Ruby treats Ava like a princess. I don't think she would do anything to hurt her." I continue to stare at Jared accusingly because I know that between the two of us, he is the only one that still tries to talk about her. When it comes to this topic, Jared acts like the adult, and I'm the one who acts like a child. I pretend it isn't real and retreat into an imaginary world that erases that part of my life. If it doesn't exist, then it can't hurt me.

"Abby, I know you don't want to talk about this, but maybe it's time we did. Ava is getting older, and if it gets back to her and we aren't the ones to tell her, it's going to damage her trust in us."

I shake my head and flop down in the chair where Kris was sitting and stare at the floor, trying to block out his words. He's right. I've always believed that avoiding the subject would keep it from being real.

The tragic death of our other sweet daughter.

* * *

Just thinking about those words makes me crumble inside. *Our other daughter—Alexis.*

Jared believes the opposite—he says that talking about her keeps her alive, and that avoiding it only erases her memory.

"Look." Jared says as he rises from his office chair and steps around to the front of his desk, closer to me. He leans back so that he's half-standing, half-resting on its edge, and crosses his arms across his chest. "We need to sit down with Ava and tell her about her twin sister."

I become immediately defensive, and my tone shows it. "We need to figure out how she heard this. It would be different if she said *I want a sissy,* but she has heard someone say that she had a sissy."

"She's supposedly been talking with your dead sister, Ally. What if the Ally that she's talking to, isn't your dead sister? What if it's A-L-L-I-E, as in short for Alexia, *her* dead sister?"

We often called Alexis Allie for short. I think Jared was the first to start doing it, and something about it felt natural. I couldn't protest, and I also didn't want to. Either way, after her death, I couldn't say her name—period.

I look deep into Jared's eyes, and something punches me in the chest. I see our dead daughter's eyes in his. It's one of the reasons I pushed him away—it was too painful seeing her eyes and not being able to hold her. Looking at him reminds me too much of everything I'd lost. Another pain stabs me in the torso, and I have to look down at the floor. I take a deep breath and shift my thoughts, but the one that follows isn't any easier. It didn't occur to me that the Ally Ava has been talking to, could be *our* Allie. But our daughter died when she was only two months old. Surely that couldn't be possible, but if it is, how the hell do we explain this to a six-year-old?

Jared remains silent, as though he's allowing what he said to sink in. I continue to stare down at the floor but succumb to the idea and finally ask, "So, what do you think we should do?"

He chews on his lip. "I think we both need to sit down and talk to her about her imaginary friend, about her ability to see people who aren't real, and her dead sister. All of it."

I finally look up at Jared. "How the hell do we do that without scaring her half to death?"

"You say that your grandmother, and possibly your mother, if rumors are to be believed, were able to see people or things that others couldn't. It can't be all bad."

"They both ended up in a mental hospital. I'm not sure it's all good, either."

"Maybe Rosemary could help us figure out how to talk to her. What about you and your sister? Did either one of you ever talk to imaginary people that weren't there—or were dead?" Jared pauses before he says the last part, as though he can't believe he's asking it.

I pause for a moment, unsure if I should tell him about Tina, but at this point, what could it hurt? "We both did. But the person we saw was the same. She and I both talked to her and interacted with her at the same time. She said that we were the only ones that could see her."

He frowns and takes a breath. It's probably a lot to process. "Did she have a name?"

"Tina." I debate on telling him more, but stop myself. There's plenty of think about already. The whole idea of it seems crazy. After watching the birthday party video the other night, I fully intended on showing him her picture to see if he recognized her, but back out every time I think about how crazy it all sounds. If I do, then I will have to tell him the whole story. I'm not sure I can talk about it out loud. I've had the conversation with him about it over and over in my head, but the words seem to have planted themselves so deep within myself, they won't surface.

Jared frowns. "When did you stop seeing her?"

"I didn't see her any more after my sister died."

"You never saw anyone else after that?"

I shake my head.

"Well, I guess you could start the conversation with Ava about this Tina, and then go from there by talking about her friend."

The idea of talking about Tina isn't something I've allowed myself to explore. I retreat inside myself, tormented about what to do. I feel as though I'm drowning inside my own head—inside this world that I've lived in all alone for so long. It's as though there's a life raft within reach, but I'm afraid to grab it. Afraid to open myself up like that.

"Abby?

I swallow hard before answering and when I speak, my voice comes out strained. "Yes." My answer isn't about just talking to Ava.

I'm finally going to tell Jared everything about my past.

36

 ared

I'M a lost cause when it comes to Abby—I can't seem to live with her or without her.

I know that something is mentally eating her alive, and I don't know how to help her. I'm all for solving complicated puzzles, but Abby is the hardest I've ever tried to solve. At the moment, she's like a mystery box, sealed with a code—a code that even the most experienced hacker couldn't figure out. I don't know why I keep trying to. Why can't I just walk away from this woman?

At the end of the school day, Abby informs me she's arranged for Ava to go home with Megan for a couple of hours so that we can talk, and my mouth practically hits the floor. I'm still trying to process her rare willingness to talk in my office today, and hadn't dared to hope that an extended conversation would be possible.

As I pull in behind Abby's car at the side of the house, I

notice right away that the side door is ajar. I spring from my car and sprint to Abby's open car door and stop her from getting out. "Hang here for a moment," I say.

"What? Why?"

"Did you leave the door open?"

"No."

I point, then motion for her to stay put. I search the ground for anything to use as a weapon in case someone is still inside the house. All I can find is a small, concrete frog. I grasp it in my hand, push the door the rest of the way open, and it announces my entrance by squeaking loudly. I round the corner to the kitchen and spot something stuck to the basement door. It's a typical piece of notebook paper and attached to it are two pictures. It's actually looks like an old polaroid that's been torn in half.

Each piece contains an image of a little girl, both of whom appear to be around Ava's age. On the left side of the page is a picture of a blond-haired girl and written in bold red letters underneath is one word. DEAD. Pasted on the right side of the page is another girl, similar in size, but she has dark hair. I recognize her right away.

Abby.

Written under her picture is another word written in red, bigger, and bolder. KILLER.

Rage fills me as I rip the page from the door, and as I do, Abby steps into the room.

"What's that?"

I hesitate, but hand it over. "I'm going to check the rest of the house."

I cautiously move from room to room, trying not to retreat into personal thoughts—thoughts about missing this house and living here. As I leave one room and enter another, fleeting memories flash in my mind like the click of a camera, and I have to close my mind's shutter. After searching every room, and once I'm secure in the idea that whoever came into the house is long gone, I return to the kitchen.

"Whoever it was, they're long gone. It appears their sole purpose for coming in was to leave that." I point to the page Abby is still clutching in her hand, which is visibly shaking.

Abby gives me a dumbfounded nod and it's obvious it's taking everything she has to hold it together. She runs her finger over the image on the left.

"Is that your sister?"

She only nods.

"Abby, talk to me. It's obvious there's someone out there with cruel intentions toward you. Hell, they broke into our—I mean, *your* house just to put this in here. Up until the other day, I didn't even know you had a sister, but someone else sure does." I can feel my voice crack from worry and fear, so I take a deep breath and start again. "Someone did this to purposefully hurt you."

Abby clears her throat then speaks, her words barely above a whisper. "Did you find anything else in the house?"

"No. I don't think they went any further than the kitchen. Do you have any idea who might have done this?"

Abby continues to stare down at the paper. "I think I do."

As I stare down at one-half of the photo with the image of my dead sister, something from my past comes back to me—the memory box and another item that was buried in it. A polaroid picture of me, my sister, and Tina. This picture, minus Tina.

Only three people were there that night, and one of those is dead. That leaves me, and someone whom I believed for years was an imaginary friend. I may feel as though I'm going crazy at times, but I know I didn't do this to myself—so that leaves Tina.

Feeling as though my legs no longer want to support me, I move to the kitchen table and sit, then Jared follows, doing the same. A mixture of his shampoo and body soap wafts toward me, and I breathe in a little deeper, using it as a distraction to calm my insides. I've always loved the way those scents mix with the smell of him—woodsy and clean. I take in another breath, feeling my nerves calm a little.

This is the second time in less than a week that Jared has been inside the house, sitting in the spot that he used to. Some habits remain intact, even when people don't. I suppose being in here must be awkward for him—it is for me. During our divorce and for a period of time after that, Jared was pretty bitter about me staying in the house. He didn't want to keep it, but at the same, time he didn't want me to have it either. Now, he'll say it's what's best for Ava, but every now and then, he'll let a comment slip about all the hard work he put into this place. I usually ignore them, but in all honesty, I do feel guilty about it. I've debated on selling many times, but this is the only home Ava knows. Going to Jared's apartment is more like a weekend getaway for her, not home.

I realize that I'm still staring at the chopped photos in my hand, and Jared is staring at me, waiting for me to say something more. "I need to show you something." I stand and retrieve the photo of Tina from my bag and hand it to Jared, then turn and busy myself making coffee. "Do you recognize her?"

Jared takes the photo and studies it hard. "She looks a little familiar. Is this someone I should know?"

I turn back around, because I want to see Jared's reaction. "That's what I want to know. Do you remember seeing her as a kid? Her name is Tina."

Jared gives me a questioning look, then looks closely. Saying her name seems to prompt Jared to look closer, and I watch his face change as he says, "Yeah. I believe I do remember her. I think this is the girl who locked me in my basement. It was in the house we lived in the first time we moved to town."

"Really?" My voice hits a higher octave, and I have to clear my throat. "She did the same thing to me, except it was *this* basement. I'd forgotten all about it until I found some drawings down there the other day."

He stares at the photo closer. "From what I can remember, she was a very strange girl. She told me that I was the only person that could see her, but then one day my dad caught me talking to her and ran her off."

"So, *he* could see her." The breath leaves my lungs.

"Of course he could see her. She was full of shit. She got me into big trouble with my father. The house we were renting at that time had a basement that was off limits. In fact, we weren't supposed to go in it at all because our landlord kept some of their belongings stored down there. There was a padlock on the basement door inside the house, and there was usually one on the outside entrance as well. That day, somehow, the lock went missing. Anyway, long story short, she tricked me into going in through the outside entrance, then managed to block the door with something to keep me from getting out. I was so upset, and I remember calling her a little bitch and if I ever saw her again, I would beat the shit out of her. I was locked down there for hours. When my father came home and found me, he blamed me, and I got my ass beat with a belt."

My mind rewinds to my own experience with Tina and this basement.

"So, what does her picture have to do with that one?" Jared points to the ripped polaroid of me and my sister. "And what did you mean when you said you think you know who put that here?"

Dread of telling him the rest of the story swells in my throat, but I force myself to swallow it down. I know I have to do this in order for him to understand any of this. I turn from Jared, click the *on* button on the coffee pot, then say, "Before we get into everything, I think we should take a walk. Explaining it to you will be easier if I show you."

Jared's face develops a curious expression, but he doesn't say anything, just nods, stands, and waits for me to lead the way. We walk around the side of the house and into the back yard, then slip through the back gate onto the walking path that runs along the stream. Jared gives me a puzzled look when I turn right instead of left. The two of us have walked along the stream many times, but always in the opposite direction. I always told him that I liked the view better that way, and he never questioned it. In truth, I couldn't bring myself to walk in this direction before because it was too painful.

We follow the tree-lined concrete path that runs along the outside of the wooden privacy fences. On the other side of our path is the rocky stream that plays a sweet and constant trickling melody, but at the moment, my racing thoughts dull the peaceful effects it usually emits.

We walk several blocks from the house and in the distance stands the monster towering above all the trees along our path. My heart takes on an erratic rhythm that can be felt at every pulse point in my body, while my breath acts as if it wants to compete. I squeeze my eyes shut and take a deep breath to prevent a full-on anxiety attack. I begin to pinch my fingers, and Jared immediately notices, so I shove my hands into my loose pockets and use my thumb to twirl the beads on my new fidget ring.

"Everything okay?"

"Yes," I lie as I swallow hard.

The concrete path leads into a flat grassy area of the old dog park, closer to the tree, and its massive size looks much bigger than I remember. I stop and stare, and Jared stops with me.

"It sure is a beautiful creature," Jared says.

I can't say anything, and instead of agreeing with him, I shake my head.

Jared turns his body toward me and looks at my face—it must be alarming because his eyes widen with worry.

"Abby, what's wrong?"

All I can do is stare and swallow. "It's where my sister died."

IV

---

*"Unexpressed emotions will never die.
They are buried alive and will come forth later in uglier ways."*
—Sigmund Freud

2 002

THE GIRL DISTINGUISHES the difference between the footsteps above, simply by their pace and the way they hit the floor. She can tell that two sets of them belong to kids and the other two belong to adults. In the mix of the stomping are muffled voices, and she tries to make out what they're saying. It all sounds more like the animated teacher's voice from the old cartoon, Charlie Brown. *Wah-wah-wah.*

She's supposed to remain perfectly quiet while she's down here, and she's already bored with being stuck in the basement for what seems like forever, even though it hasn't been that long. In her search around the stinky room, she spots a few boxes and decides to kill time by pilfering through the contents of one box labeled *miscellaneous.* She tries to sound out the word but makes one up instead—*my stuff.* Inside, she first finds an old, funny-shaped camera. She rotates it around in her hands, accidentally pressing the red button on the front. It flashes and temporarily takes her vision. As soon as the camera clicks, it makes a whirring sound, and a piece of paper spits out of the front. She pulls on the stiff square, and it comes loose from the camera. She remembers seeing one of these in an old movie she was forced to watch on movie night in the foster home.

The photo is black, so she discards it on the floor and begins to sort through the rest of the box. Her fingers brush a cool, tin box equipped with a handle. She picks it up and shakes it, hearing the rattling contents inside. Resting it down on the floor, she flips open the latch and lid, and the first thing she finds is an old, faded photograph of two women. Her eyes focus immediately on the woman on the left who looks just like her mother. But it can't be. *Why would this rich, snobby woman upstairs have a picture of her mother?*

She flips the picture over and finds two letters on the back. *M* and *S*. She inspects the photograph one more time, looking at the woman on the right. She doesn't recognize her but thinks that she looks an awful lot like the woman upstairs. The two women in the photo look somewhat alike except for their hair color. She can't stop staring at the woman on the left. It bugs her so much that she decides to stuff the photo in her pocket.

With her focus back on the box, she finds several spools of thread, buttons, and a cylinder-shaped object small enough to fit over her thumb and some chalk. Not able to figure out what the metal cylinder is for, she drops it back in the box, but keeps the piece of chalk. A place to draw would be nice, she thinks. Her teacher never lets her do it at school. In fact, there are only a few classrooms at school that have chalkboards. Most have large whiteboards where the teacher uses markers instead of chalk. Her teachers won't let her do that, either. She decides that the stone floor will work just fine for producing some artwork, but decides to draw where the woman can't see it. She might get mad.

Her eyes land on the door on the far wall of the room and she decides to see what's on the other side. As she turns the ancient-looking doorknob and pulls on the heavy door, it pops like an old person's bones—not loud, but distinct. The corners of the room are dark, and she thinks that she could draw there. It would be a long time before anyone would find her art. At least she'd be long gone before they did.

First, she draws the woman upstairs who seems to always have a frown on her face. Then she draws herself and her twin sister—someone she doesn't like very much. Next, she draws her two new friends that she met just the other day. They're not really her friends, but she just wants someone to play with.

Boredom from being in the basement continues to grow, but the woman upstairs says she has to stay down here and can't be seen by anyone—no matter what. She has a plan. The plan is to make everyone believe she's invisible. If she does it perfectly, the woman upstairs has promised she will give her all kinds of money, and a new pair of shoes. The woman doesn't know she's going to use the money to run away, because that's her little secret. So, she goes to the other corner and draws some more.

This time she adds names to her drawing, including her new friends' names. She can't remember the name of the woman upstairs, so she writes the word *witch*, because that's what she looks like.

Returning to the box, she spots the picture she'd laid on the floor and notices a smeared image—her image. Excitement courses through her and she realizes that the camera works after all, so she decides to try for a better photo of herself. This time she turns the camera around, holding it as far from her face as she can, then stands perfectly still and pushes the red button. Next comes the flash, click, and whir of the photo spitting from the camera. She holds it in her hands and watches as her face slowly comes into view. It's a very good picture of herself.

Her heart kicks into overdrive as she notices movement in her peripheral. She freezes in place. High on the wall she sees someone's face stuck up against one of the basement windows, then another face appears in its place. She realizes then that it's one of the twin sisters she'd met before. She's supposed to remain invisible a while longer, but she really wants to go out and play.

The woman upstairs has already told her some of what she's going to pay her for, but not all of it yet. She said she wants her to trick these two girls into believing that she's only imaginary, but that's all she knows so far. She's supposed to stay hidden until they can plan out the rest.

One of the sisters gooses the other and screams, *Rrrr*, and she gets mad and stomps off. That sister didn't think it was funny, but the girl watching thought it was. She decides she's going to sneak outside and play, just for a little bit.

The girl looks at the picture of herself and admires the way she looks older, even though she just turned ten. She really likes the picture but decides to leave it here in the hopes that someone else will find it one day—sort of like a surprise. Maybe even a hundred years from now. She searches for a place to hide it and returns to the dark room where she drew her last drawings and finds a crack between two bricks. The picture fits perfectly inside. After securing the picture in place, she puts all of the other items back in the box, and as she goes to put the camera back in, she debates on whether the woman upstairs would even miss it. Her final decision ends with putting the strap around her neck and hiding the camera under her baggy shirt.

As she looks at the basement steps, she thinks better of trying to sneak out that way, so she goes back to the dark room one last time. She hadn't really paid close attention before, but in the middle of the back wall, in between her drawings is another door. Something about it scares her and excites her all at the same time. She shoves it open to find a set of concrete steps leading upward, and as her eyes follow them, she sees daylight pouring in from a set of doors above her.

She pushes on one of the doors, and something about it makes her think of a scary movie she'd sneakily watched in the foster home. Her foster mom was watching it one night, so she'd sat in the hall while peeking around the corner and watched it too. It didn't scare her as much as it did her foster mom. She didn't cover her eyes once, unlike the old woman.

She spots the sister with blond hair at the far side of the back yard away from the house. To avoid being seen from the house, she darts around a bush and runs to join her. She hopes that the woman upstairs will be happy that she's going to put their plan of making them believe she's invisible in motion. Maybe she'll pay her some money sooner, and she can get out of that stupid foster home quicker.

39

bby and Ally
2002

ALLY STAGGERS into the bathroom to brush her teeth after Rosemary woke her a second time to get ready for school. Her twin sister stands in front of the sink and plops her toothbrush into the holder, then says, "Ha, I beat ya getting ready."

Ally moans her words rather than openly speaking them. "I don't care, Abby. It's not a race."

"So. I still beat you anyway."

"You girls better not be fighting, or you'll be holding hands all the way to the bus stop," Rosemary says from somewhere down the hall.

Ally drags the toothbrush over her teeth as her eyes struggle to open. She looks sleepily at the mirror, and it takes a few moments to realize that the mirror doesn't look like a mirror at all. It's more like staring at a black TV screen. She turns to look behind her, and then back at it, and there's no reflection of anything—it's just black. A hint of panic stirs as she races through brushing her teeth with no intention of sticking around to find out. She spits one last time but can't resist looking into the black space again ahead of her plan to run. She freezes when she spots movement in the middle of the void, and squeezes her eyes shut, hoping that they're playing tricks on her.

They're not.

Though somewhat blurry, the silhouettes of three girls appear in the mirror, holding hands while dancing in circles.

The image becomes clearer, but it's as though she's watching someone's dream. Two of the girls are similar in size, and the third is almost a head taller. As the girls skip in a circle, they seem to move in slow motion, almost as if they're floating. She recognizes her own face, and as they rotate, Abby's face comes into view next, then she recognizes Tina.

The scene appears happy as the girls throw their heads back in laughter, and the space around them is bright and bathed in sunlight. As she watches it, her fear dissipates a little. A few leaves fall around them, then she recognizes the massive oak tree in the distance where they often play. Ally begins to smile, then realizes that none of this is real.

Just as her smile fades, so does the light around the girls. The image begins to darken as though a storm cloud has rolled in to cast an eerie shadow on them. They release their hands, breaking the circle, and Tina runs toward the tree. She waves at Abby and Ally to follow, and they skip along behind her. The closer they get to the tree, the darker it becomes, and Ally senses something bad is about to occur. She squeezes her eyes shut, then opens them again to find only two girls standing. Her eyes take on a frantic search of the mirror and she spots the third child—she's lying on the ground. One taller girl and one smaller girl stand over her. Her breath holds in her lungs as she moves in closer to the mirror to see who's lying on the ground. Is it her, or Abby?

"Ally, you need to hurry up. You're going to be late for school," Rosemary calls from the bottom of the stairs.

Just as the dream fades upon waking, so do the images, and she wasn't able to tell who was the one lying down. Something about the stance of the two girls still standing said that the one on the ground wasn't all right. Her own image reappears in the mirror, and she's looking at her own horrified expression.

She leaves the bathroom in a trance, trying to make sense of what just happened. It's the first time she's ever experienced anything like this. She's heard voices in her head before, although she's never tried to understand them, but never has she experienced anything like this. Aunt Ruby had just told her a story a few days before about her grandmother, who lived in a *crazy hospital* as she called it, because she was seeing things that weren't there, but Rosemary wouldn't let Ruby finish the story. Now she wishes she could hear the rest of it.

She descends the stairs, and her face must give away her worried thoughts, as Rosemary notices. She meets Ally at the bottom of the stairs, and places both hands on the sides of her face, then presses her palm to Ally's forehead. "You feeling okay, Ally? Your face looks flushed."

"Yeah," is all that Ally can conjure.

Ally's walk to the bus stop and her bus ride to school is nothing more than a blur. Even spending time outside for a short recess does very little to shake her mood. When she and Abby get off the bus that evening, they walk past the gothic looking house where Aunt Ruby lives. Abby wretches and starts moaning about getting a whiff of something foul. Something that smells just like the stinky giant plant in their back garden. Ally scrunches her nose and eyebrows, because it usually only smells like that when it blooms.

As they walk along, Ally hears *pssst.* She stops and looks toward the line of shrubs that run along the front yard a few feet from the sidewalk. *Pssst.* She hears it again.

Abby hears it too and they tiptoe together toward the sound. Then Tina pops up from behind the bushes and screams, "Rrrrr!"

Both girls jump and stagger backward, and Ally snaps, "That's not funny!" as Tina laughs. A few seconds later, Abby laughs with her, although there isn't much joy behind it.

"I got you, my little pretties." Tina points and taunts.

Ally scowls at Tina as though she were actually the witch in *The Wizard of Oz.*

"Is your mom home?" Tina asks.

"Not yet. She's still at work," Abby says.

"Your mom lets you stay at home by yourself?"

"Yeah, but only because it's not for very long. She just started letting us do it after we turned seven. We have to go in and lock the door and not answer it for anyone," Ally answers.

"Ally, we'd better get home. Mom will get mad if she knows we stopped on the way."

"I'll come with you," Tina says.

"We can't let anyone in the house." Ally stops abruptly.

"Mom will never know—she can't see her," Abby says.

"Yeah—she won't know. Please. Ally, I'm bored," Tina begs.

Ally stares at Tina as if she's debating her answer, then shrugs. "I guess so." The distraction could be nice.

They make it home a couple of houses down, and Ally pauses on the second step that leads up to the front porch. She looks back and says, "You have to turn around, Tina—I can't show you where our mom hides the key."

"I already know," Tina says, and stomps past Ally up the steps. She stops in between the two concrete posts that stand on each side of the entryway to the porch. Sitting on top of each post are oval-shaped finial toppers made of cast iron and painted black, the paint flacking away to reveal some rust underneath. Tina turns to the one on the left and slides a key from underneath. "See." She holds the key up for Ally to see.

"How did you know?" Abby asks.

"I know everything, silly." Tina giggles, then walks to the front door and unlocks it. "Come on."

Ally gives Abby a puzzled look as Tina hands the key to her and leads the twins into the house. "What do you all want to do?"

"I don't know." Abby hitches a shoulder. "What do you want to do?"

"Let's play a scary game."

"What kind of scary game?" Ally actually perks up at the mention of such a game, while Abby's face shows fear.

"It's called Concentrate. Ever heard of it?"

40

"YOU WEREN'T SUPPOSED to let those girls see you—not yet."

The girl shrugs one shoulder as she swings her legs under the kitchen table, all while licking on the lollipop she'd just received. "I did what you told me. I made them believe that no one else could see me but them."

"They believed you?" The woman narrows her eyes.

"Yep," she says as she pops the sucker from her lips, making them smack. "They think I'm invisible to everyone but them. They also believe I live here, but only sometimes—like I'm a ghost."

"Well, you must be careful and do things just as I say, or I'm not going to pay you any money, and I definitely won't give you any shoes. Understand?"

The girl stops sucking on her sucker and bites her lip as her face begins to droop.

"Where are your parents?" the woman asks.

The girl shrugs both shoulders this time. She drops her hand and sucker to her lap and begins to twirl a thick strand of short hair around the finger of her other hand. "My mom went crazy, so the ambulance came and got her. At least, that's what my dad said. He said she wouldn't stop talking and babbling to people that weren't there, so he called an ambulance, and they took her away. Then my dad said he couldn't take it anymore and left a few months later. We never saw him again, either.

"So, where have you been living since then?"

"Me and my sister were put in a foster home. The first foster home wasn't bad, but I hate this one."

The woman nods and stares into space for a moment. "Have you always lived in Meadowbrook?"

"No, we used to live in Balsam, which isn't that far from here, and before that, we moved around a lot. My foster mom says we probably won't stay here long, either. The social services people want to find us a home back at our old school, so they're still looking."

"Well, I hope it works out for you."

The girl peers up at the woman. "Why do you want me to make those girls believe I'm not real?"

"Because—if they think you're not real, you can do whatever you want and make sure they get the blame for it."

The girl frowns, trying to figure out why this woman is wanting her to do such a thing. "What should I do?"

The woman pauses as though she's thinking as well. "I don't know. Do things that will play them against one another. Make them fight."

"They already do that—a lot," the girl says as she sits forward in her chair and shoves the sucker back into her mouth.

"Why do you want to pick on these two little girls? What did they do to you?"

The woman's jaw twitches, and her cold eyes fill with resentment. "It wasn't them—it was their mother. She isn't a nice person, and I think she should find out what it's like to not have such a perfect life. She lives all high and mighty in that big house which she took from me. She took everything from me, including someone she had no right to take." The woman's eyes and words match in intensity as she speaks.

The girl takes the sucker from her mouth, wraps it back up in its original wrapper, and sticks it in her pocket. "Why don't you just take the house back?"

"I will one day, but I don't just want the house back, I want to make the woman living in it miserable. The best way to do that is through her children. Who knows—if you can get those little bratty girls to fight with one another, it'll drive that woman crazy, and I can put her in a mental hospital just like she did to our mother."

"Why don't you just go get your mother out of the hospital?"

The woman's grumpy face softens. "I can't—she died from pneumonia years ago. She would have never gotten sick if she hadn't have been in that place."

The girl thinks about her own mother and wonders if she will die from pneumonia too. She brushes it off. Her mother never thinks about her. She's pretty sure her mother liked her sister more, anyway.

This time it's the girls' turn to think. The picture she found downstairs pops in her mind of the two women, one of which looks a lot like her own mother, and the other that looks a lot like this woman. It makes her curious if maybe this woman or the woman in the picture is related to her somehow. It's probably crazy, but she decides to ask questions anyway. "What was your mother's name?"

"Maria."

The girl thinks of the two letters on the back of the photo. One of them was an *M*—maybe it stands for Maria. "So, did the house you're talking about belong to Maria?"

The woman gives the girl a puzzled look as she tilts her head slightly to the side. "What's with all the questions?"

The girl flushes and looks down at the ground, but then plays it off by hitching a shoulder and saying, "I don't know. I'm bored, and I like a good story."

The woman actually semi-smiles as though she doesn't mind the conversation. "Yes. The house belonged to my mother, but my sister put her in a mental hospital and then *she* got the house."

"Was your mother an only child? Why didn't the house go to her sisters or brothers?"

"No. My mother had a twin sister, but she left years ago, and no one has seen her since."

"What was her name?"

"Sylvia. We're getting off track here. Let's get back to planning out your little job." The woman's voice shifts back to frustration.

The girl thinks about the photo in her pocket again and remembers the other letter on the back of the photo—*S*. "What did your mother look like?" she blurts.

The woman gives the girl another quizzical look. "Blond hair, blue eyes."

Before the woman can say anything else, she blurts again, "Can I see a picture of her?"

"Why? What my mother looked like has nothing to do with you. All you need to worry about is those twin brats."

"I just want to see if you all look alike. You look nothing like your sister, and her twin daughters look nothing like each other, but neither do my sister and I."

The woman frowns and breathes out for a long time as though she has nothing better to do. "I'm sure there's a picture of them around here somewhere." The woman stands and wobbles to a small stack of boxes in the living room, and the girl follows. She runs her fingers over the surface of several boxes and stops on one labeled *Keepsakes.* After lifting several different sized frames and laying them on a table next to her, she stops when she finds one that isn't much bigger than her hand. Its edges are trimmed in silver.

"Here's one," the woman says as she gently hands it over. "The blond-haired woman is my mother."

The girl looks at the two women in the photo, and once again thinks that the other woman looks just like her mother, only this woman's hair is different. But she knows that she can't be because the picture is way too old. *But why does she?* It's a question that the girl swears she'll find the answer to. She decides that stealing the photo that's now in her pocket is one of her best ideas yet.

41

bby and Ally

BOTH TWINS SHAKE their head to Tina's question.

Tina holds both her hands out in front of her and wiggles her fingers as though she's tickling the air before speaking in a spooky tone. "It's a game that tells you how you're going to die."

"I don't want to play," Abby says, taking a quick step back.

"I'll play," says Ally. "What do I have to do?"

"You have to do everything I say in order for it to work. Okay?" Ally nods.

"Good. Come with me." She takes Ally by the hand and drags her to a door underneath the stairs, then says, "It works better if it's completely dark, so we both have to go into the closet. Abby, you want to come in with us?"

At first, Abby shakes her head, then Tina clucks like a chicken. Abby frowns and huffs.

"I tell you what, we'll take a flashlight with us. Will that make you feel better?" Tina asks.

Abby nods.

"Okay. Let's do it."

Abby returns from the kitchen with a small flashlight, and the three girls step into the long, narrow closet underneath the stairs before Tina closes the door. Abby switches on the light and shines it on the ceiling. The flashlight's battery must be weak, because it casts very little light beyond the point it's being directed at, making the walls and corners feel as if they're closing in.

Tina moves around behind Ally and places her hands on her shoulder. "Okay, Ally, you stand with your back to me, and Abby, shine the light on me."

They do as they're told.

"Now, what I have to do is perform a ritual where I will say a chant, and as I say a set of rhymes, I will focus on parts of your body. When we get to the end, you'll find out how you're going to die. You ready?"

Ally nods, while Abby moves the flashlight from Tina's face to Ally's, then back to Tina.

"Here's how it goes. I'll say one verse over and over in between different verses. Close your eyes and keep them closed—no matter what, don't open them."

Ally nods again.

Tina forms two fists and begins to gently pound on Ally's back as she says,

Concentrate. Concentrate
Concentrate on what I'm saying.
People are dying. Children are crying.
Concentrate. Concentrate
Concentrate on what I'm saying.

As Tina says the words, she continues to lightly thump her fists into Ally's back over and over. Next, she moves her hands to the top of Ally's head and taps with her fists, then opens her palms before running both hands down the sides of her head. As she says the next verse, she alternates between the two movements.

Crack an egg on your head.
Let the yolk run down. Let the yolk run down.
Crack an egg on your head
Let the yolk run down. Let the yolk run down.

Tina moves her fist down to Ally's back and repeats the first verse again, then places her hands on Ally's shoulder and rubs up and down her arms as she says the next rhyme. With each new verse, she repeats the first.

She turns her fist as if she is gripping a knife and pounds a little more aggressively this time into Ally's mid-back as she says.

Stab a knife in your back.
Let the blood drip down. Let the blood drip down.
Stab a knife in your back
Let the blood drip down. Let the blood drip down.

She says the third verse, and Abby bursts out, "I don't like this game."

"Shh." Tina continues. She again repeats the first verse and finishes the last one by gripping both of Ally's biceps as she whispers in her ear.

You're standing on a building.
You're out on the ledge.
You're feeling very dizzy

and you're close to the edge.
and someone...PUSHES YOU!

Tina pushes Ally, throwing her off balance, and she stumbles forward, catching herself before she falls.

Ally snaps, "Why'd you do that? You scared me!" She fumbles for the doorknob and bursts out of the closet.

"It's supposed to," Tina says, following her out. Abby trails right behind.

"So, when you thought you were falling, what color did you see?" Tina asks.

"Color?" Ally's face twists into a deeper frown.

"Yeah, did you see a color flash behind your eyelids when you thought you were off the ledge?"

"I don't know. I think—maybe green?"

"Are you sure?"

"I think so."

"Okay. Then green means you're going to die by falling from a high place into the grass."

Ally folds her arms. "I don't believe you. How do you know that?"

"That's the way the game goes. If you see green, you'll fall to your death."

"What does it mean if you see white?" Abby asks.

"White means you'll die of old age and go to heaven, but if you see black it means you'll go to hell."

"You said a bad word," Abby says.

Tina ignores her.

"What about red?" Ally asks.

"You'll be stabbed, and yellow means you'll be poisoned."

"I don't believe any of this," Ally says, trying to sound convincing, but something about the whole game only manages to bring back the images from the mirror this morning. The uneasy feeling that's troubled her all day returns, and she no longer wants to play with their guest.

42

2 002

THE GIRL SNEAKS in through the back gate the woman had left
unlocked just for her. She's just finished burying the memory box
with Abby and Ally, but she's not going to tell the woman anything
about it because she'd put the picture she'd taken with the stolen
camera in there. She debated on putting the photo of the two
women she'd stolen too, but she'd decided to keep it. Now that
she's figured out why the other woman in the photograph looks so
much like her mother, she wants to keep that a secret as well—at
least for now.

The girl has now come up with her own plan. She'll eventually
tell the woman, but not yet. She wants to see where her plan will
lead first, and if she doesn't like it, she's making hers a plan B.

This is the first time she's gone to the woman's house in over a
week, but in the meantime, she has carried on with the invisible
act. It's been simple to do since school has just let out for summer

break. Sneaking away from the foster home has been too difficult before now, but tonight, she'd made it happen. Hopefully, she's still up.

A faint light glows in the kitchen window at the gothic house and there's hope that she's still up. The dim light makes the house look even creepier at night, but it doesn't really scare her. She's heard the stories about this house and how no one wanted to even spend a night here, but she doesn't understand why. It isn't that scary.

She used to think that the woman inside the house was scarier than the house itself, but not now. Now that she knows who she really is, she isn't afraid of her at all. She kind of feels sorry for her, and fully understands why the woman is doing what she's doing.

This house isn't the one the woman wants—it's the big house down the street. The one that the spoiled twins live in. The girl believes that she should have the house as well—it would only be right. Maybe she can help the woman get it, and they can live in the big house down the street together—then she wouldn't have to run away. One thing she's not going to do, is tell her sister about any of it. She can go on living in a foster home for all she cares.

The girl taps lightly on the back door, and she hears the woman's distinct walk as she approaches. The door opens to reveal the woman's usual grumpy face, so the girl displays her best smile and sees the woman's face shift to less of a scowl.

"I was about to give up on you," the woman barks, but the girl continues to smile. It must work because the woman steps aside to allows the girl to enter the house. "How is everything going?"

"It's been going just like you hoped. I snuck in the other night and cut up Abby's favorite toy and Ally got the blame for it. Their mother got real upset and punished Ally by making her sew it back together, plus she got grounded."

"Good. What else?"

"Well—" The girl pauses after she drags out the word. "I stayed away for a couple of days because I didn't want anyone to see me at their big party, but this evening I went to see them." The girl tells a little white lie. White lies aren't like big, dark lies. White lies are necessary if you want to survive in this world. "They still think I'm invisible."

The woman nods. "I think it's time we kick it up a notch."

"I have been—big time. I played this game with them called Concentrate. You ever heard of it?" The girl doesn't wait for the woman to answer, but instead goes on to explain how the game works. "After it was over, I don't think Ally likes me very much."

"What about the other one?"

"Oh yeah, Abby and I are much better friends than me and Ally are. I think I can convince her to do almost anything."

"Good. Then she's the one you'll focus on."

The girl pulls a questioning face mixed with some hesitation. "What do you want me to convince her to do?"

The woman purses her lips and stays silent for so long that the girl wonders if she'd heard her question. "Convince her to push Ally down on the stairs—just a few steps. Just enough that the authorities will have to get involved."

The girl almost fell over, and her eyes nearly popped out of their sockets. "So, you want me to convince Abby to kill her sister?"

"No! Lord, no." The woman pulls a shocked face. "Nothing that horrible. The girls are often home by themselves. What you need to do is convince Abby to do something that will cause a minor injury and then convince her to call an ambulance. Once she does, then you'll leave before they arrive and the EMT's will be forced to report the girls being home alone to social services."

"Oh," the girl says. She hates even hearing the words *social services*. In her book, they're not nice people, and the ones who act nice are faking. How is this supposed to ensure the two of them get to move into the big house down the street?

The girl listens, but that woman's plan is going to take way too long. She's worried that her foster mom or that evil social worker with the scrunched-up face will send her to a different foster home before she can make this happen. If she can't make this work, she'll have to go back to her original plan of running away. *Moving into that big house is a much better plan than living life on the run.*

"Do you think you can do it?" the woman asks.

The girl gives the woman a crooked smile. "No problem. I'll make sure Abby does what I say."

If she doesn't, then she'll have to do it herself.

43

bby
2002

WE'RE RACING to climb our favorite tree, each of us determined to make it to the top first. Ally and I have climbed this massive white oak over and over, but never all the way to the highest point. We're not supposed to—Rosemary forbids it. But today it's a dare that we can't back down from. This tree has a perfectly clear path of branches to the crown, and I've decided I'm going to beat my sister once and for all.

Ally is faster, wittier, prettier, and better at almost everything. She got the blond hair and blue eyes, while I got the shit brown hair, and black, soulless eyes. At least that's what our older friend Tina decided to point out one day when we were playing dress-up. I didn't like her cuss word.

Our back gate is locked as always, so we slip through the loose board in the fence that only my sister and I know about. As we get out of sight of the house, we see our target in the distance.

We make it to the tree. It looms above everything around it, proving that it actually is a mighty oak. One of the lower branches of the tree juts out farther than all the other lower branches and droops so low that it almost touches the ground, making the perfect ramp to get a good run and go.

As I'm running, the sounds of birds bounce around me, and the smell of fresh cut grass looms in the air. I take a deep breath and the smell jumps from a pleasant smell to a foul odor, like something dead—it makes me slow slightly in my pace.

Rosemary's stupid plant.

I pick up my pace again to catch the others. The smell doesn't fade; it only seems to get stronger.

I'm the first to reach the crooked limb of the tree and gallop its length like a chimp using both feet and hands. The long branch ascends at a steady angle, and as I reach the trunk of the tree, another thick branch protrudes at an angle just above it. It leads upward, and I quickly climb it too, trying to get even more of a head start. Above my head are more staggered branches, all spaced and placed in a way that it seems as though nature has designed its own version of a ladder.

Ally is right on my heels, and instead of following behind me, she moves counterclockwise around the trunk of the tree, creating her own path. Before I know it, she swings back around the tree and is now higher than me. Anger fills me, and I hear Tina call out from the branch just below me.

"Come on, Abby! You're letting her beat you."

Frustration courses through my veins, giving me a shot of adrenaline, but instead of it driving me to go faster, it causes one of my feet to slip, and I have to catch myself to keep from falling to the ground. This only agitates and slows me down more. I look up, and now Ally is three branches above me. My vision blurs with tears at the thought of Ally beating me at yet another challenge.

They soon turn to angry tears as I stare up at my sister, who's close to reaching the top.

"I can't believe you're going to let her beat you again. Look up there at her smug face," Tina says.

Her words are like that of a little devil sitting on my shoulder, gouging my anger.

"You might as well quit. She's already beaten you."

I look up one last time to see Ally straddling the last branch of the tree, looking down at me, a pompous look across her face.

"I beat you," Ally sings.

I move to another limb on the other side of the tree so that I can't see Ally's face, and rest my bottom on the branch while leaning my back against the trunk. My breath is erratic, as much from defeat as from exertion.

"You're just going to give up?"

I look at my friend and shrug my shoulders.

"Your sister just *keeps* doing mean things to you. When are you going to stop letting her do that?"

"I'm not *letting* her do anything, because she's always better at everything. I can never beat her," I say, rubbing the back of my hand aggressively across my cheek.

Tina's voice shifts to a whisper. "You know, you can fix it so she never beats you at anything ever again."

I look at her as my eyebrows scrunch together. "How?"

She looks up at Ally, then moves around the tree out of her sight. "If she fell, she might break her leg or arm, then she couldn't win at anything."

I look down toward the ground and realize for the first time just how high I am. My stomach jolts from its normal place up to my throat. I press my back and head against the tree trunk and look up instead of down.

"I mean it, Abby. She keeps doing this to you just for spite. You should teach her a lesson."

"I can't do that. What if she gets hurt worse than just breaking her leg? It's a long way down."

"Wait until she climbs back down the tree a little, then do it."

"Then she'll tell on me, and I'll get grounded for life."

"I'll say it was an accident," Tina says.

"No one can see you—remember?"

"I promise if you do this, she'll never beat you again at anything. In fact, I bet she will be afraid of you from now on."

"I'm not doing it," I snap, and cross my arms over my chest as I turn my head away from her.

"Okay, okay. It was just an idea. I'm only trying to help."

Ally climbs down from the top of the tree, then around to my side and sits on a branch above us. "What are you two talking about?"

"Nothing." I spit the word out quickly.

"I was trying to calm her down," says Tina. "She got mad because you won, and she was thinking about pushing you out of the tree. You don't have to worry though—I talked her out of it."

"What? I didn't say that!" I snap even louder.

"You did!"

Ally frowns and climbs down to a limb perpendicular to my own and stops. She leans over to look down at the ground. "That would kill me, Abby."

"I told you I didn't say that." I stand up and turn my body around to where my chest is facing the tree and hug the trunk with one arm. As I'm trying to shift my other foot around, it slips and I quickly move to grasp the tree with my other hand, but my palm slides down the bark. I cry out as it tears the flesh on my wrist, and I scramble to keep from falling. My heart pounds in my ears and the rotting flesh smell suddenly returns. It's so strong I can taste it. It almost makes me gag. I grip the tree and hold my breath.

Then the world around me blurs like I'm in a bad dream.

Ally reaches out to grab me as though she's trying to keep me from falling, and then I see Tina's hands move at the same time.

Only they don't move to save me, but instead make hard contact with Ally's chest, pushing her backward. My eyes dart to Ally's face, and all I can see is horror as she falls backwards, her arms flailing in circles, trying to grasp at whatever she can.

I hold on to the tree with one injured hand and reach for Ally with the other as I watch her fall in slow motion, yet so fast that I can't make heads or tails out of what's happening. I hear the deep thud of her body hit the ground and I stare downwards, motionless and in utter disbelief.

Her body lay there, unmoving, and the image, one leg twisted as though she's performing a contortionist act, burns into my mind. Even from up here I can see her eyes are open, unblinking, and staring back at me.

"What did you do?" Tina whispers.

I look from my sister to her and try to speak, but my words won't form.

"What did you do?" she asks me again, and I still can't say anything. "You killed your sister."

V

"A lie that is half-truth is the darkest of all lies."
--Alfred Lord Tennyson

44

 bby

"I don't want to be here." I say as I turn and stomp back the direction we just came.

Jared gently grabs my arm as he hurries to stand in front of me. "Abby, wait. It's okay." He rubs the palm of his hand down the side of my head, stroking my hair. "This is a good thing. You've been holding this in for too long." He brushes the tips of his fingers down my cheek and then rests his hand on my shoulder.

I look down at the ground as my heart thumps against my chest and a slight ringing fills my ears. It becomes louder the more I focus on it—warning sirens that I'm going to faint. Jared must sense it because he wraps his arms around me and guides me to a grassy embankment, then eases me to sitting.

"Just take a breath."

I clench my eyes shut while my teeth do the same, which only intensifies the ringing.

"Abby, look at me."

I shake my head *no,* keeping my eyes scrunched together like a child who believes that keeping them closed will make them invisible.

"Just breath with me. Breathe in slowly, breath out slowly. Breathe in, breath out. Breathe in, breath out. There you go."

I take slow, deep breaths to the rhythm of Jared's voice, and the ringing starts to fade. I slowly unclench my jaw, then the dizziness calms as well. Jared rubs his hand in a circular pattern across my back and I attempt to speak but fail at the first try. I swallow and try again.

"I don't know what is real and what is not real. All these years I was convinced that I'm the one who killed my sister, but I swear, though—I didn't push Ally. I remember Tina telling me that I should, but everything—my memory—is so fuzzy."

He squeezes my shoulders. "I know this is painful for you, but if you can make yourself sit here with this for a while, maybe more will come back to you. Maybe you can remember everything."

I don't want to remember everything. I close my eyes again as my heart flutters with the threat of running another marathon, and I breathe it back to normal. I debate Jared's advice of sitting here with my memories. I want to remember, yet I don't want to remember. It's like the anticipation of a storm. You see the lightening and brace yourself for the clap of thunder. You know it's going to boom, yet it still scares you when it comes. I fear that when I allow it to come, the impact will send me over the edge, maybe even send me to the same place my mother ended up. Where will that leave Ava?

"Abby, I know you're scared, but they're just memories, that's all. They can't hurt you. Even if you keep shoving them down, they'll find their way to the surface anyway, and most likely at the wrong time. I'm right here beside you." Jared wraps an arm around me tighter and scoots in close.

I breathe, then breathe some more. Jared's right. The past is crippling me in the present. It's taking me away from my life—from Ava. What if I let them in and I find out that I had nothing to do with my sister's death? But what if they do? The war of *did I* or *didn't I,* is in a battle with one another.

Stop it! My mind screams and I stand and walk toward the tree, glaring at it as though it were the enemy. I'm not really looking at it—I'm looking back. I slowly begin to speak, my words coming in short, choppy phrases, and Jared comes to stand beside me.

"We were racing...to the tree...all three of us. I'm sure Tina was there—I know she was. I was in front and I smelled this awful smell." I continue to talk as I stare straight out in front of me, as vivid details emerge. I can hear girls giggling and taunting—all three of us.

I'm going to beat you. Hurry! Faster! Run!

You're letting her beat you, Abby. Run faster.

I recount every moment—the conversation between Tina and me and how I refused to push Ally. "I told her no. Ally wanted to know what we were talking about, and Tina told her that I was the one who wanted to push her out of the tree. She did that often to me and my sister. She was constantly playing us against one another."

"This child sounds like a spawn of the devil," Jared says.

I huff slightly. "I think she was." After I recount every detail, all the way up to the push, and my sister's fall, I stare at the ground where her body lay back then, and I squeeze my eyes shut. All I can do is shake my head when I attempt to tell what happened next. I've never spoken of it to anyone, ever. I'm not sure I can now.

45

uby

THE CHIPPED, pink nail on my left hand irritates me, pulling my focus towards it, though I'm wee aware it isn't the true source of my frustration. My bottom is seated in the carved-out hole of the chair that wasn't made by me, although I suppose over the last two decades, I've made a huge contribution, like many women before.

I don't know where this feeling of doom is coming from, but the overwhelming dread that bad things are coming has been a fixation of my mind for the past few days.

Rosemary always described her gift as going blind for a moment, then an image of some sort would appear—sometimes the dead. They'd reveal to her when something bad was going to happen. My abilities have always paled in comparison, and my mind would manifest things as an uneasy feeling, a burst of excitement, or an intense dread, ending with a stabbing pain to my chest. I suppose most people get feelings like this, but I'm just more in tune with it. Tonight, it's an overwhelming dread—but of what, I don't know. It's like wearing a blindfold and only being able to see around the edges, and even then, not being able to make out what's around me. My so-called gift or curse is a bit like getting the scent but never a taste.

I use the broken nail to distract my thoughts as I hobble upstairs to find my manicure kit. Climbing the stairs has become more of a task these days, and I'm afraid I'm going to have to spend some money and hire someone to rearrange some rooms in the house. I don't think I can put off moving my bedroom down-stairs much longer.

I plop down on the bed and open the nightstand drawer. The four-poster bed is much like the chair downstairs, and I'm sure the stories it could tell would create a bestseller. The mattress has been replaced over the years, but the old bed has tucked away generations of women. I don't think I want to move myself down-stairs and leave it behind. It wouldn't feel right, and something about sleeping in it gives me the feeling of having my mother nearby. A mother I'd neglected, and I now carry the regret that goes with it. I'm the one who made this proverbial bed that I now have to lie in.

I'd always felt that Maria loved Rosemary more than me, but now that I'm older, I realize that it isn't true—I didn't make myself easy to love. In fact, I'm still not. I've spent most of my life living in a shadow that I only *thought* existed. The shadow of blond verses brown, gift or no gift, cursed or not cursed, or good versus evil. I'd allowed myself to believe in all that stuff, just as someone might be persuaded to join a cult.

I listened to too many far-fetched stories told by my grand-mother and my mother. I took them as gospel—real. Stories or not, I'm the one who caused my own lacking existence in this world by the choices that I made. Maria believed that my Aunt Sylvia had it all, and my mother only got the crumbs. But most of the recount was from my mother's recollection. I sometimes wonder what Aunt Sylvia would say. How would she tell the story? There is after all, two sides to every story.

In their case, the story had a slightly different twist. My mother had blond hair, but my aunt Sylvia was also born with blond hair. As she got older, Sylvia's hair and eyes shifted to brown. Despite Sylvia having brown hair and brown eyes, it was said that she still carried the gift or curse just as prominently—which means that she and my mother both had it, but I only heard my mother's version of their story. I'm sure Sylvia's version would paint a very contradictory picture. It all depends on which lens you look through, or when it comes to the women of my family, who you ask. Just like a book, a lens can also be subjective.

The choices that I've made throughout my life now seem like those of someone else. Why is it that only with the accumulation of age does someone gain wisdom and the willingness to see your own faults? I believed that Rosemary had it all, and in many ways, she did. Now, I'm the one who has everything and she's spending her days in a hospital for the mentally ill.

I suppose when I was younger, this is how I wanted it. But now, I don't. My only companion is my never-ending thoughts. Thoughts that often stay on an endless loop to nowhere. It's not the sort of companion I pictured myself with when I was younger. In fact, the only person I ever wanted was Mike. Or so I'd thought, until I had him and realized that he wasn't as amazing as my mind told me he would be. But then again, who is? People often roleplay in a fantasy story starring themselves along with the one they think they can't live without, only to find out that the real world with them is nothing like they imagined.

I sink lower onto the bed and even lower into my thoughts—or memories. This seems to be a nightly occurrence. They insist on showing me re-runs whether I want to see them or not. The one that decides to revisit me tonight is the day I found out that Mike wasn't who I thought he was after all.

"Where have you been?" I ask as soon as Mike enters the front door.

Mike pauses in a half-crouched position as he puts down his travel bag. Once he sees the look on my face, his expression shifts from neutral to that of a teenager caught in a lie. A liar can't fool a liar.

"Your boss called for you. He wasn't aware that you had to travel to meet with a client. In fact, he said that he froze all funds for travel. So, where the hell were you?"

I don't really have to ask the question, because I already know. He was with Rosemary. I know because this dreaded feeling started before he even left. The feeling had become increasingly intense over the next twenty-four hours, so I called my high school friend, Judy, and had her drive by Rosemary's house. Our childhood house.

Judy had confirmed what the pain in my chest was already trying to tell me.

Mike's shoulders slump and he drops his head. "We need to talk, Ruby."

Mike ended up confessing that he had gone to see Rosemary. He said it was for closure—for himself and for her. He felt that he owed her that much. I asked him if he'd slept with her, and he swore on his life that his visit was completely innocent. I tried to believe him—I even told myself that he wouldn't do that to me.

He's too good of a guy.

We were happy for a while, then five years later, I received a phone call from Judy saying that she'd bumped into Rosemary at the supermarket and that she'd met her beautiful, twin daughters. I guess she assumed that I knew about them, but she had no idea I hadn't spoken to Rosemary since the day she found me and Mike together.

I did simple math and knew right away the twins belonged to Mike. I was mortified and pissed off, yet not at all surprised. I knew the day would come when Rosemary would get her revenge. Maria always said *what goes around, comes around.* She was right.

What I could never figure out was why Rosemary never let it be known who the father was. Why she never used it against me or never rubbed it in my face.

I left Mike shortly after I got the news about the twins, but I never told him why. My reasoning was that I just wasn't happy anymore. He eventually moved on, and I never told him about Rosemary. I'm not sure he ever found out that he was a father. At least not then. I heard that he remarried and had a son. I didn't keep it a secret for Rosemary's sake. I just didn't think he deserved to know.

When I moved back to Meadowbrook, I had one goal—to get my mother's house back. After all, Rosemary had everything—children, most of our family's money, and the house.

I at least deserved the house.

Rosemary

WE'RE all born with the ability to be bad, but it attaches itself to some more than others. According to my mother, the women of our family, or the sisters, rather, are all born with their own curse in one form or another—gifted, crazy, sane, lucky, unlucky, good, or bad. She told me this long before she'd lost her mind, when she was comparing her relationship with her sister Sylvia to my relationship with Ruby. I'm pretty sure she was trying to help me understand why Ruby and I fought so much.

She also said that curses aren't always bad, but it depends on the person who feels they are cursed. A curse can be someone who has everything going for them—looks, brains, money, but doesn't want it. They might be the loneliest, most miserable people on the planet. But to the person outside looking in, they see not having what that person has as their curse.

I was born with the curse of voices inside my head—Ruby

wasn't. She was always jealous that I had that, and all of the things that came along with it. She saw *herself* as being cursed for not having those things. With all of that, we could never see eye-to-eye. I didn't quite understand any of it until I had Abby and Ally. Then I saw their differences and started to see those same actions in them. It only made me want to suppress myself in every way even more.

What I know now is that you can never run from your true self.

I lie in bed with my thoughts as sleep seems to evade me. When you've gone as long as I have without speaking, your thoughts often talk way too much, and right now mine won't shut up. Rotating on a loop are the three occurrences that have kept me on edge for days. My sessions with Dr. Black, my visit from my estranged daughter, and the resurrection of Ally. My mother would say each of these incidents form a perfect triangle—the ultimate symbol of completeness and each point of the triangle represents the past, present, and future. Some people may see the triangle as a humble symbol, but in this case, each meeting point connects in a disturbing fashion. I can't predict yet what is coming, but a storm is on the horizon, and it's going to be colossal.

Sleep finally finds me sometime during the night, but I'm woken by a faint whisper. It's so soft at first that I don't open my eyes, then it comes again.

Rose.

My heart kicks into high gear as the word registers in my ears and my eyes pop open. I can only see her outline, but there's no mistaking who is standing over me.

Dr. Black.

At first, confusion paralyzes me, then panic takes over as she presses a pillow down over my face with such pressure that I'm not able to take in air through my nose or mouth. She smashes my head into the mattress with such force I can't turn it in either direction.

"You chose to live here so now you're going to die here." Dr. Black's words are muffled, but clear.

Adrenaline gives me strength, but it's no match to hers. I grasp for her hands at first, then my instinct is to find and claw at her face. I flail my arms and hands at the air above me, but never make contact. I begin to kick and twist my body from side to side. She only presses down harder, straddles me, then presses one knee into my chest.

"Your mother attempted to do this to her own sister, didn't she? She told you that before she ended up in here herself. Your family is nothing but a twisted bunch of psychos. This is where all of you belong, and I'll make sure each and every one of you ends up in here."

A numbing sensation begins in my lips and face, and then it travels down my limbs and body as they realize they're being deprived of oxygen. My movements slow, and the fight in me depletes to almost nothing. Sounds around me fade, yet a ringing screams in my ears.

It's the last thing I hear.

It's pitch-black and quiet—there's no more ringing, only silence. My eyes pop open again, but this time I'm alone. No pillow, no Dr. Black. It was all a horrible dream. Instinct wants me to sit up, but the dream has left me drained of energy, and I lay perfectly still. The only thing energized is my heart and my chest rising and falling as though I've run a marathon.

I've got to get out of here. With a toss of the covers, I throw on my robe and slide my feet into my slippers, then ease my door open to peek into the hall. The dimly lit halls of the hospital make a rectangular enclosure of the patients' rooms, with my room being close to an adjacent hallway. Ewelina's room is on the opposite side of the building, but I can sneak down the corridor to my right and avoid passing the orderly's station.

I step quietly down the halls, then inside her room and close the door. A familiar smell hangs in the air, and it makes me stop in my tracks. The perfume Maria used to wear. I move my eyes around the room as though I might find my mother standing there, frozen in place.

I shake it off and tiptoe across the room before gently shaking Ewelina as I whisper her name.

She mumbles something in Polish.

"Nie wywołuj wilka z lasu."

"Ewelina."

As her eyes remain closed, this time she says something in English, and her voice is gruff. "Don't call the wolf from the forest, Rosemary."

"What?" I frown again, mostly in confusion.

Ewelina opens her eyes, not at all surprised that I'm standing over her. "You all say *don't poke the bear*; we say *don't call the wolf from the forest*. Waking me from a dead sleep is poking a bear."

I stand and huff and continue to stare down at her.

"Whatever you're planning could be dangerous, Rosemary, and I'm not just meaning getting out of this damn hospital." Ewelina kicks back the covers and flicks on the lamp next to her bed.

Compared to my room, hers is bare and definitely feels like a hospital room. The walls are a dingy white with nothing hanging, and her bed is covered in hospital-issued bedding. The only distinguishing feature from the rest of this place is the smell. I catch myself looking around the room again in search of the source. I have to shake it off once more. If I had to stay in here for very long, I really would go crazy.

I back away from Ewelina's bed as she stiffly sits up and eases her feet to the floor. She groans just as someone our age would, especially as she starts to stand, then she slides her own feet into a pair of fuzzy slippers. She snatches her faded cardigan from the foot of her bed, which appears to be as worn-out and old as she is, then sits back down and motions for me to sit beside her.

"Alright, Rosemary, since you insist on robbing me of my beauty sleep, let's see if we can figure out how to get you to your daughter."

Ewelina looks furthest from a person who benefits from a beauty sleep. Her eyes have bags under them that appear to be packed for three days' worth of travel and are colored with dark rings. Her lips droop downward into a permanent frown, even when she laughs or smiles, which isn't often.

"Maria told me you'd be coming to see me. You're nothing like your mother—she never shuts up."

I smile at the idea and picture a scene in the old movie, Ghost, where Sam Wheat chants, *I am Henry the eighth, I am* until Oda May Brown gives him what he wants. My mother could be very convincing when she wanted something.

"Your daughter came to see you because she needs you, but I think you already know that. I've told you, Rosemary, we're the same, you and me." Ewelina waves her index finger back and forth between us as she says the words, then she points to me. "It's time to stop denying your gifts. You think that if you listen to them, then you'll lose your mind, just as your mother did.

Ewelina's words are blunt, and they irritate me. I snap, "I am. Why do you think I'm here?"

"You think you're ready, but you aren't, not completely. You're scared and you're still keeping most of your gift shut out."

I stare at her, aggravated by her words, but only because I know she's right.

"I'm not going to help you get out of here until you fix yourself. Stop denying your gifts and start using them. If you don't, it might be too late to help your daughter. Screw what you think about a family curse or whether you will lose your mind if you use your gifts. Hell, what's the worst that can happen? You end up living here?" Ewelina cackles at herself.

I take a deep breath and huff, then chew on the inside of my jaw.

"It's time to get your head out of your ass."

I tilt my head at her, then roll my eyes. She's right. I feared what my gift was trying to tell me when my daughters were just babies, and I am fearing what it is trying to show me now.

"My dead daughter comes to see me. She says I need to get out of here."

"You do, but you also need to know what's coming before you step out those doors. Be patient. Open your mind again, completely, Rosemary, and then we'll get you out of here."

I stare down at the floor, knowing what I need to do. I have to open myself back up and be ready to step back out into the world.

"Now, get out of my room—I need my beauty rest."

47

uby

Dreams are like messages in a bottle, and the mind often sends them under distress as a call for help, or a warning.

I sit up in bed as another dream and a cold sweat invades my sleep—more like another nightmare. In the last week they've come nightly, sometimes several times at once. For years I was able to suppress them—tune them out or forget them the moment I wake up. Lately, there's no stopping them or ignoring them.

I fooled myself for years into believing that stepping up and raising an orphaned niece would redeem me of the sins of the past. By doing a good deed such as that, I would make up for all the bad decisions I've made—for the bad that I've done.

I flop back down on my pillow, determined to shut down my thoughts and go back to sleep, but my mind decides to pick up where it left off. It takes me right back to the past—plummeting me knee-deep in memories that have put themselves on repeat tonight. My mind often takes me on a path of its own. A path that's broken and full of jagged rocks that were laid there by me.

Most people wear their past like a suit of armor, but mine only weighs me down with guilt and regret and all I want to do is forget them. I think my mind has decided to wear the sins of my past like a blanket instead—not the comforting kind, the weighted kind. The kind that won't let me get too comfortable, and the memory that covers me the most, is a secret I've carried alone for so long. I can't get it off my chest by confessing to a priest or a therapist for fear I'll end up where Rosemary is, or worse.

The weather outside matches the mood inside as the rain peppers the bedroom window, streaking down the glass like tears. My own tears do the same. Tears of regret, sadness, and loneliness. Over the years I've allowed my heart to turn to stone, and now it feels as though it has the weight of one.

I throw back the covers, climb from bed, and unsteadily pace the floor in the dark. The feeling that something bad is about to happen hits me in the chest and intensifies quickly to a level I've never experienced before. It forces me to pause, just as a noise downstairs freezes my breath mid-inhale. The only thing moving is the thump in my chest.

The noise was quick and gone as soon as it happened. I stand quiet and frozen for what seems like minutes, then I hear a faint creaking of a door, only this time I'm certain it's in the house near the stairs. I grip a tall, slender candle holder from the bedside table and begin to tiptoe from my room and toward the stairs. A creaky board announces one of my steps, and I freeze again.

"Aunt Ruby?" comes a childish whisper.

Relief mixed with immediate concern floods over me as I lower the candle holder and limp toward the stairs. "Ava? What are you doing here?"

Ava stands at the foot of the stairs, still in her pink, princess nightgown, clutching her teddy bear, Sarah, in the crook of her arm. "My legs started hurting."

I hurry down the stairs as I lean on the railing for support. "What? Does your mother know you're here? How did you get in here?"

"You left your door unlocked."

I frown as I make it to the bottom, across the foyer, and to the front door. She's right, it isn't locked. I quickly lock it and move back to the foot of the stairs to Ava. "Where's your mother?"

Ava timidly shakes her head. "Mommy's still asleep and Daddy wasn't on the couch."

"Daddy? What's Daddy doing on the couch?"

"Having a sleepover."

I give her a quizzical frown.

Ava catches it because she pops out the words. "Mommy was okay with it."

"Okay. But what are you doing here at this hour? Mommy will be highly upset at you for sneaking out of the house."

"My legs started hurting again, then Ally told me I had to come."

"Ally did? And what's wrong with your legs?" As I ask the question, the panic that hit me in the chest a few minutes ago hits me again.

Ava begins to ramble, and I struggle to make sense of anything she's saying.

"Ally's my friend, and before my secret friends come to see me, my legs always hurt. I have two friends and both of their names are Ally, only spelled differently. Mia can see them."

"Who's Mia?"

"My real friend that I made at school the other day. She knows my two friends named Ally, too. Rosemary has a picture of one of them."

I suddenly feel the need to turn on another light, so I flick a switch. "We need to call your mother. If she wakes up to find you gone, she's going to flip out."

"But I have to find something first, Aunt Ruby. Ally said I *have* to find it—now. She said it's very important."

I ignore her plea and attempt to guide her to the living room. "How do you know Rosemary?"

"Daddy took me to meet her." Ava swings her body to the side away from my hand and raises her voice. "I have to get something out of the closet under the stairs. Ally said I have to do it now."

She swings the closet door the rest of the way open and yanks on the long string. The dark space lights up in the center, then Ava disappears into the far dark corner out of sight. I hobble to stand in the closet doorway and watch questioningly as Ava crawls around on the closet floor, feeling the individual planks of the floorboards. She repeatedly sticks her tiny fingers into different cracks.

"Ava, what are you looking for?"

"Ally said she left a letter in here for Mommy."

I feel my face flush with both fear and frustration. I know deep down this is part of the panic I've been feeling for the last few days. The skeletons in my closet that I thought had rotted, decayed, and were laid to rest forever, are about to emerge. The pain in my chest puts itself on repeat, hitting hard and fast, then disappears, only to come back again with more intensity each time. It's hitting in a pattern that says, *something is coming. Something is coming. Something is coming.*

"She said she wants Mommy to remember that girl named Tina."

The name that comes from my great-niece's lips sends a shiver of fear down my spine.

A name that I've tried to forget.

"I KNOW THIS IS DIFFICULT, Abby, but keep going. See if you can remember what happened once you came down from the tree. Please. Just try," Jared says.

I don't look at him, I just swallow and nod. I stare at the tree and, as though someone has switched on a silent film, a buried memory begins to play out in my mind. One where I'm standing over my sister's broken body. For the longest time after Ally's death, this same scene played on a repetitive loop. I've always stopped the memory from progressing all the way to the end. Today, my mind takes on its own agenda and continues anyway.

My seven-year-old body slumps to the ground in abandonment over my sister, and I kneel next to her, shake her, and scream her name.

"Ally! Ally! Please wake up. Please wake up."

I shake her harder as tears begin to sting my eyes, then I grab both of her hands as I stand and attempt to lift her to standing.

"Ally, come on. Get up! Stop pretending. Get up!"

One of Ally's hands slips from my grip, and her body falls back onto the ground like a broken doll. Tears shift from blurring my vision to sliding down my cheeks. Sobs make it hard for me to speak as I drop to my knees a second time and I wail, squeezing handfuls of Ally's shirt.

The images of me and my sister fade, and in the peripheral vision of my mind, another memory comes into view. The memory seems to come to life as my head turns to the right, as though I'm watching it play out for real. I don't want to, but it insists on showing itself to me anyway.

"She's over here!" I wail as I hold Rosemary's hand and drag her toward the giant oak tree. My sister's lifeless body comes into view, and Rosemary releases my hand and races ahead. She falls to her knees beside my sister, then slides her hands underneath Ally's already stiffening body before scooping her up into her arms as she cries out.

"No! No! No! Nooooo!" Sobs and words collide, making her words distort, but even so, her words are unmistakable. "What happened?"

"I don't know—it happened so fast. But I think Tina pushed her!" I cry out, my own words sounding far away as though I'm in some horrible dream.

Rosemary rocks my sister back and forth, and as she sobs, I too collapse to my knees next to her. She turns to look at me, her cheeks wet with tears and croaks, "Abby, how did this happen?"

My throat tightens as I try to tell Rosemary word for word what happened, but my sentences come out choppy and hard to understand. "We climbed the tree. Tina told me to push Ally because I was mad. I told her no. Tina pushed her—made her fall." I point up toward the branch.

"Oh no, Abby—you didn't. Why? Please tell me you didn't?" Rosemary screamed.

I'm jolted from the memory by Jared's arms wrapping around

me. I hadn't realized I was crying, and my cheeks are wet. Sobs consume me just as they did back then.

"I'm so sorry you had to go through that alone, Abby. No one should ever have to carry something like this by themselves. I don't know how you've done it."

My throat swells, making it hard to breathe as I cry convulsively, and Jared squeezes me tighter. It feels as though this is the first time I've truly cried over my sister's death since that day. I'm not sure how long I stand in Jared's arms and bawl, but I wouldn't want to break down like this in anyone else's presence. When I'm finally able to catch my breath and calm my crying, I step back, prompting Jared to release me.

"You okay?"

I wipe my face with both hands and shake my head as I take another step back, but turn my body so that I'm no longer looking at the tree. I clear my throat before I attempt to speak and force my voice to sound normal. "I'm okay. I guess that's been building for years," I say, faking as much enthusiasm as I can, yet avoiding looking into Jared's eyes.

"Where did Tina go after it happened?"

"I don't know. By the time I truly realized my sister was dead, she was gone. I never saw her again after that."

"That's why your mother and your aunt believed you pushed your sister out of the tree?" Jared says the words as more of a revelation than a question.

I try to steady my voice. "I think my mother wanted to believe it was purely an accident, but she was convinced there was more to it because she thought I'd made up the story about a friend—a friend that she had never seen. My mother never really talked to me about it—she never talked to me much at all after that day. As the years went by, my aunt felt that it was up to her to teach me how to control my anger, or any feelings for that matter, and was convinced that I had let my anger get the better of me. Since I never saw Tina again, I began to believe it myself."

"Now I understand why your mother is where she is. If she believed that one of her children killed the other, accidental or otherwise, no wonder she stopped speaking. No wonder you—" Jared pauses, and with the tips of his fingers, gently brushes my cheek, catching a stray tear. He doesn't finish his last sentence. "We should go to Rosemary and show her the picture. She should know what you found."

"I did when I went to see her."

"What did she say?"

"She didn't say much of anything. I'm not sure she believed me. I got the feeling that she didn't want to talk about it."

"Where did you come up with the photo?"

"I found it in our...um...the basement downstairs. It was wedged in between two bricks. So, I'm not sure how long it's been in the house, or if it was put there before my aunt moved in, during, or after."

"Was the photo you showed me the only one you found?"

I nod.

"I think this girl is back, and for a reason. We need to find out why. If she did what you say she did as a child, who knows what she's capable of now that she's an adult?"

49

I CATCH Abby's mistake of first referring to the basement as *ours* before she corrects herself. Something about it gives me hope once again that maybe there's still a chance for us. My face threatens to react, but I quickly shift it back to neutral, as if I didn't hear it.

The two of us walk away from the tree back toward the house, and I have to fight the urge to take hold of her hand like I used to. Even though we've been separated for years, it's as if the familiarity has stayed intact. The idea of doing it seems so natural.

I don't know why I can't just tell her how I feel—show her. She's confiding in me like never before, and for the first time in a while, I have hope for us.

We walk along in silence, engrossed in our own thoughts, and to my utter surprise, I feel Abby's hand slide into mine, her fingers interlacing between my own. My response to the shock almost forces me to jerk my head to look at her, but I stop myself for fear that it might make her let go. Instead, I squeeze with a tighter grip as though it might keep it from happening. We continue to walk with our thoughts, hand-in-hand until we reach the back gate, and I reluctantly let go to be the gentleman and open it. The moment is over, but it was bittersweet while it lasted.

We enter the house and head toward the kitchen, and just as Abby's pouring our coffee, the doorbell rings. "Would you like for me to get that?" I ask.

"Yeah, it's probably Megan bringing Ava home."

I'd be lying if I say I'm not a little disappointed that our daughter is returning home so soon. I open the stained-glass door to find Megan and Ava standing there, and the looks on both their faces are quite different.

"Daddy!" Ava squeals as she leaps toward me.

"Mr. B," Megan stutters. "I didn't expect to find you here. Is Abby okay?"

"Yes. Why wouldn't she be?"

"No reason, just surprised," Megan stutters again. "Tell Abby to call me if she needs me."

Megan and Abby are close, but there's something about her words and her facial expression that puzzle me. I get the impression she doesn't trust me, or as though she's afraid I would harm Abby in some way. I catch myself frowning at her, then shift my expression.

For some reason, I feel that I need to ease her mind. "Would you like to come in? Abby just made some coffee."

I ask the question, certain that she'll decline, but I'm surprised when she immediately steps past me as she says, "I'd love to."

I stand with the door open, dumbfounded. I like Megan well enough, but she's a bit of a busybody, and seems to like her share of drama. I'm regretting my invite already.

Ava runs off to the living room to watch her favorite animated show, and the three of us sit around the kitchen table drinking coffee while Megan does most of the talking. During the conversation, I learn that Megan has a live-in girlfriend she calls Kay, who's a neat freak but finds Megan's messy side cute. Seeing as though I'm her boss, it's far more than I need to know about her personal life.

On several occasions, Megan makes the comment that she feels as though she's imposing and should go, then dives into another story about her and her partner. I give Abby a glance, but she has a far-off look in her eyes and isn't responding to Megan as she usually would. I decide to be the bad guy and thank Megan for watching Ava and start dropping hints that I need some time alone with Abby.

"Well, Megan, thank you for watching Ava for us. We were just making plans before you got here about taking Ava out for dinner, but it was good talking to you."

"Abby, I think your ex-husband is kicking me out. Since when do you let him tell you what to do?" She laughs off the comment.

I look straight to Abby because there's something in Megan's tone that strikes me as odd. I get the feeling she isn't joking. She shoots me a look.

"I'm just kidding, boss." She waves her hand at the wrist, then her eyes snap back to Abby, but there's a menace to them. I'm not sure if it's directed at me or Abby. Abby doesn't seem to catch on. Maybe I'm just on edge.

Megan begins to ramble on again, diving into another story about her girlfriend taking her to some Thai restaurant and giving her a promise ring that closely matches her own. She proceeds to say something about matching mood rings and how their moods always seemed to match one another. After a few minutes of it, I find myself tuning her out, but when I've had enough, I drop a less subtle hint this time as I stand and say, "We were just about to leave for dinner. Let me walk you to the door, Megan."

She finally takes the hint. "Well, I guess I'd better be going. The squeeze and I have dinner plans as well. Of course, she knows I'm always late. It's another thing she finds cute about me."

As she stands to leave the kitchen, Abby stands too, and Megan whispers something that's not so quiet into Abby's ear. "You sure you're okay? Do you need for me to rescue you?"

"I promise, I'm fine," Abby whispers back, and I turn away as though I didn't hear. When Abby returns to the kitchen after walking Megan to the door, she says, "Sorry about that. Megan's a talker."

"No kidding." I stand and pour myself another coffee. "I don't think I want you and Ava staying by yourselves tonight. Not until we figure out who came into the house."

"We'll be fine."

"No, I mean it. I think I should stay here tonight. It's either that, or we call the police."

"No!" Abby snaps, then shifts her tone when I cross my arms over my chest, which is a stance I take when I've made up my mind and there's no changing it. "Fine—you can stay on the couch."

The old Abby's back. Earlier, she was holding my hand, but now I'm like the dog that came in wet and lost the privilege of jumping on the furniture. It's like that with Abby—you're given a bone for just a few savoring moments, then she yanks it away, leaving a lingering taste in your mouth of what you can't have.

Losing a daughter was the final wedge driven between us. For two months, life was perfect. We had a home, the twins, and each other—we were truly happy. But apparently, that happiness was only a loan—tragedy took it back. Losing our daughter foreclosed on the rest of our happiness and our marriage. Abby lost part of herself that day, and I don't think she's ever returned, while I lost my daughter and my wife. Now that I have the knowledge of Abby losing a twin sister as well, I fully understand why she is the way she is, and I need to protect her now more than ever.

I'm a lost cause when it comes to Abby.

* * *

Rain pelts down outside, tapping against the tall windows in a constant pattern. I lie on the seven-foot couch, which has a broken spring located right in the center, and no matter which way I turn my body, it invades my lower back or my ass. I've rotated at least three times since lying down and it's not even midnight. The thought of Abby being right upstairs does nothing to assist with my ability to sleep. Instead, my mind revisits the day's events over and over as if my thoughts have been put on a never-ending loop. Rain peppers against the roof, which only competes with my brain's insistent re-runs.

Just as my mind and body begin to succumb to slumber, a noise jolts me back to an alert state. I lie still and listen, unsure if the sound came from inside the house or outside. The faint sound comes again, and it's definitely outside. I sense movement coming from the front porch, and it sounds as though someone is mumbling—a woman's voice. I leap from the couch, and the spring makes a popping sound as I do, and I move straight to the front door. Without hesitation, I swing the door wide, hoping to give whoever is on the other side the element of surprise.

I'm the one who's shocked.

Slumped on the wicker couch looking drenched, is Kris.

I quickly step onto the porch and close the door behind me as my untactful words escape me. "What the hell, Kris?"

She mumbles something, and most of her words are inaudible. The only thing I understand is, "Bastard…played me." She doesn't even look up at me. I'm not sure she even realizes I'm standing here.

I look down between her legs and notice the fifth-sized vodka bottle, which is half-empty. Even if I hadn't seen the bottle, it's obvious she's drunk. I look to the curb to see if I can spot her car, and there isn't one.

"Did you walk here?"

She mumbles something else.

"I should've known you were like all the others. All of you bastards are."

She looks in my general direction, but she's so plastered, her double vision seems to be looking at the second 'me.' She attempts to stand, sways, then lands back on her ass while some of the contents of the bottle sloshes onto the porch. I move to catch her, but I'm too late.

"I knew you were still in love with her. It's so obvious—the way you look at her at work. Why did you lead me on?" Her voice keeps getting louder as she speaks, and I move to the couch to sit next to her.

"Keep your voice down. Ava's asleep."

I don't want her to wake Ava, but I also don't want Abby to find out about me and Kris—not this way. I want to be the one to tell her. Since Abby kissed me the other night, I've decided that I'm going to be honest with Kris about the feelings I still have for Abby and break things off with her—before anyone got too serious. And, to prevent any tension at work.

"You're not afraid of me waking Ava, you're afraid I'll wake *her*." She says the last word louder and whinier. "Your precious Abby."

I wince and look back at the door of the house. I shift my tone and try to approach Kris with more patience. "How did you get here?"

"I walked. You didn't answer my question—why did you make me think you cared about me?"

"Kris, we'll talk about this later. I don't feel now is the time."

"Of course it's not—she's up there." Kris points toward the ceiling of the porch, but it's as though her arm weighs too much, and it flops back down on her lap. She lifts the bottle with the other unsteady hand, and it sways back and forth in front of her mouth, struggling to find her lips.

I grab the bottle from her hand. "I think you've had enough of this. I'll take you home and then we can talk about this tomorrow."

"No—let's talk about it now," she demands with a slurred voice.

"I'm really sorry you're upset, Kris, but I think this would be better to sort out when you're sober. For now, let me take you home, and I promise, I'll call you in the morning." I tap the bottle down on the oval-glass table, wrap one arm around her soaked body and lift her from the couch.

She attempts to fight against me, and in the process, she scoots the table forward with her knee, knocking the bottle over, and the liquid pours onto the porch. Her fight isn't much of a struggle as her movements have been switched to slow-motion, and I drag her to the steps of the porch as I continue to shush her. "You need to go home and go to bed. I promise, we'll talk about this tomorrow."

"Fuck you!"

Already done that, but it's becoming obvious that was a mistake. The thought passes through my mind, but I don't say it aloud. The first time we slept together, I told her it might have been a mistake— that if anyone knew, they might think that I abused my position of authority. She was the one who convinced me that we were two consenting adults just having fun. I try to determine if I'd given her the impression that we were more at some point. Did I miss some cue on her part that it was turning into more for her? It was never my intention if I did.

Rain falls in a steady downpour, and my hair and clothes become soaked as I move her around to the passenger side of my car, open the door and assist her into the seat—maybe a little too aggressively. She continues to try to fight against me, but it does her no good. Before I shut the door, I say, "I'll be right back, just stay in the car."

I can still hear her protesting outside the car, even after I've closed the door, as I run back into the house to get my keys. The house is still silent, and it doesn't appear as though she's woken Abby or Ava. I rush back outside to find that Kris has already opened the door and was attempting to haul herself out of the car. I gently push her back in and close the door again, then race to the driver's side and climb in as well.

"Why did you do this to me, Jared?" Her words are almost inaudible through her drunken sobs. This could be a long night. Reasoning with an intoxicated woman who feels scorned isn't the kind of situation that can be reckoned quickly. Even though it isn't cold outside, Kris's teeth chatter as much as her voice does. I turn on her seat warmer and remain silent on the drive across town while she continues to tell me that I'm a bastard and I should be ashamed for playing her and breaking her heart.

When we reach her house, I assist her out of the car and to the front door. "Where's your key?"

She doesn't answer, just continues to mumble more words that at this point I've tuned out. I turn the knob and the door is unlocked. "You really shouldn't leave your door unlocked."

She glares at me and hiccups. "What do you care?"

I walk her through the tidy house to the couch and plop her down, falling on my bottom next to her as I do so. She slumps into the sofa as her head flops back limply. "Why, Jared? Why?" She whines the words, and I exhale a breath of aggravation and decide that I'll attempt to make her feel at ease before I leave her.

"I'll get you some water, then we'll talk."

50

 osemary

NESTLED into the multi-colored covers of my hospital bed, I dream of the tiny, dark-haired girl who looks up at me with her beautiful brown eyes, and I find myself transfixed on them. Her tiny form and the space all around her is bathed in ethereal light as though she isn't of this world. She smiles at me, then reaches out and takes my hand, turning it over to look at my palm. With her tiny finger she traces the letter that spreads across the inside of my hand, and it tickles.

"My sister has the same letter on her hand." When the sweet sound of her tiny voice reaches my ears, I know immediately who she is. My granddaughter.

"Isn't she beautiful?" The words seem to float on the air, and I look up to find my mother walking toward me. Maria smiles at me just as she used to when I was a little girl. She places her hand on the dark-haired girl's head, stroking her hair and says, "I see you've met your granddaughter, Allie."

I nod and my voice evades me. It's not by choice but by awe. My mother is just as I remember before her mind left her—before she left me.

"It's time, Rosemary," Maria whispers. "It's time for you to go. You've been here long enough—no more hiding."

The sound of her voice is all around me yet intensified inside my mind. Like an echo that bounces from far away—so far that she isn't part of this world, yet she is. She and my granddaughter's images begin to fade like a hologram, and all I'm left to see is a white void with only dark outlines. I lie still and listen with my eyes remaining closed for fear that if I open them, they'll fade away completely.

"Your daughter needs you. You have to go to her." Maria says the words again, only this time with a little more urgency.

"How?" I whisper, but I'm not quite sure if the word actually escapes my lips.

"They will help you."

"They?" I ask, my question filled with confusion.

"Rosemary?"

This time the whispering of my name floats just above me —closer.

"Rosemary." The voice is different—grouchier. I feel my forehead frown and release a gruff exhale. It isn't my mother anymore —it's Ewelina.

I open one eye and see her leaning over me, her face way too close. "Rosemary." This time she barks my name, sharp and fast, and a drop of spittle lands on my face.

I dart my head to the side with an involuntary wince and wipe it from my cheek.

"I'm awake!"

"You were talking to Maria, weren't you?"

"Yes, and you interrupted."

"We don't have time for you to go all fairies and rainbows right now. She told you what to do. Now, get your scrawny ass out of bed."

"She said *they* will help you. What did she mean?"

Ewelina steps aside and says, "Us."

Angie stands at the door, blocking the long, rectangular window. "We have to go now if we're going to do this, ladies. The five o'clock shift will be arriving soon, and shift change is our best chance of not getting caught."

"Don't blame me, blame Sleeping Beauty, here. She's the one dragging her ass."

I give Ewelina my best frown as I throw back the covers and roll my stiff body from bed. Angie smiles at me seemingly amused at the shock on my face.

"I'll explain later, Rosemary. Okay?"

I continue to stare as I wonder how or why Angie would be involved in this, then shake my head in a choppy manner. "Okay."

I take in Ewelina's clothing, which makes her look like a completely different person. She's wearing pale, blue hospital scrubs identical to Angie's. Ewelina shoves a set of scrubs into my hands that are the complete opposite—bright yellow and plastered with animated cats. "Here—you look like a cat lady," she says, then snorts a laugh.

I roll my eyes.

"Rosemary, I want you to put a jacket on over your scrubs as though you're going home after a long shift. Both of you, put these on." Angie hands each of us face masks, which have remained common for most hospital staff since the lockdown days. Once I'm completely dressed, she cracks the door open and peeks into the hall, then ducks back into the room. "You two ready to do this?"

I resort back to my silent days and nod my head.

"Good. The hall is clear for now." Angie hands Ewelina a pack of cigarettes. "You wait here for five minutes, then walk toward the staff's outdoor area like you're going for a smoke. Don't rush, but don't stop and talk to anyone, either. Just behave as though it's something you do all the time. They usually don't pay attention to staff going in and out of that area. I'll go out and around the hospital and come in through the door from the outside, then you'll go out. That way, if someone actually sees a person going into the smoking area, they'll see someone come back in. Like I said, no one pays attention to the smokers, especially this time of day at shift change. Chances are there won't be anyone out there. If there is, avoid eye contact and keep to yourself."

"Just don't ack like yourself and you'll be fine," I say to Ewelina and give her a twisted grin.

Angie laughs. "It's good to hear you speaking, Rosemary. It's a nice sound."

I give her a warm smile, feeling oddly shy at her kind words. "Which way do I go?"

"You're going to wait until 5:00 exactly and walk right out the front door. My friend Jonathan is going to make sure it happens. He'll be waiting for you and will distract the front desk workers. You should have no problem."

"What the hell do we do when we're out of here?" Ewelina asks.

Angie gives Ewelina a smirk. "Ewelina, do you always have a potty mouth?"

Ewelina puffs. "Don't be such a puss, Angie. You need to toughen up if you expect to survive those kids of yours when they become teenagers."

Angie rolls her eyes. "The two of you will head east toward Luna's diner and meet up in there. Wait inside—I have a friend that's going to meet you there and take you where you want to go. Any questions?"

Ewelina and I shake our heads, then Angie cracks the door open, nods, and slips into the hallway.

"You ready, Rosemary?"

I take in a sharp breath and dip my head in an unsure yes, then look at the clock on the wall. For the first time I realize what I'm about to do—step out into a world that I left behind more than twenty years.

The second hand on the clock jumps from one line to the next while its ticking seems much louder than it actually is. Almost deafening. The minute hand snaps to the center of the twelve, and the hour hand tells me it's time to go, prompting my adrenaline to kick into overdrive. I look at Ewelina, and she's smirking at me.

"Okay, okay." I mouth the words but without a sound, then open the door and step into the hall. It's clear. I breathe deep, straighten my posture and perform a nonchalant walk in the direction that will lead me out the front door of the hospital. As I make my way to the elevator and press the down button, I can't decide which is louder, the thumping of my heart in my ears or the pings of the elevator. They both manage to stretch my nerves like a piece of elastic.

The elevator door opens, and inside is a blond-haired girl, pacing and running her fingers over the metallic surface of the wall as she hums the tune of *This old man, he played one.*

I smile and my nerves are immediately calm. *I'm doing the right thing;* I tell myself and step onto the elevator.

Just as the door starts to close, someone yells *wait*, and a hand slaps between the doors. My breath catches, and I can no longer inhale or exhale. A woman steps onto the elevator as if she's in a hurry. I recognize her right away and look down at the floor while I shift my mask up closer to my eyes. She works in a tiny office on my floor where she's always wearing a headset and typing away on a computer. Not sure what her job is exactly, but it never changes. I'd find it smothering day after day.

"Nice scrubs. You must be a cat person."

I nod but don't make eye contact.

"Long shift?"

I nod again.

"Me too. I don't get to go home and sleep just yet. Have to meet with my son's teacher this morning, again. I swear I spend as much time at his elementary school as he does. That mouth of his is always getting him into trouble. It's so bad I saw the principal visiting someone here the other day and I was too embarrassed to let him see me."

She's talking about Jared. I look up quickly and make eye contact, then catch myself and look back down immediately holding my breath.

Shit!

"Which floor do you work on?"

Fear holds my words hostage. I cough and force them to the escape. "First. Brought up some paperwork for a friend who was in a hurry and had to get out of here this morning."

"Yeah, well, I know the feeling."

The door opens on the first floor, a part of the hospital I'm unfamiliar with. The woman rushes off the elevator as she says, "Have a good day."

"You too." I release the rest of my breath as I collapse back against the wall of the elevator. I take a couple of breaths and push myself back to full standing before stepping into the hall.

I look to my left down the long hallway and see the large desk with a security guard seated there. *Jonathan,* I hope. I turn to look back hoping to see Ally standing there, but she's gone.

I hesitate but begin to walk toward him as he looks up from the display of monitors that surround him. *What if he's not the one who's supposed to help me? Or, if he is, then why is he putting his job on the line to do it?* The thought rushes through my mind and I pause, then debate on running back to the elevator. He smiles at me, and I peel my foot from the floor and take another step toward him, then another.

His appearance is slightly disheveled as though he's just finished a long, uneventful shift, where his biggest challenge is staying awake. As I approach the desk, he perks up in his chair, stands, then glances around as though he's just realized who I am. I assume that my scrubs, which look as if the cat fairy threw up all over them, have given me away. I'm relieved, because he speaks first.

"Good evening, I mean, good morning, miss. I bet you're ready to get out of here after a long shift." He says the words just as another woman in scrubs emerges from a closed door marked with a tag that says *staff only*. She stops to speak to the guard, and I turn my face slightly away. I'm sure it's just my nerves, but it feels as if she's staring at me, which makes my heart pound against my chest. I busy myself by fumbling with my jacket and work to zip it up. I'm pleased when she says, "Oh yeah, you reminded me—I left my jacket in the office." She nods and turns back the way she came.

I exhale an exasperated breath and fight to keep from collapsing.

Jonathan smiles, seemingly very calm. "It turns out, I'm finished with my shift too, so I'll walk out with you if that's alright with you."

I nod but can't form the words. Jonathan opens a large drawer toward the bottom of his desk and retrieves an insulated tote, which I assume is his lunchbox. He steps to the end of the long desk, opens a small door, then steps aside for me to walk through. I oblige.

As we're stepping around the front entry desk, Jonathan turns to the woman working behind the tall counter as I continue to walk toward the front door and says, "See you later, Martha. Glad your shift's the one that's just beginning and not mine." He laughs.

She only glances up for a second and says, "Rub it in, Jonathan. Have a good one." She doesn't even look in my direction, and I release a long breath. I've made it.

He opens a large glass door, and we step out into the rain. I immediately and haphazardly lock eyes with the gentleman ascending the steps. Panic hammers my chest. He's the hospital's Chaplain. His eyes squint curiously at me as my own drop to the ground. The Chaplain is one of those people who never forgets a name or a face. For a moment, I feel as though I may faint when Jonathan says something rather loudly. "So, is that husband of yours still chasing those big catfish?"

The question throws me off guard at first, then I realize he's making an attempt at a distraction. I clear my throat and push myself to play along all the while, my insides quiver. "Oh, you know, he tells a good fish tale. *I caught a fish this big.*" I use my shaky hands to demonstrate by placing my palms close together, then spread them wide to emphasize the tale is bigger than the actual fish, and as I'm doing so try to focus on steadying them.

Jonathan lets out a convincing laugh as he opens the next door which leads outside of the hospital.

As we step outside, rain sprinkles the dimly lit steps and side-walk. The scents and sounds suddenly seem more intense than they are in the courtyard of the hospital. Bird's sing, despite the hard rain, but at the moment it feels more like they're screaming. An overwhelming urge to run back through the hospital doors threatens my ability to follow through, so I take a deep breath, close my eyes and think about what I have to do. After a few calming breaths and several urgent steps, I make it to the bottom of the concrete steps.

"Will you be okay from here, miss? I can give you a lift if you like."

"No, I'm fine. I have a friend meeting me on the corner. Thank you, Jonathan." I say the words with as much sincerity as my voice will allow.

He gives me a military-style salute and a warm smile. "Then I think I'll go home, kiss my misses, and get some sleep."

I pull my mask down, smile, and turn east in the direction that Angie suggested. As I'm walking down the sidewalk, I see a group of people dressed in scrubs walking in my direction and I duck my head low. Each of them is staring down at a small rectangular object in their hands, a glow reflecting from their faces. One-by-one, they only glance up at me for a split second, then back down. Not a single one of them actually sees me. *This was easier than I thought.*

I make it to the corner diner, which is the only thing on this street that looks familiar. In fact, what used to be houses are now convenient stores, fast-food restaurants, and something called a Vape Shop. The outside of the old diner has the same retro appearance with shiny metal walls, a multitude of windows, and a massive red neon sign that states it's a diner. The familiar smell of greasy food floats in the air, and it prompts my stomach to growl. I hadn't even thought about breakfast until now, yet a queasy feeling in my stomach tells me it's best to skip food altogether. Besides, I don't have any money.

I step through the glass door, which smacks a bell to alert my entrance, and I move across the black-and-white checkered floor to the farthest booth in the corner. The red vinyl seat makes a crackling sound as I slide into it. A waitress wearing a pale-blue, nostalgic dress with a white apron steps next to my booth and hands me a menu.

"I'm waiting on someone," I say, my words sounding more like that of a timid child. She smiles and assures me she'll check back with me later.

I glance around the diner at the people sporadically seated at the counter and in booths, and every single person is staring down at the item in their hands. Even couples seated together aren't looking or speaking to each other, but gawking downward. Cell phones were a thing when I came to the hospital—small, foldable, and typically hooked on a person's belt. People often had them stuck to their ear, but you rarely saw them staring at them as though in a trance. Now, they appear to be more like miniature televisions with a constant display of entertainment. They seem to capture everyone's attention to the point that people are functioning like robots or zombies. Even the waitress can't seem to walk past a certain spot behind the counter without picking one up to tap quickly on the screen. I'm not sure I've missed out on much of anything since I've been gone.

The door swings open, which sends the bell screaming, and the eyes of the room only look up for a second—some don't look up at all. Ewelina releases the door, causing the bell to jingle again as she spots me slouched in the corner. She plops down across from me. "Look who made it after all. I'd have bet my right eye that you chickened out before you even made it off of our floor."

I give her a disgruntled look. "I'm here, aren't I?"

Ewelina coughs out a loud chuckle. "Hanging out with me has been good for you, Rosemary."

Engrossed in our usual banter, neither one of us notices the figure that approaches our table until she speaks, then we both freeze in a wide-eyed stare.

"Hello, Mom."

51

Ruby

2002

AT FIRST, I assume I'm waking from a dream when I hear a girl talking at the foot of my bed. She's removing clothes from my chest-of-drawers by the handful and tossing them on the mattress at my feet. I come fully awake and realize that she's actually here. The realization of it makes me bolt upright and snap, "What the hell do you think you're doing? How did you get in my house?"

"This isn't going to be your house much longer. We're moving soon. Remember?"

"What are you talking about?" I throw back the covers and wearily spring from bed, irritated and exhausted. Since the funeral and sending Rosemary away to a mental hospital, the last few days have provided very little opportunity for sleep.

"Now that one of the twins is gone and the mother is in the looney bin, that big house is empty, just waiting for us."

"Keep your voice down—you'll wake Abby. She's finally sleeping for once."

"Is she going to live with us, too?" The girl fakes an English accent as if she's trying to be someone else.

I frown. "Why are you talking like that? And what makes you think you're coming to live with me? Nowhere in our deal did I promise anything other than a pair of shoes and some money." I reach out and grab the girl by both forearms and stop her from pulling any more clothes from the drawer.

The girl stops and stares up at me, her dark eyes darker than usual. "I thought since we're family it would change everything."

"Family? What makes you think we're family?"

She reaches into her back pocket, pulls out a wrinkled photograph, and shoves it at me. "Because—if the woman with blonde hair is your mother, then that makes you my cousin."

I yank the picture from her hand. "Where did you get this picture?"

"I found it in your basement and took it with me so that I could compare it to a picture that my sister has of your mother and my grandmother—Sylvia."

For a moment, I try to make sense of what this young girl is saying while my head spins in denial.

"We are tied together by blood, but we're also tied to one another even more now because the of huge favor I did for you."

"Favor? What are you talking about?"

"What you asked me to do. Well, sort of." The girl pulls her arms loose from my grip as she looks up at me with dark eyes. She opens the bottom drawer, grabs another handful of my things and tosses them on the growing pile. "I couldn't convince Abby to push her sister, so I did it for her. I think she was too scared to do it."

The air leaves my lungs. I force in a trembling breath as a shudder courses through my body. I can't believe what I'm hearing. "That's not—" My voice is even shakier than my breathing as the reality of her words sinks in. Horror pounds my chest, or maybe it's my heart, but I instinctively take a step back. "What did you do?"

"I planned for it to happen on the stairs like you said, but I didn't get to do it, so I took the opportunity when we were all in the tree. I know you didn't actually want her to die, but it just sort of worked out that way. Honestly, I think my plan was much better. If we did it your way, we'd have to wait for social services to step in, and that can take forever. Trust me, I know. Look how long I've been waiting for a new home."

I try several times to form audible words, but it takes several seconds. "That isn't what I wanted at all. In fact, the worst I wanted to happen was a sprained wrist or ankle. And if social services stepped in, they would have taken the girls and given them to me. The three of us would move into the big house together. I only wanted to teach my sister a lesson. I didn't want to take her children away from her forever, only for a short while." My voice breaks. "I definitely didn't want anyone to die."

"I really am sorry it worked out this way, but now the three of us can live in the house together—you, Abby, and me." The girl looks at me again, and I see a hollowness to her eyes. I hadn't noticed it before, but they appear as if there's no one behind them.

I continue to stare, aghast, as I fumble for words. "Why in the world would I want anything to do with you after what you've done? In fact, the only thing I need to do now is call the police and tell them what you've just admitted to doing."

The girl stops gathering clothes from the bottom drawer and turns to look at me, her dark eyes wide. "Your blood and my blood are the same. We're tied to one another, and if you try to send me to juvie or back to that foster home, I'll tell the police that you, my cousin, forced me to do it." The girl places both hands on top of one another, places them underneath her chin, and tilts her head to one side while batting her eyelashes. "Who do you think they'll believe? A sweet, innocent child, or you?"

Shock and disbelief have taken my words as I swallow hard and try to figure what to do or say. I sit down on the edge of the bed and plant my face into the palms of my hands. *This is all my fault.* The sentence puts itself on repeat over and over until I hear Abby cry out across the hall, and it brings me to my feet. I look at the girl. "Stay here and don't make a sound."

"But she might as well know I'm here and that we're all going to be living together."

"No!" As the word escapes my lips, I immediately attempt to bring my voice back to a calmer level. I need to convince this girl to stay hidden until I can figure out what to do. "We need to talk about this before we jump into anything. You seem to have forgotten that Abby was there—at the tree that day."

"Yes, but I'm pretty sure I convinced her that she was the one who killed her sister. She was pretty confused after, so I think it worked."

This child is a monster. The thought crosses my mind as I convince my face not to give away what I'm thinking. Despite the fact that my insides are quivering with shock and fear, I attempt to mask my emotions by smoothing out my words and be as convincing as I can. I have to stall enough time for me to figure out how to get rid of this girl from my life—for good.

"There are certain things we're going to have to do first, or you might not get to live with me. There has to be lots of planning to make this all work out. Just wait here and be quiet, and we'll do that when I come back. Understand?"

The girl's face shifts from confidence to contemplation. "I suppose you're right."

"You have to understand that Abby is only seven and is too young to understand any of this. Right now, she is mourning her sister, so just give her some time. I promise we'll make this work."

The girl nods. "Okay, but I can't wait forever. Social services says that me and my sister will be going to a new home soon, and we have to move in together before that happens."

This time I nod. "Good. Come with me." I rush the girl downstairs and around to the closet door underneath the steps. "Hide in here until I calm Abby down, and I'll be right back." I reach in and pull the string on the light, close the door, and quietly slide the lock into place.

I tiptoe back upstairs and into Abby's room to find that she must have been dreaming, because she's sound asleep now. Relieved, I walk as quietly as I can down the hall and back into my room. As I'm stuffing my clothes back into the drawers, I figure out what I need to do to get rid of this girl.

I ease back down the stairs and tap on the closet door. "Give me a few more minutes—she's almost asleep, then I'll come back to get you." I hold my ear to the door and hear her say *okay*, then I tiptoe to the kitchen as best I can and quietly remove the cordless phone from its base before slipping through the back door to make the call.

"*9-1-1. What's your emergency?*"

"I'd like to report an intruder. She's only a child, but I think there's something really wrong with her. She keeps babbling on and on about running away from her foster home and insists that she lives here, but I've never seen this girl before in my life. You really should hurry. I truly think there's something mentally wrong with her. I'm afraid she's going to hurt herself or someone else."

5 2

ared

I TOUCH my hand to my head, which feels as though it's being pounded by a jackhammer. I don't just have a hangover; it feels more like ten hangovers grouped into one. *What happened? Did I get drunk last night?*

I'm in a strange, dimly lit room and my bearings aren't with me. I scan my eyes from corner to corner, stopping to look at pieces of furniture. A dresser is covered with various items—jewelry box, picture frames, and a lamp. The next piece is a matching chest-of-drawers and on top of it are a couple more picture frames. The room is too dark to make out much about them. I don't even attempt to—I'm still trying to figure out how I got here.

I put my evening on rewind and sort through the list of the events leading up to this moment. *I was with Abby, she held my hand,*

I opened the gate for her, we agreed I would spend the night, couch, spring in my back, a noise on the porch...Kris.

"Kris," I say aloud. *I'm still at Kris's?* I bolt up quickly, but don't even make it to full sitting before a sharp pain shoots through my left wrist, and it yanks me back down again. "What the hell?" Secured around my wrist and attached to a bar on the headboard of the bed is a set of handcuffs. I yank hard against them and the only thing I manage to do is hurt my wrist more. The next thing I realize is that I'm completely naked. *What the hell happened last night?*

"Kris!" This time my tone of voice isn't very pleasant as I yank at the handcuffs some more.

Kris appears in the bedroom doorway wearing the long-sleeved t-shirt I was wearing when I brought her home. My eyebrows meet one another in a furious stance as I attempt to speak in a calm manner.

"I'm not really finding any of this funny. Can you let me out of these now?"

She takes a sip of coffee from the blue mug she holds in both hands. "But we had so much fun last night. You sure you don't want to continue?"

I search inside my pounding head but can't recall anything beyond the first hour after bringing her home. I fully intended on going back to Abby's. The last thing I do remember is getting Kris some water and sitting beside her on the sofa while she carried on with her crying, drunken rant about me and Abby. It seemed to drag on forever. I remember the bottle of scotch sitting on the coffee table, and in order to deal with her rambling, I turned it up and took a hefty shot. Beyond that, I feel like a character in a movie where someone might have waved a flashy object in front of me and erased my memory.

"We had some of the best sex of our lives last night. You were the one who insisted I handcuff you to the bed. In fact, you were beyond insistent about it, not to mention the things you asked me to do to you."

I still can't remember, and quite frankly, I don't want to. I want to get back to Abby's house before she wakes up. I can't let her find out this way. I suddenly feel as though someone has dumped a bucket of guilt over me at the thought of sleeping with Kris. I had no intention of ever doing it again. How did I go from wanting to break it off with her to being handcuffed naked to her bed?

"What time is it?"

Kris pulls up the long sleeve of my shirt to look at her watch. "Why does it matter?"

My face involuntarily frowns. "Kris, where's the key? I need to go."

"Why? You afraid your precious Abby will wake up and wonder where you are?"

I try to keep my frustration at bay, but it still comes out in my tone. "I mean it, Kris. Let me out of this."

"I don't think I like your tone."

My frustration grows louder and so does my voice. "I really don't care if you like my tone, because I'm very serious. Give me the key."

"So, you can go back to her? I don't understand you, Jared. You come here, sleep with me, then expect me to just let you walk out this morning and go back to your ex-wife?"

I feel as though she just slapped me. I'm not sure what to think right now. I don't think any amount of alcohol in the whole world would make me jeopardize my chance of getting back with Abby. There's no way I would have done this. What the hell did I drink?

"What kind of man are you?" Kris's face twists into a hateful expression. "I don't think I'm going to let you do it. In fact, I think I'm just going to let you lie there and think about what you're doing to me."

My arm has a knee-jerk reaction as I yank against the handcuffs and say through gritted teeth, "Kris, I suggest you let me go."

"Or what?"

I take a deep breath and attempt to control my tone, but aggravation gets the better of me. "Just what is it you want from me? I thought our little arrangement was perfectly fine the way it was. Why the sudden clingy child act?"

"Clingy child? Is that what you think of me—a clingy child? First, you call me a bitch and now I'm a clingy child. Yet, I'm fuckable. Is that how it is?" Kris picks up a pair of jeans from the bedroom floor and yanks them onto her legs.

"What are you talking about? I don't recall ever calling you a bitch, nor would I. Have you lost your intelligent mind?"

"No, but you have, and I think I'll just leave you here to think about that. Maybe you can lay here and figure out how to be less of a bastard and start treating me the way I deserve."

For a moment I'm speechless as I try to figure out who this woman is and where *fun* Kris went. This is a side of her I didn't know existed. This woman is a far cry from the buttoned-up school councilor or the fun, sexy fling I thought she was—a filler for the woman I actually want.

I continue to watch her, dumbfounded as she strips off my shirt, exposing her braless breasts, and slings it at my head. It lands across my face, and I yank it away with my free hand. When my eyes look back in her direction, she's stomping through the bedroom door as she jerks a yellow t-shirt over her head.

"Kris? Kris!"

She calls back to me, her voice fading with each word. "I'll come back when you've had time to think about what you've done." The next thing I hear is the front door slamming.

My mouth gapes open in disbelief. "What the hell just happened?" I ask the question aloud as if someone might explain it to me, but there's no answer. It's just me—naked and handcuffed to a bed.

53

osemary

I'M NOT sure what kind of face I pull, but I seem to have lost my words, despite finally finding them a few days ago.

She just called Ewelina, Mom.

I blink and stare up at Angie who is looking down at me, smiling. I know I've lived inside my head for over twenty years, but I didn't think I was that out of it.

Ewelina peers at me, her eyes dancing. "Now that we're away from that dreadful place, are you ready to hear our secret?" She slides on into the booth and Angie sits down next to her.

I slump back in my seat and fold my arms across my chest, still unable to speak, so I just nod.

"How long have we known each other, Rosemary?" Ewelina props her elbows on the table between us.

I shrug my shoulders, confused. "A few months, I suppose."

"Did you know that you've never asked me about myself, at all?"

"I've never asked anyone, anything." The sarcasm leaks from my words.

Ewelina huffs. "Well then, let me introduce myself. I'm Ewelina and this is my daughter, Angel."

I look at Angie with a perplexed expression.

"My name is Angelina. When I was a child, Ewelina called me her Angel. It's my husband who calls me Angie—so that's what I go by."

I still can't speak.

Angie continues. "When I first began working at Serenity Oaks, I was drawn to you. In fact, when I walked into the hospital for the first time, I got a tingling sensation that told me I was supposed to be there. The kind of sensation I usually get when I need to pay really close attention to what's going on around me. These weird occurrences have been going on ever since I was a little girl. It took me years to figure out why it was happening, but I've learned they usually occur right before something is revealed to me.

"Have you ever wondered why your mother, Maria, chose me to talk to?" Ewelina asks.

I blink several times, frown, then shake my head.

Angie speaks up. "She hasn't just been communicating with my mother, but she communicates with me too—not like she does with her." Angie directs her hand toward Ewelina. "It's kinda of a long story on how I ended up at this hospital—husband, job, yada, yada. I'll fill you in on that story someday, but what I can tell you is that I was drawn to this town, and then to this hospital, and then to you. The very first time I saw you; it was as if someone spoke to me. Not like, actually speaking to me, but it's like I just knew—you were important to me. I'd been searching for my mother for quite some time, and every time I saw you in those early days, I learned more and more about who you were, or are."

Angie's eyes soften. "I believe it was Maria that was showing me. Granted, I didn't realize that until I brought my mother here and she could actually hear Maria. I believe it was her who led me to find Ewelina. It just came to me one day where to find her, and sure enough, I did. I tracked her down at a hospital in Virginia where she's been since I was a young girl. I knew the moment I walked into the hospital I'd found her, because the same tingling sensation overwhelmed me, just as it did when I first met you."

I stare down at my hands, drowning in confusion. I knead them together, then open my mouth to speak. Angie continues before I can say anything.

"I couldn't tell anyone who Ewelina was when I had her transferred to Serenity Oaks for fear I wouldn't be able to work there anymore. But when I went to see her, she already knew that I'd be coming for her. As soon as she arrived here, Maria started communicating with her right away."

"Yeah, she wouldn't shut up," Ewelina blurts.

My mind spins, and I take a moment to catch my breath. "I still don't understand what all of this has to do with me?"

Ewelina lets out her usual huff. "Pay attention, Rosemary."

I give her a scowl.

"Your mother had a sister."

"Yes." I draw out the word, wondering where she's going.

"Sylvia?"

"Yes." I draw it out again.

Silence stretches between them.

"Sylvia is my mother."

My words escape me again as I stare, dumbfounded. As I look at Ewelina and her words sink in, my face shifts to a stunned expression. "She's your mother?"

Angie speaks next. "Mm-hm. I did more digging into my Ewelina's past right after she and I decided to have her transferred here. I learned that Sylvia married a military man from Poland and lived there for many years. My mother had a twin sister named Adina, who died from the flu when she was only a toddler and years later, after my grandfather died, Sylvia brought Ewelina to the United States."

I stutter. "So, you're my cousin?"

"Pfff, yeah." Ewelina laughs, followed by a snort. "Who would have guessed? You and I related. It wasn't long after Angelina found me, when your mother started talking in my head and hasn't shut up since."

I ponder on everything they've told me as I look at Ewelina and her blond yet graying hair. In this situation, one might have a hundred questions going through their mind, but my first thought was *the family curse*. "Did your sister have dark hair and eyes?"

"I don't remember much about her, but pictures that I saw of her later, yes, she did."

"Did Sylvia tell you stories of our family's history?"

"About one sister being good and the other bad, or curses and gifts, or some bullshit like that?"

I nod my head.

"She told me that your mother tried to smother her in her sleep, but Maria tells me a different story. But she said she was innocent and that all she was trying to do was scare Sylvia. I told her I didn't want to hear it because she's dead anyway. What does it matter? I told you, your mother never shuts up, and she's not going to shut up until we go see your daughter. That's why she brought us all together."

I picture my mother and Aunt Sylvia as being very similar to Ruby and me. Jealous, competitive, and taking life way too seriously. With our family, jealousy is born into us because of our gifts, or lack thereof. There have been times over the years when I've hated Ruby and missed her all at the same time. Now that I'm older, I see her a little differently, and I see that most of our history was tainted due to my own selfish feelings and beliefs.

When we're in our youth, we make our beds, then have to lie in them when we're older. We don't always make them up in the correct way, so life's proverbial bed is often full of painful lumps and bumps that we'll deal with for the rest of our lives. The women of this family seem to always find themselves on the bottom bunk of life and it's no one's fault but our own.

The bell above the entrance door of the diner bangs against the glass and startles each of us. A gentleman enters, soaked and disheveled. I glance at him and look away, then I realize who he is. "Jared?" I say in a hushed tone, then begin to wave my hand as an excited child might do upon seeing their favorite celebrity.

Ewelina lets out a *huh,* then turns to see who I'm waving at. "Who's that?

"That's my son-in-law."

54

 ared

AT THE MOMENT, I feel as though I'm a character in someone's psychological thriller and the writer is having way too much fun toying with my storyline. I have no idea how I got into this position. I have a horrible headache, and I don't remember having any fun getting it. *What the hell happened last night?*

I roll my naked body over onto my stomach and grip the vertical bar the handcuff is attached too, and shake it to see if there's any give. It moves slightly, so I shake it harder. It doesn't budge any further, so I maneuver my restrained hand around and grip the bar with both hands and give it a hard shove. The bar bends in the center and pops loose at the bottom, so I slide the handcuff free, although the other side is still attached to my arm.

I bolt up from the bed way too fast and have to sit back down again as the room moves at high speeds around me. I've never

328

encountered a hangover like this before. In fact, it feels more like I've been given a shot of morphine laced with speed. One side of my brain seems to be fighting the other while also waging a war against my bodily functions. *What the fuck did Kris do to me?*

The question runs through my head as I hold it in my hands, trying to stop it from spinning. Something about this whole situation doesn't make sense. I wouldn't have drunk that much, knowing that I'd left Abby and Ava alone just after someone had broken into the house. *What the fuck? What the fuck? What the fuck?*

After my brief meltdown, I grab my shirt, then stand up slowly and search for the rest of my clothes, which isn't much—a pair of boxers, t-shirt, sweats, and crocks. I search for my cell phone, but I don't remember bringing it with me. As I battle the chaos going on inside my head, mentally and physically, and stagger toward the bedroom door, a picture on top of the dresser grabs my attention. I yank the frame and angle it toward the lamp on the bedside table, and when I see the woman resting her head on Kris's shoulder, panic surges through me. The urgency to get back to Abby takes on a whole new meaning.

I wobble out the front door of Kris's house and into the darkness. My car's gone. *Kris took it.* "What the fuck?" My anger prompts the words to escape me out loud this time. Thoughts collide and a deep feeling in the pit of my stomach balls itself into a knot, which only feeds my hangover more. Something about this whole situation screams that something bad is about to happen. I'm struggling to believe that this is just some jealous woman's revenge.

There's much more to it than that.

I walk across the porch and the rain beats down on the metal roof above—a sound that would usually lull me to sleep, but it echoes inside my ears and causes only discomfort. *I need to get back to Abby and Ava.* This urgency seems to consume the rest of my hangover. I now realize that being here is intentional.

Kris planned this.

That thought drives me into the pouring rain and down the street. I make it one block and decide that I have to find a way to call Abby. Now is a moment when I miss the good ole days of a phone booth on a corner—not that it was ever common in my time, but I remember my mother talking about them being around. I could definitely use one now.

I walk down the potholed sidewalk underneath the dim streetlights, which does little to illuminate my path. Stinging pellets of rain force me to tilt my head downward as I squint my eyes to protect them. A red neon *Diner* sign blurs in the distance and I pick up the pace as I move in that direction while my soaked feet squeak inside my crocks. Despite the gray sky, I can tell that daylight waits just on the horizon, which means I've spent the majority of the night at Kris's with no recollection of anything beyond the shot of scotch. *It had to be laced with something.* The thought occurs to me as I rush through the hinged, glass door.

As I swing it open, a bell clangs above me, and I wince. I walk straight ahead to a long counter lined with red, vinyl stools. I step between two of them and wait for the waitress who stands with a phone to her ear at the far end of the counter, jotting down a to-go order. My patience begins to wear thin when the waitress decides to veer from the to-go order to discuss her dog and how it looks just like a stuffed toy. I take in a deep breath and let it out loudly, which does nothing to grab her attention.

In my peripheral vision I see movement and turn my head while shifting my eyes to the right. When I realize that someone is waving their hand frantically at me, only then do I turn my full attention.

My mind spins, and I feel my eyes widen in shock. A questioning look crosses my face as I walk slowly in their direction.

"Rosemary? What are you doing here?"

She smiles a genuine smile as she scoots further into the booth and pats the seat next to her.

"Um, how is this possible? I mean, that you're here?" I ask as I sit my soaked body on the far edge of the seat and dart my eyes to the two women across from her. I nod a hello gesture and prop my elbow on the corner of the table, forgetting about the handcuff still attached to my wrist.

"What do you mean *how is it possible*? She's got two legs—she walked." The other woman who I've seen in the hospital several times spits out words that seems more like a bellow. She points to the handcuffs and says, "What's the matter there, Sonny—your partner get a little too kinky for you and you had to make a break for it?"

I quickly slide both hands under the table.

"Ewelina," Rosemary says in a hushed tone.

I lean my body slightly away from Rosemary and give her an astounded look. She spoke? Abby said that she had, but to hear it with my own ears after all this time is quite something.

"Jared, this grumpy, old woman is Ewelina, and sitting next to her is Angel."

I remain in shock for a bit longer at hearing Rosemary speak and then acknowledge the other women. I smile at Ewelina, who doesn't smile back, and then catch myself looking at the woman next to her. My eyebrows shift toward one another. Something about her is familiar. I can't put my finger on it, but it's as if I've seen her or someone that looks like her before. I smile and nod my head again.

"I have to ask again—how is it you've come here? Is everything alright?"

"Speaking of which, we can't stay here," Angie says. "We should probably get going before the hospital realizes you're gone. This diner has a lot of hospital staff in and out of here all the time."

"Yes, and I need to find Abby."

I hear worry in Rosemary's voice, and it fuels my own. "Rosemary, is something wrong?" I ask, this time with more urgency. I've never really been a person who believes in the idea of people seeing or knowing things before they happen, but at the moment, something tells me that the universe is trying to warn even me. Rosemary suddenly speaking and leaving the hospital after all these years can only mean that something *is* about to happen.

Ewelina's gruff voice speaks for her as she begins to slide from the booth and scoots the young woman next to her along. "Of course there's something wrong. Rosemary grew a pair of kahunas, busted out of the hospital, and found that puny voice of hers. Her deceased mother won't shut up, and her dead daughter won't leave her alone."

I'm sure I pull a face—what kind, I'm not sure, but Rosemary pats me on the shoulder and says, "I don't know for sure, but I feel a strong need to get to Abby."

"Come on," Angie says, "Ewelina, you can finish telling Rosemary everything in the car. It'll all make sense, then."

I stand, and Rosemary slides from the booth, and straightens slowly. "Take me home."

55

bby

I OFTEN SPEND TOO much time trapped inside my own thoughts and fears, and they insist on consuming the largest part of my mind, even when I'm asleep. I feel like a bird trapped in a room surrounded with windows, but they're all closed and blocked by memories I want to forget. I can't escape them, nor the guilt that comes with them.

A loud warning wakes me, but when I open my eyes, I decide it must have been all inside my head. I'm not sure why it registered as a warning. When I finally come fully awake, I realize it was actually a noise outside.

Someone's outside. As soon as I think it, I bolt upright and jump out of bed.

I move toward the stairs and all the while my mind attempts to play guessing games with me. *Maybe it's just Jared*—I attempt to convince myself. *But what if it isn't? What if whoever came into the house today has come back? What if they're hiding somewhere? What if...?* I tiptoe downstairs and my first thought is to check the front door's lock. I begin to shake when I find that it isn't secured. I know I checked it before I went to bed, and there's no way Jared would lie down without checking it himself. I turn the deadbolt and rush to the living room to check on Jared. The covers have been thrown back, but there's no one on the couch. I move through the dark house to the kitchen, trying to push down panic. Maybe he got up to get himself a snack or something to drink. I only find a dark, empty kitchen.

I flick my index finger with my thumb as the habit of messing with my fidget ring has already formed. I'd taken it off before bed, so I resort back to my more painful habit. I push worry even further down as I check the guest room on the first floor and all the other rooms downstairs. No Jared. Fear begins to win the race as my heart behaves as though it's in one.

I pull back the curtain and look out the window. Jared's car is gone. Confused, I get a sudden feeling I should check on Ava and climb the stairs two at a time. Fear shifts to confusion and then rushes straight ahead to panic.

She's not in her bed.

No longer worried about being quiet, I flick on the lights in Ava's room, the hallway, the bathroom, then my room. Maybe she'd snuck in there at some point, and I didn't realize it.

She's not anywhere in the house. Panic shifts to terror.

I retrieve my phone from the nightstand and call Jared's mobile. A ringtone screams from downstairs—the themed ringtone that Ava had assigned to Jared's phone so that she would know when it was me calling—My Little Pony.

Why would Jared leave—better yet, why would he take Ava out of the house in the middle of the night? I begin to pace the upstairs floor, phone in hand like a caged animal. Despite gripping the phone tightly, I still manage to squeeze the shit out of each finger, making a sting travel across the palm of my hand.

My thoughts spin out of control from one negative direction to another as I plop down on the bed. *I'm a horrible mother, just like I was a horrible sister. I couldn't protect Ally and now I've failed to protect Ava, too.* With each pessimistic thought that passes through my mind, I feel more crippled by guilt and uncertainty. I jump from the bed and pace aggressively as I stare at the black screen on my phone, trying to decide if I should call the police. If Ava's with Jared, I don't have anything to worry about. But what if whoever came into my house had somehow forced the two of them to leave in Jared's car?

That doesn't make any sense.

My thoughts speed ahead with no order or direction just as my pacing does. I sprint back downstairs and search the living room for any clues as to why Jared might have left in the middle of the night. *What if he found Ava missing before I did and went to search for her? That's stupid!* I argue with myself. A new surge of panic hits me, and I run back upstairs to look for clues in Ava's room. A violent shiver passes over me when I see that her favorite Sarah doll is missing too. Wherever she is, she took it with her.

Peering closely at her bed, I notice a folded piece of paper on her pillow. I snatch it up quickly, and there's no mistaking my six-year-old daughter's handwriting.

A l e s a i d i n e d t o g o s e e a n t r u b e.

A rush of tingling washes over me as I run into my own room and throw on yesterday's clothes along with a hoodie. For some reason, Ava thinks she's supposed to go to Ruby's house—in the middle of the night. *Why would Jared go along with this? This makes zero sense.*

My pacing begins again, and I don't even realize it. *You were weak as a child and you're weak now.* The words bounce around in my head and they come across in a taunting tone. Not even in my own voice, but Tina's voice. The same voice I heard the day my sister died. *You've lost—give it up.* I shove my face into the palms of my hands and say aloud, "stop it!"

I grab my cell phone, cram it into my back pocket and decide to go through the front door rather than the dark route behind my house and Ruby's. Rain is falling quite heavily, so I pull the hood of my sweatshirt over my head and sprint across the porch. I halt in my tracks when someone speaks behind me.

"Where're you going this time of night?"

I immediately recognize the woman's voice and turn back before jumping in surprise. "Megan? What are you doing on my front porch this time of night—or morning, I should say?"

Megan is slumped on the wicker sofa with both elbows propped on her knees. I notice the vodka bottle on her lap, and most of its contents have spread across the table and onto the porch floor. Megan's hair hangs in dripping clumps while other strands stick to her face. Her pink sweats are darkened with wet spots while her wet t-shirt reveals her black bra. She doesn't look like herself at all.

"Did you walk here?"

She shrugs her shoulders. "Kay and I had a fight and she kicked me out."

I tilt my head, aiming for something vaguely supportive, but my mind is in tatters and every one of my nerves is frayed. "I'm really very sorry, Megan, but right now isn't a good time for me, either."

"Really? So that's how it's going to be? I'm there for you anytime you need me, but you can't give me five minutes?"

"I'm sorry, but I have to find Ava—she snuck out of the house sometime during the night."

Megan whispers something inaudible, and I try to decipher what I think I hear. *Brat?* I know I must be mistaken—Megan would never talk about Ava that way.

"You must be freezing. Come, you can wait inside until I get back. I'm sure Ava is at Ruby's. I just need to go see, then we can talk."

Megan picks up the vodka bottle and holds it up higher than her face, then asks, "Rough day?" She turns the bottle upside down and empties what few ounces are left in the bottle.

I assume by her words she means she's had a rough day, and I make an attempt at distracting her. "I never pictured you for a vodka drinker—I figured you as a sweet wine kind of gal."

"You saying I'm a puss?" Megan snaps, and not in a joking manner.

"No," I bark back, shocked at Megan's tone. Liquor doesn't seem to be her friend. "I'm, um, nothing. I was just attempting to distract you. I wasn't trying to upset you."

"No—say it. You think you're better than me, don't you? Just because you're a teacher with a degree and all that."

"No! You know I have never said that, nor have I ever treated you as such." Irritation takes over my voice, and I try to tell myself she's just drunk, hurt and lashing out. I swallow it down and open the front door, then hook my hand underneath Megan's elbow and guide her into the house. She allows me to help her.

The second we step through the door, a sudden foul odor forces me to hold my inhale. For a moment I think it's her, but then realize I've smelled it before. She flops down onto the couch where Jared had been sleeping, then grabs the blanket and slings it out of her way. "Why are you sleeping on the couch?"

"I wasn't, it was—" I stop myself from finishing the sentence. I step back away from Megan, but the smell doesn't fade—in fact, it continues to get worse. The smell is familiar, and I'm suddenly learning that it only comes around when the moment needs me to pay attention.

Almost like a warning.

"I bet it's that bastard boss of ours. I knew you were fucking him again."

"No—"

Megan interrupts me. "I told Kay he was fucking you both. He's a bastard just like all men—it's why you'll never find me fucking a man. Of course, at the moment, I hate women, too."

It takes a moment for Megan's words to register, and when they do, she has my full attention. "What do you mean, fucking us both? What are you talking about?"

"Oh, you didn't know, did you? Yeah, he's playing both of you."

"Kay? You mean your girlfriend?"

Megan laughs but something about it is cruel and alarming.

"You really don't know, do you?"

"Know what?"

"Who my girlfriend is."

"Yes—" At first, I start to say yes, but then I realize that I've never met her girlfriend. "I mean, no, I've never met her, but you've told me about her and that her name is Kay."

"Not Kay as in K-A-Y. I call her K as in the first letter of her name. It's just a pet name. She calls me *M* and I call her *K*. But you definitely know who she is."

I exhale loudly, annoyed beyond belief that I'm having to deal with this when I need to check on Ava, but I appease her. "Who is she, then?"

One side of her mouth lifts into a cocked smile as one eyebrow raises. "Kris."

56

Ruby

"FOUND IT!" Ava announces.

After hearing Tina's name, I'm still trying to gather my thoughts and words that seem to have scattered themselves everywhere, and not into any order to form a coherent sentence. It's a name I'd hoped never to hear again.

Ava emerges from the closet holding a yellowed folded piece of notebook paper. My forehead shifts into an involuntary frown. She begins to unfold the piece of paper, and I snatch it from her hands more aggressively than I intended. I try to smooth it over as soon as I see Ava's upset face by saying, "This has been in there for a long time—let me check it for bugs."

Ava recoils as her eyes pop open wider. She nods. "Okay."

When I unfold the unevenly stained paper, an immediate shudder rips through my body at the sight of the childish handwriting. One part of my mind tries to convince me that this is just

339

Ava playing a trick on me. I peer down at the blue-eyed, blond-haired girl, and know better.

D e a r A b b y

T i n a i s v e r y ba d. S he is no t yo u r f ri n d.

s he s a i d y o u w u r g o ee n g to   h e r t m e
e ve n k i l   me. I t h e nk s h e is   g o ee n g t o

t. ri to h e rt y o u. o r m e .

Y o u   wo n t lissi n t o me so i a m w r i ti n
it in a le ttr.   P e s e   do nt be   f rind s

with h e r a ne mo r.

L o v A l l y

I know I'm not able to hide the pale and haunting expression that crosses my face, but I attempt to.

"What is it, Aunt Ruby?"

I force my face into a lie and say, "You were right. It's a letter from Ally a long time ago."

"Let me see it." Ava reaches for the letter, but I hold it a little higher.

"I'll read it to you first. Okay?"

Ava seems satisfied and lets me do so.

"It says, dear Abby. Tina is not real. She is just an imaginary friend, so don't believe anything she says. Love Ally."

"Let me see." Ava jumps this time and snatches the paper from my hand.

I allow Ava to grab it because I assume that even though she can recognize some words, she can't read enough to understand what it actually says.

Ava stares at the paper as though she's actually reading it. She looks up at me and frowns. "Ally said that's not what it says." She begins to read the letter aloud, pausing in between each sentence as though someone is telling her what to say.

I shake my head back and forth in short sweeps of denial. "I guess I must have read it wrong. I don't have my glasses on."

Ava frowns.

The pain continues to hit me in the chest, and I know that something is coming. It hits me once more so hard that I literally jump. Ava and I both speak at the same time with almost the same, exact words.

"Ava, I want you to hide in the closet."

"Ally says I need to hide in the closet."

Just as I realize that Ava's words match my own, the lock of the front door clicks behind me and panic jackhammers at my chest. I don't need to convince Ava any further, as she goes straight to the closet and closes the door behind her. As soon as the latch closes, I hear footsteps move around the stairs toward me and turn to see an older version of the dark, brown eyes I remember from all those years ago.

Eyes I'd hoped I'd never look into again.

"It's nice to see you again, my darling cousin, but the look on your face says you're not as happy to see me."

"How did you get in my house?"

The woman holds up a key and flashes a menacing smile. "Same spot it's been for years. You and your family really should get better at stashing keys." As she's holding the key in her left hand, I notice the ring on her pinky finger, and I focus in on it more. At first my thoughts scramble to understand what I'm seeing, but as I stare at the familiar amber stone, I stifle a gasp as I realize it's the same ring I saw on Ally's hand all those years ago. My conversation with her runs through my mind. The color yellow. I remember telling Ally that when a mood ring turns that color, it means the wearer is stressed, restless, or unsure.

I swallow hard before I speak to prevent my words from coming across as weak. In knowing that she isn't as confident as she pretends it makes it easier for me to fake confidence. "What do you want?"

"You know exactly what I want. What you denied me all those years ago."

I begin to quiver inside and hope it doesn't show on the outside. "I don't know what you're talking about."

"Your little stunt of getting me taken away by the police that night sent me to a mental institution for youths. I spent six months there because of you. Then I was placed in a foster home two states away. I never saw my sister again after that, not that I wanted to. She's as boring as you are."

"I've never met you before in my life and as far as I'm concerned, you've broken into my home." I say the words as boldly as I can.

"You robbed me of what was mine and ruined any chances of me having a normal life. It was all your fault. You took everything from me."

My thoughts from earlier play in my mind on repeat, and her words remind me of my younger self. Of how my miserable existence unfolded because of the story that I wrote for myself—a story that is heading for a horrible ending. And like this woman, I blamed Rosemary for my own self-inflicted misery. "I think your own choices have ruined your life—not me."

Her eyes set themselves into a fevered stare. "I'm not that little girl anymore, and far from being stupid and naive. I will have what is rightfully mine, just as much as it is yours—or Abby's. You might have outsmarted me back then, but when I tell your precious Abby that you were the one behind Ally's death, she'll send you to join your sister—or worse. Then, as far as Abby goes, I've already set her fate in motion."

An icy chill creeps up my spine. "It was you that took it upon yourself to commit murder. I never wanted anything like that to happen."

"Oh, dear cousin Ruby—let's face it, we're cut from the same cloth. You're not all that different from me. You hated your sister just as much as I did mine, and you wanted nothing more than to see her suffer. I have to admit, stealing your sister's husband was pretty clever. To some, you might as well have committed murder —you slaughtered the woman's marriage."

Her recount of my past cuts me to the core. I try to swallow down the immediate guilt inflicted by her words and focus on the moment at hand. The fact that she knows about Mike tells me she didn't just roll into town yesterday. She's been doing her home-work, and she isn't here for a stroll down memory lane.

The woman turns and walks toward the closet under the stairs where Ava is hiding. "I heard you talking with someone before I came in. Did you stuff them in the closet?"

I limp a few steps forward as I push down fear and attempt to dissuade her. "You're mad. If anyone deserves to be locked away for the mentally insane, it's you."

She stops, then pivots back to face me, her eyebrows raised. "I am? Says the woman who has more skeletons in her closet than a mausoleum. This closet of yours holds a lot of nasty secrets, doesn't it, Ruby? After all, you forced me to hide in here because *I* was *your* dirty little secret. I wonder what other little secrets this closet can tell."

A sharp pain pounds against my chest—*another warning.*

"Would you like to hear one of my dirty little secrets?" She steps closer to me—too close—and shifts her voice to where it's barely above a whisper. "This is where I told Ally how I was going to kill her."

57

bby

MEGAN'S WORDS have crumbled the foundation beneath me and I'm beginning to fall—the only thing stopping me from actually doing so, is confusion.

Megan lets out a sadistic laugh.

"What's going on, Megan? What are you talking about?"

"You might be book-smart, but you truly are an idiot." Megan straightens her posture and smooths down her wet hair with both hands. Her appearance transforms, and I realize that her drunken act was just that—all an act; or at least, partially. "Kris was right—you're spoiled, entitled, and most of all, self-centered."

A multitude of emotions rush through me, and my mind isn't sure which it should grab hold of. Hurt mixed with anger moves to the top, but instinct takes center stage and I take a step backward, then another, as something in me screams that I should go find Ava.

What the hell is happening? The question decides to put itself on repeat in my head and I have to force myself to let it go. Flashes of conversations and interactions between Megan and myself come and go, and none of them warn me of this.

But what is *this?*

I slowly take another step backwards.

"I don't understand, Megan. Where is this coming from?" With each step that I take away from her, I count inside my head. Anything to slow my racing thoughts.

One step back.

"Just what I said, your ex-husband is fucking Kris."

Her words sting badly, but I focus. "You're hurt, so you're trying to hurt me. Is that what this is?"

Two steps back.

She shakes her head. "No. Kris fucking Jared was something we both agreed on. It's what she wanted, and all I want is for her to be happy. I would do anything for her."

I try not to react, even though my face threatens to. "I don't understand where all of this is coming from. You always seemed to despise Kris."

Three steps back.

"I guess that means I'm a better actress than I thought."

"But why hide it.?"

"It's what Kris wanted. She didn't want anyone to know until the time was right."

"Then why now?"

Four steps back.

"Well, I guess since she and your ex spent most of the night together last night, I thought I would take it upon myself to fill you in."

It feels as though Megan has just driven a knife into my stomach—or maybe my heart. Either way, her words gut me like a successfully hunted deer.

Five steps back.

"Just where is it you think you're going?"

I freeze and stand very still, but my mind does everything but. It spins out of control as I breathe and try to calm myself. I look into Megan's eyes and force my voice to sound as though it has more courage behind it than it actually does. "What do you really want from me, Megan?"

Six steps back.

Megan stands from the couch and takes a few steps towards me.

Seven steps back.

"I don't want anything." She takes another step, and another. "But Kris does, and I'm here to make sure she gets it."

Eight steps back.

"It sounds to me as though she already has what she wants— you *and* my ex-husband."

"Ohhh, that isn't all she wants."

Nine steps.

"You're not going anywhere." Megan takes several swift steps in my direction, and it prompts me to turn and run. Just as my hand grips the doorknob, she grabs a fistful of my hair, yanking me backwards. She tightens her grip, pulling me into an awkward position, then pulls my head against her chest while speaking into my ear. "I told you, I'm not letting you leave."

I press one hand onto hers as hard as I can and force her hand to collapse against my scalp as I begin to pry her fingers loose from my hair one-by-one. She wraps her other arm around my chest and attempts to drag me back into the house. Through the struggle, I keep my focus on prying her hand free from my hair, and when I'm down to her last two fingers, I grip her wrist and swing my body around, twisting her arm with me. She lets out a painful cry.

In school, we're trained on how to remain calm and break free from a student if they become violent and grab you. We're not supposed to hurt them back—twisting Megan's arm to the point of breaking it is not part of that training and is pure instinct.

I don't let up and twist harder, which forces her to drop to her knees as she cries out again.

"I'm going to find my daughter, and I suggest you go back to your girlfriend and tell her that whatever *this* is about, she'd better back off," I hiss.

Megan cries out, and for a split second, I feel sorry for her and loosen my grip. It was a mistake. She seizes the opportunity and punches me in the stomach, crippling me to the floor in a crouched position as I hug my arms against my body. I fight the urge to throw up.

Megan comes up from behind, wraps both hands around my throat, and lifts me from the floor. Instinct and training take over once more, and I raise both arms high over my head, squeezing against hers, and twisting my body quickly. I use my shoulders as leverage as I bring my arms down hard, breaking her hold on me. I step back as soon as her hands release and pivot around behind her, then I shove her to the floor and kick her as hard as I can in the side. I waste no time as I race through the house and out the back door. The back yard is pitch-black due to the neglect of replacing the bulb in the motion-triggered lamp on the side of the house.

Jared had scolded me for neglecting it, but now it plays to my advantage. I race across the lawn, fumble with the latch on the gate, and sling it open. I hurry down the path toward Ruby's, and when I get there, I bypass the gate that's surely locked, slip through the loose board, and slide it back into place. The second I step through the opening, the smell that resembles rotting flesh returns and I instinctively press the back of my hand against my nose. I don't know where the smell is coming from, but I'm starting to understand it. It means that something from my past has come back to find me, and I now realize who that someone is.

I can't believe I didn't see it. My mind attempts to scold me, and I have to force it to stop because I know beating myself up over my own naivety isn't going to help me now.

I race through the yard around my mother's fairy sculpture and the old, iron table toward the sunroom door.

It's locked.

I peer in through the windows, and like the outside, the inside is mostly cloaked in darkness, but I see a faint light at the far end of the house. I'm not quite sure what I'm seeing, but when my eyes lock on the other woman's eyes, confusion takes the front seat.

58

Jared

I SIT in the back seat of a car full of women who are all virtually strangers, yet my connection to them runs deep—we all have one common goal. To find Abby.

I've known Rosemary for more than two years, yet she's still a stranger to me. The other two women in this car are her family, yet are complete strangers as well. I suppose at one point in everyone's life; we are all strangers. Even when we're born and we look into our mother's eyes for the first time, she is a stranger. But that stranger becomes the most important person in our lives. It's the same when someone finds their soulmate, and they too become the most important person in their life. For me, that's Abby, and the need to get to her is stronger than any urge I've ever felt in my life.

Sitting in this car with these women and seeing their determination, I am coming to realize what family and love truly means. I'm learning that it really exists. For the first time in my life, I feel worthy of going after what I want. My father's cruelty and rejection isn't going to define me anymore. I deserve to be happy. I deserve to be with Abby, and I'm going to tell her how I really feel.

With this realization, I find myself growing impatient—I want to get to Abby—now. I understand why these women have a need to stroll down memory lane, but all I want to do right now is drive like hell. I patiently listen to their conversation while trying not to flip out and scream at them to drive faster.

"Do you want to tell Rosemary, or should I?" Ewelina asks.

"You go ahead. I'll focus on driving," Angie says.

I resist the urge to lean forward in my seat.

Ewelina twists her stiff body around to look at Rosemary sitting next to me. "Your daughter was right, Rosemary. She didn't kill her sister. My daughter did."

Rosemary's head snaps from Ewelina to Angie, her face twisting into confusion and rage.

"Not this daughter—my other daughter—her twin. The belief that there is one bad twin, and one good twin, is often very true. It's very true in the case of my family, anyway."

Rosemary clears her throat before she speaks, and the one word she does floats on a whisper. "Tina?"

"The girl in the picture that Abby showed you and me?" I butt in to ask Rosemary as my mind tries to catch up with their conversation.

Ewelina nods, more at Rosemary than me. "There's a reason your dead daughter started coming to see you in the hospital all of a sudden."

Rosemary turns her head to stare out the window as though something out there might help her to make sense of what Ewelina is telling her.

Angie speaks next. "When my sister and I were kids and in a

foster home, she talked about running away, or finding somewhere else to live. She never followed the rules of our foster parents—always getting into trouble and sneaking out of the house. She told me once that she was working on a plan to find a permanent home. Something about finding some of our long-lost cousins. I didn't believe her, of course, but she swore she was getting out of there one way or another."

I turn to watch Rosemary's face as she listens to the driver speak. She wears a far-off expression, as though she's staring through Angie and into her distant past.

"My sister came home one night after sneaking out of the house, woke me up, and was all excited, saying that she'd just done something that would ensure her a home for good. She said that she'd be moving into the mansion soon, and of course, I wouldn't be coming with her. She even showed me the house on a drive home from the market one day."

Angie stops the car at a four-way stop, and as the sound of rain hitting the car gets louder, so does she. "We didn't get along very well and she was always telling stories that were never true. I just assumed this was another one. It was around this time in my life I started having weird things happen—or at least, I noticed them more. That night, I got a weird tingling sensation in my lips that spread across my face and then my whole body. It was so intense that it scared me. Shortly after it hit, my sister told me one of the most far-fetched stories ever."

I catch myself leaning even closer to the front seat as I listen, waiting for the rest.

"She said that she'd found our twin cousins, and that one of the twins asked her to kill their twin sister and make it look like an accident. Again, I thought she was making it up, so I asked her, *'did you do it?'* She said very nonchalantly, *'yeah—I pushed her out of a tree.'* As she told me this story, the tingling became unbearable, to the point I felt as though I was going to pass out. Occurrences such as that still hit me today when something bad is about to happen. I felt it again this morning, and it really hasn't let up."

I feel horror steal my expression and I look over at Rosemary to find it has taken over hers as well. As I speak, I'm certain I'm speaking for the both of us. "Did you tell anyone?"

"No. I didn't believe her. I pretty much just laughed at her. As far as the physical sensations I was feeling, I didn't understand it—I just assumed I had some sort of virus or growing pain. However, a few days later, the police knocked at our door and told our foster mother that she'd broken into someone's house and that she was hysterical. They took her upstate to a mental facility for youth. We were separated from then on."

"So how is it you're both back in the same town?" I can see that Rosemary is still processing everything the woman is saying.

"Lots of things brought me here. My husband, job, school, and," she pauses and looks over at Ewelina, "my mother. I'm not sure about my sister or why she's here. She hasn't tried to look me up, or if she has, she hasn't made it known. I only figured it out after I found my mother, and as I kept digging, I found out my sister only moved here a year or so ago. I've only lived here for a short while."

Ewelina turns again to look at Rosemary. "I think my other daughter came back to finish what she started—or at least that's what Maria is telling me. I think she has plans for us all."

"Why?" I ask.

"Not sure." She glances at Rosemary. "But she's been right under our noses this whole time."

59

osemary

"WHAT DO YOU MEAN, been under our noses?"

"When does your dead daughter usually come to see you?" Ewelina asks.

I think back for a moment. "It seems she always appears when I have one of my sessions with that dreadful Doctor Black."

"Look who just got a little smarter," Ewelina says in a wise-cracking manner.

The words get trapped in my throat for several seconds. *"She's*…your daughter? Dr. Black?"

"Mm-hmm." Ewelina and Angie both nod.

"I think she got a job at the hospital to get close to you and my mother, and I don't think it's to have a family reunion. She wants something."

"But what?" Jared asks, scratching his head as if he were watching a movie he didn't understand.

"Well, her goal back then was to find a home, but now I think it's maybe to cover her tracks. Could be she's worried that someone will find out what she did all those years ago."

"Or to get what she wanted back then," I say.

Angie slows the car at a familiar four-way stop, and as I look around at what was once my neighborhood, my vision suddenly goes dark. My heart pounds, and I wait for my vision to return. When it does, I instinctively search for my dead daughter.

There she is, standing under the streetlamp less than a block from my old house. I click the lock on the car door, pull the handle, and the door flies open. Angie slams the brakes.

Simultaneously, the other passengers in the car say, "What the hell are you doing?"

"We have to go." I stiffly rush out of the car. "Someone call the police. Now."

Angie pulls the car close to the curb, throws it in park, and reaches for her cell phone.

"9-1-1 What's your emergency?" I hear from the speakerphone as I walk away.

Ally doesn't say a word but waves for me to follow. I don't hesitate.

As we make our way closer, daylight finally begins peeking between the houses and trees, and I see someone crouched on the front steps. *Abby.* Jared spots her at the same time and sprints ahead.

"Abby?" He says her name aloud, and she ducks. She sees us and hurries down the steps, confusion and relief consuming her face, and says only one word.

"Hurry."

60

bby

WE ARE ALL OFTEN FOOLED by the people that we think we know. People who pretend to be someone they're not for the sole purpose of getting something they want. It seems I've attracted these kinds of people my whole life.

I try not to think about Jared and Kris being together. In fact, if I allow my mind to picture the two of them embraced in each other's arms, I'll surely throw up. The thought of it is more than I can bear. I know I'm the one who pushed him away, and no man is going to stay single forever, just waiting. *But why her? Anyone but her.* My mind attempts to put the thought on an endless loop.

Why not? My own mother rejected me. Why wouldn't Jared choose someone like Kris over me? She's smarter, prettier, and not as messed up in the head as I am.

My thoughts keep me frozen in place—paralyzing me from making a move. I press my palms to my eye sockets in an attempt to push the thoughts away. Now is not the time to allow self-sabotage to take a front seat. I breathe and shove them down deep and tuck them away for later. I have to figure out what to do—for Ava.

I force myself to focus on the two people in front of me.

I put my face closer to the window and search for Ava. There's no sign of her anywhere. I crouch lower and watch the two women, and it appears as though they're leaning in toward one another, as though they're going to hug. I can't see my aunt's face, but I can see *hers*.

She steps back away from my aunt, and I can see malice in her eyes. The second I look into them, the foul odor returns, and I instinctively search for the large plant that used to live in this backyard. It doesn't exist, and it's as if I'm looking for the ghost of something.

That smell and this person are one and the same—vile, covered in a false beauty. Her presence looms in the air, and I think about what my mother said when she referred to the nasty-smelling plant. Creatures hide behind their beauty, fooling everyone around, but they can't hide forever. This woman appears beautiful on the outside, but she's been rotting on the inside ever since she killed my sister.

Maybe I should call the police. I crouch lower to the ground and debate what that would achieve. There's no proof that this woman has done anything. It's my word against hers.

The smell gets stronger, and it forces me to clamp my hand over my nose and mouth—it's warning me to do something now. I crouch lower and scurry around empty flowerpots and dying bushes to the side door. Also locked.

I make it to the front porch and remain crouched as I look for the key that's been hidden under the finial ornament since I was a child. It isn't there. How else did the woman get into Aunt Ruby's house?

As I'm easing onto the front porch, I hear footsteps behind me, and then I hear someone say my name.

61

*R*uby

FOR A MOMENT, it feels as though I'm going to wretch as a wave of nausea and bile burns my throat. I swallow it down, lean away from her, and look her dead in the eyes. They seem to reflect a younger version of my own, but worse—far more vengeful, dark, and monstrous. There were times in my youth that I hated life, and the reflection of that curse is vastly present in hers. The very first time I looked into her eyes back then, they were hollow—as though there was no soul behind them. They look even more soulless now.

As I move to step away from her, a sharp, searing pain pierces my stomach, and my breath stops mid-inhale. I fear I know exactly what has caused it, but instead of looking down, I try to convince myself that I'm letting my fear take over. I swallow it down, then speak.

"Get out of my house."

No longer able to ignore the pain and the warm liquid moving down the front of my body, I look down and see the knife's handle protruding from my abdomen.

"As I told you before—I *will* have what belongs to me, dear cousin."

I push down panic. *Ava.* I have to protect her.

I move one leg to step forward, my heart pumping blood at a steady stream down my lower stomach, painting my shirt dark red. I feel myself waiver and then my knees buckle, stealing the support of my legs. My kneecaps pound against the hardwood. I instinctively look toward the closet door, afraid that Ava had seen.

The door remains closed.

"Let's see what you're hiding in the closet now."

She steps toward the closet, prompting my instinct and adrenaline to take over. I scramble to my feet, amazed at my own ability to do so.

"Get out of my house!" I swing at her, and she turns as my fist makes contact with the side of her head.

She staggers backward, and I swing one more time. This time she dodges and shoves me off balance. I hit the floor, landing on my hip, which moves the knife in my stomach, and it feels as though I'm being stabbed over and over again.

Everything around me blurs as sweat beads on my forehead. Despite that, I begin to shiver violently as though I'm cold. I roll to my back, and the room spins as my vision fades. And like a lens on a camera closes, only in slow motion, so do my eyes, covering me in darkness. The last thing I hear is—

"Hello, Ava."

62

ared

"Abby?" I rush toward her as relief overwhelms me and it takes everything in me not to jump the fence and scoop her into my arms. "Where's Ava?"

"I think she's in there, but so is Tina." Her eyes flash frantically, and her face has drained of all color.

Just as Abby descends the steps, I see a woman rushing behind her, and when I see who it is, I scream, "Abby, watch out!"

Abby turns, just as Megan swings a thick branch and strikes her across the chest. She falls backward, and I leap over the wooden picket fence and grab Megan's arm as she raises it to swing again. Her eyes are wild and unseeing, as though she's possessed by something. It's a side of Megan I've never seen. She's always the happy, cheerful one at work. My mind feels like treacle, and I can't make sense of what I'm seeing.

"Stop it, Megan!" I wrap both arms around her, pick up her petite frame, and sling her away from Abby.

The three women behind me hurry through the small gate as Rosemary states, "Ally says we have to find Ava."

Abby looks up at her, still trying to bring her breath back to normal after having the wind knocked out of her. Her words come out between coughs. "She's in the house."

For an older woman, Rosemary moves quickly, climbing the steps two at a time. She bursts through the front door and disappears into the house, Ewelina right behind her.

"Can you stand up?" Angie asks as she grips Abby by the arm.

Abby nods and stands, though she looks a bit unsteady.

"Poor little Abby." Megan emphasizes the words in a mocking tone. "You've got that damsel in distress act mastered well. Too bad your knight in shining armor is fucking someone else."

"Shut up!" I snap the words and yank Megan off to the side, away from Abby, my face burning. *She wasn't supposed to find out like this.* The words bark inside my head.

"Oh—no worries, Prince Charming. She already knows about you and Kris."

I release her, and she turns to face me, straightening her wet clothes. I'm sure my face reflects a number of emotions, but I hope the only thing she can recognize is that I'm not letting her affect me. "What the hell do you want, Megan? Why are you here?"

Abby knowing about me and Kris, terrifies me. I was fooled by Kris's manipulation. Foolish to think that sleeping with her was meaningless and harmless. Something that would come and go quickly. I was wrong. Now, there's no way Abby and I can get back to anything we once had.

"I'm here to help the love of my life get what she deserves," Megan hisses. "The life that the women of this family stole from her."

Angie steps forward. "She manipulated you into thinking that about her. My sister was always good at manipulation. When she didn't get what she wanted, she used others to get it. She wasn't born with the blond hair and blue eyes, nor a gift. She couldn't stand it, so she resorted to doing bad things to get attention."

"She resorted to things that wasn't just bad, but evil," Abby says. "Do you even know anything about Kris—about her past?"

"I know enough to know that you rich, spoiled bitches took what was hers."

"You're in love with a murderer," I say.

Megan stares at me, then looks at Abby and Angie. "You all are liars!"

Ewelina's rough voice yells something frantic from inside the house. Megan turns to run as Abby and Angie run toward the front door. I grab Megan by the arm and yank her back to me, slap the free end of the handcuff around her wrist, then drag her with me.

63

bby

I STOP a few steps into the foyer, and my heart does the same as I see my daughter being held by the throat. I notice my sister's mood ring on her finger right away. Fury races through me.

"Hello, Doctor Black," Rosemary says, but her tone isn't welcoming.

Ewelina takes a step further into the room, and the woman grips her hand around Ava's throat a little tighter. "Hello, Kristina," Ewelina says, her voice smooth and calm.

"Well, if it isn't the infamous mother who abandons her children," Kris says.

My eyes land on Ruby's body stretched on the floor next to Kris and Ava, and I stare at the knife in her abdomen, rising and falling at an alarmingly slow rhythm. I choke back a sob as I take a step toward her body.

"Stop," Kris demands as she pulls Ava in tighter, and she takes a couple of steps to stand directly behind Ruby. Ava looks down at Ruby, tears swelling in her eyes. I mouth the words as I nod my head up and down, *It's okay.*

"Just what do you think is going to happen, Kristina?" Angie speaks up. "You still think you're going to possess this house? Especially now?"

"Shut up, Angelina. You've always had whatever you wanted. The last thing I'm going to do is listen to you. What do you know about any of this, you spoiled bitch? Every foster home we were in —you were the pick. They always loved you more. Little miss perfect."

"You're the one who made it hard to love you. You never followed the rules. Always blamed others for your own shortfalls. You're in this mess because of *you.*"

Kris rolls her soulless eyes. "It's easy for you to say. You were the one who got adopted by the rich family while I was moved from foster home to foster home." Kris turns to Ewelina. "And you? It's all your fault, you crazy old bitch. If you hadn't gone off the deep end, I wouldn't have had to do any of this."

"Odjebalo ci." Ewelina starts speaking out in Polish. "If anyone is crazy here, it's you. You're the one holding a little girl hostage. Why? You really think all of this going to work out the way you want it to?"

In the distance, sirens begin to swell as they move closer.

"Just run, Kris. The police are almost here. Forget these people and get out of here," Megan begs.

Kris turns her eyes toward me. "I did you a favor that day. Had I not done it, you'd have eventually killed Ally yourself. You two were just like all the other sisters in this family. You hated each other. None of us were meant to be bound together by love or friendship. We're cursed in this family before we're ever born. The universe chooses to favor one sister above the other, and by that, it decides our life's story. One gets the short straw while the other gets the champagne and caviar."

I look back down at Ava, whose eyes are wide, but then they shift far to her left as if she's looking for something, or someone. My eyes follow hers, but I don't see what she's looking at. Confusion squeezes my eyebrows toward one another, as Ava makes a slight nod of her head. What she does next sends my heart and my adrenaline into overdrive. She looks down and lifts her leg high before bringing her foot down as hard as she can onto Kris's toes. Her action prompts my own as Kris cries out and releases her grip.

Ava runs to Jared while I run toward Kris, but then Kris reaches down and pulls the knife from Ruby's stomach, causing her shirt to darken more with fresh blood. The knife slices through the air as I run toward her, then it slashes across my chest and left shoulder. I slap my palm against it as blood oozes between my fingers. I stumble backward and struggle to maintain my balance as Kris charges toward me again.

Ewelina and Rosemary springs forward, and Rosemary grabs Kristina's arm while Ewelina wraps both arms around her waist, pulling Kris back away from everyone.

Sirens grow louder and stop in front of the house.

"Kris. You've got to run!" Megan yells.

Two policemen rush through the front door. They take in the scene and quickly respond by raising their guns in the air.

64

bby

"CURSES ONLY HAVE power if you believe in them, and I don't," the good-looking actor declares with an emphatic gesture from the TV projector.

"Well, this person has obviously never met this family," Ewelina interrupts.

"Shhhhh!" Everyone whips their heads toward her as others press their index finger to their lips.

I remember thinking about this same line quoted in this movie at one point in my life—and it's true. I look around the backyard at everyone as they snuggle in with their blankets, clutching their cups of hot chocolate as the light creates dancing shadows across their faces. Just as Rosemary used to do when me and my sister were kids, a projector rests on the antique iron table, aimed at the white sheet draped across the wall of the sunroom. Tonight's movie is Practical Magic starring Sandra Bullock and Nicole Kidman.

"You know I'm right," Ewelina mouths a little louder.

We all shush her again.

My eyes land lovingly on my mother. The light from the movie illuminates the wild hairs on her head as if they're glowing and dancing along with the shadows. Ava sits on her lap, swinging her legs and munching popcorn. I'm not worried about the movie scaring her. Seeing dead people doesn't seem to faze her.

After Kris's arrest, my mother and Ewelina voluntarily went back to the hospital to face the consequences for leaving without a pass or permission. There wasn't much of a repercussion other than pulling some more time in the hospital. They were basically sentenced *in house* and given community service—similar to what a judge might give someone. In their case, they had to work in the hospital. They both also had to undergo a full psychiatric evaluation before they could be released, and as part of their conditions, they had to agree to attend therapy every week.

Sitting next to my mother is Ruby, and I can see that she's smiling—something she does a whole lot more of these days. Her wounds are healing, both physically and mentally. I suppose when one holds on to a secret so dark, it eats away at the light of someone's soul. I don't blame Ruby for what happened to my sister. She got caught up in what so many people do—always dwelling on the negative things in life and never being grateful for what they have right in front of them. I see the gratitude on her face daily now—and Ava absolutely adores her.

Ruby and I had a heart-to-heart in the hospital, and I asked her why she locked me in a closet as a child and why she'd make me watch videos of my dead sister. She said that the grief that came with knowing what happened to my sister was more than she could bear. The day that she found out she had inadvertently caused my sister's death was the day that she lost the right to be happy ever again, and her need to punish herself and everyone around her was all-encompassing. She wept over her actions and told me she didn't expect my forgiveness.

I could certainly relate to that.

It was the price she had to pay, and she had to make absolutely sure that I never turned out like her or make the same mistakes she did. In her mind, by making me hate those things about her, it would force me to be the complete opposite. Make me a better person than she. It doesn't make sense, but at the same time, I understand that life and trauma shapeshift a person far from the person that they could be or used to be.

Deep down I always knew that Ruby loved me, she just didn't love herself. She's learning to do that now.

Ewelina is a whole other kind of addition to my life. Dullness and her are two things you'll never witness together. She's very outspoken, even when you don't ask, and watching her and my mother interact with each other is better entertainment than any sitcom or comedy show. Ewelina still deals with the voices in her head, and sometimes when they get too loud, she suggests that she should go back to Serenity Oaks. At the same time, she takes comfort in knowing that she isn't alone. We also know that like my grandmother, Maria, dementia is a huge threat to her in the future, just based on the extremity of her gift, but for now, she's enjoying her family.

The doorbell breaks me from my thoughts, and Ava jumps from my mother's lap and squeals, "They're here!"

I stand and reach out my hand. "Well, let's go get them."

Ava hops a few steps, then we duck under the sheet and into the sunroom. Now that Rosemary is back, plants and flowerpots line the windowsills and hang from the ceiling, bringing life back to the house. We agreed that she'd never own another Corpse Flower. I haven't witnessed the smell that resembles it since the day Kristina was taken away by the police, and I have no desire to smell it again, regardless of its source.

Ava runs ahead through the house, then turns. "Can I open the door, Mommy?"

"Of course." Ava's been a bit clingy and cautious since that day, but she's slowly coming out of her shell. She told me that when that bad woman was holding her, Ally told her how to get away. She said that Ally told her to *stomp the woman's foot as if she were killing one of the biggest, ugliest, cockroaches, ever.*

For several days after that horrible day, she wasn't able to leave my side, and I didn't make her. We went to the hospital every day, and sometimes we'd visit Ruby at home twice a day. Even now, we have to call her every day to check on her. Ava insists.

The door swings open and Angie smiles, both her hands resting on the shoulders of each of her children. Ava and Mia both squeal as they embrace, while Mason gives at least a half-smile. It's a far cry better than what I see at school. Since he found out that he's part of this family, he's settled into school a little more, and at least doesn't try to run away anymore.

Angie ended up losing her job at the hospital, but she didn't mind. The only reason she ended up there to begin with was for Rosemary and her mother. Once the three of them were united, and now that we are all together, she feels there's no purpose for her there anymore.

Mason and Mia are the first set of twins born in this family where their genders are male and female. It took us all by surprise. Rosemary says that maybe it's the universe's way of breaking the curse. But was there ever a curse to begin with?

Just as the actor in the movie says, *curses only have power if you believe in them.* I'm not so sure I do anymore. Kristina wasn't cursed. She had a chemical imbalance and she needed help, but she never got what she needed as a child. It turns out that she took on the part-time job at the hospital for the sole purpose of getting close to my mother. She'd already secured her position at the school, and I guess she felt she could further her plan by making sure my mother remained in the hospital and out of the picture.

I suppose there was a reason Kristina went on to get her degrees in psychology because lots of people seek out the very thing they need the most. Many become therapists because they need one themselves—Kris sure did. Others pursue law enforcement because they had no one to protect them when something traumatic happened to them. Many go into the medical field because they had to watch a loved one die from some terrible disease, and they felt helpless. And some of us become teachers because *we* need that stability and love.

Grief is like a tiny stream that never dries up—not completely. There's always a steady flow of sadness, longing, and the missing of someone you loved dearly. When one loses a child or another close family member, grief will park itself in their life permanently. You just finally learn to live with it, and in spite of it. It becomes a part of you and all you can do is embrace it.

Last week, Jared and I sat down with Ava and told her about having a twin sister. We also told her that her sister Allie and my sister Ally are together—out there—somewhere and taking care of each other. Ava hadn't actually seen her sister, but Mia had and she's the one who told Ava about her. I'm not sure why my daughter Allie was making herself known to Mia—maybe she was just trying to pull the whole family together. If that's the case, I'm happy she did, and I'd like to think that she's content wherever she and my sister are. She doesn't need me, or any of us. That's what I choose to believe, and that's what gets me through it each and every day.

Now that I'm one-hundred percent sure that I'm not the one responsible for my sister's death, I can appreciate the time we had together. I can now allow myself to watch our childhood videos and instead of feeling guilt, I feel a sense of peace for her and myself. I suppose it's possible to grieve and be happy at the same time. I'm finally able to talk about my daughter with Jared and Ava without it crippling me. And I'm finally able to smile at the happy memories of me and my sister.

The three children run upstairs to play, and I return to the backyard and find Jared lying on a blanket, his head propped on his arm. He scoots over slightly, rolls to his side, and pats the blanket in front of him. I rush over and lie down, and he spoons me in close, wrapping his arms tightly around me. Everything about it seems so natural, as if we never stopped holding each other.

As it turns out, Jared and I were both just two broken people. I always felt I wasn't worthy of his love, but in turn, he felt the same way. In fact, he told me that for years he believed I was out of his league, and that he'd realized that the repercussions of his father's abuse had only made him feel unworthy of my love, or anyone else's for that matter. It crippled his ability to try to win me back. The guilt I feel for contributing to those feelings is something I will have to carry forever, but they'll make me strive to be a better wife.

I haven't wasted another moment since they took Kristina away. I've never asked Jared about her or the two of them. I didn't want to spend another moment of my life without him. I finally feel good enough—not just for him, but for me. I'm finally loving me.

Tomorrow, Ewelina and Angie plan to go visit Kris at Serenity Oaks. They're not sure if she will be accepting of them, but at the same time they feel that maybe it could be a fresh start for all of them. Become the family they never were.

As the movie is ending, Ava, Mia, and Mason burst from behind the sheet, all smiles and giggles—even Mason. They run straight to Rosemary and Ewelina and beg to have a sleepover with their grandmothers. Rosemary and Ewelina both turn to me,

Jared, and Angie, their faces begging just as much as the children are.

Jared and I exchange a look. "I'll be over first thing in the morning to get her," I say.

"Nonsense. I'll bring her home. It's Sunday—pancake day," Rosemary says with a cheesy grin.

I smile back at the idea.

Jared and I say our goodnights, then step through the back gate. At first, he turns to walk home, and when he sees me hesitate, he does too.

"I want to go this way," I say, nodding toward the path by the stream.

"You sure?"

I nod. "I'm sure."

He takes my hand, and we walk in silence for a while. A breeze begins to play with my hair, then the silhouette of the massive oak swells in the distance. For a moment, I think I hear my sister's giggle floating through the air. A sound I haven't heard in a very long time, and as it touches my ears, I know I'm going to be fine.

We are going to be fine.

ALSO BY CHERANN WRIGHT

WHERE SECRETS STAY

Kevan Renee inherits an abandoned estate from her beloved Gammie; a place which holds dark secrets. Nathan searches for his sister missing for two decades. When Kevan revisits the estate, she soon learns that secrets don't always die when we do. As haunting visions consume her, one figure stands out: a lone-little girl standing beside a still pond.

ACKNOWLEDGMENTS

Forever and always, thank you to my loving husband and two amazing daughters who stuck with me through another one.

Massive thank you to my editor Jessica Ryn. I feel as though your name should be on the cover just as much as mine is. You are amazing.

A huge thank you to my Blainiac family, who inspired the school scenes in this novel. My fond memories of working at the small country school with some of the most amazing friends and coworkers brought this part of the novel to life. I miss and love you all.

Another huge thank you to my closest friends, who are the first to read my novels and have repeatedly proven to be my biggest supporters and fans.

To all of those that have read my books and told me all the ways they enjoyed it: I love hearing from you—I can't tell you how much joy your reviews and messages bring. Thank you so much.

To all the booksellers, libraries, and reviewers for being so kind about my books.

Last, but certainly not least, my biggest thank you goes to my readers out there in the world. I wouldn't have written a second one if it weren't for you. You guys are amazing.

ABOUT THE AUTHOR

I've always had the dream of becoming a writer, but like so many others, I put my dream on hold. I went on to complete two masters' degrees in education and have taught for over fourteen years. After raising two successful daughters and sending them on their way to college, I decided to scratch the itch and write my first novel. THE TRUTH IS A LIE is my second novel and certainly won't be my last.

This is a work of fiction. Names, characters, organizations, places, and incidents are either products of the author's imagination or are used fictitiously. Any resemblance to actual persons, living or dead, or actual events is purely coincidental.

Sleuthing Sloth Press

Copyright © 2024 by CherAnn Wright

All rights reserved.

No part of this book may be reproduced in any form or by any electronic or mechanical means, including information storage and retrieval systems, without written permission from the author, except for the use of brief quotations in a book review.

Front Cover Design By: Carissa Kezen, CK Book Cover Designs

Editor Jessica Ryn

Contact Info: https://www.cherannwright.com

Digital ISBN: 979-8-9886557-7-0

Print ISBN: 979-8-9886557-8-7, 979-8-0886557-6-3, 979-8-9886557-5-6

www.ingramcontent.com/pod-product-compliance
Lightning Source LLC
Chambersburg PA
CBHW030539310726
48979CB00010B/1971/J